Grey Stone

JEAN KNIGHT PACE

JACOB KENNEDY

To my mother, who was sometimes more canine than human.
To Mark, who helped me remember the joy of spending time in magical places.
And to my three sister cats, Elizabeth, Savannah, and Emma, who keep me young.
—JKP

To my lovely wife, Cara, who had a dream that an elementary school teacher was a werewolf.
—JK

Grey Stone

by Jean Knight Pace and Jacob Kennedy

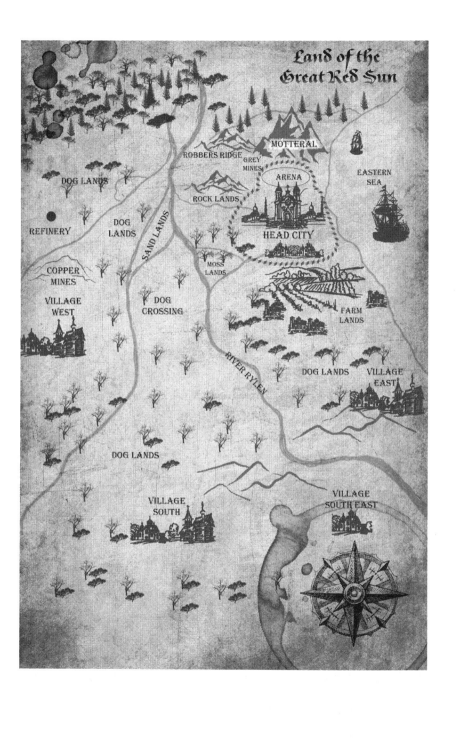

PROLOGUE

T he young witch, Zinnegael, set down her mid-morning mug of chamomile and stood abruptly. She felt the thundering of their paws as though they ran through her veins. She felt them stop. All except one. This animal walked toward the chosen.

The tea leaves drifted in the cup, steam rising, igniting the girl-witch's nerves. Her mother's chamomile never lied. Now the group formed a small triangle: boy, halfling, and leader of the pack. Of course they still needed the verlorn, but the race of dogs would not be able to help her with that.

The girl-witch crushed another handful of herb into her mug and watched. The dogs, she knew, would need to be reminded. For that she would send one of the riddle keepers. The boy would hear it first; he was the one with ears that listened. And she trusted that the leader of the pack would then know what to do.

Two of her most beloved animals stood at her side—one dark as moonless night, one streaked like rays of sun. Both were as big as mountain rams with coats soft as petals and claws much sharper than rosebush thorns.

"Go to them," she said to the sun-streaked one. The witch did not look up, but her words were kind. "Do not let yourself be seen. Not yet."

Had Zinnegael not been so accustomed to the silence of the enormous animals, she would not have known Savah had left at all. But she was used to quiet, and to listening with a deepness most girls her age didn't know could exist.

Quietly she stirred her tea. And watched.

The pup bowed.

The great dog paced.

One of many unknown things would become clear to them. The poor pup would understand it last of all and feel it most keenly.

Zinnegael may have been a sorceress and a prophetess and a master of potions, but she—barely fifteen and an orphan of sorts as well—felt her insides tremble with the young dog until finally the boy came to him and rested his hand against the pup's soft ears. "Well then, that's more like it," she said. "And Savah—swift and soft as wind—should be there shortly to help." With that, the young witch gave a final swirl to her prophetic tea, and drank it up.

CHAPTER 1

Pietre watched the red sun as it hunched over the horizon like a fiery bear about to relax into sleep; he quickened his steps. The moment the great sun set completely, the wolves of the Blødguard would be released to hunt any humans remaining in the woods.

Pietre's mother had sent him to gather mushrooms for sunset meal and had warned him not to dawdle. He had found no mushrooms, but had caught two fat fish. He planned to make a present of them to his parents. One fish could be fried that evening by his mother while the other slowly cured in his father's new drying machine—a strange rounded contraption made of the metal his father had mined during the day.

The fish, however, had caused him to be late, and now the moon sat high and broad across from the setting sun. His mother would be worried. Pietre moved swiftly through the woods that grew just outside his village. Even in the increasing darkness, he knew the lay of the creeks and ditches, the hunting grounds off limits to humans, and the coves where deer, rabbits, and squirrels sometimes hid from the weekly hunts of the wolves and their shapeshifting masters, the Veranderen.

Pietre jogged past one of the coves when he noticed a thick patch of serilla mushrooms. He got on his knees to quickly gather them and, when he did, he heard the faint sound of an animal whimpering. He paused to listen and could hear that it wasn't just one voice, but many. He crept toward the sound, into the shadow of a rock, and there on a bed of moss was a litter of pups.

Pietre caught his breath. Seeing a dog was rare enough; a whole litter of young ones was almost unheard of.

The pups pushed and pawed at each other, hungrily sucking their mother's milk. The she-dog, in contrast, lay perfectly still and even in the deepening shadows, Pietre could see a long gash along her snout. Beads of blood had dried into her light gray fur and she breathed heavily.

Pietre began to crawl backwards to the mushrooms when her soft voice came to him, the tones as gentle as those his own mother used. "Boy, the good God of the White Sun did not give dog and man the power to speak to one another so you could crawl away like a thief."

"I'm sorry, she-hound," he mumbled, trying to sound older than his thirteen years. "I did not wish to disturb."

"I know, boy, and you must not linger, as the sun descends quickly. But I can smell the fish in your pouch and I have not been able to hunt for days. You hear for yourself how the pups cry in hunger as my milk grows thin."

Pietre paused only for a moment before nervously approaching the she-hound and tossing her his largest fish. It was true that his father would have loved to try one in his drying machine, but Pietre knew that more than that his father would be disappointed if he had left a dog —much less a whole litter of them—to suffer. Pietre watched the she-hound devour the fish. He had never been so close to a dog before. Her fur was sleek, her eyes dark and soft with wispy black lashes that closed out thousands of questions. At her stomach, pushing and fighting for position, Pietre counted eight pups—little lumps of brown, white, and black. He could not take his eyes off the squirming, furry bodies. He had an intense urge to reach out and hold one, but wasn't stupid enough to grab at a dog pup uninvited.

"I'll return tomorrow with more," Pietre promised the she-hound, patting his pouch. As if in thanks, the smallest dog rolled over, let out a tiny yeep, and nudged Pietre's toe with the soft cool tip of a pink-black nose. Pietre touched one finger to the velvet muzzle and then made haste to return to his hut before dusk had fully settled.

He could hear the Blødguard assembling—the screeching howls of hunger. As the lowest class of wolves, they were kept from food for days so that when released they would be motivated to hunt without mercy. The sun was just a slice of red now against a pale purple sky and one of the wolves wandered close to the gates, waiting, his breath blowing hot into the winter air.

Pietre picked up a large rock and threw it as far as he could away from the entrance. The animal turned and when he did, Pietre ran. His head told him there was no reason for this, that the sun still shone and the law would protect him, but the tightness in his throat urged him to keep moving. He did not stop until he could see his house. Then he slowed, breathing deeply to calm himself. As he did, he imagined the tiny pup soft against his finger and wondered briefly where the she-dog's mate had gone. Usually, the father of the pups fed the females as they nursed. Pietre thought of the gash on her snout and wondered no more. Wondering did little good to young human boys, and as the world around him darkened and braced for night, he could hear the Blødguard keening anxiously as they stood at the forest edge, eager to be released to hunt for human renegades, runaways, or the unlucky straggler.

CHAPTER 2

T he wolf general Grender walked slowly down the corridor, stopping at the great iron door of his master only for a moment before pushing it open.

"Come," commanded Crespin—king over all—the shapeshifting Veranderen, their wolf allies, the free-ranging dogs, and the human serfs. The king stood in wolken form, wolfish and fierce, as he always did. Most other shapeshifters found the flesh form easier to maintain and maneuver on a day-to-day basis—smaller, simpler, softer. But his majesty was unconcerned with small, simple, soft things, and he had not been seen in his flesh form for at least 900 years. Though he stood on two feet, he could run on four when necessary. His hair was dark, almost black, and covered his body and face. His eyes were a deep russet that seemed to glow like the bauble at the tip of his staff. Many of the olders said that those eyes held even more magic than the staff— magic pulled from his foes when he rose to power nearly a millennium ago. He wore a long red robe with exquisitely worked golden thread woven throughout and an amulet of garnet around his neck. His voice, though always clear, was unusually soft—so soft that his servants had to strain to hear his important words. He was twice the size of the wolf Grender, with a hard, muscular body that stretched into slender, strong

6

paws—the nails polished like spearheads. The king stood flanked by his sons, Wittendon and Kaxon—the one tall and pale, the other broad and dark.

"You have been busy again General," the king stated, still not looking at the wolf.

"My liege?" Grender asked, tucking his front legs beneath him in a low bow.

"Please," King Crespin growled, dismissing his sons as though they were flies, and with a flit of magic closing the large doors behind them. "My spies have picked up an unwelcome scent in the western wood—pups they suspect to be half-dog and half-wolf."

Grender stiffened and looked directly at his king, but said nothing.

"You have, it seems, a penchant for the females not of your kind. This I do not understand. The dogs may be soft of coat and weak of mind, but I need you to understand that half-breeds can have no place in this land." The king turned from his subject and walked the length of the granite floor. "This has always been so, but whispers of a new rebellion grow louder. These rebels who call themselves the Septugant speak of a seventh era and a return to bygone times—times when men and wolves walked side by side. Times they do not understand. Such talk must be controlled, quelled if need be. Half-bloods of any sort will only escalate it." His sharp nails clicked with each step, the tip of his staff crackled with heat, and his fur glowed with pulses of angry magic —tiny charges of energy seeking a place with which to connect.

Grender did not move.

"See that those younglings become what all such abominations must. And see that you create no more." The king stopped, looking down at Grender. "Otherwise you shall be relieved of your position as head of the Königsvaren and the mighty Wolrijk—he who now leads the night hunts of the Blødguard—shall stand in your place."

Grender repressed a snarl at the sound of the Night Hunter's name. "Yes, my lord," he said, and bounded from the castle into the night— howling for his wolf brothers to join him in the hunt.

～

Pietre lay in bed listening to the howling of the wolves. It was not an unusual sound, but it was one he never got used to. The howls of the Blødguard were not as terrifying as those of the Veranderen—their wolf-shifting masters, but they were much more frequent, carrying into the villages night after night. Occasionally, if a human had not returned before sunset, Pietre heard the human cries as well. That was the most horrible sound of all. For as long as Pietre could remember, his mother had tucked his blankets firmly around his ears to drown out the sounds. Or try to.

But tonight the howls were particularly fierce and oddly close. The snarling of the Blødguard was mixed with the smooth well-trained howls and whispers of the Königsvaren—the king's wolf guard. The Königsvaren did not hunt for stragglers and castaways as did the Blødguard; the Königsvaren hunted for the convicted, the delinquent. They did not hunt to eat, but to avenge. Pietre tossed in his bed for the better part of the night, dreaming in blood until at last the amethyst dawn washed into his nightmares, pressing against the dagger-like sliver of a moon and waking him. His muscles ached and he was oddly relieved when his mother asked him to take a basket to the woods to gather mint and sweet leaves for tea. The stink of the overpopulated human village would wake him, the gossip of the biddies who sat by the gates would give him news, and it'd been several days since he'd been able to sneak a morsel to the she-dog—she whose name was Hannah. He tucked an egg and a few strips of dried venison in the basket and hurried out into the brisk red morning.

Hannah's growls came to him first. He stopped just short of her cove and sat behind the rock from which he had first spied her with her pups.

"Hannah," he whispered. "She-dog, what's wrong?"

She murmured no response, but her growls became snarls and snaps and Pietre could now clearly hear the dark gnarl of a wolf that had moved almost directly in front of Pietre's hiding place. Pietre spoke no more, barely daring to breathe. Further back, the pups whimpered and moaned. Suddenly there were jumps and barks and the clear cry of a dog that had been struck. "Hannah," he whispered again, and again he received no response.

Stealing a glance he saw that dog and wolf were circling, speaking to one another in deep guttural tones Pietre could not understand until he heard Hannah leap up screaming, "They are MINE!"

She struck her mark. The wolf lay still a moment, breathing heavily. She circled him panting. From the way she moved on the grass, Pietre could tell that at least one of her legs was wounded. The sounds of the wolf seemed to fade and, for a moment, Pietre thought the attacker was dead. Pietre nearly stepped into the low clearing when he heard the wolf growl again, fierce, low, unforgiving.

The wolf sprang on the she-dog, and for much too long dog and wolf were a tumble of fur and howls and low, rasping speech. Pietre heard something else as well—the sounds of the pups, creeping along toward the rock where he was hidden.

The wolf heard it too and this time when he struck Hannah, it cut desperately, deeply. Pietre, even with his weak human senses, could smell the blood. The pups began to cry, pitiful tiny sounds as the wolf jumped towards them. Hannah had fallen close to Pietre's rock—part of her body lay in his view. He could smell the fur matted with saliva and sweat, could hear her breathing, and could see the tiny ball of a singular pup at her feet.

"Take him," Hannah said in a fierce whisper. "Take him and leave." And then with a distracting roar, Hannah leapt at the wolf, kicking the small black and pink-nosed pup to Pietre's side.

Pietre did not think to do anything but obey and, tucking the pup into his pouch, he crawled away as quickly and quietly as he could.

Behind him, he could hear her again, hissing at her enemy, "They are mine." And then, not daring or wishing to hear more, Pietre took the shivering puppy and ran.

WHEN HE CAME INTO HIS HUT, HIS MOTHER, CARINA, LOOKED AT HIM. In many ways she was like a dog herself—lean, strong, with soft hair that tumbled down her back in a thick, neat wave. Her eyes were delicate and brown, but uncomfortably keen. "Pietre," she said, stopping him as he ran for his room, "the herbs."

Pietre stopped, his back still turned from the penetrating eyes.

"We slept badly last night," his mother said, "and a bright batch of mint does wonders for the head."

"Mint was scarce this morning, Moecka."

"Was it? Adventure, I take it, was not."

And with that, Pietre faced his mother. "I found him in the woods. Orphaned." He hoped it was a lie.

His mother wiped her hands on her dress and took the steaming water off the fire before moving to Pietre. Carefully, she took the pup into her hands, observing the dark muzzle, the thick tail, the odd point of its tiny ears. His mother handled the dog as though it was a delicate doll and Pietre guessed she had never seen a dog so young.

"Orphaned?" she asked.

Pietre did not dare to answer. Humans, he knew, occasionally abandoned their weak or injured to the woods to starve or die during the night hunts, but dogs did not.

"An unusual pup," she said, her voice soft, measured. She returned the dog to Pietre. "You know that dogs cannot live among us. They prefer the company of their own and the freedom of living outside city walls."

Pietre could not argue. Dog packs roved through the woods, scavenging, singing, and surviving better away from the human villages that sweltered under taxation, lack of sanitation, and the heavy hands of the Veranderen. To house a dog could put it at risk.

The dog whimpered and burrowed deeper into Pietre's chest.

His mother tightened her lips into a pale line. "He is very small. He will need to be nourished today. Tomorrow we will seek a she-hound to nurse it." She paused, pointing to a pot of milk warming over the fire and firmly repeated, "Tomorrow."

Pietre took a rag from the kitchen, twisted it into a thin rope and dipped this into the pot of milk. He lowered the dripping rag to the hungry dog's lips and let it suck until it whimpered for more. Pietre fed the dog over and over until the pot ran dry. When it did, he cradled the tiny pup against his neck and by the warmth of the fire, the two of them slept in a small heap.

Pietre awoke only when he heard his father, Jager, washing at the door. The sun, though still bright, was now beginning its descent, and the moon rested—a slender matriarch in her throne of purple sky. Each afternoon Pietre's father returned dirty and stooped from the copper mines where he worked harvesting metals to be refined and formed, then sold or sent to the head city.

Groggy, Pietre watched his father come in and move close to his mother. Without words, his father held up his palm. His mother returned the gesture, placing her own palm softly against his. It was a gesture common among adult relations or close friends. But before their hands had parted, Pietre watched his father bend down to place his forehead gently against his mother's face. They stood like that, heads pressed softly together, for several moments. They had done this for as long as Pietre could remember, but lately it had begun to embarrass him. He turned away and with his movement the silence of the hut broke and his father came over to sit by him at the hearth.

Pietre sat up, dog in hand.

"And what is this?" his father said, stunned and grinning.

"I found him," Pietre said excitedly, forgetting for a moment the terror of the morning.

"In the wood," his mother cut in. "Orphaned."

His father, too, paused to examine the unusual ears, but did not linger as long as his mother had. "Well, then, does he have a name?"

"The dog does not need a name from us," Carina said. "It's not as though the dog could be kept." She laughed at the thought.

Pietre carefully pressed against one of the dog's soft ears and said, quietly leaning toward his father, "If I could, I'd name him Humphrey."

His father whispered back, "And if you could, that'd be an excellent name."

11

His mother cleared her throat and nodded toward an empty pan.

"Apparently, it's time to see what the old hens have for us today," his father said, winking. He was gone only moments before he returned. "Carina, there's a dying she-dog out here—ripped to shreds. Grab some rags while I get water."

Pietre sat frozen, clutching the little dog against him. Both shuddered, but neither moved until Pietre's father called, "Son, bring me that pot."

Pietre did not want to obey. He knew the dog outside was the she-dog Hannah and he knew what it meant that she had brought none of the remaining pups with her. Yet when his father called once more with a harsh "Pietre" there was nothing to do, but rise and get the pot. His father filled it with water and together he and Carina methodically washed, dried, and pressed upon the bloody gashes that refused to heal. Pietre was sent to fetch more rags, to heat water, to gather bread crusts. It was difficult work, but soothing in its constancy. For a time, Pietre almost forgot the danger that Hannah was in as he moved steadily between pot and rag. And then, abruptly, his mother rose, placed the rag in the bucket and gently held the she-dog's chin. "Ah now, my dear." His mother's face was set, but her eyes shimmered, flickering like candles lit behind windows when it rained. Pietre looked away, willing his body to stiffen, but trembling.

The she-dog sighed a soft "Thank you" to all of them, and then whispered something to Carina that only just brushed against Pietre's ears. Carina listened for several minutes, her face pale but firm until finally the whispering stopped and Pietre's mother rose to fetch a blanket while his father went to feed and milk the goat.

"Bring him," the she-dog begged Pietre. "Please."

He left and returned with her pup. She placed her head on the pup's soft body as her breath came in shallower intervals.

When it seemed the she-dog had fallen into a hollow sleep, Pietre bent close to her face to listen for breath and was surprised when she spoke. "Take me outside of these walls, child. It is unwise to keep me here."

"The dogs deserve the best we can give them," Pietre said softly.

"The dogs protect their own," she said. "You should too."

Pietre pushed back a shudder and whispered, "A dog can hardly be thrown out like a sack of rotten potatoes."

"Lovely sentiment," she said, as though to scold him though there was an obvious fondness in her voice, "but not a very practical one." Hannah's breathing became slower, a dark rumble at the bottom of each breath.

Pietre turned to see his mother silhouetted in the doorway, watching. She stepped forward, stern and resolute. "Take the pup inside. His hair must be cut in the morning." Pietre stood to obey and his mother continued, her voice softening, "If the pup is to live here—and that was what the she-hound requested—then I don't want him to attract...fleas."

With that, Carina covered Hannah in one of Pietre's old quilts and hoisted her over a strong shoulder. Gently, she whispered a soft death incantation into the she-dog's unhearing ear. Then, looking straight in front of her, she carried the dog away.

The pup whined and refused to move until Pietre picked him up, cradled like a human babe, and took him to the dusty hearth. "Humphrey is a good name," Pietre whispered. The dog, able to understand though not yet to speak, pressed his nose against the boy in approval.

Pietre's father returned to get the old shovel. By the fire, Pietre and Humphrey slept to the soft rhythmic sound of shifting dirt while outside the village, the moon hung like a cradle and the world lay eerily still.

CHAPTER 3

Wittendon stood with his trainer Sarak at the gates of the great coliseum. Two thick granite pillars etched with the moon and sun formed the main entrance, and when Wittendon walked through them he felt as though their weight pressed against his shoulders. Four moon cycles remained until the centennial Motteral Mal competition, but already human slaves and Veranderen workers moved around the area preparing for the legendary tournament.

Wittendon looked up the large Hill of Motteral to the small stone basin at its top—the Sacred Tablet—the point where it had all begun, where the Sourcestone had been placed in order to grant Veranderen their power, long life, prominence, magic, and insurmountable strength.

"Don't look so terrified," Sarak said, shifting into his flesh form for the day's practice and tightening his cloak. "The Sacred Tablet is just a big bird bath that ladies kiss for love. Maybe it would help if you pictured them in their underwear."

"The birds or the ladies?" Wittendon asked.

"Whichever you prefer." Sarak winked.

At that Wittendon cracked a smile. "You know I hate these practices."

"Ah," Sarak teased, "just because you insist you have no magic—" Wittendon raised an eyebrow while Sarak continued, "Just because you practically swoon like a human female every time you think of the blades of the Shining Grey, just because you worry you'll nearly get killed and wind up going crazy and have to spend the rest of your days in an asylum?"

"Yes, I suppose that's all." Wittendon walked past another competitor, an easterner named Koll. Koll had been practicing, but was now whispering to his trainer and pointing. Softly, a word floated across the field, a word Wittendon had heard too much in his relatively short lifetime: *verlorn*—magic-less one.

Koll turned back to his training as though he'd never said a word. When Wittendon looked in his direction, Koll maneuvered the tip of his blade so that it magically sparked the grass in front of him. Koll turned to look at the prince, bringing the sword to his lips. He blew off the tip of his sword and sneered. The hair on Wittendon's neck rose up.

"Oh, and that," Wittendon muttered to Sarak.

Sarak nodded more seriously than usual and tapped his foot so that a tiny tremor rolled through the earth toward Koll. It threw his balance off just enough that his hot sword bumped against his cheek, singeing the hair. Sarak smiled and looked at Wittendon as they walked away. "Well then, cheer up. Sadora's going to be at the opening ceremonies."

In spite of himself, Wittendon's face lightened.

"At the opening ceremonies?" Wittendon asked as though to say, *Only at the opening ceremonies?*

"What?" Sarak asked. "Worried about losing your royal breakfast in front of her if she watches the actual tournament?"

"You know *they* tease me enough without you adding to it, right?" Wittendon tried to sound light-hearted, though the thought of Sarak's twin sister watching him in the tournament did make him feel a little ill.

Sarak ignored him. "Don't worry, Witt, she hasn't much heart for games like this. She'll only be there for the music and firelights."

15

Wittendon sighed. No amount of joking could change the fact that he, a royal son, was on the brink of humiliating himself in front of thousands of his subjects.

Sarak lightened up on the teasing. "Maybe if you can actually manage to look unbroody, or is that in-broody—no that sounds too much like in-breedy—well, anyway, if you could look a little more cheerful, maybe I'll let Sadora sit next to you instead of guarding her like she certainly deserves to be from such a wet blanket."

Wittendon pulled his bronze cloak about his shoulders and looked at the fat sun and hazy half-moon, which circled across the sky like partners in a dance—one fiery-gowned, rising and dipping through the day and night, the other gauzy, reserved, yet nearly constant. Though the moon moved slowly through its monthly cycles, it never set completely, hovering near the horizon when the sun hung high, waiting for its turn to rise when the sun retired to her slumber.

"Well, it would be nice to see Sadora again, if she happens to come. And if I happen to see her. And if you happen to keep your yap shut for more than two minutes."

Wittendon was about to attempt a proud, princely walk across the amphitheater for the day's Motteral Mal training, when a runner wolf entered the pavilion, bowed low at his feet, and gave him a brief message. "Your father requests your presence, oh mighty lord. There is news of deafening sadness to any kin and keeper of the wolf. Come quickly, my lord, and see."

With that Wittendon gave a quick nod to his friend, then turned and walked away, leaving the usually cheerful Sarak frowning at the long shadow that followed his prince.

WITTENDON STRODE THE IMMENSE CORRIDOR TO HIS FATHER'S THRONE room. There was only one reason his father would consider a summons urgent enough to interrupt his Motteral training: a wolf had been found dead. And if Wittendon was needed, the circumstances surrounding that death were unusual.

Before entering his father's great chamber Wittendon loosened his cloak and shifted into his wolken form—hair thickening, teeth lengthening, blood pushing through his body with extra heat and strength. His hands grew knobby and bent, much like his father's. His wolken form *looked* fierce at least. Which was good. He'd just as soon wander into his father's chamber naked as he would show up for an important task flesh-faced like a human. Wittendon entered his father's quarters, bowed quickly, and kissed his father's fist. "You asked for me, Lord King."

"The body is laid upon that table," his father said, "much as it was found."

As Wittendon moved near the dead wolf, his father followed. "The wolf Grender was one of my best and one I did not wish to lose."

"My lord," Wittendon murmured to his father, aware that Grender had been head of the Königsvaren.

His father, however, did not further acknowledge whether his general's death brought him any especial sorrow and continued, "Additionally, I find the marks most unusual."

Wittendon had noticed this as well. Most of the marks were like those from an animal with claws—scratches and crusty, bloodied gashes, while the clean cut in the hide seemed to come from a weapon. An unusual weapon. The wound gaped open, clean skin parted from clean skin, blood fresh and wet, as though it had not even tried to clot or heal.

"Father," Wittendon said, respectfully turning the wolf general's corpse and inspecting each wound. "Most of the marks are like those from a common dog. As for this," he said pointing to the cut. "It appears to have been made from a weapon containing the Shining Grey."

His father raised a bushy, black eyebrow. The rare metal was only used once every hundred years—during the Motteral Mal tournament. It was one of the few substances that could weaken, maim, or kill a Verander.

"And how," the king said, curtly, "did he *die*?"

Wittendon spoke carefully. "It is an answer I can only guess at,

Lord Father. I suspect a dog was ultimately responsible for the general's death. However, it seems that prior to that, while aiding in a practice for the Motteral Mal, the general received this wound by accident. Several of the weapon tips have been painted with the Shining Grey, have they not?"

The king nodded.

"The Shining Grey would not debilitate a wolf like it might debilitate one of the Veranderen, but it could easily weaken our wolven cousins, allowing the dog beast a deadly advantage. I can see no other explanation."

His father turned back to him. "You have a gift, my son. Perhaps it is your only gift, but at least it serves a purpose."

Wittendon bowed, not wanting to meet his father's eyes, not wanting to see in them the constant disapproval. It was true that Wittendon had a gift, a very small gift. Among his race—a race that lived for centuries and sometimes beyond—most were unused to the stiffened, cold corpses of the dead, and most were afraid. Wittendon was not. Wittendon had seen his mother laid out at a young age and remembered it perfectly. Though her body was dead, Wittendon had felt sure that something of her continued. Since then he had not been afraid to handle the dead; he had not been afraid to approach the pieces that remained of them.

The king turned away. "It is unfortunate that your gift is one that tends to be useful only in times of bad news." The king's copper eyes burned with the power of the great sun. "I will not have the leader of my wolf force humiliated at the claw of a common dog. Find the beast. And if, in battle, my wolf general has destroyed it, find the creature most connected to the dog. The murder of a wolf is punishable by death. It matters not to me whose death it must be."

Wittendon bowed, kissed his father's fist once more, and retreated just as an enormous, deeply scarred wolf named Wolrijk entered.

Once away from the king's chambers, Wittendon sighed and sent for a traveling cloak and several strips of pheasant, wondering where to begin.

A renegade dog would have very few friends and nowhere to go. It could flee to the human lands—fenced towns splattered with dirty streets and scanty huts. Or it could appeal to its own kind. Neither option seemed feasible. For a dog to enter a human city was to accept a frail human hand of help while being ostracized by its own stronger clans. And for the humans to extend help was a risky move. Yet for a dissident dog to be connected to other dogs seemed even more impossible. The humans, at least, were sentimental and reckless. The dogs, on the other hand, were careful and fiercely driven by the needs of the pack. While it was true that the dogs' strength and powers of communication were superior to many of the other races, the dogs knew that the king could destroy them. And they would never allow the needs of one dog to topple the needs of the pack.

Wittendon belted a copper canteen around his waist. He would start with the western woods surrounding the human villages. Difficult or not, the dog must be found. And if it was dead, another connected to it must be apprehended—relative, friend, or unfortunate acquaintance. On this, the law was clear. Returning without a criminal would humiliate the rules of the Veranderen nobility. It would communicate to both human and dog that a wolf could be killed without deadly consequences. That was a message his father would never allow.

Wittendon sniffed the night air and looked to the stars to lead him through the black woods, hoping to find the guilty beast soon so that no one of innocent blood had to be taken instead.

CHAPTER 4

King Crespin paced his great hall, troubled once again by a dream of the girl. She had stood nearly swallowed by a bright blue sky. He had not in his life seen a sky of blue. The red sun and its flaxen moon, which provided power to him and those of his lineage, cast the skies in a gentle purple hue—sometimes bright as summer's lavender; sometimes hazy as a female's cloak. The sky set into indigo, and rose into a ruddy lilac. But never did it blink at him with the bright blue of the humans' eyes. Never did it rise with the golden stare of an extinct cat. Never did it set like the sterling gaze of his deceased wife. Except in his dreams. Then and only then did the ghosts of his and his nation's past rise up before him and spread themselves across the skies. Then and only then did he feel fear brewing in his chest that he did not understand.

His wolf general was dead. His eldest son was sure to be humiliated at the upcoming Mal competition. His spies brought word almost daily of a new rebellion—a group of Veranderen and men called *Septugant*—the seventh era. Each week he received reports of missing serfs and wayward Veranderen, of stolen weapons and midnight gatherings. A rebellion was nothing new. He had known and crushed many in his reign. But their convergence with the Motteral Mal was creating a minor nighttime malady of his otherwise fluid senses. Inconvenient, he reasoned, but nothing more.

Kaxon, his youngest son, arrived at the hall, a steaming mug in hand. "Another dream, my lord," he asked, bowing and presenting his father the medicine.

"It is nothing," the king replied. "There is excitement in the land over the upcoming Mal competition. It stirs my blood. I trust that it ignites yours as well."

"Indeed, my lord. My training goes well."

"Very good," his father replied and, dismissing his son, took slow sips of his sleeping tonic until violet dawn began to creep through the east windows and he finally fell into slumber.

WITTENDON AWOKE WITH THE BIRDS AND A SHORT HOUR LATER FOUND the town to which the bloodied she-dog had retreated. Catching her scent had been surprisingly easy. The wolf and dog had met at a secluded hill outside this village. Other animals had been there too—young ones whose scent was that of dog and wolf combined. Wittendon did not need to dig the tiny graves left by the she-dog to understand what that meant. The wolf, Grender, had fathered a litter of half-breeds. And half-breeds could not be allowed. Of all things, King Crespin was most clear on this. Although half-breeds were sometimes born harmless or even deformed, they were often born with strange powers and were dangerous—their bloodlines wrapping about in unpredictable ways with the potential of two different races at their command. Yet, as Wittendon had trodden the tiny graves, as he had scented the blood trail the mother dog left in her work of burying her young, Wittendon could not deny that the thought of so much premature death left him colder than when he had first arrived.

Now, in the muddy morning, choking in the smells of dirty chicken pens, children's feet, and breakfasts of burned porridge, Wittendon wished he had not caught quite so many fish for breakfast. He could tell that even by low human standards this village was repugnant. The city gates themselves hung askew and unguarded, the smoke from the chimneys seemed thin and dingy, and the scent of unwashed human was so strong, it made Wittendon's full stomach turn circles.

Before entering the gate, Wittendon shifted into his flesh form. Even so, there was no possibility that he would be mistaken for a human. His wine-colored robes, which hung to the ground, were streaked with orange and lined with golden thread along the hem and sleeves. His face was young and ruddy, his eyes sharp and steely. And his stature—tall even by the standards of his own kind—was that of a giant to the mortal flesh-wearers.

Wittendon had but to look at an old, crumpled woman and she pointed toward a hut on the outskirts of the village. The she-dog had clearly retreated there and collapsed. Then some minutes later, it seemed she was carried into the gates of the hut and placed in a bed of meager grass. Near a weed-filled garden surrounded by wildflowers, Wittendon could see—as any half-blind hag could have—a mound of freshly dug dirt. Deep within it, he smelled the death of the creature he sought.

Wittendon sighed. The wolf's murderer was quite dead. Which left Wittendon to hunt out and convict the humans connected to her—those who lived in the filthy hovel before him. At least it had been simple.

"Man serf," he called, waiting only a moment before a chestnut-haired man opened the door and stood before him.

The man offered a low bow. "May I be of service to his greatness, the prince?" A woman appeared at the man's side, silent and nearly as tall as the man.

Immediately Wittendon sensed the smell of the she-dog on the woman. He was surprised at its strength considering that the dog must have been buried for some days now.

"A wolf has been found dead," Wittendon said. "I am sent to find the human responsible for this death."

"I would be happy to assist you if I in any way knew how," the man said in a way that did not convey even the smallest hint of happiness or willingness. "But no wolf has been known to have died in these parts for generations."

"I do not believe a human has killed the wolf," Wittendon responded. "Yet I am quite sure that a human is connected to the murdering dog and it is my job to find that human."

"I wish you much luck in this, good prince," the man began, trying to shut the door.

Wittendon reached out and held it. "And my job is completed at this hut. The woman at your side reeks of the offending dog. As the dog no longer lives, the woman is to be taken instead."

With this news, Wittendon could feel heat rise in the man's body as well as a gentle trembling.

"My lord," the man began, more humbly than before and with an especially low bow, "how could such a thing be?"

"You know the law," Wittendon said. "The murder of a wolf must be paid through the murder of another." Wittendon could feel the man trembling through the thin boards of the floor. Firmly, Wittendon took both of the woman's arms and led her forward. Her face was clear and open with eyes the color of forest paths. She had not yet spoken and, while Wittendon could feel sadness and a sense of fear in her, he could not grasp at any feeling of repentance.

"That dog did not belong with us," the man said, boldly stepping beside his wife.

Wittendon tied the woman's hands in front of her body. "And yet you showed it mercy."

"We were unaware of the she-hound's"—and here the man paused, choosing his words carefully—"*crime.*"

"The woman is connected to the animal," Wittendon said simply.

"The woman is a silly woman. She cannot help but be connected to the suffering." The man's voice had begun to rise.

"Come," Wittendon said gruffly to the woman, grasping her wrists and growling.

"Besides," the man continued suddenly, "*I* was the most connected to the animal. I found the dog and brought her here. I cleaned her wounds and dug her grave."

"Jager, that is enough," the woman said at last.

Wittendon looked to the man. "Your defense does you no favors."

But the man continued, "The dog was my project. This woman merely followed my instruction."

Wittendon raised one pale, hairy brow and bared his upper teeth, no longer looking as human as before. "Well, then," he said calmly, holding out his rope and tying the arms of his new captive more quickly than seemed possible. "I can release her."

He pulled at Jager's wrists.

Quickly, before Wittendon could move, Jager leaned forward, fleetly touching his forehead to that of his wife.

Wittendon felt the heat of the faces of man and wife connecting. It was something he had never seen among the humans or known among his own race. His father's only affection was a quick touch of his fist to Wittendon's shoulder in the formal greeting of nobility, and Wittendon's memories of his mother were dim and distant—snatches of flower-laden scents and bits of song that hummed into his veins when she had bent to say good night.

More harshly than he intended, the Veranderen prince turned and led his captive through the dim morning. The smells of meager human breakfast assaulted him as he walked towards the exit, the sounds of nervous mothers' lullabies bidding him farewell.

PIETRE HAD BEEN TOLD BY HIS MOTHER TO AVOID BEING SEEN AT ANY cost. Humphrey, she had said, must be kept in the room, even if he had to be tied to the bed. Pietre had gasped. To tie a dog, it was unthinkable. His mother had bit her lip nervously. "I believe that even the dogs would agree that to be temporarily bound is better than to be permanently killed. He cannot be seen or heard or it will mean death; do you understand?" Pietre had nodded, though he had not understood. Now he began to. He had peered around the kitchen door, shaking, as his father was led from the house. Pietre had seen humans taken before. They did not return.

Pietre walked slowly from the kitchen to the place where

Humphrey was tied. The dog was just learning to speak. He whined softly, looked to Pietre, and said, "No."

In the other room, Pietre heard his mother crying.

"Don't be angry," Pietre said, untying Humphrey. "I wish I could have tied my father to the bedpost too. And I'm pretty sure if he'd needed to, he would have tied me." As soon as he said it, Pietre began to cry. None of it made sense. They had done nothing wrong. In fact, they'd done everything they thought was right. And nothing good had come of it.

Pietre sat on the floor sobbing until Humphrey came and pressed his nose to the boy's hand. The dog's nose was still pink and black, his fur mostly black with patches of white on his chest, muzzle, and legs. His body was small, but his paws—also pink and black—seemed to grow bigger every day. Humphrey put a paw in Pietre's lap.

"Humphrey," Pietre asked suddenly, wiping his face on a ragged sleeve. "If he comes around again—he who shines like the midnight moon—if he comes again, would you be bound for your safety?"

"No," the dog repeated.

"No," Pietre said. "No. My father would not either." The boy sat there for a long time tears steadily trickling down his face. When his eyes were swollen, but his mind felt clear, he stroked the now sleeping dog in his lap. They had both lost a parent now. It didn't make Pietre feel better exactly, but it made him feel less alone.

FOR WITTENDON, THE DISTANCE TO THE HEAD CITY WAS A MERE hour's run through woods and pasture, but with the human it took several hours of walking along paths and badly paved roads before they arrived. At a small patch of dilapidated huts outside the great wall of the city, Jager asked to stop at a well. "Please, my lord," he said, his voice cracking from thirst. Wittendon consented though he told the prisoner to hurry. On this, the west side of the head city dwelt the most destitute and desperate humans. They clustered together—outlaws, beggars, and thieves—messy camps of men who lived no better than barnyard beasts, and did not seem to want to.

Wittendon waited impatiently for the prisoner to draw water. The prince did not wish to have beggars pulling at his robes, holding out their filthy palms, and muttering for a crust of bread, but just as Jager finished his small drink, an old man tottered before the prince, bowing in an exaggerated fashion. Wittendon opened his mouth to say that he had no food to give when the old man suddenly spit at Wittendon's feet.

Calmly, Wittendon stepped over the spittle, pushing the man aside and walking towards the western gates of his city.

"Haven't time for me, eh, Lord *Werewolf?*"

Jager drew in his breath.

Wittendon stopped and turned slowly to face the man. "What did you say, old man?"

"I said," the man repeated, stepping so close that Wittendon could see the three rotten teeth that dangled from his upper gum, "that those of mighty blood and impenetrable hide have little time for the humans who make their tools and send their rations in grain, sweat, and blood."

Wittendon drew himself to the full height of his flesh form and faced the man squarely. "We give more time than we wish and more care than some deserve, you toothless, drunken fool. But that is not what you said."

"I said," the beggar whispered, moving closer, "a name deserved by those who shift from man to wolf and wolf to man and give more care to one race than the other. *Werewolf,*" he hissed.

"And," Wittendon said, with a seeming calm, "you will not say such a word again." In a moment, Wittendon was holding the old beggar's throat, but the hand he used was no longer that of a man. The fingers had grown long and gnarled. Coarse hair rippled like a wave of shimmering water along his back and limbs, a thick, slate-colored mane. The shifter's teeth grew sharp, white, and strong. His hands were human-shaped, but as muscular as a man's arm with thick nails like polished iron tusks.

He held the old man by the throat and lifted him so that the man dangled in the air like a dead goose. Wittendon held him until the man's skin turned gray and his breath came only in slow, thin wheezes. "Perhaps now you will remember that the Veranderen are a mighty race that oversees—despite the seething, often ungrateful nature of their varied kingdom—many kinds of subjects." He dropped the man to the ground. "And that they are not the ancient, limited, verlorn beasts whose name you so carelessly speak." Wittendon growled low, his skin softening, his back, chest, and arms shrinking back into the tall, thin form that was the pale prince. Only his teeth remained sharp and wolken. Wittendon smiled, baring them.

The man held his throat, gasping and nodding. Wittendon shook his head, dropping a thin gold coin at the man's feet. The old man bowed again, still coughing, and scratched a bit with his foot in the dirt.

Wittendon walked ahead, not noticing that the man did not pick up the coin. The prince jerked the rope connected to Jager's wrists. Jager stumbled forward, falling into the dust where the old man had sketched a small, rickety '7.' Wittendon pulled the rope again, without turning back. Jager quickly swiped his hand through the dirt and stood, the remnants of the dusty '7' clinging to his skin.

CHAPTER 5

The 6th Era began at the end of the 11,100th tournament of the Motteral Mal. It did not begin peacefully.

Born a son of one of the king's sorcerers, Crespin had barely ranked high enough to compete in his first Motteral Mal. Fortunately, rank did not concern him. He had strength, and magic more powerful than anyone had seen since the changing of the suns.

At age sixteen, Crespin stormed through the tournament, defeating Veranderen decades older with years of training. In the years of the 5th Era, the winner of the Motteral Mal would become head of the great Council of Elders, the highest-ranking official in the land.

As Crespin continued to conquer, moving up each round, the Council grew more suspicious. They were concerned about an ancient prophecy having to do with one who could control the Grey, one who could change the suns, overturning their way of life.

When Crespin left the final hill, bloody and victorious, they did not greet him as a victor. Rather, they examined his skin, his blade, his eyes, his urine. Nothing was amiss. Crespin was not one of the Greylords as they had feared. Even so, the members of the council were concerned to see such a young, inexperienced Verander ascend to a rank higher than their own. At the last moment, one of the most esteemed Veranderen, an elder known as Tomar, found an old scroll stating that competitors under the age of eighteen could be made to wait until the next tournament if the Council deemed them too young. An elder named Naden supported the motion and after a unanimous vote, Crespin was deemed too young—too impetuous, too *rash*.

The elders would come to regret their decision. One hundred years is a long time for a talented, driven Verander to practice. And plan. At the next tournament, Crespin easily took his victory. And then, after the tournament, feasting at the victor's place of honor, alone with the great elders who would be decorating him with leaves of the Crimson Maple, Crespin produced a long straight blade—tipped in over three inches of the great Grey. The elders stood, scattering, trying to summon the blade away from Crespin. With a burst of magic Crespin divided the blade into twelve long deadly slivers, slaying all but one of the elders—the very one he had most wished to kill. That Verander— Tomar—fled the land, never to be seen again.

It didn't matter. Crespin came forth from the chamber of the elders covered in blood and crowned himself as leader: the first king. That night, during a speech at the celebration, Crespin declared that his people did not need bureaucratic councils. They needed leadership. He had just defeated eleven of the most powerful Veranderen of the land. Leadership was what they got.

In the years that followed, assassins flocked to Crespin, only to be killed before they had so much as glimpsed a hair of the king's precious face. Crespin could sense them. He could feel their weaknesses. He could destroy them. Through the years, murder attempts came less and less and finally not at all. Rumor whispered that the king had power to seize the spirits of the most vicious and powerful assassins, bending their ghosts into his service, though none could know for sure. Most of the Veranderen now living did not remember life with the Council, or a time when any would openly threaten the king. King Crespin had been, in his way, good to them. The Veranderen now lived in a golden age at the height of wealth, comfort, and security.

If not loved, King Crespin was respected. If not honored, he was feared. And each Verander depended on the king's strength, his cunning, and his talent in government. He was a masterful politician, a perfect swordsman, and a magician like none had ever seen.

CHAPTER 6

The gates of the palace stood open, awaiting the arrival of the prince. Jager gasped at the height of the bronzed doorways carved with glyphics of the deep red sun. He followed Wittendon, stumbling up steps that were too tall for regular men. As they marched through the gardens of the palace, Jager noticed that there was no horse dung to step over, no muddy straw stuck to his boots, and smells so fresh and lovely he could not quite believe they were within a city. Many of the sweetest smelling roses were thick-caned, deep in color, and masterfully wound around trellises and trees.

Wittendon walked impatiently, shortening the ropes on his slave's wrists, while a servant disappeared with a missive to the king.

Jager was almost too stunned by the greenery to remember the ropes that held him. He knew that his wife, with her simple garden bed of nettle and purslane, could never imagine flowers like this. "How old, my lord, are the roses?"

"Older than you, human, and many of my kind as well." Wittendon paused so long that Jager considered the conversation ended. Yet, after some minutes, Wittendon spoke quietly. "The oldest roses were tended by my mother, the beautiful Loerwoei, and then later a human female who was my father's servant." Wittendon seemed to sag at the thought, and said nothing more.

Jager looked around the garden. He knew the tale of Loerwoei. She had sickened among a race that never grew sick and died among a people who often lived through millennia. Some among his race whispered that she had carried a curse. If it was true, it hadn't been passed to the flowers, which bloomed like maidens. "Carina would quite love this," Jager whispered to himself.

"When you speak in my domain," Wittendon said harshly. "Do it loud enough that your prince can hear."

"I meant no disrespect, Lord Prince. I only noted that my wife would have found such gardens similarly soothing."

"Your wife would have found the gardens soothing until she tired of the work and fled like my mother's useless she-gardener did."

Jager bristled, pinching his mouth closed.

The prince's eyes hovered like stormy clouds above the straight line of his mouth. "The roses that still live are tended as though they are babies, but new roses will never bloom again in this garden. My father forbade it after my mother's death."

Jager spoke no more and the two continued quickly to the great hall, Jager trotting behind the tall Verander in an effort to match the long, silent strides.

Wittendon left the prisoner in the hands of the guards. He needed to escape from humans and roses and memories. In not too many minutes, he found himself in one of the Motteral training rooms. He was surprised at where his feet had taken him. The Motteral Mal was not something that excited or soothed him.

Wittendon wandered to the weapons wall and ran a sharp fingernail along the long curved blade of one of the scythes. The scythes were over three feet in length, the curved blade itself being well over a foot long and sharp on either side. Today, the shimmering tip was only steel, but at the real tournament, the tips would be made from the rare and poisonous metal his people called the Shining Grey.

Wittendon lifted the scythe from its rack and swung it around. He cut and jabbed at the air from all directions. Even for those with magic, the Grey could prove deadly. It could disfigure, tear, poison, or cause pain so excruciating that the nearly immortal Veranderen could barely withstand it. For him…Wittendon didn't want to think about it. His own body was tall and strong, his hide tough, his torso lean and hard, but even after years of his father's tutelage and then months of intensive training with Sarak, he could not make the smallest amount of magic come forth. Such a weakness would ruin him at the tournament. With every swing he could feel his father's disappointment at having a magic-less—a *verlorn*—son.

Wittendon balanced the blade of the scythe on his palm, feeling the cool of the sharp metal against his skin. Sometimes when he dreamed, he remembered a time when prickles of magic sparked at the tips of his fingers and surged through his body. But then, that's what dreams were made of—illusions, wishes. He sighed.

One thousand years ago his father had won his first Mal tournament at the tender age of sixteen. Wittendon tossed the blade, letting it flip mid-air so that he could catch it again flat in his palm without getting cut. He held it for a moment, then lifted it over his head and swung it in tight, powerful circles. His father was every bit as strong now as he had been then. Stronger.

Too bad he was a lousy cockroach of a father. And husband. Crespin had married the beautiful Loerwoei less than three decades earlier. Already she was gone. Wittendon's father never spoke of her. Never explained her death or her illness in a race that rarely sickened.

Wittendon dropped his blade carelessly on the floor.

From a chest in the corner of the room, Wittendon pulled out one of the practice dummies. If he was going to stand in a practice room, feeling angry and swinging a three-foot long curved weapon, he might as well have something to hit. Wittendon let his body relax and expand —felt his skin tighten and toughen as the fur grew in thick, though still fair, across his face, trunk, and legs. The tall, stuffed dummy stared at him with glass eyes. Wittendon circled the dummy, and then lunged—centering his weight at the stomach of his unmoving victim. Weak or not, strange or not, his mother had been strong and steady in her kindness and love to him. In the few memories Wittendon could recall of his mother, she had shown more love than he'd known in the nineteen years with his father. He remembered his mother's sweet smell, her hair, and the way her eyelashes had brushed against his face and nose.

Wittendon raised the scythe at the dummy and struck. Again and again he angled the blade into the flesh of his pretended opponent. The more he thought about his father and his dead mother, the deeper his blade went. A pale blue-ish purple rose had been her favorite—*sterling roses* the human gardener had called them.

"Sterling," Wittendon whispered to the shredded dummy—the same color his mother's eyes had been, nearly the same color as the deadly Grey.

And on that thought, the stuffed dummy suddenly lifted its arm. Wittendon gasped and stumbled back, only to hear Sarak laughing.

"Sarak, you crazy dog," Wittendon said, turning toward him. "Do you mean to kill me with shock before I even make it to the tournament?"

"Might save you some embarrassment," Sarak wheezed through his laughing tears.

Wittendon paused for a moment to look at his oldest friend. Watching Sarak laugh was better than drinking a relaxation tonic. Wittendon felt the tension seep out of his neck and shoulders, felt a smile creep onto his face. "You're laughing harder than you did when we went on that campout as kids and you lined the opening of my canteen with serentaug venom. It burst as soon as my mouth touched it. My lips were numb for days."

"And the gasses from the explosion made it so you had to tell the truth," Sarak added. "Let's not forget about that. Oh, that was the best."

"I should have had you arrested then."

"You did better than that. You told Mericina that I liked her. And I couldn't deny it because everybody knew I'd made you tell the truth. That was the end of potions for me. I went back to regular magic."

"Yeah," Wittendon said, smiling just a bit. "That was a piece of sweet revenge. Too bad I couldn't taste it because my lips were numb."

"I just couldn't help it," Sarak said, still laughing. "Then, or now. Finding you alone in a practice room was strange enough. Whispering to a thoroughly mutilated practice dummy was just too much. I could see you weren't going to give him any advantage, so I decided to." Sarak wiped his tears with a hairy hand and then raised both of his arms, magically moving the arms and body of the dummy so that he walked around strutting like a chicken.

"Hilarious," Wittendon said, sitting down on a bench, still holding the scythe.

"Oh, but it was." Sarak let the dummy fall to the ground and sat beside his friend. "You should have seen yourself. What were you telling it anyway—that you planned to use its stuffed ribs to pick your teeth?"

"Not exactly," Wittendon said, standing and righting the dummy. Sarak had been raised by his half-crazed nanny and an ancient lady of the court—a woman he had called 'aunt' although many said she was no more than a distant cousin. As a lower lord with unclear parentage, Sarak couldn't compete in the Mal, but his magic was powerful.

"How'd you do it?" Wittendon asked.

"What do you mean?" Sarak asked. "You know the principles of magic."

"Yes, I do," Wittendon said, thinking about how his father had hammered them into him for as many years as he could remember. First you've got magic—that's good. Second you understand the science of what you're trying to manipulate—that's better. Third you have experience with the thing you're manipulating—that's best. "But," Wittendon said.

Sarak raised an eyebrow, waiting.

"But how does it *feel*?" Wittendon pressed.

Sarak stood, a little more serious now. "It fills you up. Say you want to make something hot. You think about how heat works—the molecules speeding up, racing through you; you think about your experiences with heat—a sweltering day, an angry heart. But it happens quickly—it fills you; it becomes you. For this dummy, I concentrated on the arm, the way muscles and sinews work, the way my own muscles felt. But that wasn't all that connected me to the dummy. For a moment all those thoughts, all those feelings about muscles became me; and I moved the dummy. For some it starts slow and they have to really concentrate. For others, it comes in a flash, and they connect themselves to the magic."

"And for those with no magic?" Wittendon asked.

Sarak sighed. "Then there is no connection, regardless of the level of concentration."

Wittendon frowned.

"Look, maybe we should start at the beginning. Shift into your flesh form and let's start where the tournament does."

The Motteral Mal began in the Verander's weakest form—the flesh. Then as the match progressed, one of the competitors would suffer a defeat or reach the point where he needed to shift to his wolken form to survive. Which also signaled a loss. Round two was fought in the wolken form, but without magic. It was only in the final round that magic could be used. Magic and the Shining Grey—the two things Wittendon feared the most.

"No, let's go to round three," Wittendon said. "I've spent enough time in that cursed flesh form today."

"Now you sound like your father," Sarak said.

Wittendon kicked the dummy. His mother had shifted with ease. As most of the nobility did. But his father was called The Unshifting—he would not be seen in any form that was not pure strength.

"Seems like you had a rough day," Sarak said, rescuing the stuffed dummy from further abuse.

Wittendon paused. "My father sent me to collect a wolf killer. Only the man I got wasn't the killer."

"Well, that's about as clear as a crow's foot pie," Sarak said, tossing the dummy to the side of the room. "Don't waste your pity on humans. I can assure you they wouldn't waste any on us. In fact, I really doubt they bother to waste any on their own."

Wittendon thought about Jager's face as he pulled him away from his wife and wasn't so sure.

Sarak snapped his fingers, bringing Wittendon back from his thoughts. "Okay, round three it is. It seems you've already given round two all you have and more anyway," Sarak said. "Now let's work some magic." Sarak raised his hand and a weapon from the wall flew into it. "Do not neglect your scythe in the final round. Magic alone is not enough. Magic, in fact, is best used to enhance your blade and everything else around you." As he said this, Sarak's scythe began to glow. "You can make it hot, cold, flaming, trembling, leafy, or ticklish for all I care, but make it something."

And before Wittendon could think Sarak had sprung at him, hot blade in hand. It tipped Wittendon's shoulder and he winced and stepped back a pace.

"Come, friend," Sarak said. "Concentrate and strike."

Wittendon did and while it was a fierce strike that met Sarak's blade with a clang that went to his bones, nothing—hot, ticklish, or otherwise—happened beyond that.

"And again," Sarak said, growing more focused.

Sarak's hot blade swung over and over at Wittendon's scythe. Wittendon could feel the heat from Sarak's blade warming the metal of his own, but still he could not change the temperature of the blade himself.

All at once, Sarak's blade turned as though to ice. He struck Wittendon's now warm blade and with the sudden change in temperature from Sarak's icy blow, Wittendon's blade broke solidly in two.

Wittendon threw it to the ground, but with one deft movement, Sarak kicked the jagged hilt into the air, so Wittendon could catch it. "Do not give up so easily. Even the hilt can help you. Heat it," he commanded. "Heat is the easiest to master, since usually a battle inspires such emotion. Focus your energy and your anger into the matter of the thing you hold."

Sarak struck, again circling his friend, stabbing at his side, shoulder, neck, and hide—jabs that all would have weakened Wittendon if they'd been done with the Shining Grey. It did make Wittendon angry—hot.

He focused on that heat, thought everything he could about heat, and tried to center it on the jagged-tipped hilt.

Sarak was light on his feet, but Wittendon was just as quick. He jabbed at Sarak's hand, scratched his cheek, but no heat came from the weapon. As Sarak's blows became fiercer, Wittendon felt his father's disappointment leak into his thoughts, *Your magic is weak, my son, if it is there at all.* And then, he heard the whispered word that had hovered around him since childhood. "This one," they murmured. "Verlorn."

All at once, Wittendon turned and again tossed aside the hilt. "It is enough," he said, but Sarak continued to thrust, nicking Wittendon's ear and then nearly drawing blood from the wrist.

"Pick up the hilt," Sarak said, his voice a low, threatening rumble. "The fight continues."

"No," Wittendon said, folding his arms and holding his ground.

"Do it," Sarak shouted, lifting his free hand so that, with a tossing motion, his magic sent the hilt flying at Wittendon's throat.

"I said enough," Wittendon shouted back, catching the hilt and growling as a sudden image of his mother in her garden flew through his thoughts and he saw a rush of the metallic blue roses. At the final word, Wittendon crushed the hilt. It fell in pieces, like petals to the floor.

Sarak stopped and leaned on his scythe like a cane, all the battle-fury gone in an instant. "Well, then, I suppose it is."

Wittendon glared at his friend—surprised at the strength that had poured out of him, though he knew it still wasn't magic. "I haven't got it," he said furiously, dusting the metal from his hands.

Sarak bent down to examine the pile of shavings from the metal hilt.

"Do you know much about flowers?"

"Nothing at all."

"Metals?"

"A good bit more, but still not enough to perform the simple act of heating it."

"Yes," Sarak said. "So it seems." He touched a flake from the metal hilt. "Something is stopping you from the magic. Something I don't understand. It's like your desires are turned elsewhere and your magic is lost within them."

"That's ridiculous," Wittendon said, turning his back to his friend. "I've spent my whole life working to find my magic."

"But working does not always equal desiring."

"And I've desired nothing more this last half hour than to send a hot bolt of it shooting through your backside."

"Now that I *am* glad to hear," Sarak said, gathering several bits of the destroyed hilt. Sarak stood up with a handful of metal from the ruined weapon. "Rather like rose petals don't you think?"

Wittendon ignored him and said flatly, "Whether it's desire I can't find, or magic, the end result is the same. Nothing comes out."

"Oh, but something does," Sarak said. "The blades practically hum now at your presence. As though waiting for your magic to be released."

"That's not funny," Wittendon said, kicking the pile of metal that was once his hilt.

"You're right; it's not," Sarak said, "and that is most unfortunate because I do love something funny."

Wittendon waved an irritated hand in his friend's direction. "They're going to kill me—at the tournament."

"No," Sarak said. "You might not win—don't get me wrong, but creatures strong enough to crush metal into petals *without magic* don't wind up dead. Plus," he grinned, "I think you'll impress the ladies."

As Wittendon turned to leave, Sarak called after him, "Do you mind if I take these to my sister. She'll think they're pretty."

Wittendon rolled his eyes and called back, "Take all you want. Compliments of his majesty, the verlorn prince."

WITH THAT, THE MAGIC-LESS PRINCE WALKED OUT THE DOOR AND almost directly into Sarak's sister, Sadora.

39

"Pardon me, Lord Prince," she said dipping her chin to her chest in a graceful bow. "I am come only to find my brother."

"No," Wittendon stammered. "It is I who should apologize. I was not looking and I...I..." She wore a simple green gown and a plain locket, but her light cinnamon hair was shot through with honey-gold strands so that when she moved it was like watching the red sun itself.

Sarak came out of the room and tapped his sister lightly on the nose. "Old Witt's just been squeezing in some extra practice. Apparently, he's worked so hard, the blood now fails to run to his brain."

Sadora smiled shyly. "I am sure the blood runs where it must for these things. And how goes your training, Lord Prince?"

Wittendon didn't even bother to speak and looked to Sarak for an answer.

"See," Sarak said. "What'd I tell you?" He took his twin's arm and began leading her to their quarters. "If you must know, the metal sings when it is in Wittendon's hand. Not quite literally of course, though that would impress the gentlefolk of the court. Oh, but that reminds me that my dear friend's practice has landed me with a gift for my sister." He reached into his robe to retrieve the leaves of metal.

Wittendon turned to leave before he could see Sadora's reaction, although he was not out of ear shot when he heard her gentle voice murmur, "You tease me brother. It seems barely possible to crush a hilt. And to shatter it into something of such beauty...A hilt," she said again, and laughed.

Her laughter was just as honeyed as her hair. Wittendon unconsciously slowed his walk in the hope that he would hear it again. It was no wonder Sarak cracked so many jokes if that was the sound that greeted him when he did.

Sweaty and tired, Wittendon walked to his chambers, not feeling exactly good, but not feeling quite so hopeless either.

CHAPTER 7

Pietre laid out his findings from the day—five small minnows and a satchel of greens. Most of the fat fish had swum further upstream to mate, and though greens were bountiful in the wood, they did little to keep the belly full. His mother had remained home to do a bit of mending and laundry for their crotchety old neighbor. His mother worked well with a needle, but since the visit from the prince, most people had been hesitant to give Carina work. It wasn't that they were cruel. They were just afraid.

No one came to the door. No one stopped them on the street to share gossip. But occasionally, several slices of bread would show up near the door or a bucket of berries drizzled with a few spoonfuls of milk would be hung on the gate. On those days his mother would weep. Pietre knew why—whoever had left the crusts or berries would likely go a little hungrier that night. There was not much that grew well in their village. The woods were shared by animals and humans; animals claiming the better part. With the way things were, there was not always an abundance to share. So when people gave a little—even when they avoided being seen helping the unlucky family—they were really giving quite a lot.

One morning, an anonymous vial of oil with a fat clove of garlic had appeared at their doorstep. The sharp, slick dressing made things taste a little better, but today it didn't make Pietre feel any less hungry after sunset meal. Pietre went to bed early.

Humphrey came to him and tried to lie on Pietre's chest as was his habit, but he was getting too big. Instead he rested near Pietre and laid his head on the cot in the warm spot between Pietre's shoulder and head—the soft black and white muzzle and wet nose tickling Pietre's neck. Usually Humphrey fared better than the humans—he could eat foods their weaker stomachs could not. But tonight Humphrey had gone just as hungry as everyone else and his stomach growled. Humphrey didn't seem to mind and fell into slumber almost as soon as he'd tucked his head next to Pietre's. But Humphrey's grumbling belly kept Pietre awake—wondering. Over and over he heard the words of his mother on that first day he'd brought Humphrey to their home. *As if a dog could be kept.*

Pietre tried telling himself that Humphrey wanted to be here, but in his heart he knew that Humphrey had not been given the chance to be anywhere else.

Pietre wrapped his ragged nightshirt around his skinny chest as the howls of the Blødguard filled the night. He knew the Veranderen starved the Blødguard in order to intensify their hunts. Pietre still couldn't find a place in his heart to pity the vicious wolves, but as Humphrey's stomach growled so hard the cot seemed to tremble, Pietre found a sliver of understanding for the half-starved beasts that he'd never known before. The Veranderen would starve their friends to get something out of them. Was Pietre doing the same thing in keeping Humphrey close instead of returning him to the dogs?

Deep into the night, after the wolves had fallen silent, Pietre knew what he needed to do. He curled into his thin quilt, holding it to his ears so he wouldn't have to hear the grumbling of Humphrey's belly; and finally fell asleep.

~

A GOOSE SLATHERED IN HONEYED CREAM SAUCE AND SHOWERED IN huckleberries sat untouched in the king's chamber. King Crespin rose from his bath and dressed, though most of the nobles in the palace were likely laying out their bedclothes. The sun dropped low, slipping beneath the earth and pulling his thoughts to things departed. Most of the Veranderen lived so many years that those who didn't sat like stones in one's memory. Crespin picked up the ten-foot staff with the translucent ball at the top. He fingered the smooth wood gently, then touched the ball, which lit with a subtle hum.

Crespin did not wish for things, but he wondered occasionally how it might have been if Draden—the only Verander he'd considered fit to be his advisor—had not fled shortly after the slaying of the elders. Draden had been both sorcerer and scholar, master of the old language and the new. None had known more of metalwork, minerals, and magic than Crespin's renegade friend.

Draden had crafted the staff that Crespin now carried—a staff that could shift with mood to act like any weapon, except the Grey, for any circumstance except to kill Draden. The king smiled—it was just that sort of thinking that he had liked about his old friend.

The moon hung high as Crespin exited the palace. He followed its light through the northern woods and into the forbidden grove. No one knew it was forbidden; no one knew it was anything unusual at all. But nearly fourteen years ago when something had been taken from Crespin, he had enchanted it. Now, if any of his subjects happened upon the grove, the ground pulsed with danger and the air hung heavy in their lungs. The unwitting trespassers' thoughts would begin to spin with their darkest memories and deepest fears. Those who didn't leave immediately were escorted off, and though they often had to spend several nights in the mental infirmary, they never quite remembered why.

Crespin laughed to think of it and then stood in the center of the grove, indulging in a few minutes of silence—no buzz of insects, no hoot of owls, no breaking of twigs, nothing in his bewitched patch of earth except his own thoughts.

Draden had had his reasons for fleeing. In the slaying of the council, Crespin had taken from Draden many men whom he had revered and one he had loved deeply. Still, the cleansing of the council had been necessary. Crespin had tried to explain this to his friend—his friend who was hardly opposed to a brutal act when necessary. Yet Crespin had been unable to sway Draden to his side with arguments of the power and renewal the two of them could accomplish together. Draden had fled to distant hills to eat herbs and tree bark until he withered away—a victim to the weakness called love. Crespin would not be such a victim. After Draden left, the king had burned Draden's letters, his portrait, and any of his belongings left in the palace. Crespin found that memories were harder to destroy, but he had carefully pushed the defector's face and voice from the forefront of his mind, remembering only those things most practical—Draden's tactics in battle, his ferocity, and his ability to mold the powers of those he defeated, to shape them into something useful.

Crespin took a deep breath, the cool air sharp and refreshing in his lungs. The partial moon hovered brightly, and Crespin let his staff dim, the memories of his old friend settling, hiding. Crespin walked several paces southeast, the trees thickening around him until he came to a damp, vine-hung crag. Crespin clicked his staff to the ground and the vines parted, revealing an opening. Then, letting his wolken body grow as large as possible, Crespin walked, stooping, through the cool mouth of the cave into its warm middle. Water sounded in his ears as he trod over the sludge, then the rock-like bits, and deep under the earth into his great room. The torches within lit up as soon as he entered, revealing neat towers of coins, artifacts, weapons, and jewels. The room was a storage shed, a treasure chamber, a sanctuary. Or it had been for most of his reign. Now, though the room was still bursting with riches, a jewel stand at the center of the room sat empty, its four claw-like Pallium prongs filled with nothing but acrid air.

Crespin struck his staff to the floor—a shock of light bursting from its tip like a small star. Quivering green smoke snaked around his feet, as though bending, bowing. "My lord," three voices hissed from the mist. "An honor, a delight, a joy."

The king scowled. He had captured these spirits many years ago

44

when his reign was still young. Most assassins had been conquered with ease. Crespin had drawn their strength into his staff and then used their own power to kill them. These three had given him an especial challenge. As their reward he had given them a special punishment: to live as *Mördare*—half-lives—protecting the treasure they had wished to claim. They could not die; they could not live. It was a fine, and particularly cruel, piece of enchantment.

Staring at the mist that began to take a slinking humanish form, Crespin asked, "Have any breached this chamber since last I visited?"

"Oh, no, our Magnitudinous One. No." The three voices wound over each other like maggots, their wispy ghost forms scraping the ground.

The king scanned the room, inspecting each gem, each breastplate, the twelve thin spears, then nodded. "And do you now wish to tell me who it was that took the stone those years ago?"

It was a question Crespin asked every time he entered the cave, though every time he was greeted with the same reply. "You have bound us, oh Almighty Master, to protect, not explain."

Crespin gripped his staff, the tip a sickly green. "You've done such a marvelous job protecting," he said very quietly. "I can see how I shouldn't pester you in asking for explanation."

"Such a small stone," they hissed in unison. "Why should our Infallible One need it?"

"Clearly I do not," Crespin said, waving his staff so that the phantoms stood before him in full bodily form. "But just because I do not need a thing does not mean I do not wish to know who took it." And then he smiled, leaning toward them. "Remember," he said, "that to tell me is to alter the terms of our arrangement. To tell me is to be released from your lovely little stewardship here."

The Mördare bit their rotting wrists, pulled out tufts of hair, scratched at their own eyes. Crespin knew it took all their efforts to refrain from telling him.

"It would be so easy," he said sweetly, "just a few simple words."

The Mördare ground their teeth, pulled at their tongues, dug their nails into the hollows of their cheeks. Of course they wanted to tell him. Of course they wanted to be released from their bondage. But to tell him would be to lose the one piece of power they now held against the king, the one small portion of themselves they had retained. Crespin had not thought a theft possible. Because of this, he had bound them only to report any who *sought* the stone. And according to the Mördare no one had sought the stone; someone had simply taken it. Now, they held this bit of knowledge as their only revenge. And no matter the prize, they would not let it go. Crespin understood. What did freedom matter if you held no power in it?

"Please, our Thunderous One. Magnanimous. Colossal." The ghouls twisted their bodies in a misty circle around Crespin—swaying, bowing. "We did more than any others could have against a force more powerful than any in the land," they moaned. "And the force is now gone. We have killed it." The Mördare stood, smiling—the green ghoulish lips curling over putrid fangs.

"So you have told me," the king said. "Many times."

The Mördare seemed to laugh.

"But the most powerful stone of this land is gone and you have given me no one to blame. Thus your servitude must continue."

The ghouls stopped laughing. "No, our lord. It is too long already. Release us to the life beyond. Do not force us to always remain in this in-between."

"You will be released," the king said, "in the year I or one of my lineage has access to the stone."

The ghouls moaned and shrank, hissing and shrieking until the king stamped, and they were gone.

WHEN CRESPIN CAME BACK INTO THE FRESH NIGHT AIR OF THE forbidden grove, his head felt clear. The Mördare could retain their secret and their bondage if they wished. Eventually Crespin would have what he wanted. Eventually Crespin always had what he wanted.

When the stone had been taken almost fourteen years ago, Crespin had enchanted this wood. All would be repelled by it. All except the heir of the one who had taken the stone. Should such a creature exist, he would be drawn to the cave; and thus to his death. Crespin would have more than revenge; he would snuff out the bloodline that might be strong enough to rival his own.

But none had come. Not yet anyway.

CHAPTER 8

Humphrey bounded through the wood. The morning was fresh and clear, the sky a deep periwinkle that signaled the winter rains were over. He could smell the coming of spring in the land at his feet and in the darkening leaves of the trees.

He had understood language since he was a babe, but in the last few weeks his speech had come to him clear and strong. In it he felt a connection to his mother and his race. Every morning when he and the boy scoured the woods for mushrooms and dandelions, wild asparagus and chicory, Humphrey thought of his mother and felt the beginnings of a song in his head. He had not quite got it right yet and he would not bring it forth until he did. It would be his first—his hondsong.

"Humphrey," Pietre called out harshly.

Humphrey felt the hair on the back of his neck stand up. It was true he was quickly outpacing the boy; still, he didn't like to be scolded like a common chicken. He ran further ahead of the boy, until he could barely hear the scuffling walk of his friend. And then, suddenly, he could hear it no more. The dog stopped, pricking his ears, listening. At once the morning seemed very very still. Humphrey raced back to the boy, worried that he'd been overcome by a wolf, or a bear, or the wolf-turned-man that had come to the house all those weeks ago. Humphrey could not see the boy, could not hear him; faintly, though, he could smell him. The dog followed Pietre's scent until he came to a small opening between two rocks where Pietre sat.

Between those dark boulders of the earth, the child looked pale and small. In the last weeks he had eaten little. Humphrey had tried to help —finding old carcasses crawling with tasty maggots, chasing the scavenge birds away before they got the best parts. But the dogs, Humphrey was learning, could eat many things that the delicate humans could not. Pietre clearly longed for bread and fresh beef. This longing had begun to show in the dark circles of his cheeks and eyes.

Now as the child sat in the dim cave with his face toward the stone, Humphrey could not deny that he looked more ghost than boy.

"Go on," Pietre said, gesturing to the thick woods. "Your mother would not have wished you to die with us."

Humphrey did not immediately understand, but sat at the boy's heels and looked into his face. When the boy failed to acknowledge him, Humphrey lay down and curled into a ball. Where they sat between the boulders, the sky could not be seen, the spring could barely be scented, and shadows cast over the boy and dog as though night was on the horizon.

"Go on," Pietre said again.

Humphrey paused, looking into the boy's eyes and feeling for the right words. "To whom?" the dog said finally. It was true that Humphrey's legs longed to run outside of the boundaries of walls and houses, that his lungs ached for air that was not crusted by chimney smoke and goat dung, that his heart wished to know those of his own— their ways, their foods, their rituals and friendship. But he had also come to love the boy and the sweet Carina who had become his mother. It seemed impossible to simply separate those two parts of himself and leave this one behind. Gently, he placed his head on the boy's bare foot.

The boy put a hand to Humphrey's head and then in the distance the two of them heard the sound of running and barking and sniffing. From far off, the dogs began to sing—their call coming to pup and boy as a sort of travelling tune, lifting through the air, forcing spring's advent into the cold, dark cavern.

Pietre stiffened. "To them," he said, even more sadly than before, taking his hand off Humphrey's head, and turning again to stare at the boulder behind him.

∾

EVEN AMONG THE DOGS, MARKHI'S SENSE OF SMELL WAS RENOWNED. He could track things from the smallest hint of scent. He could find food or water where others thought none existed. Pack leaders often asked him to help seek out dogs who had gone missing. He had found numerous lost pups, waylaid messengers, rebellious youth, and the remains of more dogs than he cared to count. Weeks ago, he had been sent to seek the she-dog, Hannah—a task which he had undertaken with much duty and some dread. He had known her well, though he had not seen the she-dog for years.

Hannah had always run to her own rhythm and Markhi knew that many years ago, she had desired to spend time among the humans, learning of their ways and aiding them in seeking food. After she had disappeared several months ago, all the nearby human villages had been searched and when she did not turn up, her mother had sought out Markhi, now as muscled and sleek as a dog could be and leader of the great pack known as Sontag.

Markhi had used every trick he knew, but Hannah had been careful to cover her tracks and her scent. Perhaps she had known Markhi would try to come for her. Until this very week, he had neither known nor felt anything of his old friend. Then, quite suddenly, as he and his pack had come to a clearing seeking fish, she had been there. Not in the flesh, but in the scent of everything around him—the bushes, the rocks, the mosses. He knew she had birthed young ones and he under-stood then why she had left her home, family, and pack. At the birthing spot, he could also smell wolf—wolf mixed so fully with dog that Markhi feared the worst. He knew the pups had been killed and he knew Hannah was hurt if not dead. The other dogs, he trusted, did not fully understand what the confusion of smells on the lonely hillside meant. He wished for it to remain that way. "There has been conflict," he said.

The dogs ran on, their paws and nails clicking with the rhythm of animals so accustomed to each other that their bodies joined into synchronized movement.

They had been following Hannah's scent to a nearby village when Markhi noticed the wolf-dog smell again and the smell of human. His ears pricked up, and he paused when he could see two boulders rising high above the earth. Two small voices, arguing in hushed tones, carried across the wind.

Markhi ordered his dogs to stand down.

As Markhi trotted to the boulders, he was not sure what to do with the creature he expected to find. A half-blood dog could never be accepted into the pack and would even be a danger to a human village. But he doubted he could kill one so young, especially when he suspected the animal was all that was left of his friend Hannah.

PIETRE CAUGHT SIGHT OF THE GREAT DOG FIRST AND SUCKED IN HIS breath. The mighty dog was a good bit taller than Humphrey's mother had been and almost twice as broad. His face and legs were a dark sandy color, which faded into black along his back like a dark robe. The dog and his pack were what Pietre had been both hoping for and dreading.

Pietre wanted nothing more than for Humphrey to stay—nothing in all the world, except to get his father back. But to keep the dog with him, to convince the young animal that there was nothing outside of the rotting walls of his village, well, that may have been true for Pietre, where only death waited for him every sunset outside the gates. But for Humphrey there was a life of freedom and song, of friendship and family. And of food—all the food he could think to need or want. Pietre knew his friend should not have to suffer because he did. And yet he hated to give him up.

"Good day, younglings," the large dog said, dipping his head in greeting.

Humphrey stared at the great dog as though the God of the White Sun had just descended in front of him. Neither boy nor pup could find their voices to reply and the dog came closer, walking a half circle around the two before Pietre finally spoke. "Good day, great one." At that, the big dog seemed to smile and stopped his pacing.

"My name is Markhi," the dog said. "I don't suppose that either of you could lead us to a town with some victuals."

"No, sir," Pietre said. "I hope you will forgive my honesty, but I really don't suppose we could."

"Honesty is nothing to forgive," Markhi said, staring now at the sunken cheeks and thin frame of the fair-haired boy.

"Victuals," Humphrey whispered, as though in awe of the enormous word just as much as he was in awe of the enormous dog. Slowly the pup had inched forward until he was close. And then, without thinking—in an impetuousness that the young of his kind were inclined to—he touched his paw to the great dog's neck and gave him a playful push.

Markhi pulled away.

Humphrey tucked his tail and sat down.

"Pup," the large dog asked abruptly. "Where is your pack?"

"I am Hannahszon and live, for now, in the human village."

"You are Hannahszon indeed," the great dog said, and the tone of his voice made the fur on Humphrey's back prickle with pride.

"You know her," Pietre asked, surprised.

"I did," the dog said simply. "I was sent here to seek her."

"You needn't seek her more," Pietre said with a sad bow of his head.

Markhi sighed. "I suspected that as well, child. I know—unfortunately—many things that I do not wish to know."

"Do you know my father?" Humphrey asked, his tail beating the earth.

For a long, uncomfortable moment the dog looked at Humphrey. "I did not know your father, although I know much of his kind."

Humphrey's tail slowed, and finally in the silence that followed, it stopped. Pietre looked at the pup as though seeing him for the first time; he looked at him the way his mother had that first evening he had arrived. Pietre saw it then, the way Humphrey's ears rose to a point, the way the fur on his chest had already begun to come in thick and course.

"No," Pietre whispered softly.

Humphrey did not seem to understand. He turned to dog, then boy, then—looking confused—he curled into a heap and lay as though scolded.

"It is not of your doing," Markhi began.

"What's not?" the pup asked.

"Humphrey," Pietre said, kneeling gently by the dog and putting a small hand between his ears. "I think your father may have been a wolf."

Humphrey jerked his head back. "No," he said. "She hated wolves. She hated that wolf who came and—" Suddenly, Humphrey was quiet. Pietre knew that Humphrey understood it too—the way his mother had growled, *They are mine.* Why would she need to claim them? Unless another had come who also felt he had claim on them, another whose claim would have been to destroy, not protect.

Humphrey put a paw over his snout and closed his eyes and stayed there, barely breathing. Markhi and Pietre let him sit until finally he said, "There is no room for me then."

Pietre looked away from Humphrey and avoided Markhi's eyes. He did not want to see that the pup did not, in fact, have a place. He would be killed by the wolves or Veranderen if they found him. He would be shunned by most of the dogs and an embarrassment more than a comfort to his grandparents. He would be a danger to any humans who sheltered him. And yet, when Pietre finally glanced down at Humphrey, catching his eye, Pietre knew that he could not abandon the pup.

"Room can be made, Humphrey," Pietre said. "Room can always be made."

As he said it, an odd breeze caught some of the leaves at their feet. In the breeze, Pietre thought he heard a whisper and in the whisper a word—unusual in its tone, old and forgotten. "Rotherem," the wind seemed to say. Pietre looked around as he was sure the word had been spoken, but saw no one.

Markhi stopped and his ears stood upright. Even Humphrey raised his head.

"Markhi," Pietre said softly. "Did you hear that?"

Markhi did not answer. Instead he looked through the boulders to the light outside. A shadow danced over a spot where sunlight had dappled the ground just moments ago. "I have just been reminded of an herb," Markhi said, glancing sideways at Pietre. "An herb that was once shown to me with a warning, for it can mask the scent of even the most foul-smelling wolf. You must find this herb. It consists of a stalk of tender green with five small leaves that grow out of it. Even dried, the herb can be crushed and used to disguise a wolfish scent."

Markhi stepped from the cave and Pietre followed. "A stalk of tender green?" Pietre asked.

Markhi nodded.

"With five leaves, somewhat dark and mostly round with just a bit of a point?"

Again, Markhi dipped his head, this time more inquisitively. "Do you know this herb?"

"When you break the stalk, a milky white comes out, but just a bit. And the smell is almost sweet like anise?" Pietre continued.

"But with something just sour underneath," the dog replied. "You do know this herb. But how? Its use is not common, especially among the humans."

For several moments Pietre did not speak. Of course he knew this herb. He had gathered it every morning at his mother's request. Since Hannah had come to their hut to die, his mother had insisted Pietre harvest it every day, even when it rained. And every day, his mother had combed a bit into Humphrey's thick coat. She had told Pietre that this was to keep the fleas away. Ever since Hannah's death, his mother had become obsessed with fleas. Now Pietre understood. His mother had known who Humphrey was.

"My mother has been using this herb for Humphrey," Pietre said simply. "Only recently, since my father was taken, she has been forgetful. That's why you could smell Humphrey at all."

"This herb?" Markhi asked. "It can be found in these parts?"

Pietre nodded.

"Find this herb," Markhi said. "Collect as much as you can. Crush the leaves gently and use it on the pup every day. Every time you come across it growing, take it all. Dry any you do not use and keep it safe. No matter the cost. If the wolves find him, he will be killed. Not only that, he will be a danger to your village and especially your kin. As for the dogs, I'm not sure that even I could convince them to rescue one who is not fully our own."

Pietre nodded gravely.

Markhi turned back to the cave and spoke to Humphrey. "As for you, growing one. When my duties bring me to these parts, I will come to you and teach you some of the ways of our kind. You have a strong heart. And a soft one as well. These are traits your mother shared. You must value and use them as I trust she did."

Humphrey looked up at the great dog, holding himself straight and tall and asked, "So I cannot come with you?"

"Even if you wished to—and I don't really think you do—your place, Hannahszon, is not among our kind. Fate has taken you to the realm of man. Strangely, it is the place your mother often wished to go. Perhaps there is some piece of destiny in this."

"But if I wanted to come with you?" Humphrey asked again, as though needing to hear something he knew he wouldn't like.

Markhi raised his head, the coppery eyes kind but firm. "The pack cannot hold you. It cannot protect you from others, or even, in some cases, from its own. There are those who have been hurt by wolves, those who cannot—or do not—forgive." Looking to the pup, Markhi bent down so he could speak to the young dog face to face. "Do not look so low. It could not even hold your mother, though she was fully of our kind. There are some with missions beyond the pack. It is up to you to find yours."

Ahead of them a shadow again fell across a place where sun had been. They heard a rustle in the leaves, a sound so slight it could have been the wind. Markhi's ears stood tall and he sniffed the air.

Humphrey sniffed as well, and then shrugged. He turned to Markhi, but the dog was already running back to his pack. "What was it?" he asked Pietre.

Pietre looked to the place Markhi had sniffed. "The shadow," he murmured. "It was strange. It looked just like a cat." His voice sparked like a small light, just lit.

"And what is a...*cat*?" Humphrey asked, his young tongue clicking against the sharp, new word.

Pietre looked away suddenly and shook his head. "Something that doesn't exist," he said, all the light in his voice snuffed out.

Humphrey didn't ask more questions. Pietre put a hand to the dog's strong back.

"I won't eat too much," Humphrey promised.

"You'll eat every bit as much as you need," Pietre said. "Moecka wouldn't have it any other way. Besides," Pietre said, smiling slyly, "bloodied lizard tails are not my favorite supper."

"That's because you don't know a delicacy when you see it," Humphrey said.

"Delicacy, huh? How'd you learn that word?" Pietre asked, starting to jog.

"My mother said it," Humphrey answered, "when she couldn't hunt and we saw her eating slugs." Humphrey began to run too and the two of them bounded toward the village—to the place they would both call home.

CHAPTER 9

The king was adorned in robes of fiery red and held a staff nearly as large as a man. He sat in an immense chair fashioned from iron and wood, which extended up into a carving of a wolf's head—mouth open, teeth exposed, the grains of wood spiraling across the face like a combination of fur and flame. Behind Crespin stood two Veranderen guards while Crespin's newly appointed wolf general waited at attention—forepaw tucked to his chest. The general, Wolrijk, was the most marred, gruesome, deformed wolf the king had ever known. His entire snout was a mass of mottled gray scar tissue so thick that his left nostril was only apparent when the wolf inhaled. Under Wolrijk's chin ran a crude line of pink as though his entire face had been torn off and then sewn back on. Even so, his most disconcerting features were his eyes. One drooped, yellow puss filling the recess while the other was half-covered with a torn, hairless eyelid that could never fully close. Crespin hated that eye. Which is one of the reasons he had selected Wolrijk. The truth was that his face was so malformed it was difficult to look at without turning away.

The general's paws and legs were not much better. The front legs were more muscled than any normal wolf and the fur of his front quarters was patchy with dark tufts of fur mixed with smooth stretches of exposed skin. The yellow nails that grew from those deformed paws looked like they had been grafted in—claws that would shred his own mother to pieces if that was the king's command.

After the handsome Grender, an ugly, vicious general was just what Crespin needed, but that didn't mean he wanted him hovering next to him all day long. Especially on such an unpleasant day as the first of the month. The king struck his staff to the floor and the ugly wolf moved back two paces.

JAGER WAS ESCORTED TO THE JUDGMENT HALL BY TWO OF THE Königsvaren—wolves with fur so dark it was nearly black except at their chests where it faded to a dull charcoal. Tucking their right paws, they each bowed to the king before stepping several paces back and leaving the prisoner to stand alone before their monarch.

Wittendon sat on a tall wooden chair to the king's right—as far away from the general Wolrijk as possible.

The prisoner looked thin and smelled like mold. They'd been holding him for nearly two months in a small cell as he awaited judgment day, which came on the first day of every third month.

One of the wolves stepped forward a pace and began reciting the crime for which this trial was taking place. Had he been holding a scroll, it would have dangled to the floor with the fussy language of judgment. Finally, as Wittendon covered a yawn, the wolf concluded, "Thus, he who herefore stands is to be held responsible for the murder in cold blood of the great wolf, Grender, general of the king's forces. The human is charged, also, with providing an asylum for the guilty she-hound and an honorable burial for said dog."

King Crespin stood then, as he had for every trial that morning, and said, "Do you, Jager Wilhelmszon, admit to harboring a dog and providing for her burial?"

"Yes, my liege," the man said.

"And in this," Crespin continued, stepping down from his great chair, "did you expect to escape judgment?"

"I did not expect to experience judgment at all, my lord," Jager said.

"You did not?" the king said.

"The dog came to us at the brink of death. We did what any human of good upbringing and merciful heart would have done." The more he spoke, the steadier Jager's words became.

"And you did not ask how she had gotten to such a point?" the king inquired, staring down at the human.

"I did not," Jager said so clearly and calmly that one of the wolf captains began to fidget.

The king, just as calm, raised an eyebrow. "Your ignorance will cost you, human. Surely you know the price for such a crime. Do you not regret it?"

"No, my lord," Jager whispered firmly.

Wittendon could feel his father grow hot. Even Jager must have seen it in in the way the king's staff began to glow with embers smoldering inside the round crystal.

"Well, perhaps you will feel it more keenly when, one week hence, you are escorted to the gallows, and there granted the privilege of crossing into the great beyond to greet your much-honored canine friend."

Jager was wise enough to remain silent, though he did not bow his head or make any other gesture of penitence.

The king met Jager's gaze and after several seconds, he said, "You will want your family, I presume, to be notified."

"My family?" Jager asked, his voice stumbling finally.

"Of course. I make a point to send a messenger to the families of those executed. We are not barbarians, human, though your kind persists in imagining us as such." The king sat down and Wittendon looked at his father's solid profile and then over the prisoner's head. The prince did not wish to meet Jager's eyes.

Jager said, "I am sure my family will be notified sufficiently by my continued absence, Lord King. No messenger wolf will be necessary."

"Truly?" the king asked. "You wish to leave them ever wondering what has become of you—whether you are slave or free or dead.

Whether you have not been released and simply failed to make your way home, having found other pastures in which to sow your precious human oats."

"Lord Father," Wittendon suddenly injected, looking to the human. "If you wish, I will tell those who remain of this one's fate."

Wolrijk did not move, but Wittendon could see that he was sneering at him as the king turned.

"I wish no such thing," Crespin said sharply. "It is not the duty of princes to wander about giving their condolences to the families of the human dead."

Wittendon lifted his head in acknowledgment and then looked away.

The prisoner spoke again. "If a messenger is to be sent," Jager said, "and if it would please the king, I would ask that the messenger leave my many precious tools as they are. They are fashioned, good king, of the best metals—metals I have mined and crafted with my own hands in a manner passed down through my family for five generations."

The king blinked. Wittendon noticed it, surprised. His father never blinked.

Jager took a breath, and waited.

"You fancy yourself mighty in the making of tools?" the king asked.

"I do not fancy anything," Jager said. "Not only am I an expert at my craft, but I am skilled in the finding and mining of the ores as well. Forgive the boast, good king, but there are none who know metal as well as I. My grandfather fashioned the pattern for the chain mail you wear upon your breast. My father fashioned the tips of your boar-killers—those mighty spears used to tame and domesticate the race of pigs. And you need not explain the Shining Grey to me because there is lore of it told in generations of my family. I know that it cannot be mined more than two moon cycles before the Motteral Mal tournament. I know that it is scarce and, under the glare of the great sun, volatile. I know that if mined too early, it will weaken and corrode, sometimes becoming so unstable that it will glow in the heat of a battle, leaking a slow venom into its handler. I know that because of this, the Grey cannot be saved from tournament to tournament and re-used. Instead, an expert smith must be employed to make the blades quickly and well in the weeks before the competition. I know much," Jager said, his chin thrusting forward.

For several moments, the king paused, fingering the glowing bauble at the tip of his staff. Finally, he quietly bent down to Wittendon as if to consult and said, "Examine him."

Wittendon arose and was about to take the prisoner to another room for questioning when the king said, "Not in words. Use your magic if it happens to exist and examine this slave's memories. Tell me whether it is truth that nestles among his words. Or lies."

Wittendon put his hand to the man's head as he was expected to do, but as usual no magic poured forth. Instead he looked into his captive's eyes and saw fear and hope, rebellion and desperation crossing like stars tumbling through the night sky. "I believe he speaks true," Wittendon said.

His father sighed audibly, clicking his staff to the marble floor so that the sound echoed throughout the hall. "Believe nothing. You must know." In a bound, the king came forward and placed his palm to Jager's temple. Jager paled and staggered backwards.

The king nodded as though an idea had been confirmed. He motioned to his Veranderen guards to hold the weakened human up so he could look to the king. "You are aware that this year we once again celebrate the centennial tournament of the Motteral Mal."

"Yes, Lord King," Jager whispered.

From beside the throne, Crespin took a Grey-painted scythe and placed it in front of the prisoner. Slowly, deliberately, he lifted the tip and with it, cut a line along Jager's hand. Jager winced as a trickle of blood rose to the surface, but he did not cry out. Indeed the shock of the cut seemed to revitalize him and he regained his footing.

The king replaced the weapon and looked steadily at the human. "A tip of any kind can harm a human, but only one made from the mighty Grey can affect those of my kind. Its very presence weakens those of my race. Your kin, inept as they are with magics of any kind, are surprisingly unaffected by the power of the Grey. You will mine and then produce these weapons for our tournament. Exact measurements and qualifications will be given you by the captain of my guard, and you will be escorted promptly to the forge for a night's rest. Thereafter, you will be taken to the mines."

Jager did not move to go with the guard, but stood solidly before the king and said, "And instead of tidings of my death, food and firewood will be sent to my family."

The king paused, a hint of amusement in his eyes, as though he thought the prisoner was joking. With a wave of his hand he dismissed him. "You ask too much."

Jager did not move, even when the wolves of the Königsvaren flanked him on either side. "I have very little to lose, your majesty. And, as you must know, I ask but little."

Wittendon stared at the prisoner, remembering again the heat he had felt as the man had touched his head to that of his wife. On the other side of his father, Wolrijk's lip curled up, revealing blood-red gums and long incisors. Several of the general's teeth were cracked and jagged, yet still strong and sharp like multi-bladed swords.

Sitting on the great chair, the king asked, "You consider your own life so little to lose? You would go to the executioner rather than work at my forge for free?"

"Whether I live or die makes little difference if food is not sent to my family. At least," Jager paused. "It makes little difference to me, good king. To you, it would matter a great deal more. The smiths of your race cannot fashion the tips. Doing so weakens them to the point of sickness and even death. I know, too, of your ancient and ailing human blacksmith. Rumors run in the villages of his crumbling bones and the withering muscles that can barely lift a hammer to strike."

Wittendon braced for his father's anger. He could feel it surge through his father's bones like a current of lightning through a metal rod. And then, just as quickly, it stopped, halted by his father's calmest, quietest voice. "And what," the king asked so quietly it seemed almost gentle, "makes you think I will need to comply with such a petty bargain. You care much for your family. You wish wood sent. You wouldn't want them to be *cold*. Well, then, if you feel so deeply for their welfare, consider this. If you do not mine and smith for me, I will send wood to your kin and much of it. Your wife and child will be strapped to a stake and burned at the center of your village where the fire will then be allowed to spread to as many straw-lined huts as it can before the slovenly human forces can subdue its flames. Now," the king paused, smiling, "give me one reason, one tiny reason, captive human, why I should not do this if I wish for your compliance."

Jager paused, and the whole room seemed to quiet. Wittendon watched the human, as he stood pale and perfectly still. Wolrijk licked his lips.

"Kill us," Jager said at last. "And find another to mine and fashion your metal as well as I would have."

The king sat silently for several minutes before speaking.

Wittendon was surprised. Usually his father was swift in his decrees and merciless in his judgments. At last the king spoke. "It is good," the king said, "that I have forbidden gaming halls of any variety in your villages. It seems you are a gambler."

Jager looked straight at the king. "But you, my lord. You do not take chances. Certainly not with things of great importance."

The king did not speak, but smiled slightly and stared directly into Jager's bright blue eyes. Jager began to tremble.

The king moved to Jager and held Jager's chin in his paw—the long, golden nails extended up the cheeks of the human, as though Jager's face was framed with daggers. "I do not take unnecessary risks," the king said.

Still holding Jager's face in his hand, the king signaled for a servant to take a message with instructions. "Your family will be sent food and wood, but that which they receive will be deducted from that which would have been given as rations to you. Do you understand?"

Jager nodded.

"If, for any reason, the lack of remaining rations leaves you unable to do your job and do it well, no more food will be sent. I do not need my smith fainting into his own fire. At least not until after the scythes are complete."

Again, Jager nodded. Sweat had begun to drip from his forehead.

The king flicked it off, leaving four long scratches. Crespin turned to Wolrijk. "Watch anything he touches. He will live until the blades are completed at which time we will fulfill the requirements of the law." The king stamped a piece of paper, leaving Wolrijk to oversee that two cabbages and a duck be sent with half a cord of firewood to the family of the enslaved.

After Jager was escorted from the room, his wrists still in chains, the king turned to Wittendon. "Pity does a prince no favors and often leaves him dead at the end of the day. Is that clear?"

Wittendon nodded, surprised at the rebuke.

His father snorted with disgust and continued, "Nevertheless, this human's skill as both miner and smith exceeds any I have yet known. He will indeed be worth more to us alive than dead. For a time."

When his father left the room, Wittendon felt as though he were the slave while Jager was the esteemed son. The prisoner had a skill his father valued and a bold, almost reckless courage that could not be denied. While Wittendon had a weakness called pity. Somehow it didn't seem to compare.

CHAPTER 10

"Why is it that the humans are unaffected by a metal that can bring a Verander to his knees. Or lower." Wittendon fastened the weapons belt onto his practice tunic and looked to his trainer for an answer.

Sarak shrugged as they walked to the weapons room to retrieve their practice blades. The clouds hung low in the skies, threatening rain. Today they would practice on the Hill of Motteral—the point at which the third round of the Mal would begin.

"If they had access to it, the humans could even wear such a metal upon their wrists and necks as a type of adornment—the way our women wear gold and bronze."

"Women like shiny things," Sarak said, obviously distracted. They retrieved their weapons and began to walk towards the tall hill. The tips of their scythes had recently been painted with one inch of Grey by the ailing smith—not yet the real weapon, but enough of a taste to make their practices challenging and more real. Beneath the point of the mountain where they would practice was the only mine where the Shining Grey could be found. Under his very feet, Wittendon knew that the slave Jager was bent over the stones with a pickaxe in hand, searching for the dangerous ore with more fear of cave-ins than of the metal itself.

They walked on until the skies began to rattle with thunder. Sarak frowned. "We may have to alter our practice today. This mountain pulses with the power of the Grey and I do not like the idea of great bolts of electricity above us trying to reach the metal beneath."

For most Veranderen, practice on the hill was exhausting. Wittendon, on the other hand, found it exhilarating. The grass and sky and fresh air, even if it was filled with cracks of thunder—it worked on his nerves to make him feel stronger than he ever felt in the stone-walled pavilion below. "Just a few rounds, perhaps," he said to Sarak.

Sarak nodded, though not without glancing once again at the threatening clouds just north of them. They stopped about a mile from the Sacred Tablet—now empty of the Sourcestone that had once empowered their race. Without the Sourcestone, the Tablet was, in its way, also verlorn—a simple monument—a place where eager travelers lined up to kiss it or touch it or scrape it for luck. Yet for the duration of the Mal, the Tablet would become hallowed again. No crowds would go near it and it was there that the winner would be crowned Chancellor, second to the king.

A crack of thunder sounded nearby and Sarak quickly raised his blade. Wittendon met it with a fierce clash and the two began. Today Sarak's blade was not hot, but it pulsed with electricity. "I can tell what you're focusing on," Wittendon laughed.

"Well," Sarak said, catching his breath. "It's like I said before—if there's an emotion close to the surface that can be useful to you, take it. And use it." At the last word, he struck Wittendon on the shoulder, sending a powerful bolt of electricity through his arm. Wittendon withdrew several steps, breathing heavily and trying to recover. Rain began to pelt his face and it roused him.

"Think soggy thoughts," Sarak said, breathing heavier than he ever did in the practice rooms or pavilion. "Perhaps you can make your scythe like a wet towel and swat me with it."

Wittendon charged at him and when he struck Sarak on the wrist, the blade cut straight and long. Wittendon gasped.

Sarak staggered back. "You are a terrible student. That was possibly the worst soggy thought I have ever experienced." Sarak was still smiling, but his lips had paled to a near white and he sat upon the hillside, his wound dripping blood.

"I'm sorry," Wittendon stammered.

"Just fetch me a towel," Sarak said. "And some of my sister's tonic from that bag. It should have me recovered far more quickly than any yammering from you." Sarak's words were good-natured, though his lips were nearly gray now.

Wittendon hurried to get the tonic, and a bolt of lightning struck nearby. Sarak groaned and slumped down. Wittendon could feel it too —the connection of the bolt to the ground beneath them—the buzz of energy as fire connected to rock and metal. Quickly, Wittendon poured Sadora's tonic into Sarak's wound. The tonic was yellow and smelled of year old goose eggs, but as soon as he applied it Sarak began groaning again. His cheeks took on some color and Wittendon helped him up.

"Well, this has just been a smashing good time," Sarak said. "As you help me down this hill like I'm an old man, I'll take comfort in the fact that your father won't have me hanged for neglecting your training. You do well, my friend." Sarak hobbled over to his bag. "Oddly so, actually."

Wittendon put his arm under Sarak's shoulders and supported most of his weight as the two made their way back down the hill. The worst of the storm was over and the rain took on a sweet smell.

"Take these," Sarak said, handing Wittendon both of the scythes. "Return them to the weapons room. I'm going to see if Sadora hasn't saved me a bit of berry tonic and then put my feet up for a bit."

Wittendon took the weapons from his friend. When he did, Sarak looked steadily into Wittendon's eyes with an intensity that made Wittendon uncomfortable and asked, "Are you not affected by it at all?"

Wittendon stepped back, wishing to break their gaze. *By what?* he was about to ask, but Sarak spoke again before he could.

"Never mind," Sarak said, back to his jovial self. "I've been too long on that ridiculous hill. My mind stumbles back to the myths and nursery tales of childhood. Soon I'll be wandering around muttering to myself like an old nanny."

Wittendon put the weapons over his shoulder and released his friend. "Tomorrow," he said. "At noon."

"I suppose—if I'm not stitching some stockings and sharing gossip with the local grannies—that we can practice once more on that blasted hill."

Wittendon smiled, dropped his friend off in his quarters, and turned toward the practice room just as Sadora exited a chariot pulled by four servants. Her gown was a swirl of blue and when she caught sight of Wittendon, she gave a low curtsy. He raised his hand and she rose gracefully, her bracelets gathering around her slender wrists—several on each arm, all blues and greens. Wittendon had seen other Veranderah of the court adopt this fashion, but none wore it so well.

"Good day, Lady Sadora," Wittendon said. Normally, he would have gotten tongue-tied after that, but his fight on the hill had made him feel strong. "That color," he said. "It suits you quite well."

"Yes," she said in her voice that always seemed to be laughing. "I rather like it myself." She moved a step closer and he could smell the scent of moonflowers that always hovered around her. "The human slaves spin the silks in the east, then the Veranderen peasantry weaves it into fabric outside the southern gates. It's dyed with the brightest dyes from the berries and roots imported from the mountainside villages in the south, and then finished and shipped from the Veranderen seaport, of course."

Wittendon smiled politely. Maybe his brother Kaxon could have maneuvered through this conversation, but Wittendon knew he was in over his head. Sadora smiled and looked Wittendon in the eyes. "Imagine the labor that goes into such a dress." Sadora paused, staring hard at Wittendon.

Wittendon looked down at his shoes, all his battle confidence lost in a discussion over blue fabric. When he looked up, Sadora was still staring at him with amber-colored eyes that shimmered and swam like layers of drizzled honey. He held her gaze without speaking for longer than he'd intended, until she blinked and laughed.

"Good day, my prince," she said, curtsying again before gathering her skirts and hurrying to the art wing to meet a cluster of females all wearing similar bracelets and dresses.

Wittendon sighed. He'd heard some of the older servants cluck that the weight of Sadora's gowns had squeezed the brains right out of her head, but Wittendon wasn't so sure. Somehow whenever he was with her, he felt like the witless one.

CRESPIN HAD NEVER INTENDED TO FALL IN LOVE. LOVE WAS A weakness of the senses, a clouder of the mind, a drug worse than the human liquors. A fact that his departed wife had seemed intent on proving. She was the most loving Veranderah he had known, and the weakest of any of his race. He had been well aware that she had not wished to marry him. But he was unaccustomed to worrying about the wishes of others. They had wed two weeks after he had first desired it. Her station had improved. He had given her all she could ask and more. Yet still she refused to look at him. So many times he had stood in their quarters, holding her soft face in both of his hands while her eyes, ever, were cast down. Until several months after their marriage when she came to him at midday. She looked him directly in the face and spoke. "I come, my king, bearing flesh of your flesh and blood of your blood. The magicians and midwife both believe that several months hence I will bear a son."

He had been pleased. Veranderen children were rare—born only to females between the 300th and 303rd years and usually only to those who had been long-wed. It had not occurred to Crespin that he had married a Veranderah within that window, and even if it had, he would not have expected a child to come forth from such a short union. A rush of magic and something new shot through his frame and he pulled his beautiful wife to him. But she resisted, looking him again in the eye. "A king always rejoices for a son until that son rises in gifts and power. You are great, my king. And cunning. And your reputation is one of neither mercy nor meekness. I will not have you destroy my children."

He stepped back, surprised. "My dear, he will be our *son*."

"Which will make him both a threat and—when he is young—an easy target."

For the first time since discovering her, Crespin paused to consider the Veranderah who stood before him. "I take what is good for my kingdom and I remove the rest," he said.

"Perhaps," she replied. "But your flesh is now carried in my body. You will make me a promise. Or I will destroy that which is your own twice over—my life, and his."

The king could have crushed her, but he rather enjoyed his pretty wife and now that he knew she would soon produce for him something rare, he recognized—as he did with many of his most unique prizes—that he wanted to keep it. Furthermore, he was not much concerned over the babe she carried. It would be his and he would rule it as he did everything else. No other in his reign could usurp him; why then his child?

The king shrugged. "I will not destroy the child."

"A promise," she said. "A promise with an unbreakable spell."

Her eyes, he noticed then, were the steely blue of a sword on a clear day. "Very well," he said. "A promise."

It had taken several days to craft the magic. Covenant spells demanded concentration and care; otherwise you wound up giving more than you intended.

Finally, just as Loerwoei's belly began to press at the seams of her gowns, Crespin went to her and, with the powerful words of the ancient tongue, he cast the spell by the fire of her bedchamber.

Blood of my blood, flesh of my bone,
Wizard's spine and shining stone.
Those come forth by mother's womb
Protected now from father's doom.
As he from them will be secure,
If they the filial bonds ignore.

After all was done, Loerwoei looked at him occasionally, sometimes even with sweetness. It reminded him of the friend Draden whom he had lost—that feeling of closeness. And he had, foolishly, allowed himself to enjoy this one connection with his wife, this flourish of emotion, this weakness called love. A year following that first healthy child, she bore another. Perhaps another would have followed except that there had been an accident in the woods. Even his strongest magics could not control the unseen wound within her, and he had gone to the gardener for a potion. Her remedies of herb and mineral worked well to abate the sickness and Crespin and the gardener had spent many hours together, trying to concoct a permanent solution. Perhaps too many hours.

And then the gardener had left. A little abruptly for Crespin's taste.

After that Loerwoei died quickly.

Leaving Crespin to raise two young children. Alone.

CHAPTER 11

Pietre and Humphrey trudged home. They had only a basket of dandelion greens and several ugly mushrooms. The old goat had ceased in her milk and now they wouldn't have so much as a pat of butter to cook it all in. Pietre could feel the way the mushrooms would press like spongeweed against his teeth.

Before he reached his house, Pietre wiped his face with an old rag, as his mother had taught him, though he hardly saw the point. He hadn't had time to bathe in weeks and all the rag could possibly do was smear dirt and sweat into different places. Humphrey looked better, but smelled worse.

As soon as they reached the old gate, Pietre heard his mother by the chicken coop—sobbing. Humphrey pushed open the gate and rushed in, but Pietre dragged behind. He knew the news that must be coming; the king had surely passed judgment on his father by now. He felt sick to his stomach and wished to turn around and run back to the woods, but Humphrey had already gone to Carina, and was nudging her hand.

"Sweet Cari," he murmured. "Do not cry. All will be well. I am bigger now and can help with hunting and Pietre is man enough to gather wood, water, and herbs."

"No, no," she sobbed, wiping her face with an old, sopping handkerchief. "You don't understand." Humphrey stood back slightly as though acknowledging that he did not. And then Pietre's mother laughed, which set both dog and boy on edge. Perhaps she was descending into madness.

"Mother," Pietre had said. "Moecka." He was trying to choke in his own tears at the terrible news he expected to hear.

"No, no," she said again. "Look." She gestured in through the open front door to a table set with a stuffed bird and a bag of bright, purple cabbages. Humphrey nearly swooned.

"He lives," she said, rising and taking Humphrey's front paws as though to dance with him. "And we shall too." Humphrey cast a quick glance at Pietre as if to say, *She still might be mad.*

"Not only does he live to mine and work in the service of the king, but he has arranged to have food and firewood sent every week." Still holding one of Humphrey's paws, she pulled a paper from her apron pocket that was stamped with the king's insignia—a wolken head with a flame rising from its brow.

"But how?" Pietre asked, now coughing back happy tears, so he didn't start blubbering and dancing with animals like his mother had. He doubted any of the chickens would appreciate it.

"His skill," she said, her bosom swelling with relief and pride. "The dreadful wolf who brought the provisions bore a message saying that he would be mining and fashioning the metal for the great tournament of the Veranderen."

The Shining Grey, Pietre thought. His father had spoken of the ore at times. It was said to weaken any of the Veranderen who were exposed to it, heightening the challenge at their great game.

His mother finally let go of Humphrey and came to kiss Pietre on the head. "Come," she said, "let us feast."

And they did. Pietre was sure he had never been so full in all his life. At the end of their dinner, his mother stood and fingered one of the cabbages as though it was a flower. "Beautiful, isn't it?"

Pietre shrugged and yawned. He would have eaten it even if it had looked like an old man's toe. He went to his room behind the kitchen and looked through the small open window to the stars that were said to have guided men in the time before the rise of the Veranderen—in the time of the high white sun. Pietre had heard talk—talk of the Grey mine in the east, talk of madness and ghosts, gasses and cave-ins, terrifying talk. Still, Pietre looked to the stars, following the constellation of the serval that pointed east, and he wondered.

CHAPTER 12

P ractice had gone well. Ever since his triumph on the hill, Sarak had been wary of Wittendon's blade and had even gone so far as to say that Wittendon commanded it better than many Veranderen who'd had centuries to practice. But magic. Magic was another matter. It seemed that the more control Wittendon gained over his scythe, the further he got from making anything besides strength come out of his arm.

Wittendon walked slowly to the weapons room. From down the hall, he could hear two wolves laughing like jackals. He sighed. He had hoped to try a bit of magic in the weapons room where he felt he could shut himself off for a few moments from the stares and gossip of the other competitors, but he was sure he couldn't do anything with a couple of giggling wolves standing around.

As Wittendon got closer, he could hear them boasting, and he wondered if they'd gotten hold of some of the human liquors. Wittendon was about to clear his throat and push open the door when a familiar name caught his ear.

"I can still hear Grender begging," the first began.

"*Oh, please, help me friend,*" the second joined in, using a voice affected and high so as to sound like that of a weak, whining wolf. *"The she-beast has nearly destroyed my hide."*

"What a pity," the first laughed as the second wolf snorted. "All scratched up by his wench-hound."

And there the name was again. Wittendon pressed his ear to the door.

"That ape general Grender. He had a penchant for she-hounds and wolf-women alike," the first said, clucking his tongue.

"Especially wolf-women that were already mated to another," the second said, without any humor in his voice. "He stole her from me. Only to leave her as well and go off after that she-hound."

Wittendon could hear the first wolf snapping his teeth together. "Well, he never will again."

"True," the second said with much satisfaction. "Not since he was pricked by a little Grey-painted tip in his philandering hide."

At that they laughed and Wittendon stepped forward into the weapons room, bearing the scythe across his shoulder.

"Cousins," he said, and they bowed.

"Lord Prince," they mumbled. "We were unaware of thy noble presence."

"That, it seems, was quite clear. Do you find the death or your own kin so very amusing?" He removed the weapon from his shoulder and carefully put it into the weapons rack—a wall of scythes with Grey-painted points facing out and upward, glistening like the back of an enormous metallic porcupine.

Weaponless, he turned to face the wolves. They had risen from their bow. The first was a dingy gray with fur that looked as though it had not been washed for some time. The second had a bright, fine coat of rusty orange and eyes shot with red like he had spent too little time sleeping. Wittendon recognized both as members of the Blødguard, and neither had tucked his right paw in respect as the wolves generally did in the presence of a prince. Wittendon began to wonder if re-racking the weapon had been an overly confident gesture.

"We find," the dingy one said, facing his prince with eager, hungry eyes, "the death of traitors most satisfying indeed."

"And is it for you to determine who is a traitor?" Wittendon asked, widening the stance of his legs as Sarak had taught him during training.

"It was not our idea in the first place," said the first, securing his own footing.

Wittendon wanted to ask him what he meant, but the other wolf was pacing slow half-circles around him.

"And it was a very *good* idea," added the second. "There are, my prince, treacheries other than those committed against the king."

"Although treachery against the king and his kin," the first said, moving carefully, almost casually forward. "We could understand as well if it became necessary to protect our own."

"Your own?" Wittendon asked. "It does not sound as though you are highly concerned about your own."

From deep within the throat of one of the wolves, a low rumbling growl could just barely be heard. The fur of the gray wolf began to rise along his neck, like the fin of a shark rising from the water.

The other looked at Wittendon and said, snarling, "He stole my mate. And then left her to go after such rubble as a she-hound. He was not worthy to be called our own."

It made sense now—Grender's unusual wound. It had not come *before* he went to seek the she-hound. It had come after. And it had not been an accident. "A trial will be set," Wittendon said firmly, although he didn't dare turn his back to them and leave.

The wolves ignored him. "By your own mouth, Grender's wound was but an accident," the first wolf said. He took a step forward, smiling, "And accidents," he said quietly, "they are terrible things."

"Especially when the mighty Grey is in use," the other added.

"Especially when a young prince is as weak in magic as the lowly wolves."

The two wolves advanced on him.

"You would threaten me, cousins?" Wittendon asked, aware of his vulnerable position in front of a wall of weapon tips.

"The penalty for killing a wolf is death," said the dingy one. "And a prince's word would go far."

"The penalty for killing a Prince is greater," said Wittendon.

"True, but the penalty for him being a clumsy verlorn oaf is nothing," said the orange wolf. "At least it is nothing for us. Though the cost might be steep for him."

"And you know that his poor father has been expecting something tragic from his dunce of a son," taunted the dingy one.

"Ever since his weakened mother died," said the second, clucking his tongue in mock pity and ramming his shoulder against Wittendon, pushing him toward the rack of scythes. Several weapons clattered to the ground. One nearly grazed Wittendon's arm; another touched his leg, though it didn't break skin. Wittendon was relieved. Even a small wound might have weakened him enough for the wolves to pounce. As it was, he felt plenty strong.

"Oh dear," mocked the first wolf. "It looks like the mighty prince has stumbled."

The rusty, bloody-eyed wolf circled around him. "You know it was just a jab of the Grey—a bit from a painted tip—that killed our own brother, weakened as he was from his fight with the she-hound. Grender came to us whimpering, he did, begging for help. We helped him." He sneered. "Helped him to his death." The wolf pressed forward another step.

"And now with a whole rack of weapons at your back, perhaps we can help you in much the same way." The rusty wolf lunged at him.

Wittendon jumped away faster than he thought possible. The other wolf sprang at him knocking Wittendon again against the rack that held the curved Motteral blades so that Wittendon fell. This time a blade pricked him, though not deep enough to draw blood. Wittendon wasn't sure what a scratch like that would do. He closed his eyes, remembering the way Sarak's wound had bled, but he felt okay. In fact, he felt good. The wolves must have been mistaken about the spears. These ones, it seemed, were not yet tipped in the Grey and were merely blades of everyday steel. The wolves advanced, trying to see if one of the blades had struck home.

Wittendon remained still, appearing to be unconscious until they were quite close and ready to strike. When they did, he jumped up and away as they threw themselves against the practice blades, which pierced them, though not very deeply. Wittendon figured it would hurt, but not kill. He wanted to teach them that the oldest prince was not as easy a target as they had supposed.

"How dare you?" Wittendon said. "You are spared by this harmless steel which you mistook for a metal that would murder me…"

His last words were drowned in the screams and cries of the wolves.

"Demon prince," said the one with the dirty coat. Both wolves were frothing at the mouth, red bubbles foaming from their lips. "Murderer."

"I…" Wittendon began, confused. "You." he said, backing away and expecting this to be a trick. Yet in moments the wolves screams had gone silent and their sides ceased heaving and spasming. Wittendon moved slowly forward. "But how?" he asked himself, picking up a scythe. "They are just practice steel." He touched the gleaming blade, careful not to pierce his skin. Contact with the metal made his body quiver. Perhaps they weren't just steel. Wittendon shuddered at his mistake. If he had grown careless and let the blades pierce him, then…

The two wolves bled profusely and Wittendon felt their last word like an echo. "Murderer."

"But I'm not," he spoke to himself. "They killed themselves."

Yet even as he called for the Veranderen guards, shouting that there had been an accident in the weapons room, he could hear the wolves' accusation repeated in his mind and his guilt rose up. Steel blades or not, he had lured them to it.

CHAPTER 13

For the third time that week Pietre could have sworn he'd seen a cat. There had been the flash of orange hair, then later a pointy-eared shadow. The third time it was more a sound and a feeling than anything he'd seen—he could have sworn he'd heard the gentle thud of a great, but graceful animal jumping down from a tall tree. It had sounded just like a ghost, and in a thrilling, terrifying way, Pietre had begun to wonder if it actually was. Some of the old story-tellers liked to say that the cats had existed once, but had been hunted by the wolves until they were extinct. Of course, they also liked to say cats could land on their feet—even when falling or jumping from great heights. That made Pietre smile and shake off the teasing images of his imagination. Imagine an animal that could do such a thing. The only thing crazier was to imagine the ghost of an animal who could do such a thing.

Pietre rested in the woods, gently brushing the milky white salve into Humphrey's fur. Humphrey lay on his back, perfectly content. "You know you could open a business doing this for dogs," he said. "I bet they'd pay. We could call it Humphrey's Haven."

"What about Pietre's Palace?" Pietre asked, stuffing the rest of the herbs into a basket to take home.

"I like mine better," Humphrey murmured, drifting towards sleep.

Pietre rubbed his belly. Humphrey had quadrupled in size since Pietre first knew him, his voice now deep and rich. Pietre's mother told him tales—tales that in the days of the high white sun, dogs did not grow so quickly or live so long. Humphrey was already nearly to adult-hood. Even so, his size was unusual. Humphrey stood up to Pietre's waist and was barrel-chested with paws bigger than Pietre's own palm. "You're going to make vegetarians of us, Humph," Pietre's mother would say, tossing him a fish head or chicken liver. Though now, with the weekly rations of meat and fish, it wasn't much of a threat.

Humphrey's coat was a shiny, soft black, though his face, neck, and legs were marked with white. Pietre could tell he would be a handsome dog. He rested his hand on Humphrey's belly.

In the cool silence of the shade trees, Pietre considered the possi-bility of travelling to the head city to find his father. The road would be dangerous. If he wanted to travel it, he would have to set out as soon as the sun rose in order to be back before dark. But darkness wouldn't be his only enemy. The thieves, rumored to roam the roads in the light of day, were just as deadly as the Blødguard of the night. Pietre sighed. He was willing to take the risk, but first he would have to know where he was going. It was said that the roads leading to the Grey mines were a disorienting web of covert pathways and steep ridges—meant to be travelled only by those the king intended.

Suddenly, from just behind his back, Pietre heard a deep voice say, "Good afternoon, fair child. It seems you have put Hannahszon under a spell of contentment."

"Hello, great Markhi," the boy said, shaking off his worries and rising to greet the dog. "Humphrey wishes to open a retreat of sorts for dogs. He says your kin will pay."

Markhi smiled. "Well, perhaps when our great race fluffs about on nails painted pink." Markhi laughed with a deep resonating sound that was like the largest bells on feast days. "As for today, we fight."

Humphrey opened one eye.

"Stand, young one," the great dog said. "I made a promise to train you and this afternoon finds me in your wood." The large dog began circling Humphrey. "I see that you've grown. That is good." He lunged at Humphrey, tripping him so that he toppled over almost before he was fully standing. "But more weight and height will do nothing but pull you faster to the ground without speed and wit."

Humphrey sprang up more quickly this time. Both dogs circled. Pietre stepped away.

Markhi held his head low and growled, but Humphrey refused to bow his head and stood straight and stiff. "Your pride will be of little use, youngling. Your neck stands exposed like the trunk of a young sapling."

"And your words wax long," Humphrey said, pouncing, though not quickly enough. Markhi stepped aside and Humphrey soared through the air like a javelin gone off course.

"Head low. Move like an arrow," Markhi said. "Are those sentences short enough for you?"

Humphrey lunged again, much like an arrow, this time hitting his mark and barging into Markhi's shoulder.

"Yes," Humphrey said, smiling at his accomplishment, though it was only a moment before Markhi knocked him off-balance again and pinned him to the ground.

Pietre gasped and stepped back several more paces.

"Throat, gut, even ankles are good points to attack or weaken a dog. Shoulder, nape, and back—they do little."

Humphrey was breathing hard when Markhi let him go.

"I think that's enough for today," Markhi said, but Humphrey barreled towards him again.

"Or we could go another round," Markhi said, clipping Humphrey in the side.

Again and again the dog and dog-wolf fought until finally, Humphrey knocked Markhi into a tree and pinned him by his neck against a root.

"Well done, child," Markhi said. "If I were a human, I would end today's lesson on this positive note." Then, like a flash, he bit Humphrey's ankle, gaining a few seconds to pull the young animal down. "But I am a dog and will not take defeat for your benefit."

Pietre might have spoken in defense of his race except that Humphrey had risen again, teeth bared—ready to fight once more. His mouth was frothing from the heat; even the pads of his feet had begun to sweat, leaving wet marks in the dirt. Markhi stood still and straight. "I see persistence is a lesson you have quickly learned," he said. "But it is time to stop. My pack awaits my return and you, young one, grow too tired to learn more at present."

Humphrey growled and advanced, but Markhi stood firm. "No, young one. A dog fights hard, but knows when to stop. A wolf," he said pointedly, "does not."

Humphrey snarled again, but stopped his advance.

Markhi bowed to him, tucking a paw under his chest. For a terrible moment Pietre thought Humphrey—in his defeated anger—was going to charge the older dog. Yet after a moment, Humphrey took a deep breath and tucked his paw as well.

"There is much to learn," Humphrey said, not even bothering to hide his sadness at the defeat.

"You have learned much already," Markhi said. "And I was wrong —you were able to learn one final lesson today." After a pause Markhi added, "Your mother knew quite well when to stop and when to fight."

"Did she?" Humphrey asked with sadness, his head tilting up.

"I've no doubt of it," Markhi said, looking Humphrey directly in the eyes. "Ah, but you do grow unusually big. Already we are face to face."

Markhi turned to Pietre. "You have done well with his scent, child. I cannot smell even a trace of wolf in him. And if I cannot, none can."

Pietre nodded.

Just as he was about to leave, Markhi added, "I have heard the news of your father, boy, and I am glad of it."

"But how have you heard," Pietre asked.

"The mines are not so very far from my home," Markhi said. "News travels quickly among dogs; they love stories almost as much as the air in their lungs."

"The mines," Pietre said with a quickened hope. "Can you lead me to them?"

The older dog looked at the boy for a painfully long minute. Pietre stood as tall as his skinny frame would allow, and held his face straight and firm like he thought a man would.

"No," Markhi said. "You are young, child, and the mines of the Grey are deep. You will find your way when the fates lead you there. No sooner."

More quickly than seemed possible, the dog was gone.

"He does make a good exit, doesn't he?" Humphrey said, nursing his front paw.

Pietre gathered up his basket of rotherem, feeling like a little girl.

"Well, that's two of us then," Humphrey said, seeming to understand Pietre's thoughts and limping slightly on his left forepaw to follow.

They had walked nearly a mile when a voice spoke—soft as silk, but clear as summer.

Well met, good child, is met indeed.
But better met when voice you heed.

Pietre stopped, his breath sucked out of him. Humphrey's hair had risen and his teeth were bared.

The fates may call to places hollow,
Only when whispered words you follow.

They saw nothing. And then Pietre heard it again—the gentle sound of an animal landing in the soft grasses below.

"A spirit," Humphrey whispered. But as they listened to the soft swish of the grasses, Pietre wondered.

"The old tales speak of cats as masters of agility and silence," he said to Humphrey.

"Well, yes, but did they ever mention rhyme?" Humphrey said, scratching an ear.

Pietre glared at him.

84

"Well, did they?" Humphrey asked. "Rather annoying, actually. Imagine a race who always spoke like that. It's just strange."

"Almost as strange as race that could always land on their feet," Pietre said, considering his theory.

"Yes, well, that's pure myth," Humphrey said, a little vainly. "And quite honestly, I don't see what makes it so extremely special..." he began, but was cut off by the voice.

Well met, good child is met indeed.
Five days hence beneath these trees.

"Five days," Pietre said. "The fates waste little time."

Humphrey sniffed. "More of a slant rhyme, that one." And, ignoring his hurt ankle, he bounded ahead toward home.

CHAPTER 14

Dreaming of quiet meadows, flowing waters, vine-hung caverns; it shouldn't have been a nightmare. But it was. Always. The meadow was deeper than stillness—soundless, mute—pulling him towards it, enfolding him in its void. And then the screaming of the water, a siren call that drew him, thick-footed towards itself and then towards the cavern—cool-mouthed, hot-bellied. Through it he walked, stiff, dragging himself down tunnels that enfolded him like layers of blankets over his eyes and mouth—thick, strangling, voiceless.

Since his mother had died, his dreams had always started like this —a black abyss, a cavern, a cave. Strangest of all, when he woke, he always felt deeply sad that the horrible dream had ended, and found himself—inexplicably—wanting to go back.

Tonight, into the dark abyss of his nightmares flowed the screams of the dying wolves. And then Wittendon heard his own voice command the human Jager to kill the wolves.

Wittendon bolted up in bed, shaking, and tossed off his blankets, hoping the chilly castle air would calm and cool him. He had spent the week wondering who he was—what kind of Verander would feel pity for a human and kill—however unintentionally—two wolves. Of course they had fully intended to kill him. The taunt 'verlorn' hung in his head next to the ancient word 'werewolf.'

He got out of bed and pulled on an old bronze cloak. His hair was still matted with sweat and he was quite sure a bath was in order. But no one would be up at this hour and he wished to walk and calm his nerves.

Wittendon's head and shoulders ached from lost sleep and he wandered the castle halls aimlessly. Before long he found himself in the art wing. It was dimly lit with only a few lanterns hung along the walls. He walked along a display of ancient, conquered countries and peoples, then through the pictures of extinct animals and mythical creatures when a slight movement caught his eye. Too late he realized that he was staring at the soft hair and delicate back of Sarak's sister.

He did not think she'd seen him and had decided, quite conclusively, to leave when Sadora said, "Hello, Wittendon. What brings you to this quiet corner at such an hour?"

Wittendon took a deep breath, and walked towards her. "Lack of sleep, I'm afraid to say."

She nodded without taking her eyes from the cluster of portraits she was admiring. He came closer and stood at her side. "And you?" he asked.

She shrugged. "I have never been one to tire early and have become a bit smitten by our distant history." She gestured to a painting of an enormous cat. "The records of the time before the golden age are —" She paused. "—spotty." She leaned back a bit, tilting her face up towards one of the paintings. "I find some of these portraits helpful in connecting pieces of the myths to an image I can better understand."

Wittendon nodded, remembering with regret that he hadn't bathed. He patted down a sweaty patch of hair and stole glances at her profile. Her chin was a bit too square, but he found he liked it that way, especially with the wisps of cinnamon-honey hair that fell down around her face. Her eyes very nearly matched the color of her hair and he liked that too.

"What do you think of this one?" she asked, and Wittendon remembered he was supposed to be staring at art. The cat in the portrait was sleek, the body twisted into curves so tight yet graceful that it made both dog and wolf look clumsy and bulky in comparison.

"She is very beautiful," Wittendon said.

Sadora laughed her tinkling laugh. "And how do you know it is a she?"

Wittendon wished very much that he had taken a bath and mumbled, "Well, I, it's something in…" but he could not place it and his words dropped off.

She laughed again. "Don't worry, I thought the same. You are not like most others, good Wittendon."

"There are not many who consider that a virtue."

She nodded almost imperceptibly.

Wittendon wiggled uncomfortably and then turned. "The hour grows quite late. May I walk you to your quarters?"

In answer she gracefully put an arm through his.

"Do you think they really existed?" she asked as they left the hall.

Wittendon had focused once again on the color of her hair and was caught once again off guard.

"The cats," she said.

"To tell the truth, I have thought of them but little."

She smiled and when she did, he could see the smallest creases at her eyes. He had to suppress an urge to reach forward and touch them.

"Nor had I until somewhat recently," she said. "Did you know that some scholars claim that the cats were the keepers of riddle and prophecy, that the knowledge they held in their long-stretching memories could fill more libraries than even this palace could contain."

They were nearly to her quarters when Wittendon turned to see another, much smaller painting of a cat to the left of a dim lantern. He was about to ask Sadora why she had become interested in this point of history when the cat in the portrait moved. Wittendon gasped and Sadora looked over. What they were both looking at was not a portrait, but a small mirror.

"I hope that reaction wasn't at my expense," she said, glancing in the mirror and adjusting a perfect lock of hair.

"No," Wittendon said stupidly. "It wasn't you. You're…you're. It was. I thought." He looked at Sadora's smiling image in the mirror. "I am sorry, my lady." Above him in the beams of the ceiling, he thought he heard a soft swish. He shook his head to clear it. "The hour does you great favor, lady Sadora, but I fear my brain sizzles and spits like hot grease at this time of night."

When they reached her quarters, Wittendon quickly took her hand and touched it to his forehead in a polite good-bye.

"Perhaps," she said as he released her hand, "we can meet again sometime when the sun still grants her benevolence to your senses." She smiled teasingly.

"That would be," Wittendon said, "very nice."

WITTENDON WALKED THROUGH THE HALLS IN A HAPPY DAZE UNTIL, turning a corner, he nearly bumped into his brother.

Kaxon raised an eyebrow at him, noting the direction from which Wittendon was walking. Wittendon cleared his throat. "I couldn't sleep; I went to the art wing," he stammered.

"Of course," Kaxon said. "Where else would you have been that is in that exact direction?"

Wittendon's face grew hot and Kaxon smiled. "Well, if you need it, I can have the kitchen maidens concoct the same sleeping potion our father has ordered. Unless, of course, it's thoughts of a certain pretty someone keeping you awake. In which case, I'm going to assume you want to be left with your thoughts."

"Is it too obvious?" Wittendon asked, not even bothering to pretend he didn't know what Kaxon was talking about.

"Idiotically so."

Wittendon sighed.

"Don't worry, brother. A lady appreciates a little adoration."

Wittendon smiled. He and his brother had never been extremely close. Their interests and friends were almost as different as the colors of their fur. But his younger brother could always laugh off his father's criticism and Kaxon had a keen eye for a beautiful face. In this way, Wittendon sometimes felt he had an unlikely friend in his brother. Of course, Kaxon would throw Wittendon into the mines if it meant winning the Motteral Mal. But to Wittendon, that determination was part of his brother's charisma.

They walked past the gardens and into a corridor that led them along statues of famous Veranderen, then past the door of the vault where the great books of magic were kept. After ducking into a dim hall, Kaxon turned into the kitchen. "Sure you don't need a bit of a tonic?" he asked laughing. "I hear some of the girls can concoct a wicked love potion."

Wittendon waved him off, pretending not to hear, and walked to his room. That night, the black cave of his dreams still beat against his skull, but through it flickered mysterious felines, honeyed hair, and eyes with creases so soft his mouth went dry to think of them.

King Crespin sat up abruptly in his bed. He dreamt of her almost nightly now—she who stood surrounded by that unceasing expanse of blue sky, she who should not have been. Years ago, before her birth, his best wolves had been sent to kill her mother. Indeed, they had sworn most convincingly that they had. But a dead mother could not have birthed the child that beckoned to him so persistently in his dreams. She was the same as her human mother in stature and figure, but the hair that fell to her waist was distinctly wolken and when she turned, he was met by a keen copper eye that matched his own. He woke in a rush, dressed, and began to pace. After an hour, Kaxon knocked at the door, steaming tonic in hand.

The king did not even look to his son, but snarled, "It is no good."

Kaxon bowed and was about to leave the room when his father turned suddenly. "Bring me the wolf Wolrijk."

"Yes, Lord Father," Kaxon said, setting the tonic on a small table near the door.

After Kaxon had left, the king walked over to the drink and carefully poured it into a small flowerpot. "I do not need a useless potion," he said to himself. "What I need is an assassin."

CHAPTER 15

Pietre wound his way up the high road with Humphrey. At each bend, his pulse quickened and he expected a daggered thief to jump at him.

"You shouldn't have lied to your mother, you know," Humphrey chided him.

"What was I supposed to say? I'll be heading off to the mines now, through dangerous forests and up Robber's Ridge. But don't worry because I'm following a strange voice from a being I've never seen." Pietre gritted his teeth, listening for that very voice. She had promised to warn him if any evil waited ahead of them.

"I don't know," Humphrey mumbled. Pietre could tell that Humphrey disliked this last leg of their journey, disliked the spectral voice with the constant rhyming that had led them there, disliked telling his sweet Cari that they would be spending the day hunting with a nearby pack of dogs. "At any rate," Humphrey said, "you shouldn't have dragged me into your lie."

"Well, I beg your perfectness's pardon," Pietre said, but before Humphrey could fire back, a hiss came from behind a rock that was just ahead and the sound froze both of them. It was followed by three distinct scratches. After a moment the voice called out,

Proceed now with gentle speed.
Around the bend you'll find what you need.

Humphrey rolled his eyes and Pietre let out a relieved sigh. "Thank goodness," he said. "I thought something might have gotten her." He rounded the final corner and was struck suddenly in the back by a hooded, toothless man who sprayed dust in Humphrey's eyes and then grabbed Pietre by the shoulders and shoved him to the earth.

JAGER BENT LOW IN A LONELY TUNNEL OF THE MINE. HE WAS SURE IT was here. He could feel ore in the way some could sense water in a desert, but no matter where his pickaxe struck, the walls stared back at him black as night. Finally he threw the pick down and sat to eat his sackful of stale crackers. "Compliments of his highness," he mumbled. "He who threatens me with smaller rations every day that cursed metal eludes me."

He crunched on his meager victuals and the sound of his own chewing seemed to echo through the mines. He missed the way Carina had cooked salted meats into bread and wrapped them in paper to take to the tunnels. He missed watching her long fingers fold the edges. He missed the heat of her face near his. At once, he shivered. The mine seemed very quiet. He stood, hunching to strike again at the dull rock when he thought he heard a voice. He paused to listen. Most of the miners refused to go this deep into the rock. They feared poisonous gasses, avalanches, and the ghosts they believed haunted the tunnels under the ancient battlefields that were the Hill of Motteral. Jager did not believe in ghosts, though he had known more than one man driven to madness by the silent enclosure of thick, stone walls.

He struck at the stone again and this time he was quite sure that the sound he heard echoing back at him was not the sound of axe on rock.

"Speak," he said. "Or if you are the voice of my own faltering mind, then be still."

Silence greeted him and he let out the breath he didn't realize he'd been holding. He raised the axe to strike again and just as his arm flexed to come down, he heard it and stopped.

The wall you strike is rich, my friend.
But only from its other end.

"No," Jager murmured. "I will not lose my sanity to this tomb." He sat and rubbed his head. Then, reaching for his canteen, he heard it again. The voice was soft, clear, and distinctly inhuman.

Go north, stand left.
Trust heart, not head.
In tunnel's bowel
You'll find more than lead.

"I am mad," Jager said, standing. He moved back through the tunnel, due north, stopping when he came to a wall and then, taking a deep breath and wanting nearly to cry, he took a step left. As he did, a small crack came into view. How he had missed it before, he could not be sure. Raising his pick, he struck at the fissure of stone. It trembled, dust crumbling, and from the wall a small, round stone fell at his feet. Pulling a handkerchief from his pocket, Jager picked it up. Except for bits of rock that clung to its edges, it was as smooth as glass and ribbed with delicate lines of bright metal.

Jager leaned his head against the wall. "Thank you spirit or angel or whatever you be." He put the stone in his pocket so that when he came to the surface and reason kicked in, he would remember the mystical voice that had helped him.

Then with a mighty blow, he struck at the wall again, revealing a large pure vein of the Shining Grey.

~

"Enough with the screamin' boy. It rings off them rocks like glass in my ears," the man said, glaring at Pietre and Humphrey from under his hood. He pushed aside a large rock and, with the strength of someone half his age, easily dropped Pietre through a hole.

Humphrey lunged at the man, who stepped aside even faster than Markhi had, so that Humphrey also plunged into the darkness of the hole.

The man followed, a dim lantern hanging at his waist and said, "Everybody okay? It's a steep descent."

Humphrey growled and prepared to attack again, but the man just laughed. "Easy, does it. The mines are closer than you think. And ol' Winterby is gonna take you there."

Being thrown into a hole had temporarily stopped Pietre's calls for help. He was surprised to find that it wasn't just a pit trap dug into the earth, but some type of elaborate system of tunnels. As his eyes began to adjust to the dim light, he could see a long narrow stair leading down and to the east. He struggled to take it all in. "You are," he asked, "*not* a robber?"

Again the man laughed. "If I was, I'd be a mighty bad one, picking off two ragged pipsqueaks like you and expecting a coin to fall from it."

Pietre pursed his lips and Humphrey growled again, low and threatening.

"Hey now," the man said. "I ain't gonna hurt you. Them mines is less than a mile from here. Woulda took you a good hour through the switchbacks up above. And then you really mighta got robbed by some deadhead. Besides," he continued. "You can't just waltz up to the Grey mines and let yourself in." He moved up ahead, holding the lantern. "That Savah—she's the best guide there is—but even she can't lead you past the guards to see your old man, now can she?"

"Who's Savah?" Pietre asked.

The old man paused. "Your guide," he said, then after a minute, "and a keeper of information. As is her sister. But no information is going to get you through the Königsvaren that surrounds that mine. I got ways down here that'll go right under them."

At that, Humphrey finally stopped growling.

"Seriously," Pietre said. "You couldn't have said that in daylight."

"Ah now, but where's the fun in that?" He winked, but Pietre didn't look amused. "Come on, boy, ya gotta give this old man a break. You live under the earth long as I have and you get a little bored. Not to mention the fact that the sun off them rocks is something fierce and you were screamin' like a steam whistle."

"I was not," Pietre said under his breath.

Winterby looked sideways at him, and in a couple of minutes said, "You two wanna snack?"

Suddenly, it didn't much matter if he was crazy friend or crazy foe, both dog and boy strode up to him with a boldness that only two hungry youth on the brink of manhood could possess.

WHEN JAGER CAME INTO THE SUN, HIS OWN CHILD WAS STANDING behind a large boulder near the mouth of the mine—a dog at his side that could only be Humphrey, though he'd grown into a great barrel of a creature.

"How is it possible?" Jager whispered, fingering the handkerchief that held the stone in his pouch, and looking to the line of unsuspecting guards far below him on the mountain. Quietly, he stepped behind the large stone.

Pietre stepped toward his father. Each stood silent. No tidings of the last weeks, no tales of voices or guides, no explanations for anything. Finally, Jager held out his palm in the greeting adult men and women give to one another. Pietre placed his own smaller palm against his father's and then almost at once his father embraced him weeping.

"Come," he said at last and turned to lead his son quickly into the mine where the guards would not think to look.

Jager led them deep into the earth, wandering through the tunnels as though walking his own backyard. Pietre followed in much the same way, touching the walls and breathing deeply. He picked up rocks like they were flowers and ran his fingers over wet walls of stone.

Humphrey, on the other hand, lagged behind, panting. Jager slowed his step and fell into line with the dog. "Thinking you might want to make a break for it and take your chances with the wolf guard, eh?"

Humphrey tried to smile. "What? When I could wander deeper into this crypt with you two?"

Jager laughed, the sound scratchy and foreign to his own ear. "Ah, the dogs were born to run free in the sun, not to be encased by stone."

"I have gone through worse today," Humphrey said. "The boy and I took an unexpected path to get here."

"I'm not sure what other kind of path could have gotten you here," Jager replied.

"Our path ended in a tight stone hole—one that unfortunately no grown human could ever fit through. The boy squeezed through like a lizard, but with every breath I took, the stone squeezed me back, trapping me in its hardened clutches. I had to claw my way out."

"That is true," Pietre said, winking. "And he whined like a little girl."

Again Jager laughed.

"I'll do it again if we have to go much deeper into this catacomb."

"Lucky for you," Jager said. "Your dignity will be spared. Here it is." He stopped, and turned to a wall of stone.

Humphrey stared at it. Pietre's smile closed up and he looked sideways at his father as though concerned.

"Lovely, isn't it?" Jager said.

Humphrey cleared his throat.

"Father," Pietre said, "it is only black stone like all the rest."

Gently, Jager took Pietre's shoulder and moved him several steps to the side until the boy's face opened up again. "The Shining Grey," he said, touching the glimmering thread of a line that widened into a river of metal.

"Yes, child." Reaching into a pouch wrapped around his waist, Jager said, "Take this." He put the small stone into Pietre's hand. Even in the dim light of the tunnel, it seemed to shimmer with thin streaks of metal. "In a way this stone led me to the vein. It was the first that fell from the wall and, when it did, the large streak of the Grey became visible.

97

Pietre rubbed the gift gently with his thumb. It was a bit rough on the surface, but smooth underneath. "Thank you," he said.

The three returned to the mouth of the mine where they rested away from the eyes of the guard, but in full view of the afternoon sun. Pietre gave news of his mother, the village, and the spring vegetation. Humphrey told of Markhi and his first training. Jager looked continually toward the south with a slight unease. Finally he said, "Someone will come soon to take me back to my cell. Today bears excellent news, but still you must be gone before he gets here."

Pietre nodded, clutching the stone in his pocket. "I will return," Pietre said. "Even if you forbid it, I will come."

"I do not forbid it," Jager said. "Though you must take care. These many weeks, I alone have been in these tunnels. But with news of the Grey, many human slaves will be sent to the mine and the guard increased. You must not be seen."

Pietre nodded and placed his palm again against his father's. Humphrey bowed to Jager just as he had to Markhi, before they turned away.

Jager watched them step behind the boulder and then, a few paces later, they both seemed to vanish. It was hardly the strangest thing that had happened that day.

When Jager turned back to the south, a figure stood on the hill watching him. Slowly the figure advanced. When he was quite near, Jager was surprised to see that the tall, pale prince stood before him. The prince did not seem to have seen the boy and dog. All he said was, "I hope you have excellent news. My father grows impatient. And surely you grow hungry."

Wittendon turned and a small onion dropped from his cloak. He looked east as though he hadn't noticed it fall.

Jager tried not to look at it, though its scent wafted upward, making his mouth thick with saliva. To Wittendon he said, "On the morrow, send all the human miners you can. I have found a vein, thick and long."

Wittendon nodded joylessly and turned.

Jager bent to pick up the onion and held it out. "My lord."

"A bruised onion is of no use to me," Wittendon said curtly.

Jager stepped in front of the prince, the onion now a bulge in his pocket. The prince walked heavily behind him.

UP ABOVE ON A SMALL PRECIPICE WHERE THE WHITE MOONFLOWERS were known to bloom, a pair of honeyed eyes watched the two descend. She had noted Wittendon's slow advance. Of course he *had* seen the boy. He had watched the palm of father and son meet. Perhaps he had wanted to rush forward and, in jealousy, punish them. But he had not. The youth who had braved the journey here and the father who had risked any safety that remained to him were left seemingly undiscovered. And of course she could not have missed the onion.

"He is different than most," she murmured.

"More different than you know, pretty one," the cat said, coming to sit beside her.

"Good eve, Savah. Have you no rhymes tonight?"

"You know I do it mostly to aggravate the dogs," she replied, cleaning a delicate paw with an equally delicate tongue.

"Of course." Sadora said, smiling.

Then the two of them stood, quiet as trees and graceful as birds, and retreated together deep into the woods.

CHAPTER 16

Seven wolves fanned out in front of Crespin, ready to assist him in his search for the girl. He had not told them of the dreams— only that there was a young traitor who must be found. Wolrijk had gathered a posse of wolves from across the kingdom to assist in the search. Crespin disliked this tactic. He disliked councils of any kind, preferring to work alone or to appoint a trusted specialist. Groups, he believed, led to slowness, to indecision, to endless bureaucracy. Wolrijk had argued that with so many they could cover more ground. Which should have been true.

Yet already one of the wolves—the head scout, Rorof—was injured. A dead branch had fallen, catching the wolf squarely in the paw. Just before it had happened, Crespin had noted a breath of movement. The injury forced them to set up camp nearly an hour ahead of schedule. It had also left the wolves feeling spooked.

Zinder, a nearly white wolf who ranked second to the general, stood in front of Crespin instructing the others in the set-up of the camp. A pond was nearby and they took turns going for drinks. They went in pairs, their ears pricked upright, an edginess to each step. Never could a foreign creature be seen or even scented, but at times a twig broke or the grass seemed to swish in a direction opposite the blowing of the winds.

"Spirits," he'd heard a few of the wolves mutter, and had silenced them with a stern look. Ghosts, he knew, did not exist unless he willed them to exist. Whatever this was, it was of the flesh.

As the injured wolf nursed his swollen paw, Crespin paced around the camp. To make matters worse, a pack of dogs traveled several miles to the north. It seemed they had also set up camp. Just as the wolves were bedding down, the dogs' hondmelodie began to carry over the hills. Wolrijk cursed audibly and the two wolves on guard stiffened. Crespin could not hear most of the words the dogs sang. Rather it was the melody—smooth and story-like—and the eerie spirituality of the harmonies beneath it—that crept under the skin of the wolves.

THE DOGS SAT ROUND THE FIRE—SOME ON THEIR HAUNCHES, SOME resting with their paws tucked under their chests. A young one opened his mouth into a long steady howl and soon the others joined in. The song, as song it was, was not intoned on one trembling note as their ancestors had done in millennia before, but on many notes that blended together into harmonious hondsong. Some moved the tones up and down and as they did, one picked up a story and began to spin it. As he sang, the other dogs continued to hum and howl, their voices dancing like the swaying rhythm of the fire.

"Many years before the fathers of our fathers of our father's fathers, the great Dog of the First broke from the wolves—following the call of the Great White God, fleeing to meadows low and long until joined by others of his brothers, sisters, cousins, friends."

The howls of the dogs were like a deep drone beneath the words.

"They gathered together—this Pack of the First, and left the blood-lust of the wolves behind."

"Behind," the chorus of voices echoed. "Behind."

"Many a time the great wolves came, muzzles dyed in blood. And many a time we pressed against, fighting alike to save the pack. And so we spread."

"Like the waters in flood year, so we spread."

Five gray dogs began to circle the fire, chanting and stomping—the embers rising up as though in obedience to the rhythm.

"The Great Prophet rose from lowly clan. White vision from his tongue: kindness, loyalty, bravery, family, love."

The dogs chanted their creed, the words swirling in circles until the sounds met, each dog stomping the ground. The crescendo of the voices seemed to fill the clearing like the rounded barrier of a shield.

"The God of the White, his face fell black; the God of the Red increased." A long moan broke over the valley, pressing with weight into any who heard it.

"Tethers, tethers to the dogs." The dogs in the circle swayed, like long grasses pressed by a wind, unseen, but heavy.

"Tethers, tethers break."

The swaying stopped. A long, still silence filled the night until after many minutes a hum began, low and long, and then the lead singer sang out, "White God rise. A sacrifice. White God rise. A test."

"Kindness, loyalty, bravery, family, love." The song broke on the final word and the dogs fell silent at last.

LATE IN THE NIGHT, KING CRESPIN WALKED INTO THE GRAY WOODS beyond their camp, hoping the night air would clear his senses. The stars lay dusted across the black sky—the brightest sitting to the right of the moon—an anomaly that happened once every hundred years. The moon was full and he could feel it pour its golden strength into his tired bones. He stood alone, covered in a black cloak, gazing into a dark pond. He stared at his reflection in the waters, the moon hanging in the sky at his back. It brought him some relief.

He bent to the water to take a drink. When he rose, wiping his mouth, the silhouetted figure of a woman stood on the other side of the pond. Cautious, he walked toward the figure, but by the time he reached the opposite bank, she was gone. Turning back to his camp, he heard a voice that made the skin rise along his neck and back. It called his name. As fast as any Verander, he pivoted toward the sound, but saw nothing.

"Crespin," she whispered, her voice a murmuring echo in his head.

Again he spun around to see no one, and again through the wind in the trees, he heard the voice of the woman who had been his wife's gardener and potion-maker. "You betrayed me King Crespin—a betrayal that led me to the point of death."

Dizzy and sick, he tore at the trees, searching for the owner of the voice. It seemed to be above him, around him, surrounding him.

"And that," the voice said, nearer now, as though just over his shoulder, as though inside of him, "led to the death of your beloved Loerwoei."

Furious he turned again, raising his staff above his head, the bauble at its tip glowing with daggers. "Show yourself, dark magician."

Spinning his staff in the darkness he struck at a tree just as he heard a quiet footstep behind him. He turned, weapon raised, to see the cloaked figure. He leveled his staff at her and she pulled the cloak off of her head to reveal the face, not of his dead potion maker, but of another woman—hair and eyes in shadow, lips and nose white in the moonlight.

"Impetuous human witch," he shouted, raising his staff to thrust a ball of energy at her.

She laughed. "Sorceress, I may well be, but human I am not entirely."

As the golden ball of energy hurled toward her, a branch of a nearby tree seemed to bend in the wind, deflecting it.

Again, the girl laughed and again the king leveled his staff at her, gripping it hard.

Slowly, she raised her own staff. "The ridiculous dead wood of your staff can do nothing to me," she said calmly. "My influence begins to exceed your own. And I am set on the destruction of your kingdom."

He found he could no longer lift his staff as the woman transformed into twelve metallic cats who lunged at him.

He awoke on his bedroll, screaming. He could hear the band of wolves as they sprang up, running to him.

"Go back to sleep," he called. "It is nothing."

The wolves slunk back to their places while Wolrijk stayed up to keep watch.

WHEN THEY WOKE IN THE MORNING, ROROF THE SCOUT HAD A PAW THE size of a small head. "It is badly infected," Zinder reported to Crespin. "He will have to turn back."

"How can that be?" Crespin snapped. "His paw was struck by a tree branch."

"It is most unusual," Zinder replied uneasily. "To be honest, I am not entirely sure he has ever been injured during a hunt."

Zinder was interrupted by Wolrijk. "I have instructed the scout to remain here while we move on. A messenger bird has been sent to the kingdom and a healer will come to retrieve him. We need not waste more time waiting."

"Waste time?" Zinder retorted. "Our injured are not a waste of our time."

"I have sent for a healer," Wolrijk growled. "What more would you have us do—rock him to sleep?"

Crespin pounded his staff on the ground so that both wolves snapped to attention. "And who will now lead us in this hunt?" he asked.

Zinder turned to the king, tucking his paw. "That would be me," he said. "I am not quite as skilled as Rorof, but very nearly so."

The king could not help but notice that Zinder looked nervously to the trees, as though he recognized that it was not mere coincidence and bad luck that had waylaid the lead scout so early in their quest.

"Very well," the king replied. "We leave in one quarter of an hour."

CHAPTER 17

Pietre settled by the fire with the tin of hot hibiscus tea his mother handed him. He had snuck to the mines for the second time that week to be with his father. Each time the trip got faster, but his feet and legs were tired, his back ached, and his eyes hurt from squinting—first from the glaring sunlight of the rock lands, then from the darkness of the tunnels, then from the sun when he came to the surface again. He curled into the ragged chair, almost too tired to sip his tea.

"Rough day hunting with the dogs?" his mother asked, folding an old blanket.

He hesitated, not sure what she was talking about until, after a cough from Humphrey, he said, "Oh, yes, very."

His mother paused in her folding, but Pietre didn't notice.

"Moecka," he began. "Have you ever seen odd things in the forest?"

"I don't know what the forest is if not a collection of odd things."

"No," Pietre said, sitting up just a bit. "I mean really odd. Like—" Pietre stopped speaking and dropped his gaze to his tea.

Slowly his mother rose with the blanket and a small bundle of clean rags and Pietre continued, "I don't mean weird plants or oddly shaped trees, but maybe a strange animal or even a ghost or...or... maybe a cat."

His mother almost laughed. "'Tis naught but fairy stories," she said, putting the rags on a shelf.

"But—" Pietre began again.

"Have you seen one?" his mother asked, cutting him off.

"Well, no, but I—"

"Have a very bold imagination," his mother cut in.

She looked into Pietre's face and he turned away.

"If you are going to believe such things," she continued, a hard undertone creeping into her voice, "then you might as well believe in the God of the High White Sun of whom the dogs often speak—the one they believe will free all from Veranderen rule."

Pietre had heard some talk of the God of the White Sun. Long ago the White God had given humans and dogs the power to communicate. At least that was how the stories went. And then the God of the Red Sun had risen up pushing his white brother aside. That was all Pietre knew. "Free us?" Pietre asked.

"Put us on equal standing," she said.

"I do not know this tale."

"That's because I haven't told it for many years."

It was true. When he'd been young, his mother had filled their evenings with story after story, but it had been many years since she'd told any of the legends of his childhood. "Tell me, Moecka," he begged, fingering the rock from his father that sat in a deep corner of his pocket.

His mother hesitated only a moment before unfolding the blanket and placing it on his lap. "Once," she began, "at the dawn of time, a bright white light ruled this earth. It gave to us a sky of blue and carried in its power a bone white moon that pulled the waters in when its face came near and released them when it stepped back. Man walked among shifter. Dog and wolf ran in packs over green grasses. All worked side by side to till the earth, plant its bounty, and unmold and re-shape its metals." His mother paused and glanced toward the small window.

"But none were happy," she frowned. "The shifters felt themselves torn between two races—their forms moving from human to wolf at the push and pull, the wax and wane of the glowing white moon. They were then called"—and here Carina only mouthed the word 'were-wolf'—"a term now unspoken by any who wish to keep their necks out of the stocks. The shifters wished for more control, for autonomy from the seasons and tides, for the strength and power such control over their forms would give them.

"Men felt themselves the weakest among the races—lacking sharp teeth and claws, thick skin and fur. They felt their 'equal' duties fell heaviest on their backs. Though expert in tools and invention, they wished for others to lighten their load. They wished it too hard, as they were willing to exchange a measure of freedom for what they hoped would be a measure of ease. The shifters and wolves agreed to carry a heavier load, but only in exchange for free use of the human's tools and ideas, and only for a tax that they swore would not grow heavy.

"The dogs' wish," she said, nodding at Humphrey, "was the simplest. They wished to run free through the land without thought of others' mouths to feed. They wished to be absolved from their duties to the other races and felt they could promise, in return, to ask nothing of any either.

"The wolves wished almost the opposite. They wished for protection. Strong and fierce, the wolves hunted much and often—sometimes without cause. The other races often complained that they took more than their share and did not give sufficient in return. In fact, some wolves were subjected to trials held at the hands of the humans or dogs. They were accused of abusing the balance—killing too freely and too much and leaving too little in the lands. If found guilty these wolves were killed with their families too, and fed to those they'd left hungry in their greed. The wolves wished for an easier way. They wanted only to be fed and harbored, even if it meant life in villages with masters to lead them. In exchange they would gladly use fang and nail to protect and defend whoever was willing to feed and shelter them.

"A deal was struck. Four representatives, one from each race, were chosen. The human would fashion a stone from pure metals. The shifter would empower that stone with magic that increased as the full moon rose to its place in the sky. Then before the embers of the sun extinguished into night's blackness, all four would place the stone at the highest point in the land, a point known as 'Motteral.' In this way, each would add a touch of his essence to the new world so that each would receive a fair measure of what his race desired.

"But whether through confusion or intrigue, the human and dog arrived late. Already wolf and shifter had come to the Sacred Tablet and touched the empowered gem, which began to glow red in the night. Quickly, dog and man moved toward it—dog reaching it first. They touched it in an effort to add their essences to it, but things were changing. The shifter was strongest in the moonlight. He fought the human away. The dog fought back, but the wolf struck at his back. Before long, a battle had ensued. Relatives and friends from each race were called to the great hill. Through an unspoken alliance, dog and man fought shifter and wolf. Blood and gore were spilled as they had never been before and never have been since. But all was already lost.

"A new sun rose—red as the bloodied hill of battle. The great race of Veranderen was born. Shifters could now change form at will, resist injury or disease, and their lives lasted centuries and longer. They rose quickly in dominance. Their alliance to the wolves held fast. Even the dogs were allowed a measure of freedom as long as they obeyed Veranderen law and stayed out of their way. But the humans, now the weakest of the races, began to be repressed, misused, and heavily taxed." His mother paused, folding her hands in her lap.

"The humans maintained a small victory. For the Sourcestone had been created at their hands. While it caused the Veranderen to rise in power, it also saturated the hill with Grey that seeped slowly into the ground, like roots, extending deep into what are now the Grey mines."

Pietre no longer felt sleepy and had abandoned his tea. Even Humphrey lifted his head, both ears upright.

"It is said," Carina concluded, "that when two are found—one as strong and one as pure as the gemstone of that lost age, that the fate of the sun can be reversed and the face of the White Sun will shine again. Though dog and man will speak no more."

Humphrey sat up. "Come again," he said.

Carina smiled. "'Tis naught but a tale," she said, stroking his fur.

"You tell it too well," Humphrey said, settling down uneasily.

"A great compliment from a noble hound such as yourself," she replied.

"But Moecka," Pietre asked interrupting. "Could it really be so—could such a gift as speech be lost? And why?"

"I suppose if it was given it could be taken," his mother said, tucking the blanket firmly around his legs. "But it is just a tale, youngling. And one I apparently should not have told."

"But if it was true?" Pietre asked.

"Well, perhaps a mutual language would no longer be needed if there was a dawn of equality," she said, although she could see that Pietre looked unconvinced. "I have heard it told that some of the dogs believe it to be a sacrifice; a test to see if they will keep their creed. And I suppose one gift might need to be exchanged for others. Just like the bitter greens must be boiled with sweet meats for balanced soup."

"But that would be terrible," Pietre said, stroking Humphrey's undercoat and lying down beside him.

"Terrible on one count," his mother responded, touching Humphrey's nose gently. "But wonderful on other counts. Imagine a world where man and wolf walked an equal path—no Blødguard, no taxes...no slaves." She gave Humphrey and Pietre one final embrace and stood to leave. "No matter what the color the sun might come to, I've never known life to be anything other than terrible and wonderful wound together in different ways." At that she placed a hand on her forehead where Jager had last touched it. "Language is more than words. I don't believe dog and man could ever lose their ability to speak to one another, even if speech no longer came in the way we know."

She looked out their small window into the darkness. Pietre pulled the blanket up over his shoulders, covering his ears to keep out the sounds of the Blødguard, and draping part of it over Humphrey.

As his mother turned to leave, she murmured to herself, "But you needn't worry about white suns and lost languages. In the story two great ones are needed to change the skies." She lifted the candle and held it in front of her face. "And great ones, sleeping child, are rare in the best of times and especially scarce in these." She spoke softly to herself. "Any great ones who dare to exist are taken or lashed with burdens so heavy that changing the color of the dawn is as far from their minds as the fairy stories of their childhoods." With that she extinguished the candle and walked from the room.

Perhaps she thought that Pietre, with his blanket tucked ears, would not hear her. Indeed, as he turned his face into Humphrey's soft back, he didn't seem to hear. Yet like so many boys for so many centuries past, he did hear, and when he fell into sleep, it was with dreams of great ones and imaginings about where such a person might be found.

CHAPTER 18

Crespin looked grim. For several days their hunt had led them around in convoluted circles. And now that he felt they drew near to the girl, two of his wolves had fallen within hours of each other—one with fits of vomiting so severe that even Wolrijk had seemed concerned; the other cut in the face by a branch, which would have been nothing except that within the hour an oozing rash had broken out along the wound. The afflicted wolves had been left to await help.

The rest of the party stood at the edge of the dogs' territory. It would not normally pose a problem to travel through peacefully, but the day had been bewitched and even in the best circumstances, dogs and wolves were not great friends. Yet to go around would mean an extra day's travel. Crespin pressed forward.

The woods the dogs called their home were thick and lush. Herbs and flowers lined the path while trees as tall as the sky itself, and wider than three Veranderen, seemed to reach up at every turn. The wolves ran quickly and were almost through when one named Dorak stumbled on a ragged root, howling in pain. His companion Gog tried to help him up, pulling a splinter from the wound with his mouth.

Crespin turned on the pack, facing Wolrijk and screamed, "Have you assembled a company of clowns? Am I to believe luck is so moved against us as to trip every devil of a wolf you have brought to me? Is this the best your race can afford?"

For just a breath of an instant, Wolrijk bared his upper teeth, but the white wolf Zinder stepped forward. "It is different than luck, good king. I sense evil among the trees and at each ill event I smell odors unnatural for this vegetation."

As if to demonstrate, Dorak let out a yowl and Gog groaned.

"So this root has jumped forward to poison the wolf who now howls at my feet in pain while this other wolf whines with some sort of sympathy suffering."

Crespin and Zinder looked at the wolves—Dorak's breathing was labored and Gog's eyes seemed to have dilated, which was odd. Zinder opened his mouth to respond when the sounds of branches breaking stopped him. The diminished party of wolves looked up to see that they were ringed by a pack of broad-chested dogs.

"I suppose they're poisonous too," Crespin hissed.

"My lord," the head dog said, tucking a paw. "What brings you to our quarter of your great land?"

The king stepped forward in the formal way of the dogs. "Today, good dog, we travel forth on the urgent business of our kingdom. Pray let us pass quickly, as one has just become injured on this path."

The head dog raised two hairy eyebrows and was about to stand down when, without warning, Gog sprang upon one of the dogs, attacking.

Both sides were so stunned that for a moment none moved except the attacked and the attacker. In a moment, however, the dogs let forth a war cry and leaped at the wolves.

The injured wolf Dorak was quickly tossed out of the way with a cut to his face and back.

Two dogs attacked the wolf Gog who now foamed at the mouth, uttering nonsensical curses as he tried to claw at his opponents. One of the dogs took off a chunk of his ear, while the other bit at his neck before the attacked dog—a sentinel named Silva—threw him back, cutting his belly, so that it nearly tore open. Gog moaned, still foaming, and his eyes rolled back into his head.

The dogs flew to the aid of their brothers who were fighting the remaining two wolves. Wolrijk dealt a blow to the head dog's face, which drew blood, but did not run deep. The head dog moved to the side and advanced again, now joined by Silva.

Zinder spoke softly, but in a threatening whisper as two dogs circled him, snapping at his heels. He jumped forward to a nearby tree, which shuddered above him though there was no wind. Zinder nearly choked on his breath and ran back towards the dogs, barreling into one so hard the dog was knocked to the ground where he lay gasping.

The king raised his staff and hit it against the ground with such force that a shallow vein of earth opened at his feet and the dogs and wolves paused in their struggle.

"Enough," Crespin said, the bauble atop his staff glowing with heat. The wolves fell back and the dogs stood, growling, until their leader stepped forward. "Is this part of your urgent business, King Crespin? A surprise attack on an innocent dog?"

Crespin's staff glowed red as blood. His words were soft and measured. "The wolf is mad, and had you waited in your attack you would have had your due retribution. As it is, you have had your revenge and we will, for now, consider it an even trade." The king moved close to the head dog, breathing heavily and drawing himself up to his full height. "You, however, would do well to remember that I am king and this is my domain. The dogs are not above my rule. I will move among my land as I wish. Is that understood?"

The head dog tucked his paw, nodding. But as the wound from his face dripped blood onto his upper lip and teeth, he looked anything but meek. "I am Markhi, good king. It is a name that I pray your lordship will deign to remember the next time we have the honor of meeting upon this terrain."

The king turned without responding, leaving dogs and wolves behind. Wolrijk moved to retrieve Gog, but found the wolf could not walk. Wolrijk growled low, scowling at the pack of dogs and then at the crazed wolf. Markhi nodded to Silva, who went to Gog's side.

Using their shoulders, Markhi and Silva crouched low, lifting the insane wolf up enough to drape him unceremoniously onto Wolrijk's back. Wolrijk left without another look to find his master. Zinder pushed Dorak to his feet and helped him back to the path. But before leaving, Zinder turned to the head dog, looked him in the eye, and quietly tucked his paw. Markhi nodded back and said shortly, "The herb willowmeier will help to stop the flow of blood."

Once in the clearing King Crespin commanded, "Zinder, you stay with these two. Await help. Wolrijk, you will continue with me alone; as it should have been in the first place."

"But my king," Zinder said, standing before his lord and bowing low. "All is not well. All is not normal. The trees shudder when there is no wind. The earth and branches bleed poison into your most loyal subjects. The wolf Gog seems to have been crazed merely by extracting the splinter that debilitated Dorak. Will you now continue in this mad quest for a creature of whom you know so little?"

The king moved close to Zinder. A red blade seemed to dance inside the stone of his staff and Crespin moved this stone just under Zinder's chin. A word of magic and a flick of his wrist would have cleanly sliced open the wolf's jugular vein, but Zinder did not bow his head.

"You are brave," the king said. "And you have scouted well through these treacherous lands." The king looked northwest, the muscles of his mouth stretched in tight lines. "What you say is most true. Poison, sickness, and madness have followed us through this journey. However, I see them only as reasons to follow this quest to its end. There is one who seeks our destruction. I will not rest until she is found and killed. Do you understand?"

"Yes, my lord," Zinder replied.

"Good. Then I leave the healing to you, and the killing to one who is more suited to such work." He turned to Wolrijk who—with bleeding scratches along his face and body—looked every bit his part.

"May the God of the Red Sun grant you speed," Zinder said, bowing again. The king snorted at the sentiment. He and the general were soon out of sight.

A few minutes later, Zinder found the leaves and thin branches of the willowmeier bush. He tore the leaves into tiny bits with his teeth and dropped them along his companions' wounds, careful to avoid contact with the flesh that had been affected by the root—a root that had afflicted one wolf with pain and the other with madness. After that, Zinder sat off several paces by himself and waited.

CHAPTER 19

Wolrijk scouted slightly ahead of the king, running into the afternoon as though chasing the sun, which sat on the horizon like a mouth that gaped open, waiting for a meal. Wolrijk salivated at the thought. The day had been unusually hot and the path they'd taken wound through beds of red rock that seemed to pull the rays of the sun into them, making it even hotter. Wolrijk's extra-thick skin made the temperature even less bearable. As the sun melted into the horizon, Wolrijk reached a meadow just in front of a forest. Out of the wood and flanked by two willow trees ran a small stream which collected in a pool, clearer than any they had seen. "We can make camp here," Wolrijk said, turning to the king who followed close behind him.

As rock gave way to dead leaves, then moss, then the outer trees of the wood, a scent invaded the air that was distinct.

"She wishes to be found," the wolf said.

"Yes," the king murmured, pressing his long nails against his chin.

Wolrijk sat down and chewed bits of bramble from his fur. The king turned away and Wolrijk smiled to himself. Crespin could never look at him long before turning away, and Wolrijk liked that—liked that he could repel even a bloodthirsty king, enjoyed the power his hideousness gave him.

A squirrel scampered past. Wolrijk reached out faster than an arrow and grabbed it, breaking its neck in the same motion. "We will need our strength," he said, passing their supper to the king. "I'll go for water."

Wolrijk walked to the pool of water and for the first time that day, he paused. The water was so clear he could see each rock at the bottom, even where the water was quite deep. The rocks were of all colors—blue, orange, rose, quartz. They appeared to dance in their liquid basin. Normally, Wolrijk could not have cared less about the color of a few rocks, but somehow these were different. Thoughts of his older brother crept into his mind. He shook them off as he always did, but this time they came back. He and his brother used to skip rocks, right over the surface—like magic the way they flew from water to air. His brother had been fast and bright, and Wolrijk had loved him as he had loved no one before or since, but in a bloody political plot his brother's life had been cut short. Wolrijk leaned forward, running his marred paw through the clear waters. The gentle chill of the water seemed to erase the pain of his brother's death, the loneliness of the past many years. It seemed to erase everything.

CRESPIN HEARD THE SPLASH TOO LATE. HE RAN TO THE POOL AND when Wolrijk's head bobbed out of the water, he grabbed him by the nape of the neck and pulled him out.

Far from being drowned, the killer Crespin had chosen—the fiercest, strongest, most deformed, blood-thirsty wolf in his entire kingdom—lay curled into a tight ball; asleep. When Crespin attempted to wake him, he only rolled to the other side, murmuring sounds that rocked like nursery tunes. The posture, the slight smile on the wolf's lips—they reminded Crespin of his old friend Draden—that face he had taken such pains to forget.

Cursing the enchanted waters, Crespin kicked the wolf hard in the side. Wolrijk only muttered a sleepy sigh. Crespin left the general on the ground and faced the wood. As he did so, he heard a voice, lilting like the stream that fed the bedeviled pool of water.

And now, o king, we meet at last.
Shadows all and ghosts long past.

A cat appeared at the edge of the wood—larger than most of the she-wolves of Crespin's kingdom. The cat's face was a ruddy orange with a coat of different colors that streaked along her back like golden-toned lightning bolts. Crespin stared at the extinct animal. She smiled.

Consider yourself honored, Wilhelmszon.
Most feel my breath and then I'm gone.
You get to see, though but a moment.
Some that comes at prophecy's fulfillment.

"All this," the king said, gesturing to his slumbering general. "It is your doing?"

The cat laughed, a humming purr,

All that you have recently seen.
It is the doing of my mistress queen.

"Now," she said, breaking from her rhyme. "Come."

Crespin had no intention of obeying the animal, but when he turned his back on the cat, a wall of trees had grown up where clear meadow had been only moments before and Crespin found himself weakened to the point that he struggled to keep from shifting into his flesh form. The cat walked ahead of him and he grudgingly followed, gripping his staff and allowing it to glow with all the ferocity of the red sun.

When at last they came to a clearing in the impossibly dense wood, Crespin noticed a small, crude hut surrounded by flowers, herbs, and vegetables of every sort. In the midst of it, facing away from the king, sat a tall chair fashioned of twigs, branches, and flowers that had been bowed and bound together to form shapes and designs of birds and butterflies—as ornate as any he had seen in his kingdom. Next to the chair sat a small table and on it a tiny teapot carved from the narrow trunk of a dogwood tree and stained at the tip from much use. Two white cats rested on either side of the chair, enjoying the last rays of the day's sun.

"Good evening, dear king," came a voice from the chair. "Won't you sit down and have a cup of tea?"

The king did not move.

"Well, then," the voice said. "Manners were never really your strongest suit." From the chair a girl stood up, as tall and thin as the willow trees at the edge of the forest. Her skin was perfectly pale, except for two round pink cheeks. Her teeth were square and straight and too large for her mouth, and though it was clear that she had only just entered into womanhood, her hair hung long and gray past her waist. The king took in her features, assessing her from head to toe, meeting her gaze last.

Two eyes blinked at him. They were as distinct from each other as the red sun was from the white. The right eye was a copper disc—the same Crespin had seen in his dreams; the other was a green circle streaked with gold—the eye of the gardener he had known too well. To see both at once was disconcerting; to see only one was worse. Each eye brought out different features of her face, so that every time she turned, you got the impression she'd just become someone else.

Crespin looked at her for a long time before noticing a gangly staff that rested next to her, a staff which she occasionally touched with affection.

"Come now, good king, and kiss my cheek; it has been long since you have known of my presence and surely we have much to talk about." She leaned forward, turning her green eye to him, as though she truly believed the king would kiss her.

Instead he spat upon the ground at her feet and held his staff firmly in front of his face.

"As I was saying about the manners," the girl said. "I'm sure your dear Loerwoei never would have approved."

"How dare you speak the name of my departed queen," Crespin whispered, his voice as taut as a hangman's rope.

"Come. She was an old friend to my beloved mother. Almost as sisters, those two."

"You will stop with your frivolous, blasphemous talk of the queen," the king said, lowering his staff so that the round crystal was at the girl's eye level. "You know nothing of her."

"Do I not?" The girl turned her chair to face him and sat back down, pouring a cup of tea. "You know they say that reunions are always awkward events. I guess they're right." She placed a saucer of milk and several small fishes on the table for the cats. "It was my mother who helped to keep your beloved Loerwoei alive all those months. Your magic of course was useless. A pity my mother had to leave. Do sit down; I've got muffins in the oven; they'll be ready soon."

The king pounded his staff upon the ground just as he had in the dogs' territory, expecting the same result, but in the dense woods it did not even make a noise, much less scar the ground.

"Goodness. Don't be so sour. I'll pour the tea. One lump or two?"

As she reached for the sugar dish, the king shot a blast of heat from his staff, which knocked the dish to the ground. "You will cease your careless talk of she who was dear to me, and you will bow as all do who stand in my presence. I am Crespin—king of humans, dogs, wolves, and those who shift shape. I am king of all."

"Oh dear," she replied, casually stirring her tea. "I am Zinnegael—and you see I don't quite fit any of those definitions, so you'll pardon me if I stay sitting and just sip my tea."

The king growled and leapt at the girl, only to find his legs immediately entangled in morning glory vines. He stumbled forward, falling before the witch girl.

"I didn't say you needed to bow to *me*, though it is finally a bit of politeness," Zinnegael laughed. With a wave of her staff, the vines at his feet were gone. "These weeds can get out of hand so quickly."

"Who are you?" King Crespin demanded, rising slowly and

watching as an insolent cat in front of him casually flicked its tail, cleaning a paw.

"Do you not know? Really? Now I thought you'd have it figured out by now," the girl replied. "You know I think you really have guessed it, although—" She paused, her voice losing its playful tone. "—you do, of course, wish that you hadn't."

The king made no reply though his eyelid twitched.

"Perhaps you will recall my mother. She was very tall for a human, almost as tall as the Veranderen and ten times more beautiful, although I admit to acquiring many of my looks from my father's side." She tossed a course, gray lock over her shoulder and turned the copper eye toward Crespin. "My mother's hair was as red as the sun and she worked in the gardens of the king. She grew things of all sorts—beautiful, deadly, useful. And she became an expert in potions, an art so close to actual magic that it could catch the attention of a Verander, even a king."

Zinnegael fixed both mismatched eyes on King Crespin. "Her parents lived in a hovel outside the werewolf capital." The king growled at the word 'werewolf,' but the girl ignored it. "In order to keep them safe and well-fed, my mother learned to be fiercely, perhaps we could call it desperately, obedient."

The witch walked from the front to the back of the king, pacing like a cat. "My mother gardened with the queen, helped her when she fell ill, and loved her dearly. But she did what her king commanded her. In all things. Even those that were surely distasteful to her."

With that a vine topped with a flower of deep purple and streaked in black grew up before the king. The blooms multiplied, forming themselves into delicate cups shaped like the bellabud flowers from which hummingbirds drank. One flower climbed to the king's lips and when it did, he could smell not sweetness, but the poison stench of the purple-black nectar within.

"Will you not drink, my lord?" laughed the witch.

He twisted his head as the nectar came to his lips, the smell foul and strong and oddly intriguing in the beautiful chalice.

"When it became clear that my mother was expecting a child, a child that sprang—as the king well knew—from his own loins, he ordered her to concoct a potion that would destroy the unborn babe."

The king's lips were stiff and deadly white. The poison flower tipped its nectar to the earth where it sizzled.

"Perhaps you remember the story now," she said, taking a sip of her tea. "When my mother refused—an act of insolence new to the king—he banished her. Though we both know that banishment wasn't quite enough, was it? No, he sent wolves to her village. They hunted her parents, burned huts to the ground. And then they chased the garden servant deep, deep into these woods."

Zinnegael paused in her story to add a drizzle of cream to her cup. "Your wolves are excellent hunters, Lord King. They found my mother and attacked. First they tore at her hair, and then they maimed her gardener's hands. At that point they intended to finish their work, but something unexpected happened. Have you guessed it?"

The king looked to the cats in front of him. One of the felines licked its lips.

"Yes," the witch girl said. "More ghosts from your past. A race you thought you had eliminated sprang from the trees and attacked your wolves. Attacked and fought until the wolves retreated."

"The hunting of the cats was not my doing," the king said.

"You gave your permission."

"The wolves found great sport in it."

"Ah, a game was it? Well, I do love a good game. How exciting. A population almost extinct in the name of sport." With that, one of the cats arched its back as though to stretch—the black pupils of its eyes like daggered slits.

The girl continued, "The wolves told you their task had been accomplished—the woman with child was dead. You can hardly blame them. To have failed would have meant execution at your hand. Besides, it was almost true. My mother was very nearly dead. The cats carried my mother deep into the forest and laid her on a bed of soft bark, expecting her to die. But bark was something my mother knew. The cats brought her water to drink and the nectar of honeybloom to ease her mind. But instead of drinking, she formed a poultice of bark and tears and sweet nectar. She drank the liquid from it and put the softened bark paste on her hands and wounds. She was no longer quite so beautiful, but for several years she lived. And so, as you can see, did I." With that, the witch let out a coarse laugh.

"When my mother finally did die, it was her wish to be buried under the gardens." The witch gestured to the trees, flowers, herbs, and vegetables all around her. "Even in death, she grants life to me. While you—even in life—you wish to evoke death."

The king met her eyes—both of them, then spoke. "Half-bloods do not belong in the kingdom. It is not in the natural order."

"Indeed," she said, laughing and tapping her staff to the ground so that a bright flame, flickering with green sprang from its tip. "Indeed it is not." She threw the flame at the king. It clipped off the hair on either side of his cheeks.

"It might create creatures expert at both potions and magic."

"She devil," he hissed.

"What?" she asked innocently, burning the cut hair into dust. "You know I could have done much worse than that. You saw what I did to your party of ridiculous wolves."

The king growled.

The witch looked at him mildly. "Do you wish to fight me?" she asked, her eyes laughing.

"No," he responded calmly. "I wish to destroy you." With a mighty effort his nails and teeth grew longer and he leaped at her.

Just as quickly a wall of roots formed in front of her. He hit the wooden barricade and fell to the earth. The king groaned and tried to stand.

"Oh, but you can't destroy me," she said, smirking as he unwillingly sank back to the ground. "Someone saw to that."

Slowly, thick roots began to grow from the ground around the king.

"Do you see this staff, dear king? Or perhaps you would prefer it if I called you 'father.'"

Crespin growled, but did not move. Indeed he could not as the roots were now beginning to grow around his chest and legs.

"This staff," she said calmly, causing the roots to thicken. "I formed it from the same bark that healed my mother. The wood and I —we go rather well together, don't you think?"

"Do you plan to kill me then?" he asked, feeling the weight of the roots press down on his lungs.

She laughed, just like the girl she was and said, "Oh, I don't have to." And then in a voice that was her own, but wasn't, she hummed,

He who eleven did defeat,
shall find in the twelfth his life complete.
The first born of the surviving foe,
Shall hunt the king like lion to doe.
Conqueror conquered now descends,
To meet his own most bitter end.

The witch Zinnegael paused, her posture relaxing, and tapped her staff against the earth.

With that, the roots tightened across the Crespin's chest until the mighty king gasped and fainted.

WHEN HE WOKE, CRESPIN WAS IN HIS FLESH FORM AND HIS MOUTH tasted of oak, cedar mushrooms, and lemoned mint. His interview with the witch came to him in misaligned pieces. He had come with only dreams and he left with much the same. He did, however, remember her divination perfectly. "The first born of the surviving foe/Shall hunt the king like lion to doe." Tomar—the elder who had escaped when Crespin had killed the council—his son would hunt Crespin. The king smirked. The witch surely meant to undermine him with her bit of verse. But Crespin had gone against prophecy before, and won.

Above Crespin, the wispy clouds seemed to form a seven in the sky. As he shifted into his wolken form, tracking the sun to his realm, he cast a breeze to the skies, blowing the clouds into a fine mist that fled across the horizon into nothingness.

CHAPTER 20

Pietre bent down to the creek and took a long drink before filling his bucket. The dogs could be heard singing miles away. They rarely rhymed, but somehow their songs still rang with a cadence that lilted even better than the bards' couplets. When the dogs could be heard singing, the human villages fell still and listened. It was a rare treat—a tendril of colorful light weaving amongst the dreariness of their days.

Yet when Pietre looked at Humphrey, his friend seemed tense—his jaw set.

"What's wrong," Pietre asked. "Are you afraid of another training session?"

"Hardly," Humphrey replied. "I'm full-grown now. And I've been practicing." Humphrey winked at Pietre, but Pietre couldn't miss it—the way Humphrey's jaw clenched up again as soon as he stopped talking.

"Something wrong with your mouth?" Pietre asked, a little concerned now. Pietre had heard of the jaw sickness that sometimes afflicted those dealing in old metals and lately they'd been moving Jager's tools to boxes. Pietre knew that a scratch could cause the sickness and Humphrey wasn't one to complain of scratches.

"My mouth is fine," Humphrey said.

"Humphrey," Pietre pressed.

"It's fine," Humphrey said louder—his voice deep and rich, carrying down the waterway. The sound seemed to startle him and he shut up again.

The hondsong came nearer—snatches catching at their ears.

Humphrey's body swayed with the sound, but still his face remained tight.

"Not even a hum," Pietre said, trying to tease. "You afraid Markhi will have to train you in your singing, too?"

Humphrey looked at him, not smiling. "Wolves cannot sing."

Pietre stared back, not understanding.

"And if I open my mouth and no song comes out, then…then—" Humphrey stopped.

"Then you will be found out."

"Perhaps. But it is more than that." Humphrey looked in the direction of the dogs. "If I try to sing and cannot, then I will hear it myself —the side of me that I wish wasn't, the part that is only ugliness."

Pietre wanted to say that surely there were wolves who weren't so bad; wolves who would spare and not destroy. But he couldn't think of any, so he clamped his own mouth closed.

THEY'D HAD STORMS FOR THE PAST TWO DAYS AND, ALTHOUGH Wittendon knew that Sarak was eager to get to the practice fields, his trainer refused to brave the thunder and lightning that ravaged the hill. At the end of the second day when darkness settled, so did the skies. Stars broke out and the moon rose thick and bright. Wittendon went to bed with his heavy curtains open so that the constellations lay over him like a blanket. He watched them for over an hour as they slowly moved across the sky and then, when Wittendon finally fell into the black cavern of his dreams, a light broke through—shimmering and piercing. His mother stood before him pink-fleshed and as alive as she had ever been—a star of a woman in his bedroom.

"Mother," he said and she, humming, turned—her face awash in light until at once she blinked—the thick lashes covering the bright eyes. And then she was laid out on her funeral bed, hands crossed— pale, cold. Dead. She was dead.

He woke mourning it with the same dark ice in his heart as he had felt that day. Dead.

She did not have to be dead. If the gardener had not run off, his mother might have lived. The gardener had made tonics and teas; everything had flourished under her care. Yet she—she who had claimed to be his mother's friend—she had left when his mother had needed her the most. For this Wittendon had never forgiven the gardener. He rose from his bed and snapped the drapes shut.

SARAK TOSSED HIS BLADE DOWN ON THE GRASS. "FIGHT LIKE THAT AND they'll kill you, my friend."

Wittendon sighed, leaning on his own scythe. "Why do I have to do this anyway?" Wittendon looked to the path he'd seen Sadora take not five minutes ago. She often went that route to pick wildflowers in the morning and Wittendon often wished to follow her. This morning a post-rain musk hung thick in the air and the lush scents of his land hovered in the moisture like an invitation.

"Because you're the son of a king, that's why. And don't tell me it doesn't have its perks." Sarak nodded to the same hill Wittendon was looking at.

"You think she only notices me because I'm a prince?" Wittendon asked, angered by the idea and worried by it too.

Sarak sighed. "Hardly," he said. "Although you wouldn't have too much of a chance with her if you were just a common shifter. As it is I suppose she's the one who should be worried about having a chance with you." Sarak said it with just an edge of irritation in his voice.

Normally, Wittendon wouldn't have even noticed, but since Jager's arrest he had been wondering himself about the inequality in his kingdom—among the different races where it was obvious, but also among his own people who, though free, were divided into clear castes —most of the verlorn living in huts outside the city—digging ditches and cutting grain. "And that bothers you?" Wittendon asked.

"Look, don't try to change the subject Witt," Sarak said, managing a smile. "This conversation is about you getting killed because you're clearly love-struck and cannot bring yourself to focus on the fact that in several weeks there will be a deadly blade in your hand. And, more importantly, in the hand of your opponent."

"But does it bother you—the difference classes among our race?" Wittendon asked, picking up his blade and readying his stance.

"The Veranderen in power are those whose ancestors fought for our kind on this very hill. The others hid and hoped for the best." Sarak picked up his own blade.

"So the story goes," Wittendon said slowly. "But even so, it was the ancestors who didn't fight, not those shifters who now remain in huts and farms around the head city."

Sarak shrugged, advancing on his friend. "All are well cared for."

Wittendon wondered. The lowest class of shifters did *seem* to be well cared for, and yet among the peasants of his kind there was a strange emptiness. They had clothes, food, and shelter. They worked in their appointed positions within their communities and yet something about them seemed fractured. Few, if any, had maintained their magic and because of this they often lived shorter lives than their magical counterparts. If they did live long enough to reproduce, most peasant families were divided so that they could work more efficiently. Family relations were a privilege of those in the upper classes—those, as Crespin put it, who had the education and the intelligence to under-stand when familial allegiance swerved from affection into distraction. Wittendon moved forward, swinging his blade.

Sarak easily deflected the blow and tried to strike Wittendon's ribs. He was surprised to see Wittendon avoid his hit for the first time that morning.

"You know, I've been going to collect the miners in the evenings," Wittendon said.

"Nope; hadn't noticed," Sarak replied sarcastically.

Wittendon ignored the sarcasm. Of course Sarak knew, as did anyone with a mouth to gossip. Sadora spent her evenings picking flowers and watching the moon lift from the horizon, rising over the hill just above the mines. Going to collect the slaves was the perfect excuse for Wittendon to watch her. Every tittering maiden in the kingdom knew this.

What they did not know was that it was hardly the only reason for Wittendon to be attracted to the mines. He'd also wanted to observe the prisoner Jager and his child. The humans thought they were hiding the boy, and maybe they were from the wolf guard, but they underestimated the sharp senses of a Veranderen prince. Wittendon couldn't figure out how the boy had gotten to the mines, but that wasn't what distracted him. Rather, Wittendon had spent the last couple weeks wondering what kind of child would risk the journey through thief-ridden roads and dangerous territory to see his father. He wondered what kind of father could command such allegiance. He wondered what kind of race could be bound so tightly that separation and even the threat of death did not weaken the connection. In fact, it seemed to strengthen it. Wittendon glanced toward the Grey mines, then again at the path Sadora had taken.

Sarak struck him to the shoulder and then pinned the blade to his neck. "Yup. Dead," he said.

"I..." Wittendon began, but couldn't think of an excuse.

"Go on, then," Sarak said, sheathing his weapon. "Go on and woo her or whatever it is you intend to do. Although you better be good to her or I *will* kill you."

Wittendon just stood there looking stupid. Sarak seemed to derive a little pleasure from that and softened. "Go on," he said again, picking Wittendon's weapon up off the ground. "If you can find her, of course. There have been evenings I've wandered those hills in search of her myself, only to give up and find her at home eating supper. She knows every inch of that land. So take comfort or torment in this: if you find her, it will be because she willed it to be so."

Sarak cleaned Wittendon's blade. "Just promise me this—whether you find her or she avoids you like you have mushrooms for skin, you will be here next time with your head out of the clouds. Deal?"

"Deal," Wittendon said slowly, barely hearing the words.

"Great. A commitment made with his head in the clouds. And you will also give me two million pieces of gold upon your return. Deal?" Sarak said.

Wittendon turned to him and smiled. "We'll see what kind of a mood I'm in."

Sarak laughed. "Let's just hope that good mood or bad, you're ready to fight." Then, holding both blades on his shoulder and smiling to himself, Sarak walked down the hill.

JUST BEFORE SARAK REACHED THE PALACE GATES, A LONG, PERFECT trumpet note rang out followed by four short blasts. The bustle of the head city fell silent. The king, absent for nearly a fortnight, had returned. At the sides of the road, wolves tucked their paws while Veranderen and humans bowed—the humans lying prostrate, faces against the ground; the Veranderen on one knee, hands clasped behind their backs. The private guard of the king—half of them black wolves, half of them fair Veranderen walked on either side of the king. Through the procession, Sarak could see that the king looked pale and oddly unkept.

Sarak kept his distance, kneeling. Yet as Crespin swept through the palace gates, the king caught the young trainer's eye. Crespin stared for one long moment into Sarak's face before Sarak sank into a lower bow, and the king stormed into the castle, pushing aside the page who held open the gates. Sarak paused a moment longer before looking up, then shuddered like an animal who had narrowly avoided the hunt.

CHAPTER 21

Wittendon caught a glimpse of Sadora on the pathway that led outside the palace walls. If what Sarak said was really true, then she had been seen because she wished to be.

Wittendon followed several winding footpaths, got spider webs caught in his fur at every turn, and still could only catch the faintest snatches of Sadora's scent as the sun proceeded to set. It seemed ridiculous to stay in the woods all night in search of a Veranderah who might—for all Wittendon knew—only want to keep the town gossip going.

He stopped by a stream to take a drink, bending his head almost completely into the cold water when he heard her laugh and jerked his head up. Still he could not see her, which seemed puzzling as she had sounded so close. Perhaps it was the sound of the water in his ears playing tricks on him.

He bent down to drink again, but before his mouth hit the water, he heard it again. "Sadora," he called, standing.

The sound was coming from a hill to his right. A narrow path led up the rocky slope. He stepped cautiously onto the loose rocks, hearing high above him the faintest sounds of her voice. Quickly he climbed the hill, careful to keep his footing. By the time he reached the top, he had to stop on a flat rock and pick thorns out of each of his paws.

"Nice," he said to himself. "She's clearly in the mood for a romantic rendezvous."

And then the laugh again, only this time it echoed as though bouncing off the sides of tall thin rocks. Had she not been laughing, Wittendon would have been worried for her. They had come far from the palace, far from the verdant vegetation of the woods he knew she loved. As Wittendon pulled the last thorn from his foot, a thought occurred to him—a thought he couldn't quite dismiss. Perhaps Sarak had been wrong. Perhaps Sadora hadn't known he was following her and she'd led him here unintentionally. Perhaps her rendezvous was with someone else. The idea sat like a brick in his stomach. He hoped he hadn't come so far to see Sadora wrapped in the embrace of another Verander. He shook his head to free himself from the unpleasant image and tossed a rock down the hill, wondering what he should do. The rock hit far below and when it struck, it echoed in just the same way Sadora's voice had.

Wittendon stood. There was no use sitting here pouting about losing a Veranderah who hadn't really been his anyway. Grumbling to himself, he said, "At the very least, I can make sure whoever she's with will meet Sarak's approval."

He strode down the hill, following the path of the stone he had tossed and all at once, the rocks gave way to a flat surface that felt solid yet strangely…empty. He tapped his foot against the earth and sure enough, a tinny sound tapped back at him.

"Sadora?" he said. "Are you there? Are you alright?"

Her laughter came again, clear as a hundred bells, though Wittendon didn't hear it completely since the ground beneath him had suddenly vanished and he was tumbling down some sort of metal chute that seemed to go forever through the earth.

When he reached the bottom, not one, but six Veranderen stood to greet him, along with three men, two women, and one enormous black cat. Sadora stood among them in flesh form and when Wittendon saw her, she offered her hand in just the same way she would have had they been standing at a dinner party eating tiny sandwiches with a bunch of stuffy, starched governors.

"No, dear Wittendon," she said as he unthinkingly took her humanish hand with his wolken one. "Sarak probably wouldn't approve."

WITTENDON'S YOUNGER BROTHER KAXON SAT IN THE DUSTY OLD library. He had sworn in his school days never to return to a library if he didn't have to. Unfortunately he had to. And he didn't even have the good luck of going to the library in the history wing—the one with the pretty Veranderah at a desk in the center. No. There were many libraries in the castle. This one was the oldest, dirtiest, and dullest. No one ever came. Most had forgotten it was there at all. Wolrijk had sent Kaxon after some old scrolls that would supposedly help the king find sleep. Apparently, the tonics weren't working well enough anymore, which was a pity because the kitchen wenches with their red-lipped laughter were a lot better company than the cobwebs and cockroaches of this ancient place.

"This ought to bore him into a proper coma," Kaxon muttered, tucking the scrolls of ancient history into his satchel and turning around. Just in front of him sat a great book, resting on a tall stand with pages etched in gold. Even in the dim library the illustration on the front gleamed. A drawing of twelve long, perfectly thin spears stood side by side. In the drawing, the spearheads seemed to glitter and they were all tipped in blood, except for one. They were so life-like that Kaxon swore he saw a bead of blood slip down the edge of a blade.

Without thinking, he walked to the book and opened it, hoping for more pictures. Unfortunately he was met by nothing but words. "Bah," he said. Kaxon was about to close the book when the pages moved, flipping to the center of the book where a large sketch stared at him. The blueprint was of one spear, stretched along the page with measurements marked at intervals.

Kaxon paused. The tip was obviously the Shining Grey, but it was clearly marked at three inches. The Mal only allowed one inch. Kaxon was about to close the book, but all at once it seemed too heavy to move and his right hand was pinned underneath. A magical book was not unusual in his father's kingdom. In fact, Kaxon had owned several as a child that would color and then erase themselves. But a book resting on his hand that couldn't be lifted was less charming. Slowly, Kaxon found that he had the strength to move one page at a time. On the next page, he saw the same blueprint of a spear, only this time the bottom two inches of Grey had been covered in enchanted paint so only one inch of tip gleamed at him. Had the drawing not been marked, Kaxon never would have noticed the painted Grey.

Kaxon thought of the scythes he was more familiar with. He thought of the slave Jager and his renowned skill in the working of metals. Kaxon thought of his own royal position, his skill in leadership, his desire to be appointed Chancellor. He thought of his need to defeat the powerful Veranderen at the Mal competition; he felt the weighty importance of it all.

All at once, he could close the book, and he did so.

When he came to his father's quarters, Wolrijk was there, standing guard. "Set them here and I'll get them to his lordship," Wolrijk said.

Kaxon nodded, distracted, as he fidgeted with a clasp on his robe, shifting from one foot to another. He disliked being bossed by a wolf. He disliked Wolrijk in general with his torn up face and distorted paws. Yet he didn't care to stand around arguing.

Clicking and unclicking the buckle on his cloak, Kaxon handed the scrolls to Wolrijk.

"You seem quite animated, my lord. Have you seen something of interest in those old shelves?" Wolrijk asked.

Kaxon jerked his hands down to his sides. "There is much in old libraries, but little for me," he said. "I am merely thinking on a new strategy for the upcoming Mal."

"Very good," the deformed wolf said. Then, looking casually to the king's bedchamber, Wolrijk added, "Your father has requested that next week you go and fetch the slaves from the mines. Your brother grows overly distracted with that female."

Kaxon nodded, picturing the human Jager. As he turned to leave, it almost seemed like the ugly wolf smiled.

WOLRIJK WATCHED THE YOUNG PRINCE WALK AWAY. IT WOULD SEEM there was something besides pretty kitchen maids that could catch the eye of the youngest prince. Which was good. Wolrijk had not worked magic for many centuries; indeed it was a bit of a secret that he could work magic at all. It had taken much of his strength to enchant the book enough to keep the youngest prince reading. Wolrijk had failed when he had tried to get a long blade made for himself. Stirring the idea into the youngest prince's head seemed the next easiest way.

Wolrijk tossed the scrolls aside and walked silently from the chamber.

CHAPTER 22

"Do not be offended, good Wittendon, but your eyes must be covered for the duration of this journey." Sadora reached up and quickly wrapped a coarse burlap covering over Wittendon's eyes.

"You tie up my eyes and ask my *pardon*," he said. He could feel the tips of two blades pressed firmly into both of his sides, though with his eyes covered he could not tell if they were tipped in Grey or not. The black creature that stood at Sadora's side—he could no longer see it, but now he could more distinctly hear the animal purring, an unusual sound, an impossible sound.

"How?" he asked.

Sadora did not answer, but she moved the guards with blades away from Wittendon and took his hand, leading him through a maze of winding tunnels. He did not resist. Even as he lost count of the turns and bends, dips and ascents, his curiosity pulled at him more than his fear.

After nearly an hour, they stopped and Sadora reached up to remove the binding from Wittendon's eyes. Wittendon saw that they stood in a large room, lit with curious lanterns that released no smoke.

He stepped back into a damp corner and said, "Sarak knows nothing of this?"

"No," Sadora said, a deep line forming just above the bridge of her nose. "I do not enjoy keeping things from him, but this he would not understand."

Sadora, he noted, stood in her flesh form at the head of a long table made from the same earth, stone, and clay that streaked the walls of the room. The other members of the council, as council it seemed to be, lined up on either side of the table, taking seats that seemed to be appointed to them, although the large black cat curled up at Sadora's side and continued to purr.

Wittendon stared at the feline, letting the shock sink in. A cat—assumed extinct by all among his race and every other—sat no more than five feet from him, smoothing the fur of her ear with a wetted paw. The animal looked surprisingly like the one in the picture Sadora had admired in the art wing. *Our ancient history indeed*, Wittendon thought, and just as he did so, Sadora began the meeting by addressing him. "I have not, I realize, brought you here in a way that will inspire your trust in me, yet it is that trust that I hope to earn from you."

"Well, perhaps you could whisper sweet nothings into my ear so that I dissolve into a blubbering puddle and you can have whatever you wish," Wittendon said.

Sadora narrowed her eyes in a way that made her resemble the cat. "Perhaps you think it is joy to me to wander about the palace acting as though my only cares are petticoats and the dribbling romantic gossip of my fellow ladies of the court when, in a few short weeks, the fate of our race, your family, and the entirety of our world could be changed."

"Changed?" Wittendon asked.

"The Motteral Mal celebrates an important time in our history, a time when the earth shifted from the high white sun to the heavy red sun with its constant moon. A moon that grants the Veranderen significant power."

"Yes," Wittendon said.

"At the cost of the power and often the dignity of others." Sadora leaned forward.

Wittendon did not trust himself to reply.

"What you should know, but have perhaps forgotten or never been taught, is that every hundred years when the solstice and the full moon coincide, there is a possibility to change the worlds again," Sadora said.

Wittendon snorted. He had not been taught that, but he'd heard tell of it from drunken humans and crazed soothsayers. "Such talk is not even reputable enough to call a fairy story," he said.

"So the royalty maintains," Sadora replied.

Wittendon looked at Sadora with her human hair tied back into a loose knot at her neck—golden strands woven through the fiery red like rays through the sun. "It is madness," he said.

She sat back in her chair and pressed her fingers together until the pads became white. She stayed there for so many minutes that Wittendon figured he could have just up and wandered the tunnels if he had wished. The rest of her council sat just as still. Wittendon looked at Sadora, wishing he could see through the sculpted stillness of her eyes. Finally, he said, "I will not submit to such insanity, but supposing I did, what exactly would you expect your *verlorn* prince to do?"

Wittendon didn't think the room could get quieter, but somehow it did. Finally, Sadora spoke, "The blades of Crespin."

Wittendon did not reply, wondering what she wanted with the blades his father had used to kill the council.

"They are the blades of rebellion. And revenge." Sadora turned to the cat. "Ellza." The cat looked up and Sadora nodded. With a voice like a wraith, wispy yet brittle, Ellza began to chant.

> *Twelve Grey blades of needle-like thinness.*
> *Eleven bespotted with the blood of their victims.*
> *One pure and clean awaiting its destiny.*
> *Seeks he to whom it has fidelity.*

Sadora continued, "The blades are more powerful than any known before or since in the kingdom. The Grey of their tips does not deterio-rate with time, maintaining both brightness and strength. One of the blades is especially strong, and empowered by magic to destroy the elder Tomar—he who escaped your father's plot—or his descendants."

Wittendon just stared at her.

She smiled at him. "And there is someone I know who would be better suited than any other to wander freely through the castle looking for those blades. Someone who can stroll into libraries and cellars and tunnels without turning a glance."

"You want me to find the blades?" Wittendon asked.

"Each spear is tipped in three inches of the Shining Grey. Each is nearly indestructible, and could be used by human hands."

Wittendon could not help but growl. "Used by a human against a Verander?" The idea was repulsive. Until now, he had not been truly afraid, but now he stood, raising his voice, bracing to run if he had to. "You wish to allow the humans to kill our own kind?"

Two of the humans rose, holding daggers at their sides, but Sadora didn't move. "I wish no such thing. But the humans must be able to hold some power in their hands. They must stand as some kind of a threat. Look at them," she said gesturing to the two who had stood. "Both are brave, large men. Both are trained to fight and willing to do so. Both could kill any man who defied them. And yet both would be torn to pieces by our kind in mere moments. Look at them Wittendon; they tremble before you."

Wittendon looked. It was touching, in an odd way, that they would stand as though to protect Sadora—much like a brave and noble child might stand to protect his parent.

"The blades of Crespin would be weapons," Sadora said. "Powerful weapons. But more than that, they would stand as symbols. The spears represent revolution. Your father himself would recognize that. With such weapons in our hands, your father would begin to see these rebels —the Septugant—as something more than doodled sevens."

"But why?" Wittendon asked fiercely. "If it's even possible— which I doubt it is—why change everything?"

Sadora looked at him without moving. Deep in the earth, she looked too still, too pale, a figurine of herself. "The races are strongest when they work together. This rebellion, I believe, proves that. But

Crespin and those who came before him have perverted that relationship—yoking the humans, manipulating the dogs, coddling the wolves. Even among our own kind there is a certain inequality. Those who care to look will notice powerful family lines vanished or verlorn. Even that of the elder Naden, one of the strongest lines, is completely gone after your father's friend Draden disappeared. Others of powerful Veranderen lineage are in asylums, slums, or impossible to find. Your father is a cunning monarch—one able to control, to contain those who might defy him. Which explains better than anything his treatment of the humans."

Feeling almost as weak as the humans in front of him, Wittendon said, "The humans have what they need."

"Ah, and now you sound like Sarak." She looked off into a corner of the room. "Although my brother has not yet realized this, he and I do not agree on what ought to be the fate of the other races, particularly the humans. He has, unfortunately, seen much of their darker side."

Wittendon raised an eyebrow and Sadora continued, "Do you know that when he was twelve, his assignment was to open the gates for the Blødguard when they returned in the morning. Often he would hear their laughter and speech. They spoke of conquest of course, but just as often they spoke of those who had been abandoned by the humans— the elderly and infirm, the deformed babies and handicapped youth— those who were purposefully left in the woods to be consumed by the Blødguard."

Wittendon nodded. He did know this.

"Sarak's responsibility, too," Sadora continued, "was to dispose of the tiniest bones left from the hunt—those of the humans so young that the wolves could not consume the bones for fear of choking. It was…" she paused, "sobering to say the least. Scarring. Fortunately, Sarak's skill with magic was soon noticed by the court and his assignment was changed. But no type of magic could erase his memories of the baby bones picked clean by the wolves. The Veranderen, as Sarak sees it, are not a race that abandons its own. A point on which I also disagree."

Wittendon had not known this last part of Sarak's story; his friend had never told him. "And these people who murder their children and elders are the people for whom you plan to fight?" Wittendon asked.

"No," she said, looking to her council. "I fight for the rest. I do not believe it good to forget a majority merely because a disgusting minority often exists. I believe, in fact, that that minority would be reduced if their lives were less harsh, their fates less cruel. It is difficult to extend mercy or to nurture those less fortunate, when you have known naught but hunger, filth, and disease. The fact that most of the humans would protect their own and even others is actually what I find so extraordinary. You have walked the villages, Wittendon," she said. "You have seen what Sarak refuses to see."

It was all she had to say. Wittendon could see Jager and his wife as their foreheads met; he could see the golden-haired boy's figure as he retreated from the mines. He could see the miners—sweaty, hungry, and about to return to a dim cell instead of a warm fire in their own homes. He could see beggars he had rejected and disregarded throughout his life. He could smell the human hovels, built up on the most infertile lands in his father's kingdom. He could see the mutilated remains of the unlucky humans who had been hunted after dark.

Wittendon snarled, feeling himself waver. Yet just as he did, he suddenly saw his mother's gardener sitting side by side with his mother, and then he remembered vividly—as he hadn't in many years —his mother in tears alone in the garden, and then his mother in bed, sick in a way that those of his kind had never been sick before. "They have done evil to our kind."

The cat sniggered softly. "Have they?" the feline asked, standing and stalking toward Wittendon. "Have they hunted your kind into near extinction? Have they taken your furs to hang on their walls, encased your faces and bodies in glass at museums? Have they killed litters full of your helpless young and laughed at the victory?"

Wittendon stood, facing the cat. "They have done evil," he repeated, holding onto his hate for the gardener, even as a scent flooded his memory—the fresh graves, left by the she-hound accused of killing Grender—her innocent babes caught in the crossfire of the king's commands.

The cat looked without blinking into Wittendon's eyes. "There are those of your kind," she said steadily, "who do not need assistance in doing evil—to others; or their own."

Wittendon growled, placing his hand on his hilt. The cat did not move. No one in the room moved. Wittendon looked to the Veranderen of the council, expecting that they were just as angry at the cat's words as he was. He was surprised to feel a pulse of magic coming from their bodies—a magic that was prepared to fight. And not on his side.

"Wittendon," Sadora said at last, "if you do not wish to join us, I understand. You have much to lose. Though I think you might be surprised at what you'd find to gain. Nevertheless, if you wish to leave, a Verander of the council will show you the way out. I ask only that you agree to smell a flower. It will cause you to forget this interview unless I wish for you to remember it."

She stood in a way that signaled she did not expect discussion on the matter.

"No," Wittendon said with a firmness that surprised even him. "You have tricked me into these caverns and asked me to commit a crime against my own father. This creature has insulted my race. If you wish to keep me as a prisoner, that is your choice, but if you wish to release me, then release me—no strings attached."

Sadora was silent for several minutes. Wittendon watched her gaze as it slipped over the faces of the leery humans and uneasy Veranderen.

"Do you plan to let him leave, my lady?" asked a small, thin human who sat in the corner. Two Veranderen had quietly stepped into protective positions in front of the door. Wittendon put his hand on his sword and, like mimes on feast day, they imitated this action, never looking at Wittendon, never acknowledging they had any intention to fight. But preparing.

A weather-worn Veranderah—one who looked to be one of the verlorn peasants—placed a five-petaled flower on a small wooden stone. With the hilt of her dagger, she crushed the petals flat, so that the fragrance would be pungent when placed near Wittendon's face.

"I will not willingly smell it," he said, looking straight at Sadora.

"Is this what you do? Trick creatures? Capture them? Then force them to forget?"

"No," said a sturdy human with a long scar through his left eye. "That is not what *we* do."

"Really," Wittendon said. "Because that's what it looks like you're going to do."

The human jumped up and ran at Wittendon. Wittendon drew his sword. A Verander disarmed the prince just before Wittendon attacked the human. Wittendon regained his sword by kicking it into the air as Sarak had taught him to do and then the rest of the council got up, several running at the prince.

Sadora stood and from her fingers, she shot a burst of light that shattered against the walls in a blinding whiteness. Everyone stopped and when they did, the solid stone floor turned to thick tar beneath their feet. No one could move. No one except Sadora. Her fur thickened and grew—deep rust that ran down her back and arms, her back broad and strong, her fingers like arrows. Her eyes were a shiny copper, her teeth long, narrow, and sharp as iron nails.

The cat, Wittendon realized, was also free, though she chose not to move, instead carefully cleaning each pad of her foot as though politely trying not to notice the others' entrapment.

Sadora walked freely through the room on all four of her limbs. "Is it," Sadora asked, "comfortable to be stuck, unable to attack, unable to move freely in the way you feel you should?"

No one spoke.

"I understand the feeling," she said calmly, rising onto two legs. "I feel it much more clearly than many of you can understand. The purpose of this council, of this rebellion, is to allow each of us a level of freedom, of progression." She looked at each face, pausing to stare for a long time at Wittendon. "If we would like to succeed, we have to be able to move. And if we want to move, we have to find solutions, preferably ones that do not involve gutting each other."

Sadora released the floor, which returned to stone. The members of the council fidgeted, sheathing their weapons and returning to their chairs except for the two Veranderen who remained near the door. Wittendon stood, his sword lowered, but still unsheathed.

Sadora slipped back into her flesh form like a woman taking off her shoes. At last Sadora's gaze settled on Ellza, who looked back through narrow slits of eyes. "You must let him go," the feline said.

> *To keep him here, would serve but brief,*
> *to this great cause to bring relief.*

"Nice rhyme," Wittendon said.

"Nice repartee," Ellza replied.

"Oh, good Grey," Sadora said. Ellza and Wittendon both gave her a strange look. "What?" she said. "I can make things rhyme, too. Anyway, I believe that what your new friend means," Sadora said, turning to Wittendon, "is that if we cannot trust you, all may well be lost anyway."

"Besides," Ellza said, forsaking her rhyme and addressing Sadora. "There is a loyalty to this cause that I suspect runs through his blood."

Wittendon looked at the cat quizzically, speaking to her as politely as he could manage. "How so?"

The cat turned to the prince,

> *Your father's blood,*
> *But half of you.*
> *The other part,*
> *runs flower blue.*

She might as well have chanted in another language for the look Wittendon gave her.

"It is true that if he doesn't join us, we will certainly fail," replied the scarred human. "But it is also true that at this point, our necks will only break in the noose if he talks."

"True," said the tallest Verander. "At his word, we will all hang. Or worse," he said, giving Sadora a pointed look.

"You could always read his thoughts, captain," said the flower-holding Veranderah. "His precious memory would be spared, and we would know where we stand with him."

Sadora stood and walked forward as though to place her hand on Wittendon's forehead as Wittendon had seen his father do with hundreds of prisoners. But she did not touch him. Instead she stood only inches from Wittendon and stared straight into his eyes for several long moments. "So go," she said at last. "Verander Bray will escort you through these tunnels."

"A very complex form of magic," Wittendon said bitterly. "To read my thoughts without a touch to the head." He was not even sure his father could do it.

"Complex indeed," Sadora said, turning from him. "I call it trust."

The black cat nodded approvingly, though several of the council sucked in a quiet breath. Wittendon actually laughed. "Very well then," he said. "You may trust me, and I will not betray that trust," he said, looking to the council around him. "But I hope you know that I still do not trust you."

WHEN WITTENDON CAME INTO THE LIGHT, HE STOOD—NOT ON THE rocky path that had dumped him into the tunnel—but on the Hill of Motteral, below the wolf guard that protected the Grey mines.

"How'd we wind up here?" he asked the Verander who had escorted him.

"The tunnels are vast," was the only reply he got.

"Do any of them lead into the actual mines?" Wittendon wondered if a Verander could actually wander to his death.

The Verander shuddered. "Thankfully they do not. There is, I am told, a small crawlway that leads nearly to the mouth of the mine, though not directly in. And none of our size would ever fit through that passage anyway."

"Just in case we wanted to," Wittendon mumbled.

CHAPTER 23

Pietre set several of his father's tools in the old wooden crate his mother had brought him. Humphrey was out hunting and Pietre missed him. He didn't like doing this task alone. Packing up his father's tools felt like preparing him for burial. Yet, with a member of the wolf guard coming every week, his mother was nervous about having any of his father's things confiscated. Or noticed in the first place.

Pietre picked up a long, narrow-headed object used for driving screws through heavy metal. He turned the simple tool around in his hand, touching the flat pointed tip with his finger. No wonder his mother was concerned. Pietre glanced over his shoulder to make sure he was alone before thrusting the long screwdriver forward, burying it into a block of wood in front of him. Seeing it embedded in the wood, Pietre suddenly understood how little separated a tool from a weapon —one thing really, and that was the hand that held it.

Pietre jerked the screwdriver out of the wood and hurriedly packed it into the crate before grabbing a small jar of the various sized screws that went with it. The honed tips of the screws clinked against the glass and Pietre realized that they looked even more vicious than their parent tool—small, but undeniably sharp. The screws would have to be, of course, to wind through metal and wood as they did, but if they could go through metal, they could go through flesh. Pietre pulled one from the jar and pressed it against his finger, then threw the screw down like it had bitten him.

It was illegal for the humans to own or form weapons when not under the supervision of a Veranderen master. Pietre knew that, but until now, he hadn't thought that the very tools used to *form* devices and weaponry might be used as weapons themselves. Looking at the room filled with sharp, heavy, sometimes bladed tools, he realized how suspicious it might look to the Veranderen and wolves.

Pietre grabbed mallets, saws, wrenches, chisels, weights, and bevels from the shelves. He tossed them into the crate, not bothering to wrap them first. How had his mother allowed the tools to be kept out for as long as she had? If a wolf had happened into this room and seen them—Pietre stopped. If a wolf had happened into this room and seen them, there would have been very little that he could have done. He would have been trapped in a room full of sharp, heavy objects, and if a person was there who knew about the tools and how to use them— Pietre didn't dare finish the thought. To kill a wolf was death. To betray the Veranderen was death. To go against the king was death. Even if it was to preserve oneself, one's livelihood, one's dignity, even one's family. It was death.

Dusk was settling, and the howling of the Blødguard rang sharp and brittle in Pietre's ears. Pietre set several of the tools around him on the floor, then shoved them back into the crate. They might be able to hurt one wolf, but they could never stop a force as powerful as the Veranderen, never even slow them down. Pietre fingered the small stone in his pocket, then opened the crate again. There was something about holding a tiny force in your hands, a small piece of power, even if it couldn't save you. At least you would not be destroyed so easily— like a spider who, before being trampled, opens her mouth to insert a small shot of venom into her destroyer. It was no more than a pinch, a pinprick, a nuisance, but it was also a reminder—a reminder that had the spider been a good bit larger, she could have been the destroyer.

As soon as the darkness had settled, Pietre took the case of tools into the room where his mother had fallen asleep, a puddle of mending in her lap. She started when he entered.

"Where should I put it?" he asked, setting the box near her feet.

She shook her head, as though willing the sleep to fall away, and opened the crate, fingering each tool like it was a piece of Jager himself. She slipped out a small iron file. "Your father made me this," she said, touching its thin edge. "For times when my nails broke from work." She ran it over her rough fingernails several times, smoothing the tips, then set it back in the box.

If Pietre had had any doubt, it left. The file had flashed like a tiny dagger.

His mother looked at the box, her eyes heavy as leaden shingles. "In the morning," she said, "perhaps you should bury it."

Pietre nodded, though he knew he would not obey his mother. As soon as the sun glanced over the horizon, he would take it to the chief elder to see if he knew of any in their village who might make good use of such tools, those who might appreciate their quality, and understand their potential.

CHAPTER 24

Crespin walked through the great hall so quickly that his black wolf guards had to trot to keep up with him. His nails had been trimmed, sharpened, and polished to a shine. With each step he clicked importantly, and with every third stride his staff came down on the tiling with a loud thud that echoed through the chamber.

Wolrijk met the king at the door and bowed low. "The great wolf Gog will soon be released from the asylum. They tell us that with a few more treatments any lasting effects should be minimal. He'll be back to his docile, level-headed self in no time." Wolrijk paused pointedly. "As long as they complete the treatments."

Crespin dismissed this news with a swat of his hand. "Tighten the security outside the human villages and starve the Blødguard an extra day. Our watch-wolves and hunters grow lazy. Send the white wolf Zinder to the dogs; he communicates well with them. Tell Zinder to make sure the dogs do not come to the humans' aid against my orders." For a moment the king hesitated. "And," he began, looking sideways into Wolrijk's eyes, "have them dismiss Gog immediately. I'm sure that his healing is sufficient for my needs."

The wolf smiled. "Yes, my lord."

"Oh—and the scout, Rorof—has he recovered his ability to run?"

"Yes, lord, though he tires easily—"

Again, the king waved his hand. "Send him to find the witch's wood. Give him the hem of my traveling cloak to smell if you must. Instruct him to go around the dog's land; I do not wish for them to know I have an interest in the land outside their borders. Is that clear?"

"Entirely, sir."

"Good," the king said.

Wolrijk bowed low and left without a further word.

The king had spent the last several days in his quarters recovering and handling matters that had been neglected such as the never-ending flow of merchandise to the north port, and a communication with the governors overseas about transportation to the upcoming Motteral Mal. He wished for as much of the kingdom as possible to attend. He wished for it to be a display of his power and dominance over the kingdom he had spent most of his life shaping. It was the first time in the last several centuries he had felt the need to openly exert his strength, and he wanted masses there to see it.

Daily, his guards and spies brought news of the Septugant. As if the graffitied sevens weren't irritating enough, three of his human prisoners had been mysteriously freed this week, and an ancient document taken from his oldest library. The Septugant's acts were desperate, almost pitiful—the paper they'd stolen had been nothing more than a historic report on sediment. Yet he had learned in his lifetime that pests are best controlled before they grow into pestilence.

This morning he had signed a decree—any human, Verander, dog, or wolf found in alliance with the Septugant would be hanged without trial. Any leaders were to be publicly beheaded. It was gruesome business and there was some possibility that a few innocents might get caught in the fray, but at this point Crespin did not have the time or forbearance to wade through the trials of those who were hoping to unravel the tapestry of his rule.

Crespin thought about the witch girl's final prophecy about the firstborn of Tomar—the "surviving foe" that, according to her, would defeat him. Crespin knew the witch hoped to cripple his confidence. He had no intention of allowing her to succeed.

Crespin waited for the tailor to arrive and fit his ceremonial robes. Making a strong show at the Mal would serve him well with both witch and rebellion—it would display his assurance to the witch and his invulnerability to the Septugant.

The old tailor arrived with a low bow and a blue measuring tape. The king stood straight, grateful for a few moments of forced stillness. In the last week, he had thought through several elaborate plans for destroying the witch and had finally decided on a classic, simple approach. He would burn the witch's forest. It was wood. And it would burn. The thought brought him some satisfaction since he was certain that burning would add insult to the injury of her loss. She wouldn't be able to stand losing her precious garden and tea chairs. Crespin would send Gog to do it. The wolf was, at this point, the perfect candidate. He was mad as the March wind. Which was just what Crespin needed.

After the witch's wood was gone, Crespin suspected it would be even easier to locate members of the underground rebellion, to stamp out their fight for equality.

The king grunted as the tailor pinned the fabric along his shoulders, the cloth falling in red rivers down his back. His people had no idea what equality meant, what it was like to live in a world where every burden was supposed to be the same. They did not remember what the ancients had written and warned about—the humans' disdain for labor, the packs of wild dogs claiming land after land as their own, the wolves' incessant hunger. They did not read or remember the primitive texts about those who were once called werewolves, those who could control neither their shifting nor their destinies. They did not understand all the reasons things had needed to be changed, controlled, and even—at times—repressed.

The tailor draped a long length of cloth over his forearm. "Would you have, Lord King, a smaller robe designed for your most noble flesh form?" he asked, pinning and tucking.

The king looked into the mirror to the tailor behind him. "You have tailored my clothes often, good Verander, have you not?"

"Yes," the tailor answered, taking a small step backwards.

"And have I ever desired a smaller robe made for my, as you call it, 'most noble' flesh form?"

"No, my lord," the tailor replied, beginning to tremble. "I only thought that with the upcoming tournament you might require one for certain ceremonies. Or, perhaps to impress the vast groups of governors and ladies that will travel to these parts."

"And you believe my flesh form necessary for this?" the king asked, resting the tip of his staff against the mirror.

"Well, of course not, my lord. I only thought that perhaps some protocol or tradition or…Or that perhaps his lordship would need, well, something further."

"No," the king replied very slowly. "I need nothing further." He pulled his staff from the mirror and when he did, hundreds of shards flew towards the tailor's delicate face and hands, stopping mid-air and hanging there ready to burrow into his flesh.

"Does it seem," the king asked, "that my flesh form could ever bring me anything greater, anything *further*, than what now stands before you?"

"No, good king," the tailor said very quietly.

"Good," Crespin replied. He nodded and tapped the mirror, sending the glass back to it, sealed and fixed.

Shaking, the tailor finished with his pinning and the king stood, adorned from neck to floor in a blood red robe that shimmered and caught the light with the smallest movement. The garment was heavy and when the king moved, his clothes rustled and swayed with purpose.

Crespin held his staff and smiled into the mirror at his trembling tailor. It was a robe kings could respect and that even the foolish Sadora and her gaggle of admirers would be forced to appreciate. Pity he would have his tailor hanged as soon as the robe was complete.

CHAPTER 25

S arak stood silhouetted against the dawn. He was not as tall as Wittendon, but so lean in his torso and long in his legs that he often appeared taller. His shoulders against the rising sun looked disproportionately wide. As Wittendon walked the hill toward his friend, Wittendon felt a little sick. It'd been several days since their last practice, but still his head wasn't focused on the tournament. It was in tunnels with beautiful traitors and talking cats. It was thinking about the twelve blades his father had hidden.

Sarak was looking at him now—a long, slow stare that Wittendon could not meet. Wittendon had given Sadora his word that he would keep his mouth shut, but he didn't like hiding things from his closest friend.

"Soooo?" Sarak said, tapping the hilt of his practice blade. "How'd it go with Sadora?"

Wittendon looked away, but that didn't stop Sarak. "So bad you don't want to tell me or so good you don't dare?" he asked.

"It went," Wittendon said, pausing to unsheathe his blade, "very differently than I expected."

"Different can be good," Sarak said.

"Hmm," Wittendon muttered.

"And different can be bad."

Wittendon didn't even respond.

Sarak paused. "Well, as stimulating as this conversation is, maybe we should get to practicing." When he said it, he seemed just a little annoyed. He raised his blade before his face and Wittendon did the same. They circled twice and Sarak lunged. Wittendon met his attack with a ringing clang of his blade and they sparred for several minutes in silence, neither of them gaining an advantage over the other.

After several minutes, Sarak put down his scythe. "Well, at least your head has come out of the clouds," he said. "You fight well."

Wittendon shrugged and Sarak sighed. "Look, I'm sorry if she broke your heart. If it brings you any consolation, she has broken many."

Wittendon shrugged again, but after a pause he said, "She didn't break it exactly. It's like...it's like she poked it."

Wittendon felt like he had spilled out some deep secret, but Sarak tipped his head back and laughed. "Well, friend, then it could have been much worse. Just think—if you get only poked and not broken at the Mal, you'll be in good shape."

For the first time that week, Wittendon cracked a smile. "Glad this is so entertaining for you," he said.

"Yeah, well, I've been worrying about it for months. My friend. My sister. Ah. You have no idea."

They drank from their flasks of water and rose to fight again.

"You know your sister loves history," Wittendon said.

"Oh, good Grey, tell me she didn't spend the whole evening talking your ear off about that."

Wittendon blocked Sarak's hit without answering.

"History is a new thing with her. Well, sort of new." Sarak angled his blade, nicking Wittendon's hand, and taking a step closer. "It started a couple years ago when she wanted to find out more about our parents and was doing all this research—since our aunt died, there is no one to actually ask. And then all that time in the history wing, it just got to her brain. I think it was the dust."

Wittendon smiled, but it was a weaker one this time. Sarak started moving in more with his blade, snipping at Wittendon's wrist and shoulder.

"Lately," Sarak said, nearly pinning Wittendon's arm, "she's been obsessed with the history of weaponry and metallurgy. I told her she must be getting into the Mal after all, but she just stuck her nose back in her smelly old scroll; it was some ancient text about how sediment can carry metals or something."

Wittendon didn't respond. Even if he'd wanted to, he was too intent on blocking Sarak's blade—a blade Sarak kept using to reflect sun into Wittendon's eyes.

Sarak jabbed, pricking Wittendon's side. "I'm just glad she loves the gardens and woods so much. It keeps her away from the books enough to add some color to her cheeks."

Wittendon cleared his throat. It kept her away from the books alright.

Sarak's scythe circled like a ring around Wittendon's neck, the tip just touching his jugular. "Gotcha," he said. "It's good your opponents won't know my sister as well as I do. Otherwise they could distract you hopelessly."

Wittendon wanted to tell Sarak everything—the tunnels, the rhyming cat, the deadly blades of Crespin, but he stood there still as a stone and said, "Well, she has the parties to keep her nose from her books, too."

"Ah, yes," Sarak said. "Is that the reason for the sulking, the distraction? Does it bother you to think of her dancing with others, laughing?"

Wittendon couldn't believe how easily Sarak had just filled in a blank that hadn't been there.

"And there is the Fortune Ball coming up. She'll be there with bells on. Maybe even literally depending on what's new in fashion." Sarak smiled at his friend. "Come on then, I'll take you to the village for some food. It's on me, good prince."

Wittendon did not really want to spend more time with Sarak right now, but there was nothing to do but accept. They cleaned and sheathed their weapons and began the walk down the hill. "She'll probably have a warm supper waiting for you," Wittendon said, looking for an excuse to skip out on lunch.

"After this morning, I should have appetite enough for both. Come now, you need some cheering up."

~

CRESPIN WATCHED HIS SON AND SARAK WALK DOWN THE HILL. HE HAD chosen Sarak for his skill with a blade, his unusual prowess in magic, and the easygoing attitude Crespin knew would be helpful to Wittendon. Watching them walk, then run down the hill in their wolken forms, Crespin noticed something that had escaped his eye before. On every other bound, the young trainer lifted his right leg higher than his left. It was an unusual trait for one of such speed. And a trait he had seen in only one Verander before.

Crespin met them at the bottom of the hill with a nod just as they shifted into their flesh forms and tightened their cloaks.

"How goes the practice this promising day?" the king asked, briefly acknowledging his son, but addressing Sarak.

Sarak bowed. "Quite well, my lord. Your son has improved exponentially since our first meeting."

Crespin stared into Sarak's dark eyes, noting the way a ring of yellow seemed to surround each iris. "Yes," the king said. "I have been watching. Do you know, good Sarak, that you move in a way that recalls to me someone I knew many moons before your birth?"

"A dear friend, I can only hope, my king," Sarak replied with a flattering bow.

"A peer," the king said. "And a man I was forced to respect." The king turned with an enigmatic swish of robes and left.

When he was gone, Sarak turned to Wittendon. "Well. I can see now how you and the mighty king have communication issues sometimes."

"That was more of a compliment than he's ever given me. I'd take it if I were you," Wittendon responded, handing their weapons to a servant before the two friends headed into the village to eat.

156

CHAPTER 26

The dogs kicked mud at each other. It was something Pietre couldn't quite get used to.

He and Humphrey had come for a training session with Markhi, but instead were met by the sight and sound of dozens of dogs who had gathered around a field by the creek bed. The field was comprised entirely of thick black mud and filled with paw prints and skid marks. Dogs and pups rested among rocks on a high bank overlooking the field.

Although Pietre had been lying to his mother for the last month about hunting with the dogs, he'd never actually seen more than a few at a time, standing at a distance as they waited for Markhi. The noise of all those canines barking and talking made Pietre's head hurt, but it excited Humphrey who couldn't seem to keep his tail or tongue from wagging.

Markhi stood in the middle of a huddle with eight large dogs. When he lifted his head, he saw Humphrey and Pietre and gave a curt nod. Pietre rubbed the stone in his pocket as he'd become accustomed to doing when nervous. A smaller, heavyset dog came hurtling toward them, ears flapping with every bound. Humphrey stopped wagging and stood with head erect and body still. The small dog rammed to a halt and stood right in front of Humphrey. He looked up at Humphrey's bulk with nothing less than disdain and said, "Markhi, the arch hound of the great pack Sontag, welcomes you. The great captain Markhi invites the dog Humphrey to play mudball. Will you accept?"

Humphrey tossed his head back, looking to a host of lovely young she-hounds on the upper bank. "Yes," he said, confidently.

"Excellent," the dog said, with a sly smile that made Pietre lean over to Humphrey and whisper, "You sure?"

"Of course," Humphrey replied. "Look how small and old most of them are. I've totally got this."

Pietre smiled in almost the same way the little dog had. "Okay," he said and went to find a place for himself among the rocks and spectators. It proved to be a little harder than he had expected. Every time he saw a small spot of grass or a nice flat rock, one of the dogs seemed to move into it just before he did. They never looked at him, just drifted over into the available space. He stood there awkwardly for a minute, hoping Humphrey's reception was better than his, when he heard a soft female voice whisper, "Come human. You can sit right here."

The dog's fur was cream-colored and thick, although when he looked into her face, he was met by the blackest, roundest eyes he had ever seen. He sat nervously on a rock and she seemed to smile at him. "I am Alekas," she said. The dogs around her looked away, clearly not thrilled by their new seat-mate.

~

HUMPHREY WALKED TO THE MUD PIT. MARKHI DIDN'T ACKNOWLEDGE him, nor did the other dogs. There was barking and snarling among the eighteen or so competitors. "Hey, flea bag," a voice said loudly into Humphrey's ear. Next to him stood an enormous dog, obese and ugly with tiny eyes shrouded by dirty brown fur. "You go to that end with the other butt sniffers."

Humphrey lifted his lip in a snarl and was about to say something, but behind him a dog shouted, "Hey newbie, over here." Humphrey gave the fat dog one last look before turning to the dog who looked like the team captain.

"You ever played before?"

Humphrey shook his head.

"Well," the captain said, "see that ball in the middle. We run for it. When we get it we take it past the line at the other end. Got it?"

What wasn't to get? It sounded like the easiest game on earth. Humphrey nodded and his captain looked at him skeptically. "Oh, and that dog who was insulting you—you probably want to keep a safe distance."

Humphrey snorted. He doubted that fatso could catch up to him if he tried.

Humphrey's team lined up and a little yapper next to him said excitedly, "Keep your head low. Fake. And block. And fake. And block." The dog bounced around like he was made of springs. "And fake. And block."

The crowd was pounding on the rocks and barking. Competitors at each end puffed their chests, jumping and sliding. Humphrey stepped into the mud—it was like trying to walk in six inches of porridge. He searched the bank to see Pietre and caught sight of him just before the dog refereeing barked twice and the mud went flying.

"Is it safe?" Pietre asked Alekas, once the roar of the crowd had died down a little.

"Safe?" she said. "That's not a word we use much." She smiled, but Pietre found he couldn't quite return it. Humphrey might have been full-grown, but he was young and too confident.

"Oh, don't worry," Alekas said. "A strong dog like your friend— he'll be fine. Now where do you hail from?"

"A village," Pietre said, trying to catch a glimpse of Humphrey through the mud. "A few miles south. We—" he paused, not quite sure how to put it. "The dog Humphrey and I travel together."

She laughed. "Yes, well, obviously, he's not from around here."

Her dark eyes glistened and she added, "He's huge. And he doesn't carry himself like the dogs in this pack."

Pietre knew Humphrey had grown big, but until now, Pietre hadn't realized that even among the dogs, Humphrey's size was an anomaly.

Just then, the ball slipped away from one of the players on the field. The spectators screamed, barked, and howled like lunatics—especially the women. "Come on Borl!" several of them were shouting. "Silva," a group of others yelled.

The younglings and pups in the crowd were tackling each other and growling, eager to seem as tough and big as the grown dogs. Some of the youngest and oldest just wandered around sniffing things—grass, mud, old fossils, even the dung. Pietre grimaced and Alekas asked, "You humans don't revel in the joys of smell like we do?"

"No, I guess not," he said.

"You are missing out," she replied. "You can learn a lot with your nose. It brings much pleasure, like tasting food."

"Some things are better left untasted," Pietre said, looking at a small speckled dog sniffing at another's back end.

Alekas laughed. "Ah, boy, there are no bad smells. Just interesting ones. And you can learn things from them all."

THERE WAS A LOUD ROAR AND THUNDER OF FEET AS THE DOGS stampeded toward a mushy leathery ball at the center of the pit.

Humphrey charged out, but was late to the first tussle, where dogs and more dogs smacked into each other. As the other dogs collided Markhi cut right then left as his opponents lurched for him. Two of Humphrey's teammates lunged at the same time, and at the last second Markhi ducked and the dogs crashed long ways into each other and flopped into deep mud. The crowd roared with delight. "Markhi!" they shouted.

As his mentor darted forward, Humphrey became more and more determined to stop him. Markhi approached the end of the pit and Humphrey anticipated what the dog captain would do—a quick recoil and a head fake to the right. As Humphrey lunged out of the mud, at least five feet in the air, there was a gasp from the audience. Markhi braced for impact as Humphrey's legs stretched out, ready to tackle the leader. In his mind, Humphrey could practically hear the she-dogs swoon.

It was too bad he didn't hear Pietre shouting, "Look out!" because just before Humphrey hit Markhi, a glint in his peripheral vision became a gnarly, fat face. Borl's 200-pound body smashed into Humphrey's ribs, taking his breath and sending him face first into the black mud. He felt like he was suffocating, although he knew he must still be alive because he could taste the mud as it filled his mouth, nose and throat. Humphrey got up, spit, gagged, and tried to shake the mud out of his ears. It stuck there stubbornly, making it hard for Humphrey to hear. Unfortunately, he didn't need to hear to notice the crowd laughing and cheering for the opposite team.

Markhi rose out of the mud, with the ball in his teeth. He had scored.

"NICE MOVE, STUPID," BORL SNARLED AS HUMPHREY LIMPED BACK TO his side of the field. "Next time, save yourself the trouble and just run the other direction."

Humphrey kicked up his heel, flicking a blob of mud right into Borl's mouth. "Score," he whispered, as the dog spat and coughed.

When the referee barked for round two, Humphrey was ready. He had stopped thinking about the she-hounds and stared straight at his opponents.

When the ball came near, he charged. Markhi still beat him to the ball, but it was close. Humphrey's teammates stopped Markhi and forced him to pass to a black dog with a wiry frame and a lot of grit—a sentinel the crowd called Silva. The dog ran towards the goal, as their captain yelled, "Wolf sniffers!" but after a few yards Silva was tackled so hard the ball flew out of his mouth into the air where it was snatched by the little bouncy dog on Humphrey's team. The bouncy dog ran faster than anybody else. He almost made it through the thick line of blockers until Borl knocked him in his head. Before he went down, the little dog tossed the ball straight to Humphrey. Borl and the bouncy dog landed with a slurp as the blockers stumbled on top of them.

"Dog pile," the crowd roared gleefully.

Humphrey didn't hear. He just ran toward the goal. His ribs still hurt, but he knew Markhi was right behind him and he ran with everything he had. He was only feet from the goal, but he could feel Markhi at his heels. Even on solid ground it would have been hard to outrun Markhi. In thick mud it was impossible. Humphrey slowed for just an instant and set his hind legs as firmly as he could. Using all his strength he sprang forward. Markhi saw it and jumped too, but Humphrey soared past him and across the goal line.

For a split second the crowd was silent and then the entire pack of Sontag broke into noise—barking, stomping, banging, and yelling.

Pietre whistled above everybody else.

Humphrey shook off the mud and tossed the ball in the air, trotting back to his team.

"Beginners luck, punk," Borl said, but he was smiling.

Markhi came over to him. "Not bad," he said, looking to the sun, which had begun to sink.

Pietre came over to them and also looked to the sun. Humphrey supposed that they would need to hurry if there would be time for a bath in the creek before dusk. But when he saw the she-hound at Pietre's side, hurrying suddenly fell off his priority list. Besides a few brief memories with his mother, he had never actually seen a she-hound up close. This one, he decided, was an excellent specimen to begin with. He tried to say hello, but all that came out was a strange sort of yip.

Markhi nudged the boy as they walked back to the path. "Do you think the Veranderen are the only ones who can participate in sport?" he asked laughing.

"I think the Veranderen tournament would pale in comparison with yours," Pietre said smiling.

"Indeed?" Markhi said, not quite catching the joke in Pietre's tone. "You know, I've always thought much the same thing."

Humphrey said nothing. He hadn't stopped staring at the she-hound.

She smiled at him, sniffing courteously at his ear, and he was about to try to say something again when Markhi looked once more to the sun and said a bit more urgently, "The hour grows late." Just as he said it, a woman came into view, holding her skirts and hurrying down the hill. Humphrey turned, surprised to see Carina pink-faced and out of breath.

"She has never come after me," Pietre whispered. "Not in all my years."

"It is nearly dark," she panted, ignoring the pack of muddied dogs who were all staring at her. "There have been wolves around the village all day. They're tightening the security. We must go. Now."

For the first time, Humphrey noticed the sun, sagging like a tired child toward its bed; for the first time Humphrey realized how far the mudpit was from the village. And for the first time, Humphrey saw the fear in Carina's face drip into her stature and voice. She looked old.

"Now," she repeated.

"Stay for another round?" a dog called to Humphrey. And for a small moment Humphrey paused.

It was Markhi who actually stepped in and said, "No, we must get this woman and child back to their village as quickly as possible."

"But what of the wolf Zinder's new restrictions?" a fat gray short-hair asked. "We are forbidden from helping that kind."

"We have put this human at risk," Markhi said. "Zinder instructed us not to offer our protection. He said nothing of helping humans in their haste. Now move."

To Carina he said, "The boy can ride on one of our larger dogs, but you, good woman, are too large and long. You must simply fly."

Alekas and Humphrey slowed to run alongside Carina. Even so Carina—fit and strong from years of labor, but running on two human legs instead of four canine ones—could not keep up.

"Take him," she said, gesturing to Pietre. "Take him and leave."

In her words, Humphrey heard the voice of his own mother as she had tossed him to Pietre while fighting a wolf.

"No," Humphrey said. "You will not be left behind. Get on my back."

"I cannot," she huffed. "I'm too long and too heavy."

"Hold your legs up along my sides and bend your head low. We will make it."

She climbed onto the great animal and held his shoulders, bowing her head so that it touched his neck.

As the pack neared the village, a sliver of dim sunlight remained above the horizon, but the Blødguard and several of the Königsvaren had begun to gather around the gates of the village. They stood there, a gray and black line of fur and fang.

"We will make it sweet Cari," Humphrey said, breathing hard. "You will see; we will make it."

They arrived at the gates just before the sun sank, but an enormous wolf with wild eyes and a frothy mouth stopped the company. He ignored the dogs so completely that Humphrey was surprised. He asked only to see the humans' papers.

"Papers?" Carina asked, her breath coming out in raspy hiccups. "The people of this village have no papers. Most cannot even read."

"Today, houses were searched and papers were issued to all humans by order of the great general Wolrijk," the wolf said—his eyes wandering over the woman as though he stood before a buffet table. "If you have none, you may not now pass." A line of drool dripped from his lip.

Humphrey felt Carina sag beside him. Markhi stepped forward. It was clear that Markhi recognized the drooling wolf, and that something about that recognition made Markhi angry. "This is ridiculous," Markhi said. "The humans have been caught up in the wood; let them through."

"You," the wolf general Wolrijk said, striding out from behind the dilapidated city gate, "have no jurisdiction here. In fact, you are not to be aiding humans at all. You will leave at once or you will suffer severe disciplinary consequences."

The drooling wolf let out a howl and Markhi whispered, "The lunatic who attacked Silva. He is even more deranged now than before."

Wolrijk smiled.

Markhi paused. Humphrey knew Markhi was trying to decide if he should stay or go. The safety of his pack was at stake.

"The law given to us," Markhi stated slowly, as though trying a bit of diplomacy, "was that we not protect the humans if they were caught out after dark. It says nothing of aiding them in a safe return."

Wolrijk growled at him. "The idea behind the law—as I see it," he said, "is that you are not to give them aid at all. And how I see it is all that matters."

The line of the sun blinked once—dull and sleepy—and then the light went out.

PIETRE FELT THE DARKNESS LIKE A HAMMER. TO BE OUT AFTER DARK— it was death. Pietre gripped the rock his father had given him—patches of it were still quite rough. He held it so hard it seemed to make his palm buzz. His mother's eyes were wet, but she did not cower or hide her face.

"And now even the literal reading of the law is no longer on your side," Wolrijk said, staring at Markhi. "Tonight I will see that both dog and human pay the price for breaking it." He advanced as the wolves began to form a circle around the dogs and humans. "I owe you," Wolrijk said, "for this fine streak of pink scar that now runs along my pretty back. I thank you for adding it to my collection."

"A fine collection indeed," Markhi replied, his voice deep and rumbling. "You must be proud as it seems you are determined to add more." Markhi lowered his head inviting the challenge and Wolrijk pounced. The two animals met chest to chest with a crack that sounded like both must have broken the other's collarbone. They rolled on the ground, Wolrijk now covered with much of the mud that had been on Markhi. Markhi tore at the wolf's ear, ripping a piece off which he spat into the leaves. Wolrijk stared at him, straight into the eyes—the scars along his face almost glowing when he sprang on the leader of the dogs.

The wolves stood in a circle around the humans and dogs, although the wolves did not attack. Pietre was confused, but Carina whispered, "They wait. They wait to see which of the beasts comes out victor."

Softly, she began to hum. Her voice rose and fell in a steady melody. Behind her, Alekas picked up the tune and added her own voice. One by one, the other dogs joined in, the song twisting and dipping, the noise pressing against the line of wolves that surrounded them.

Wolrijk struck at Markhi's back, dragging his nails along the spine, blood beading and matting into the dirty fur. "There, now you have something to start your own collection," Wolrijk sneered.

Markhi did not reply and that made Pietre nervous.

Markhi ran at the wolf general and then, just as Humphrey had done in mudball, he slowed, shifting his weight to his back legs, and leaped forward, landing on top of Wolrijk. Wolrijk howled in pain and it seemed the fight was nearly won when the foaming wolf Gog came forward screaming, "I will feast this night!" He tore at Markhi's head, ripping the flesh from his cheek so that it flopped around like a butterfly lighting upon a flower.

Carina gasped and the song broke. Alekas bowed her head with a low, sick moan. Several of the dogs howled as the wolf Gog came in again for another bite. "No," Pietre screamed. Pietre ran toward Wolrijk and Gog. Gripping the stone his father had given him he used it to strike at two other wolves that stepped forward to stop him. He hit one in the side and sent the animal sprawling away, then nicked the other in the neck. The wolf Gog paused in his attack on Markhi, turning to Pietre with a growl so deep that all else fell still.

Humphrey did not hesitate. Pietre could feel him running—his feet pounding the ground with a freedom that seemed to surge through him —a freedom at being neither dog nor wolf, a freedom at being bound by none of their laws or restrictions. He jumped at the wolf Gog— tearing at his eyes and scratching into his forehead. And then, just as though the wolf were as light as a dove, he kicked him to the ground and pressed on his ribs until they bowed and threatened to crack.

The other dogs growled and stepped toward the party of wolves, but just as they did, Wolrijk flipped the unconscious Markhi over and tore into his chest. Pietre ran at Wolrijk, screaming, and hit him soundly in the head right between the eyes. The stone was not sharp, but on impact the rough edges bored into the wolf's skin and a tiny prick of blood appeared. Pietre braced for the wolf's attack, pulling his arm back and preparing to strike again.

But to Pietre's surprise, the wolf did not retaliate. Instead he toppled over, weak and moaning. In fact, it seemed that all the wolves paused, looking as though their blood had thinned and their bellies turned. Pietre brought his arm up—the small rock so light it felt as though it had joined with his hand.

"No," the wolf moaned. "No more. I have greater battles to fight than this. You may pass, boy. You and the woman also."

"First let the dogs return," Pietre shouted.

Wolrijk paused, looking to the still figure of the unconscious Markhi.

"Let them return," Pietre repeated. "And know that it is quite dark and that you are quite uncertain of who they are."

"Quite," the wolf replied weakly. "Now go."

Humphrey stayed behind, but the wolf general looked at him. "Are you deaf, stupid hound? Go."

Humphrey paused and looked to Pietre. Pietre nodded to him, wanting to cry, but knowing it would be safer for Humphrey with the dogs now than with him.

Humphrey turned with the pack and followed them, helping to bear the unconscious body of their leader on his back. When Pietre turned away from the dogs, he saw only Wolrijk—his eyes filled with shards of hatred like tiny promises for revenge. Pietre stepped into his village pressing the stone tightly as the wolf general slumped into a helpless pile of fur and blood.

CHAPTER 27

Kaxon ran to the top of the hill that led to the mines. He tried to run everywhere now. The beginning of the Mal was just a few weeks away and he wished to be as strong and fast as any Verander. Today he planned to be a little more cunning as well.

He stopped at a distance. He could see the cartfuls of rock and metal being brought out by the human slaves on this final day of mining. He could feel it too—so much of the Grey in one place. He was relieved it was as yet unrefined—the rough-hewn stones were not as potent as the finished Grey. He walked past the wolf guard and gestured to the head miner, Jager, who walked slowly toward him down the hill. When Jager arrived, Kaxon was relieved that he didn't see or feel a trace of Grey on his person.

"Well met, good human. How goes your work?"

Jager stared at him for a long moment. "It goes quite well, my prince. Tomorrow the refining and smithing will begin."

Kaxon nodded absently. "Yes, it is about that that I wish to speak."

He paused and Jager waited in perfect silence, though he cast a glance up the hill at least once.

"The usual tips are made of precisely one inch of the Shining Grey."

"Yes," Jager said, looking the youngest prince in the eyes.

Kaxon gathered his strength, surprised at how nervous he felt in front of a mere human. "This year there is a need for one of unusual length. I am commissioning you to make a blade of no more or less than three inches of the mighty Grey."

Jager bowed respectfully, but said, "A similar request was made by another only a short time ago."

Kaxon took a quick step back, curious and angry that someone else might be trying to do what he was doing.

"And you did not wish to inform your king of his identity?" Kaxon asked.

"His identity was and is unknown to me," Jager said. "He wore a dark cloak over his person, which completely shrouded his face. I did not recognize him as any of the competitors I have seen practicing on this hill."

"Such an exchange should nevertheless have been reported," Kaxon said, pacing.

Slowly Jager looked at the prince. "I did not consider it of importance as his request was promptly *denied*."

Kaxon stopped in his pacing and met the human's gaze. He was not used to pushing around his name. Usually he didn't have to. Pulling his shoulders back and holding his neck high, he said, "Well, this time it comes by order of one born to the great King Crespin—one with the power to reduce your rations."

"And *generous* they are my lord," Jager replied, his cheeks sunken, his face taut with hunger.

"And those to your family."

Jager stood for some minutes, his shadow lengthening with the quickly lowering sun, and then said, "Has the king himself then made this request?"

The question irritated Kaxon. "The son of the king has made it; it is very nearly the same thing."

"Very *nearly* indeed," Jager replied, pausing again before speaking. "Of course, if what you request were to be done, I would want to protect my assets."

Kaxon smiled. "You wish for gold," he asked. "Extra rations?"

"Continued food for my family," Jager replied. "If I am ever…If I am *gone*."

Kaxon nodded. "I wish to have the blade no later than three weeks hence."

"It will be delivered to your quarters."

"No," Kaxon said, turning suddenly. "You will have it taken to a small chamber to the left of the weapons room. The handle of the scythe, will be marked with a moonflower. You will place the marking here." He pointed to a specific place on the hilt of the weapon he carried.

Jager bowed. "As you wish, my lord; it will be marked."

Kaxon had already turned. "Your men may conclude for the day and follow me," Kaxon said, beginning down the hill.

Jager stood still for a few more moments before he turned back to the mine to retrieve the men.

WOLRIJK WOKE LATE IN THE AFTERNOON WITH HIS HEAD STILL throbbing and his mind swimming in fog. He did not enjoy being humiliated and manipulated by a human child. As soon as he got the chance, he would kill the boy. Unfortunately it seemed the little brat had gotten hold of a stone with Grey in it. Wolrijk shook his head— unusually potent Grey. Wolrijk knew it hadn't been smuggled to the family with their ration of food because he personally inspected every package and he was sure they'd been free of rocks. Or anything else odd. Yet it also seemed impossible that the boy could have gotten through the wolf guard at the mines. The guard stood two thick and completely encircled the hill just below the mine's only opening.

Wolrijk wandered to his bathing quarters and dunked his head in a basin of cold water, the small nick from the stone burning. Suddenly, he jerked his head out, shaking off the fur. He had heard, he remembered, rumors of a sighting. Some of the wolf guard near the mine claimed to have seen a young ghost—scrawny and pale as clouded moonlight. He appeared as a glimmer and then was gone. Now Wolrijk wondered.

Unfortunately, he could not wonder long. The king would expect him in less than an hour at the entrance of the Fortune Ball. Just before sunset the Motteral competitors and other guests would begin arriving. Wolrijk groaned and dunked his head into the basin again, wishing it was a bucket of cement instead of frigid water.

If there was anything he hated more than the Shining Grey, it was a ball.

CHAPTER 28

She was not there with bells on. Rather Sadora stood, glowing at the entrance of the ballroom, in an amethyst colored cloak that parted at her neck to reveal a delicate lilac gown and a gaudy metal necklace strung with what seemed to be dozens of platinum petals that clinked together merrily every time she laughed.

Wittendon stared at her so intently that he didn't realize Sarak had come up behind him until his friend said, "It couldn't have gone too badly then. She's made a necklace of the hilt you broke."

"By the moon," Wittendon said. "You nearly gave me a heart attack."

"You always were a little too easy to surprise," Sarak replied. "We'll have to work on that at our next practice."

"Is it really the hilt?" Wittendon asked.

"I can't think what else it might be," Sarak paused, staring at his sister. "You should be very flattered. Sadora rarely wears anything over the locket our parents left to her. Come to think of it, I've never actually seen it covered at all."

Wittendon nodded. Already, Sadora was being swarmed by Veranderen, and he wondered if he would have a chance to dance with her at all that evening. He needed to, he told himself, just so he could get a closer look at that necklace.

As though reading his thoughts, Sarak said, "Oh, honestly, Witt, do I have to help you with everything? Come on." He led the prince through the throng to his sister. "Pardon me, gentle beasts," he said politely, while firmly nudging Sadora's admirers to the sides. "First dance goes to her brother." Sadora smiled, her eyes flicking up to Wittendon before she took her brother's extended hand.

The two siblings walked to the dance floor and as they passed Wittendon, Sarak whispered, "Give me one minute for this crowd to thin a bit and then feel free to cut in."

A waltz began and Wittendon stood there while Sarak and Sadora swirled through a crowd that was still oohing over Sadora's gown. Across the room, Wittendon saw Kaxon come in with a pale, wispy female at his side. Kaxon caught Wittendon's eye and winked. Which reminded Wittendon it was time to cut in.

"May I," he said, feeling like an idiot, and holding out his hand for Sadora to take. As soon as they were together, Wittendon felt that a collective female swoon caught all the ladies of the court. Kaxon's date was staring at them completely gooey-eyed and whispering behind her hand to another Veranderah.

For the first time, Wittendon understood how Sadora might prefer a dark tunnel filled with a group of sworn friends to the lights and sparkles of celebrity.

"Welcome to my world, good Wittendon," she said. "I am glad you are here."

"I am often at the balls," Wittendon responded. "My presence as prince is required." He kept his step simpler than the swirling pattern that Sarak had chosen.

"Yes, but then you are here *only* as required and tend to hide by the food and drink. That is not quite my world."

"Perhaps not," Wittendon said, "though I am not now convinced that this is really so much your world either."

"This, good prince, is a vitally important part of my world. Without it, no other could exist."

Wittendon was not sure what she meant. He was also not sure he was still in step with the music. But looking at the adornment around Sadora's neck, he was quite sure that it was the hilt he had managed to break.

"Do you like it?" she asked, moving so as to put their feet back in time with the waltz.

"You are as a flower tonight," he replied, thinking of the pale purplish-blue of his mother's roses. When he did, the final rhyme of the cat in the tunnel wound into his memory—*Your father's blood, but half of you. The other part runs flower blue.*

"Thank you," she said, the music slowing to its conclusion. She curtsied; Wittendon bowed. A short, dark Verander moved in beside Sadora to take his place for the next song.

"You will save me a dance near the end, won't you, good prince?" she asked.

Wittendon nodded, not quite trusting himself with a response, as the woman who was the head of the Septugant rebellion spun away, smiling like she had no other care in the world.

Kaxon came up to Wittendon and clapped him on the shoulder, grinning in every way like a wolf.

"You look like you're going to eat me," Wittendon said.

"With any luck, Sadora will get to you first," Kaxon replied, laughing.

"I think she already has," Wittendon said and laughed although inside he felt there was nothing funny about that fact.

"You ready for the opening ceremonies in a few weeks?" Kaxon asked a little abruptly.

Wittendon could sense that his brother was nervous. "No. And you?"

Kaxon grinned again. "Not quite, brother, but I took care of some business recently and I think I will be." With that Kaxon's lady came up with a delicate éclair that she pushed into his mouth, giggling.

"Enough talk," she said, nodding briefly to Wittendon and leading Kaxon out to the ballroom floor.

Wittendon wandered through the throngs of people—the dance

floor glittering with reflections of the gems and finery of his race's noble class. He felt just as lonely as he would have if it were a great, dark wood.

~

WOLRIJK STOOD NEAR THE KING'S THRONE, WHICH WAS ELEVATED above the crowd. Wolrijk noticed each guest who walked through the door—the adornments, the gossiping, the ridiculous, expensive ignorance of them all. He also noticed that Crespin seemed much more interested in it than usual. After several dances, the king motioned for him. "The young Sarak," the king asked. "Do you know of whom I speak?"

"The trainer for your eldest, my lord—yes, I know of him."

"His sister draws close to Wittendon," the king said carefully, "and my son seems to return her affections."

Wolrijk nodded, waiting. Young couples danced like snowflakes on the floor below them.

"The parentage of these two siblings is quite unknown. They came here eighteen years ago with nothing but a half-dead nanny and a note addressed to a lady of the court—the second cousin of their mother. We have welcomed them into this realm, given them every privilege two Veranderen could enjoy. And they—in turn—have been respectful and helpful to the kingdom. However, respect and beauty alone are not enough to deserve the hand of the prince."

Wolrijk nodded. The king paused for a moment, watching Wittendon and Sadora dance while the trainer Sarak looked on.

"I leave it to you, Wolrijk, to learn more of their mysterious parentage. If all is honorable, I see nothing wrong with letting this piece of *romance* grow. However, if there is ought in their ancestry that is not befitting for the bride of a prince, it is best that we halt this before it goes too far."

Wolrijk noted that as the king concluded, he looked—not to the lady Sadora—but directly at her brother. "And the priority of this investigation?" Wolrijk asked.

"High," the king responded, meeting Wolrijk's eyes for just a moment before turning away. Crespin held out his hand dismissively. "You need not do it yourself. You have my permission to appoint it to another if you feel there is one more suited to the work."

Wolrijk looked one last time to the dance floor. Sarak kissed his sister on the cheek and whispered something in her ear that made her laugh. Then he left the hall. The king's eyes flicked to the trainer as he walked out the door.

Wolrijk followed the king's gaze. "It shall be done by me, good king," Wolrijk said with a bow. "His majesty's priority is nothing if not my own."

～

Just before dawn, Sadora slipped her hand into Wittendon's. "Have you saved me one last dance?" she asked.

"It has cost me several painful hours of my life," Wittendon said. "But yes, I suppose I have."

She held his neck tightly and pulled him close to her. He could feel the sharp edges of the necklace she'd created against his chest. He could smell her perfume and the scents of every other Verander she'd danced with that night. But underneath it all he could smell her—the sweat, the earth, the grasses and flowers, the water she drank from a stream at the top of the hill, the musk of the tunnels underneath. She leaned in and pressed her cheek against his neck, pushing his hand firmly against her waist so they were as close as Wittendon had formerly dreamed them to be. So close, in fact, that Wittendon wondered for a moment if her other suitors had been bringing her wine all night long. They hadn't. She moved her lips near his ear and whispered clearly, "I'll meet you at the ledge above the mines exactly ten minutes after midday. You will be there or one more persuasive than I will be sent after you."

"I assure you, good lady, you are quite persuasive enough," Wittendon replied, brushing her ear with his lips and wishing just a little bit that it had been too much wine that had caused her to press close to him.

He pulled away as soon as the dance had ended and bowed stiffly. She smiled brightly though something like hurt blinked through her eyes. Wittendon wished he could have caught that look and held it there just as she had held his ear to her mouth when she needed to speak. As it was, she gave him her hand, which he touched to his forehead, and then she was gone.

A WOLF HAD NOT BEEN FOUND DEAD. BUT A WOLF HAD BEEN FOUND with an awl to the eye. The news flowed through the villages like rains off a roof, dumping the stories at Pietre's house. The human—an impetuous youth just half a decade older than Pietre, had been caught in the woods well after dark on an overgrown path that led to a deep wood. He had been killed of course—his body picked clean. But not before he'd jabbed an awl into the eye of the wolf.

Pietre's mother pressed her lips together when the story came to them on the wrinkled lips of the toothless old maid who was their nearest neighbor.

"No good will come of it," Carina said, as the old woman hunched over her knitting, counting stiches.

"Perhaps not, but it warms my bones to hear it," the old woman said, pulling out a row and beginning again.

"It will warm your bones, till those needles have been confiscated by the Veranderen and you can't clothe yourself."

Beyond their hut, the tall legs of two gallows had gone up. The king was having them built in every town, ready for any who pressed in the smallest way against his rule. The workers were supervised by Veranderen, then paid with gold and liquors so that at the day's end, their minds could forget the work of the day's hands.

The clicking of the old woman's needles had begun again—rhythmic, soothing—a song, a story in the clatter of the age old task.

Pietre, Carina, and the old woman stared out the small window, watching the work on the gallows. Pietre's mother looked away. The old woman only knitted faster—something in her eyes was deep and frightened, but flickering like the pages of a book blown in the wind—pages that fluttered and flashed with words from a story Pietre couldn't quite see to its end.

CHAPTER 29

W ittendon met Sadora at the ledge just as promised. She had changed from her gown and necklace into a rust-red cloak with the simple locket she always wore.

"Come," she said simply when he arrived.

He followed, obedient, but annoyed. "So the necklace last night," he said, "a clever symbol of your power over me."

"Do you think so?" she asked, shifting into her wolken form and sprinting over rocks and twigs towards a tall, bare hill ahead of them.

Wittendon shifted as well and followed. "I see, too, that you don't need it here now that you are back in your own comfortable realm."

"I have never needed it," Sadora said, stopping and looking her prince squarely in the face. "And as for it being a symbol of my power over you, you are very much mistaken. If anything, I have begun to wonder if it is just the opposite—a symbol of your power over the rest of us." She paused and looked to the hill ahead of them.

"A Verander who can break a hilt?" He laughed, angry. "Hardly the most powerful thing ever accomplished."

"A Verander who can break a hilt into slender, metallic petals." She paused, lifting her nose into the breeze. "Something to think about."

They crested the hill in silence and before them stood the darkest,

179

greenest wood Wittendon had ever seen. The trees stood thick, yet shadows moved between them as though the branches were ever changing.

Sadora stopped just outside of it, next to a stream flanked by two willows. "I have brought you," she began, "to someone who might better be able to explain who you are—you who can empower a metal with his mother's essence in a place where only his father's influence should be felt." She stood by the stream, panting, though she did not drink. Wittendon bowed by the clear waters, but she stopped him. "Things here," she said, "are not at all as easy as they seem. Do not yet drink until you have made your choice. Within those woods lies— possibly—a great key to your past and parentage—who you truly are and your potential in the kingdom at this time. It is also a place where great burdens are placed upon the shoulders of those hoped great enough to bear them. You do not have to go in. You do not have to comply with me, my rebellion, and my ideals."

Wittendon laughed. "Of course not. I'm sure I could refuse and thereby choose to be murdered by those of your band before I reveal any precious secrets."

"No," she said firmly, placing her hand on his and leaving it there for longer than Wittendon thought necessary. "A few draughts at this stream and you will forget all. When you wake, I will sit here with a picnic basket and sweet meats. You can go back to being the king's son in pursuit of a beautiful, frolicsome, frivolous girl. Or you can join us, as I believe one of those dearest to you would have if given the chance. Enter the woods with a commitment to find yourself and meet your fate. Or drink and forget."

"And may I ask a question?"

She shifted to her flesh form and nodded formally.

"Which of those dearest to me might have gone on with me? Not my father or brother. Not even my own closest friend—your twin."

Still without looking at him, she said, "Surely you do not believe that your mother was only a pretty face?"

Wittendon paused. His father had chosen his mother on account of her face. Wittendon, however, had barely noticed his mother's face.

Instead he had felt her love, heard her laughter, relished their evenings in the nursery, and felt in some indescribable way that she would have run through demons to get him if she'd had to. These were the pieces of her that had remained after her physical face had settled into the dust. These were the things that her death had not been able to take from him. "She was," he said slowly, "a source of goodness."

Sadora turned from him, her gown catching in the wind. "It is time to make your choice."

Wittendon realized suddenly that he had made very few choices in his short life and none of any importance. "This choice," Wittendon said. "You cannot give it to me."

"No," she replied. "I merely open your eyes to it."

Sadora walked several steps away from him, adjusted her hair with a golden comb, and set out a picnic basket, which came magically from a pocket in her cloak.

He looked at her cinnamon hair. For two years he had wanted to touch it. It would be easy—wonderful in a way—to forget who she really was, to put behind him all the confusing things that had happened in the last several weeks. To stay would mean to have the pretty girl everyone wanted and with that a bit of the acceptance he'd never enjoyed. To stay would mean more practices with Sarak and a shot at maybe finding his magic, at performing solidly at the Mal, a chance at pleasing his father.

To stay would mean having anything he wanted—as long as what he wanted was not virtue or love or goodness, as long as what he wanted could be bought, promoted, or pried from the hands of another.

In front of him Sadora had spread out a red silk cloth stacked with the finest foods his kingdom could offer. Her hair had been pinned back, showcasing her bare slender neck. She looked every bit like the lady of the court he'd thought her to be. Wittendon did not look at her again. He turned to walk toward the wood. He did not need a frolicsome girl any more than he had needed a frolicsome mother. A shadow shivered in the wood. It seemed to breathe and he followed it.

SADORA SAT IN THE EMPTY SILENCE OF THE WOOD. SHE ATE A FEW OF the sweet meats by herself, then magically folded the picnic basket into the size of a coin, and began the long walk home alone. She had a feeling Wittendon would be several hours in the wood and that he wouldn't be much interested in seeing her very soon afterwards. Encounters with the witch Zinnegael could be...jarring.

Sadora walked in flesh form, happy to slow the hours down. As she walked she fingered the locket her nanny had wrapped around her neck all those years ago. In the one half was an image of her mother—young, beautiful, with the same deep russet eyes Sadora had grown into. In the other half, instead of a portrait of her father, was an elabo-rate coat of arms—a circle of rushing water that surrounded seven tiny flowers, each with seven tiny petals. At its center was a long thin line that pointed upward. She had spent years looking for a crest similar to this one and had so far been unable to find such a design among any of the royal writings, history books, or pictures.

Lately, she had begun to wonder if she even really wanted to find out. Not knowing who she was had allowed her to be many people—to slip almost effortlessly from socialite to soldier. Knowing might change all that—might set her arrow to a course nearly as straight as that of the great Wittendon himself. Not that she didn't envy her prince. Even when he did not fully realize who he was, he moved forward instead of jumping back and forth between different selves. He was as steady as the star that hung to the moon's right every hundredth year, and she suspected he would always be.

Fingering the crest on the inside of the locket, she could almost feel it hum in her hand. That feeling had been growing stronger in recent months—as though the metal itself was trying to tell her something. She dropped the locket so that it hung at her heart. That was, after all, where it belonged. On the back was an inscription, written in a language so ancient her dying nanny had barely been able to interpret it. *"Key to my heart,"* her nanny had whispered softly.

Sadora smiled at the sentiment. It sounded a good deal better in the old language. In her own tongue, it seemed something to be hung out at a souvenir shop run by silly, tottering women. Yet she wondered—she suspected—that it really was somehow the key to her heart, the thing that would hold her on a steady course, and give her purpose. Many would argue that as spy and the leader of the Septugant she had plenty of purpose already. Yet she knew that a shifting girl was always a shifting girl. At some point the façade would have to end. At some point, she would have to take a stand. She had done so with Wittendon already. She had shown him who she really was and, although he would never believe her now, this had made her feel closer to him than any late night conversation or clinging dance ever could.

The locket hummed against her bosom. Soon she knew she would have to follow its call, and then there would be no returning to the girl she oft pretended to be. This afternoon, however, she murmured, "Hush, now, I wish to walk for a few days more with the grass under my feet and the dew in my hair." Obediently, almost lovingly, the locket fell still.

CHAPTER 30

Pietre didn't dare call it luck that the General Wolrijk had not yet reported him. Luck had nothing to do with it. The wolf was waiting for him. Planning. Twice Pietre had seen a guard wolf on their property going through their things when he was only supposed to be dropping off food. And lately Pietre had felt something too—the impression of footsteps behind him, the hint of air on his neck like breath that wasn't his own, the terrifying instinct to run.

This morning he walked past the newly finished gallows, the teardrop ropes swaying in the wind.

It had been foolish for Pietre to attack the wolf—foolish when it meant that he or his mother could hang for it from a noose braided by the hands of their own friends.

But what else could he have done? The wolf had planned to kill them anyway.

Pietre walked out of their village in search of firewood for their breakfast. He passed the gravesite of Humphrey's brothers and sisters —now a flat piece of land with flowers and grasses springing up. He fingered the stone in his pocket, then went to the creek and bent to take a drink. He heard the crack behind him first. And the crack above him after. He stumbled over sticks, running along the creek. Behind him he heard hard breathing, many footsteps, and then a curse. The sound of pursuit stopped.

It was idiocy to turn and look, but he couldn't help it. He needed to see what followed him, what wanted the stone. When he turned, he saw two nearly black wolves—not a surprise. And in front of them stood two enormous cats—one dark as midnight and one fire-striped like the noonday's sun. Deep in his bones Pietre had known the wolves wanted something from him just as deep in his bones he had known the cats existed. But seeing them all there and facing off made his head swim.

"Can it be?" one of the wolves said to the cats, lurching toward them.

"Of course not," the black cat said. "We've been killed and then forgot." The cats moved lightly, dancing away. They might have seemed perfectly at ease except that Pietre could see the hair along each of their backs rise, like the spikes of the desert lizards. He couldn't stop looking at them—these creatures from the bedtime tales of his childhood. They moved slowly at first and then like wind. Their claws seemed to work much the same way. When they brought them up to strike, they started off as fluffy, padded feet and then out sprang five nails, sharp as mine picks. Pietre gasped. He had never seen an animal do such a thing. The largest wolf jumped at the black cat, biting at her paw. She scratched his face, but that only made him laugh.

"We have not come for you," the large wolf said. "Our general sent us only after the boy. But if you wish to fight, it will be our pleasure."

"Our race has destroyed you once," the smaller wolf chimed in. "It should not be too hard to do it again."

"And we trust," the flame-streaked cat said, calmly looking to the large wolf and then the smaller one, "that you will do just as bad a job now as you did then."

"To the hunt," the smaller wolf growled. He ran at the flame-marked cat. Pietre could feel the speed and weight of the wolf as his feet hit the earth. But she was quicker, streaking away like a beam of light. The wolf changed direction to cut her off and caught her shoulder, knocking her down so that she skidded and rolled through the dust. It seemed to make her angry. Her eyes were orange, except for tiny slivers of black that ran from top to bottom like a poisonous snake's. Pietre stepped back, but the wolf did not. He was running again toward her, but this time she ran toward him as well, springing over the wolf and using her back claws to scrape him before jumping off his back. Pietre sucked in his breath as all four of her paws hit the ground at the same time. "It's true," he whispered to himself. "All four feet. Humphrey will never believe me."

The black cat had scratched the large wolf's face into ribbons of blood, though he had torn a piece of her ear. Pietre couldn't help but think she looked like a princess with a ripped gown. Both of the cats met and stood shoulder to shoulder now. They walked slowly forward and began to talk.

> *The race that rises from the dust,*
> *Surprise for king and country must*
> *Awake the fear and awe of those*
> *Who years ago tried to dispose.*
> *And now if it is up to us,*
> *We'll skin your bones, and hind legs truss.*

The wolves growled, but Pietre could tell they hesitated in their attack. The cats moved forward again, repeating their words, louder and with a hum to their voices that made Pietre's skin rise in tiny bumps. The largest wolf struck first. It charged between the cats, as though hoping to knock them both down like pins in a game. Instead each cat raised a paw and scratched the wolf in even lines from his muzzle to the tip of his back—deep scratches that began to drip blood as he fell moaning.

The other wolf barreled forward. He chose the flame cat and landed on her with a howl and a thud that Pietre knew would have broken his own back. The cat hissed and yowled—a sound Pietre had only ever heard in his childish nightmares, but the black cat jumped onto the wolf, holding his flesh with her claws as though he was a tree she intended to climb. She opened her mouth and Pietre could see the thin white spears that lined her gums. She inserted them like ivory needles

186

into the wolf's neck and just like a man being bled by a human surgeon, the wolf collapsed, rolling to the side, without a moan.

"Sister," she said to the striped cat, and to Pietre's surprise the streaked cat rose, with a gentle whine. The black cat licked her sister's wounds gently as the flamed cat tested each paw against the ground. "Stupid beast," she said. And then, as one, the two cats looked at Pietre.

During the fight he had not thought to fear them. The cats moved like the women of his kind. But now that their slitted eyes stared straight at him, he stepped back.

"You, child," the injured one said, "should come with us."

Pietre turned without thinking and ran. Behind him the gentle swish of footsteps began to follow him. He ran to the narrowest point of the creek and splashed through. He ran over roots as thick as his waist and past trees older and rounder than the red sun itself. He ran over barren rocky earth and into a dry and desolate stretch of land. His legs and back and shoulders ached in a way he had never known. He had brought no water and the sweat of the midday heat poured off his face and hair. His tongue felt thick and his stomach hurt. He did not know how much longer he could go. Then, all at once in the middle of the dry cracked land, the footsteps behind him stopped. Pietre ran a small length further and then paused, putting his hands to his knees and breathing steadily, trying to persuade any food that was left in his belly to stay there. He listened carefully and still did not hear them, his breath coming a little easier. He lifted his head to see if there was a stream anywhere near and there, only inches from his face, stood the cats. His vision blurred, the world spun; he stepped backwards, and fell.

CHAPTER 31

The white wolf Zinder watched from a distant hill as Gog set patches of meadow on fire—starting with the long brown grasses and then moving to several of the stubby dead oak trees that marked the end of the dogs' territory and the beginning of a verdant, dark wood.

The wolf Gog was mad, sick. Perhaps the king was too—sending the crazed wolf out there with a torch in his mouth. Yet that was just what the king had done. Crespin wanted to destroy the wood that belonged to the traitor he had hunted. He wanted it and so it was done, regardless of the potential cost.

Of course Zinder would not stop the deranged wolf. That was not his place. His place, if he had one, had not been found. It was not here in the beautiful lands of the dogs, nor was it within the palace walls that offered him life, work, and protection in exchange for a word as simple as compromise. And it definitely wasn't in the middle of a burning meadow trying to reason with a crazy wolf who held a log of fire hanging from his mouth like a deadly pipe.

The fire was rising now and spreading to things that were not dead —the short white meadow flowers, the crusty barks of ancient trees. It licked at the lush wood behind it, though it did not eat, preferring for now the easier stalks of the meadow and thin trees of the woodland's edge.

The humans called fire hungry. They should know. It had often feasted on their thatched homes, their spindly villages. Yet to be hungry, Zinder thought, meant that you—at some point—could be filled. And fire never was. It swept through the earth leaving neither bone nor marrow, scraps nor ends—leaving only an ashy tailwind that would take centuries to settle and sprout.

Gog spit out the end tip of his torch and then he laughed, running wildly in circles before taking off to the south where the fire had not yet blown.

Zinder stood undetected and alone— watching until a slight movement at the edge of the dogs' territory caught his eye. Two forms rustled against the grasses and small trees; they were blinded by smoke and running. A gust of wind caught the thick mass of flame and threw it into them, the closest dog falling into that fiery belly that could not be filled. He howled in pain and the scent of burning grass turned to something thick and sour. Dropping to the ground, his companion whimpered in grief and terror, crawling forward then back, unable to see where the fire would strike next, unable to see the one clear path Zinder could see from his hill—the one path that might lead the dog to safety.

WITTENDON HAD BEEN WALKING MUCH OF THE AFTERNOON. HE WAS now very lost. The woods were full of shadows; they shuddered and changed faster than seemed possible. After a few hours of wandering, Wittendon said, "If whatever force that rules this wood wishes to speak to me, it can have the decency to show me the way."

"It could not have been said better by my mistress herself," a small voice spoke from a tree.

Wittendon looked up, but could see nothing.

"She is preparing a batch of her finest oatmeal cinnamon crispies as we speak. And of course there's always the tea. It's a favorite, even among the cats." The voice paused and an animal stepped from the shadows and cocked her head at the shocked prince before her. "Of course, normally one of the biggers would have been sent for you, but they are quite busy right now." The animal leapt from the tree. Wittendon had seen the giant black cat, Ellza, at the council, so the sight of a cat was not entirely shocking. This one, however, was small —no more than a few pounds. Her fur was sleek and gray and it looked as though she could easily fit in the lap of one of the humans.

"A house cat," Wittendon said in awe. He had seen pictures in his history books—small cats the humans used to keep in their homes or barns to hunt mice and rabbits.

"Hardly," the animal answered in a purr that sounded like a laugh. "I am a wild cat. There are but few of us left upon the land."

"A wild cat?" Wittendon asked, almost laughing himself. "Are you not all wild now?"

"Some of us more than others."

The cat wove itself between Wittendon's legs as it spoke. "When first hunted by the wolves many of the biggers formed a great band, enlarging the tunnels of the rabbits and foxes on which they preyed, and then hiding themselves therein. By the time my mistress's mother came to this land, the cats had been mostly forgotten and thus enjoyed a little part of this deepest wood. And then of course when my mistress grew and perfected her craft, they no longer needed to hide, though the tunnels have found good use. But the wilds, we did not settle and hide. We merely transferred from place to place when needed. We are movers, runners, messengers, nomads."

This cat did not rhyme as Wittendon had heard the large, black cat do, but its voice and words were still like a song. Wittendon found himself shaking his head to keep from feeling entranced.

It was good he did, because without another word, the cat was leaving. Wittendon knew if he wanted to meet the mistress of this animal, he should follow.

WITTENDON NOTICED THE FAINT SMELL OF SMOKE AS HE AND THE CAT entered the clearing. No one else seemed to notice or care. In front of him, the table was set for tea. Two cups rested on saucers and several cookies sat on a tray as though travelers stumbled to these haunted woods every day. Sprawled behind the table lay two large white cats. They sat up when the newcomers entered, but did not bother to look in their direction.

"Good afternoon, prince," said a voice that came from a little hut to the right of a large garden. "The scones are a bit dry today; I do hope you will forgive that. Don't worry, I've spread them with chocolate to make up for any lack."

A girl entered the garden, stepping across the stone path as though every bump had been memorized a lifetime ago, though she couldn't have been more than fifteen. In one hand, she held a tray that was piled so high with pastries he could not see her face; in the other she carried a vase with pale purplish-blue roses.

"Good afternoon," Wittendon said, finding his voice and staring at the flowers.

"Well, then," she said, putting the tray of scones next to the cookies and the roses next to Wittendon's face. "Already I see that your manners improve upon those of your father. Very good. Perhaps we can talk."

When she turned to him, he took a step back. Her hair was as gray as an ancient wolf, her figure as slight as a human girl, and her eyes were mismatched—one copper and common, though familiar some-how, the other green, wide, and spotted with gold in a way he had only seen in one other person, a person he had never expected to see again. He looked to the roses—sterling roses—and then to her green eye and said, "You are the gardener? My mother's gardener?" He attempted to draw a weapon from his sheath only to find that both weapon and sheath were gone.

"Now, now, don't bother with flattery, good prince; of course I am not *that* gardener," she said. "Do come and have some tea."

He stood still and she rolled her mismatched eyes. "Well, if we must speak of family resemblances, I can now see your father in your manners. Please," she said, gesturing again to the table.

Still Wittendon did not move, but he felt as though the forest behind him grew thicker—pushing him forward. "You are not she?" he asked staring at the roses and again at her face.

"No more than you are the great King Crespin himself," she responded.

He smiled and seemed to relax. "Well, that seems a safe enough comparison as most would say I am barely his blood at all."

"You are half his blood, good prince," she said, sitting down across from him and stacking a delicate plate high with confections, "and half that of your angel mother. It is sometimes easy, even desirable, to forget a bit of our parentage. But that, dear, is something we must not do."

He paused, looking to the pastries. Sadora had warned him of the charmed stream and he wondered what else might alter his mind in this place.

"Eat," she commanded. "I know you are hungry, and from the smell of the north wind, I begin to guess that our afternoon will be fuller than even I expected." She popped a cookie in her mouth as though it was a tiny grape and then went in for more.

"Don't neglect the tea, dear," she said, pushing his cup towards him. "It is the best there is and will give you much strength for the day."

He did not neglect the tea. He had had nothing to drink since that morning and the brew was every bit as good as she'd promised.

"Your eyes," he said, his mouth full of chocolaty scone. "They do not match."

"There are few things about me, my prince, that do."

"And the one is the same as a woman I have known and cannot forget."

"That is because half of that blood runs through my own," she said, setting her cup down.

He choked on his cookie, spilling his tea. "Then perhaps we will not be quite the friends I was beginning to hope."

"Perhaps we will be better," she replied, eating again.

"Why?" he asked. "Is this the blood you wish to forget, but take care to remember?"

She laughed and the blossoms of her garden seemed to open their heads at the joke. "No, my prince, it is quite the other half," she said. "I have taken great care to remember both my parents, though for entirely different reasons. You would do well to remember both of yours as well. It is for this reason that I have brought you here."

Wittendon looked at her, puzzled. She poured him another cup of tea, but he did not drink it.

"You know I grow all the ingredients in these gardens," she said through a mouthful. "Well, all but the chocolate. That is a little bit *imported*." She winked at the wild cat and then she paused, surveying the garden like a lover. "A gift from my mother, these grounds."

At last Wittendon pushed his cup away and stood. "I would prefer it if we did not speak of your mother," he said.

"Well, what you would prefer is not always best for you," she replied. "In your mind you have created a person you believe my mother to be. This image has been encouraged, perhaps even formed, by your father. But you did not *know* my mother."

"Nor do I wish that I had," Wittendon interrupted.

"My mother did not leave the palace on her own terms," the young witch said, ignoring him. "She left the palace because in her womb she carried a child that your father did not wish to be known among his people."

Wittendon was not highly experienced in these matters, but he understood talk of a half-breed when he heard it. "My father has no patience for half-breeds," he said.

"Well, on that we can certainly agree. At least halfway. Won't you have another oatmeal crispie?"

Wittendon shook his head, trying to clear it.

"Besides my right eye," she said abruptly, "look at me and tell me what you see." She paused as though posing for a portrait.

Wittendon looked at the girl. She was pale and wiry, muscled, but so thin you wouldn't know it unless you stopped to really look. Her hair was an anomaly, but her cheekbones were familiar somehow as was something about the way she moved her forehead up and down. When she turned her head so only the copper eye shone, her face seemed to fall together and Wittendon gasped. He looked down to think, glancing at the girl's hands when he did. The bones were thin, but with distinct bumps on the middle knuckles. The ring finger was nearly as long as the center finger and the smallest finger crooked in as though it had been broken, though looking at it, Wittendon knew it had not.

"Dreadful, aren't they?" she said. "I daresay they'll never ask me to model the latest diamonds."

"A half-breed," Wittendon murmured, holding up his own hand.

"It really was quite imperative that my mother leave," the girl said, holding her own hand up so as to mirror Wittendon's. They did not quite touch, but it was plain to see that one hand was a smaller, but perfect model of the other.

"They are just like his."

"Oh, yes, our lord has distinct fingers now doesn't he," she said.

"And your eye. The brown one." Wittendon's head pulsed. The smells from the north seemed to cloud his judgment—acidic and smoking, but he couldn't focus on them quite now. "You are a half-breed," he said again.

"Yes," she said, "I believe we have established that."

"And the other half is from my father." He felt drugged by the words. "Which means—"

She drummed her fingers on the table. "Come now, good brother, and out with it."

"That you are my sister," he finished.

"Quite," she said. "Well, yes, not *quite* as in entirely, but *quite* as in, yes, you've figured it out. I am your half-sister to be exact. Our mothers were not shared. Not in body anyway. I believe in heart they were really quite similar."

"And your mother grew the roses?"

"Only because your mother taught her how."

"And your mother—she had to leave," Wittendon said.

"Yes. And almost didn't make it. The cats saved her," the girl said briefly, passing an oatmeal crispie to the wild gray cat she called Emie. Looking to the north sky, the young witch then shooed the little cat inside and quickly cleared the table. "There is little time now for discussing business so let us be about it quickly, brother." The vegetation thickened around them, forming a sort of wall on all sides. "Sadora has told you of the plan to get the spears?"

Wittendon nodded, then looked at her and said, "And if such a plan succeeds you will have twelve spears. Twelve symbols of power and rebellion. What more? It is a plan without hope."

"Oh, there is much hope," the girl responded. "Much hope that hangs from unlikely places." Turning to Wittendon, she said, "Your mother—tell me what you remember of her."

"First tell me your name," Wittendon said suddenly.

She smiled, a deep wide smile that Wittendon couldn't deny reminded him of Kaxon. "Zinnegael," she said. "And now think please —and a teensy bit quickly—of your mother."

This was not hard for Wittendon. He had thought of his mother much throughout his life and even more in the last several hours as he had walked the wood. "She was kind. She spoke to me every day and sang songs under the moon in the evening."

"And her eyes? What color were they?"

"The same as my own," Wittendon responded.

"And have you ever seen such eyes in the entire kingdom?"

"They are less usual than the browns and coppers, but common enough."

"Are they?" Zinnegael asked. "Think. Think about when she sang to you under the fullest of moons."

Wittendon did think. He had been so young—four or five at the oldest. He remembered her hair better than her eyes. It had brushed his cheeks as she sang. And her smell, which was of chocolate and— Wittendon paused, surprised—and of tea. The same tea which he just drunk—quite perfectly like it. Wittendon looked up at his half-sister.

"Family recipe," she said, though he hadn't told her what he was thinking. "Now I hate to rush you," she said, looking to the skies that were becoming hazy with smoke, "but try to remember your mother's eyes, in full moonlight. She was always there with you on those nights, was she not?"

She had been, Wittendon remembered now. She had always come to the nursery to sleep on the nights when the moon was fullest. He closed his own eyes, heard her song, saw the lashes—longest in the land—as just before he fell into childish slumber they parted. "She glowed," he said slowly, opening his own eyes. "Tiny flecks shot through the blue and they glowed like the star to the side of the moon."

"I had hoped so," the girl said calmly.

The small gray cat came over carrying a thin dagger in its teeth. It handed this to the witch and she thanked the cat. "Now go, Emie dear," she said to the animal. "The winds smell ill—find cover in the cellar if you wish. I've some pretty dried fish there waiting for you." The cat did not need to be invited twice.

"Lovely species," the girl said. "And so neat." She took the blade, held it firmly for a moment, and without warning cast it solidly at the right side of Wittendon's chest. It sank into his flesh with a pop and he staggered back. One of the big white cats yawned.

"You have not forgotten my father's blood then," he said, staring down at the blade, which shimmered with the sheen of a metal he had come to know well in these last weeks before the Mal. "All this time, you have wished to isolate me in order to destroy me."

Again she laughed, the herbs and blossoms by her feet swaying at her mirth. "Brother," she said, stepping forward and pulling the blade from his chest with a sucking sound that made Wittendon feel sick. "Let me know when you are dead."

For a moment the wood fell still, as though every insect paused in its motion. Wittendon put his hand to his wound. He had expected to feel warm blood, tender skin. Instead, he felt a small dent that grew shallower and narrower as the seconds passed.

"I do not bring creatures to this garden to destroy them," she said, dropping a cube of sugar into her tea. "I bring them here so they can realize who they are."

"Surely it is not the Grey," Wittendon said, taking the weapon from her hand as if it were a toy.

"It is indeed and more than a little," she said. "Our father has very few weaknesses, but I will tell you of two. First, he forgets to look for things in unlikely places. It's a foolish failing, actually, for what does one ever find in the likeliest of places. Certainly not one's lost kitchen shears, I can assure you of that. Those I found under the fallen petals of the hardy hibiscus last summer. Hmph. Who would have thought?"

Wittendon just stared, still touching his wound, which was now a blot of shimmery flesh. He rolled the Grey blade in the fingers of his other hand.

"And second, he forgets some of the oldest rhymes. Or rather he ignores them. Our father is old, but he is hardly as old as this land and even younger than the land before it." Wittendon struggled to focus as she spoke, still touching his chest as she continued. "It doesn't help that, until recently, Crespin believed the riddle keepers extinct." Zinnegael looked to the two white feline sentries and smiled fondly. "If he has heard the rhyme, it would have been when he was quite young."

"What rhyme?" Wittendon asked.

Zinnegael ignored the question for a moment, watching as Wittendon felt his chest. "It's quite gone now, brother. You know, for one our father claims is expert with the dead, you seem to have a hard time understanding that you are *not*." Zinnegael turned again to the north, sniffing. "And, yes, the rhyme. The cats do not forget. And neither should we."

> *When two worlds meet,*
> *An era complete,*
> *And one sun assumes the day;*
> *The other ordains,*
> *His own captains,*
> *The moon Lords of the Grey.*

Wittendon had stopped touching his chest, but looked no less dumbfounded. "Did you mean to explain something to me?" he asked. "Or just spin my head in circles?"

Zinnegael pressed her lips together for a moment before speaking. "In the times before your father's time when this world was young, the Greylords were established; and quite feared. They could change the course of the new world if they thought it wise. If you believe, as the dogs do, in the God of the White Sun, then you will believe that this was one of the things the White God ordained when he stepped aside for his red brother—"his own captains" as the rhyme goes—those who could reverse the suns or alter this world if the need ever arose."

Wittendon looked skeptical and Zinnegael continued, "If you do not believe in the White God, it is nevertheless true that there were those among your kin capable of resisting the Shining Grey and capable of handling its mother stone, but very few. These special ones —these Greylords—were so feared that soon enough they were hunted. By the time the Council was established, it was firmly believed that they were all gone. But bloodlines are funny things, passing along traits in a skipping, summery sort of way. You carry it good brother. A gift from a lost time that comes when lost things must be found."

Wittendon stared at her with his mouth wide open.

"Truly you are not completely without our father's manners," she said. "But manners are not your only weakness."

"I know," he said quickly. "I have no magic."

The witch made a piffing noise with her nose. "No," she said, "that is *not* your weakness. What inhibits you is rather the opposite of what inhibits our father—you neglect to look for things in the most likely places. You, dear brother, ignore the things you know. How often have you thought of your mother and seen her as more than a pretty simpleton? How often have you thought of my mother and felt that her disappearance never fully made sense? How many times have you come near the Grey to find your veins singing with strength in its presence? You have felt truth, but ignored your instincts. Ignore them no longer."

Wittendon looked at Zinnegael for several very long moments before saying the only thing he could think to say, "But my eyes don't glow."

She smiled. "They will, brother, they will. As soon as you find your magic."

Before Wittendon could argue, a rustle shook the trees behind them and two more large cats appeared before the witch—one, the black animal Wittendon knew as Ellza and a fiery striped one Zinnegael called Savah. It was the fiery one that carried an unconscious boy face down on her back.

"Ah, the dear," Zinnegael said. "Take him to the cellar with Emie. I've a plate of cakes that will do him good."

The cats obeyed, hurrying the boy to the cellar before Wittendon could get a good look at him.

"And now, Wittendon," she said. "Our father strikes. In a way uncharacteristically desperate for him. That is good."

The winds from the north blew down in a great gust, as though Zinnegael had suddenly chosen to release them.

"Fire," Wittendon said. "We must leave."

"No," she replied. "It will not reach its mark, though it will do much damage. To whom, in the end…well, that remains to be seen."

Wittendon did not bother asking what she meant. The scent began to choke him.

The girl picked up an old staff in one hand and her cup of tea in the other. She began to mutter.

"Go below," she said calmly. "The boy is one you'll want to meet."

Wittendon did not resist.

The witch Zinnegael sat in her chair, taking a sip of tea as she watched the skies. "I could have done with another cube of sugar," she murmured, tapping her staff to the earth as the forest grew up around them.

CHAPTER 32

Markhi stepped into the clearing where just a few short weeks ago he had fought the king's wolves. There was nothing left. He walked through the gray dust, the dead coals staining his fur and the pads of his feet. He kicked at an ashen stump and it fell with a soft plunk to the earth. For several hours, he had been looking for the remains of his two missing sentinels. They had been stationed here on the edge. They would have had very little time to retreat from the fire, very little time at all. The fire had torn through the land like a rabid phoenix. Markhi lifted his paw and blew at the dust. Every insect, leaf, and worm was dead.

The land was not the only thing changed. Markhi's face was stitched together crudely—the work of a kind human healer who had barely the supplies to string a thread through a needle. Markhi had avoided infection only through memories of his grandmother's herbs. So while he had never considered himself a great treat to look upon, he now saw in his face the same type of pink tracks that covered the wolf general Wolrijk. And Markhi hated that.

He walked to a clear pool in the middle of the wreckage. Its beauty was striking in this valley of death. He stared into the water and noticed how his scar zigzagged along his face like a switchback up a mountain.

"I think the she-hounds like it," Humphrey said, coming up behind him. "There's nothing that says warrior like a big old scar."

"Good thing I can smell well or you would have scared the bark out of me," Markhi said grumpily. "And the she-hounds will not like this." He looked over the burned valley and then sat on his haunches in a slumping way that made him look old.

Humphrey sighed.

"I cannot find them," Markhi continued. "Not so much as a bone. Silva and his brother. They were my friends. Now their families will have no peace. Our people will have no body to bury, no ritual to close this tragedy. Only our song."

"Which is more than others have," Humphrey said, looking across the land to the wall of healthy trees at the boundary of the dogs' territory. The trees stood straight and tall, every leaf in place and bursting with green. "The winds shifted the flames suddenly, didn't they?" Humphrey said, noticing a movement along the edge of the trees.

"Perhaps," Markhi replied, his heavy eyebrows pulling down into a frown.

At that moment the moving object took shape and a large cat came forth from the trees. She walked slowly and deliberately, carefully placing her paws so as to keep them as clean as possible. Markhi sighed and stood, his neck long, his eyes set firm.

Humphrey just stared. The fairy stories he'd heard of this race could not have prepared him for the actual sight. The she-cat was larger than either of the dogs with short hair streaked in orange, red, and gray as though she herself were the flame that had lit the land on fire.

"Evening, Savah," Markhi said curtly, and now Humphrey turned to stare at his leader, looking a little hurt that such a secret had never been shared.

The cat nodded her head gracefully in reply, but her eyes were thin slits.

Will you now join,
The cause that will,
Destroy the force,
That your realm kills.

"You may dispense with the rhyme, Savah," Markhi said. "The pup will figure out sooner or later that you don't always speak that way."

Humphrey did not take the time to be offended at being called a pup. "Your voice," he whispered. "You are the voice who led us to the mines."

"No," she said. "That was the human Winterby."

"Yes, but you—"

"Do not think me rude," she interrupted, "but I haven't time for reminiscences at present."

The cat calmly smoothed a whisker and again faced Markhi. "Will you join us?" she asked again.

Markhi looked at her, his scar a little pinker than usual. "Why?" he replied, trying to stay calm, though his voice was rising. "So we can cry to your mistress any moment trouble rises in the air? So we can be guarded in exchange for obeisance? So we can follow her about eating crumpets and growing fat?"

The sleek cat opened her mouth, baring two extremely long, extremely sharp incisors, but said nothing.

Markhi sighed again and the muscles on his neck relaxed some-what. "I am sorry, Savah. I do not wish to give offense. It's been a difficult day."

The cat's face did not change. She stood perfectly still, awaiting an answer.

"The dogs run free, good cat. Any allegiance, however noble, however seemingly helpful, will compromise that. We cannot join your Lady. Any dog who wishes may join the resistance as we will not inhibit the freedoms of our own, but do not expect our kind as a group to join your mistress or the Septugant rebels she supports. It cannot happen for those who wish to remain free."

The enormous cat laughed. "Free?" she said. "Your land burned

202

without cause by a king you cannot oppose or contradict. Your sentinels missing with no chance for retribution. Your face mauled by a wolf"— Savah moved close, her whiskers brushing Markhi's nose —"that you cannot by law kill." She stepped back. "You may have your freedom, dog. I will take my rebel band."

She bent for a drink from the pond, her tongue flicking out so delicately to catch the liquid that none at all splashed onto her face or whiskers. "Let me know if you change your mind, Markhi, arch hound of Sontag. And tell your comrade it is bad manners to stare with his tongue hanging out like a dead goose's neck."

Humphrey put his tongue back in his mouth as the cat walked delicately across the dead meadow without looking back at them.

"You know," said Humphrey. "I *did* think her a little rude." He sat for a minute and then turned suddenly. "You called me a pup."

For the first time that day, Markhi smiled. It didn't even hurt his face anymore. Until he looked over his land. The dead dust that stared back at him made everything hurt.

Humphrey stood beside him. "Do you really think it would be bad to join them? Just sometimes?" Humphrey asked.

"That's the problem," Markhi said. "You can't join sometimes. You can't put *just* a toe in the water. Soon, they will pull you in. There will be duties. There will be fees—not in money of course, but time spent away from the pack. And they wish us to fight with them, for them. There is talk of a great war brewing. War costs much more than time— injuries, lives." Markhi licked his scar. "You must consider all aspects of a decision when you are choosing for a pack."

"But look around," Humphrey said. "Injuries, death; they've happened. What if the cause leads to a better place? What if it means less destruction in the long run?"

Markhi paused before answering. "We may not have the most rights, yet among all the races we run the most free. The humans and wolves are subject to the Veranderen—providing labor, tools, protection, food, information. Even the Veranderen are tethered by the needs of their peoples—forced to worry about diplomacy, taxes, foreign relations, plagues. But we live alone, work alone. We care for our kind. We have land, food, air on our backs. There are few things that threaten our way of life."

"But the king? This wood?"

"It is true that the king can command us if he wishes. But he rarely does. Truth be told—he doesn't dare. Again—he is tethered—finding it easier to avoid civil war with a force as strong as ours than to manage the wreckage such a disaster would bring."

Humphrey stamped an irritated paw in the ash so that a puff of smoke rose around them.

"And this," Markhi said, answering Humphrey's wordless accusation. "This I believe was a mistake. A disaster intended for another group." Markhi looked across the land to the untouched wood.

"Which doesn't make it less of a disaster for us," Humphrey pointed out.

"We will adapt—it's what we do best. This will grow—lush and young and green, and my bet is that if well-handled the king will reimburse us grandly for our loss."

"Right," Humphrey said. "Because you're free from diplomacy and stuff." He shook his paw, which was black from the ash.

"You are too much like your mother," Markhi said, just a hint of fondness leaking through the annoyance in his voice. "And you do not fully understand our ways. You do not understand our traditions, our history. You were not raised with our kind."

He expected Humphrey to come back with something snarky, but Humphrey only looked into the reflecting pool in front of them. "It's true," Humphrey said at last. "I've always been a creature of different worlds—worlds that will pull me to pieces if I'm not careful. I should have realized it earlier when my mother and siblings were ripped from me, when Pietre and my sweet Cari were left behind."

Markhi paused. "Different worlds," he said thoughtfully.

Humphrey looked up at him.

"You," Markhi said, "will be our toe in the water."

Humphrey looked at his ashy foot with a confused look on his face, but Markhi didn't notice.

"Perhaps the dogs are not ready for a rebel band, but you can be our ears that listen, our eyes that see." Markhi laughed. "It will be a mission like your mother used to dream about."

"A mission," Humphrey said, tasting the word, his eyes bright.

"A mission indeed," Markhi murmured, looking at Humphrey and thinking of Hannah, the scent of her death creeping into his memory. Markhi turned abruptly and when he did, he saw a shape move to the south. He narrowed his eyes and sniffed, but could sense nothing more.

ON THE SOUTHERN HILL, THE WHITE WOLF ZINDER STOOD VERY STILL. His position hadn't changed much in the last day, but the entire world around him had. An unconscious dog lay at his feet—the animal's fur singed, his skin burned in various places. Zinder had dragged the dog sentinel from the fire just as the dog had collapsed from fumes the day before. Zinder had covered him with cool mosses from the hill, watching him drift in and out of fevered dreams throughout the night. If the general Wolrijk ever found out, Zinder would have his throat torn out as all traitor-wolves did. Until now Zinder had not thought of himself as a traitor. Until now, he had thought of himself only as an observer—as one who saw things others of his kind often refused to. Yet lately the things he noticed had become more and more alarming. Watching the flames threaten the innocent dog sentinel, Zinder had abandoned mere observation and stepped into action.

Action was the one thing he and the General Wolrijk held in common. It had given them a mutual ground to stand on when they otherwise could not see eye to eye. But now, at last, Zinder's actions had deviated unforgivably from Wolrijk's ideals. Zinder supposed his treachery had been brewing for a while. It made sense when one had the tendency to save, the other to destroy.

The damage from the fire stretched on for several miles. Zinder watched the two dogs in the distance as they surveyed the wreckage. One was the head dog who had fought Wolrijk in the clearing; the other he did not know. He watched them until they ran back through the blackened trees, deeper into their lands. They swam through the creek that had halted the fire, and at last disappeared into a part of the wood that had not been destroyed.

Zinder sighed. Having a paw in different worlds was not a task for the weak of heart. Turning, and carefully stepping over the unconscious dog sentinel, Zinder headed east to the palace. It was his job to report to the king. His lordship would not be pleased to find where his fire had spread. And where it had not.

CHAPTER 33

King Crespin was tired. It had burned. It had burned plenty. But it had burned nothing he had wished it to burn. The dogs would now have to be appeased. There was even a chance he would have to send food to them for a period of time, though it would have to wait until after the Mal. At this point he needed any extra resources for the tourists and dignitaries who would be arriving shortly. Crespin felt like his veins were burning. Several of the ships with food and supplies necessary for the large gathering at the Motteral would be arriving late—another reason the dogs would have to wait to receive food supplements. Wolrijk had no news about Sarak; Kaxon was slinking around like a criminal; and Wittendon was nowhere to be seen if not with that female. Stress was nothing new. It was the cost of being king of everything. But on nights like this, Crespin missed Loer-woei. Her touch could calm him better than any tonic Kaxon brought up from the kitchen. At least before she had gotten sick.

His mind ticked back to times past. He had tried to destroy it—the stone of power his wife had found, the stone of source. She hadn't known what it was, of course, and he hadn't told her. He had simply sent a servant to relieve her of it. It had killed that servant, and in the few days Crespin had possessed it, he had found himself weakened. He had taken it to the place of treasures. There he had brought forth the gram of precious Pallium that had been panned from the River Rylen. Pallium was a metal of containment. Crespin had been hoping to use it to protect himself as Tomar had. But such things could wait. Containing the Sourcestone could not.

Magically, he had crafted the bits of metal into four thin prongs on which he placed the stone. The prongs clamped around the gem, holding it fast and dulling its strength.

Crespin smiled, feeling better in the memory. Being born the son of a court magician may have been a lowly position, but that magic—honed and perfected—had served him well during the years of his reign.

Crespin sighed and folded himself into the down-filled blankets, the clean sheets soft against his tired, wolken body. At least there were *some* perks to ruling.

He was drifting to sleep when he saw her, not Loerwoei whom he had wished to meet in his dreams, but the awful other. She sat perched on his windowsill like an enormous owl, staring with her ill-paired eyes. He rolled over, hoping to change the dream to something more pleasant, but then she spoke.

"Hello, father."

He buried his head in his pillow.

"It was rather warm yesterday in the gardens—unseasonably so."

He shook himself and sat to try to wake up, but when he did, she was still there, her legs dangling to the floor. He growled and held out his hand for his staff. It flew to him like a bolt of lightning and he stood, tapping it to the ground in a way that made the room shudder. "How?" he said fiercely. "How are you here?"

The girl leaned forward on the windowsill like she was going to whisper a secret to a close friend. "What you should be asking," she said, jumping to the floor and holding her own staff casually in her hand, "is how I got into your dreams. It's much more complicated magic, you know."

"As a matter of fact," he said, moving very close to her. "I do."

She held her head high, but he could tell from her posture that she was not quite as safe here as she had been in her wood. He tapped his staff to the ground and a golden cup came into his hand. "Perhaps I should offer you a cup of tea," he said, sneering.

She clamped her teeth together, pulling her neck as far away from the cup as possible. "That's terribly kind of you, but at this time of night, I fear it would keep me awake for far too long."

"I doubt that," he said, laughing as he dropped the cup at her feet. The liquid turned red and thick and ran like blood through the stones around her. He smiled. "This is my land. This is my realm. This is my room. What do you want?"

The fluid had reached her feet. It climbed her shoes like a deadly glue. She murmured a few words, her own staff glowing, and the poison retreated through the cracks in the stones.

"What," he repeated, moving his face only inches from hers. "Do. You. Want?"

"What I want," she said stepping back, "is my mother back, my grandparents, the world I should have been born into. But since you cannot manage that, oh mighty king, I would like you to refrain from smoking up my wood. You know you left quite a mess."

The bones of the king's knuckles turned white around his staff and he glared at her. "You pulled me to your wood in the first place," he said. "So it's hard to believe you really wish to be left alone."

"Well, then," she said, every inch of confidence returning to her voice. "I must be here in order to taunt you, haunt you, watch you crumble like a stone through which water flows and then freezes, weakening it and then, in time, breaking it apart." She stamped the stone floor, and the bricks beneath her cracked.

Crespin laughed at the gesture and spun his staff towards her so the floor became ice, slippery. She stumbled, catching herself on the windowsill and dropping her staff.

He kicked her staff up with his foot, caught it and snapped it in half. She ground her teeth, stumbling again, and he threw her staff through the window. When he heard it hit the ground he leapt at her, howling. He grabbed her neck with his golden fingernails—sharp and long as talons, but still less deadly than his teeth, which he bared inches from her face in an ugly smile. She would snap even more easily than her staff and this part of his day, at least, would have been productive.

Letting his power increase, he grew wider and taller until he stood several feet over his prey. "You were not content to hide in your enchanted wood, conceited child. If you really wanted to *taunt* me, as you say"—he tightened his grip on her neck—"then you should have remained in my dreams." Bowing over her, he pressed the nail of his thumb against her throat, drawing it down in a straight line from her jaw to the base of her neck, his eyes glowing as red as his staff. A line of blood ran from her neck, the drops falling to her dress in a steady stream, but still the green and brown eyes stared at him as though nothing had changed. Her face became white, but her breaths continued as steady as they ever had been.

With one hand she held the windowsill; with the other, she carefully reached under the king's enormous arm and quietly touched his staff. It shuddered from the pressure of her hand and the stone at its tip went black. Crespin threw her to the floor with a curse and she stood, holding three fingers to her neck, stopping the flow of blood. He snarled at her, gripping his staff harder.

"If it's any consolation, *father*," she said, rising to her feet and summoning her staff just as he had first summoned his. "I can't kill you either." With her free hand, she gripped the two pieces of her staff, holding them together like a doctor setting a bone. "My mother revealed to me many things in our time together in the woods. There is a magic that keeps you from destroying me." When she took her finger from her neck, the wound had healed except for a small line of red.

"Your mother was a human," the king snarled. "And she is dead. She protects you from nothing." He grabbed his staff and sent so much power into it that the gem at its tip relit and caught fire.

"My mother was a healer," the girl witch said. "But I did not say that it was she who protected me. You seem to forget, Lord King, that my mother is only half of who I am. You," she continued. "You are the one who protects me now."

"I?" the king said, laughing and raising his staff.

"You," she said again. *"Those come forth by mother's womb. Protected now from father's doom."*

He lowered his hand as though he'd been struck in the stomach. "That was," he said. "That was—"

"That was not for me," she concluded. "I know. Covenant spells are tricky little beasts. I never mess with them myself—promises provide too much margin for error."

She pointed the tip of her staff at the tip of the king's. Both weapons trembled as they met and then both went still. "We are an even balance," she said, giving the king time to realize he could not move against her any more than she could against him. Then she drew her weapon back and turned from the king.

He roared, reaching for her, but found himself stumbling on his own icy floor. She jumped onto the windowsill and steadied herself for a moment. "An even balance," she repeated. The king rose and she looked at him eye to eye, opening her palm to show that her staff was now whole. "Though I expect that soon I will add a weight to my end that will tip things in my favor."

With that she stepped purposefully backwards out of the window just as he raised his staff over his head to crush her. He waited to hear the sound of her body hitting the earth, but she was gone, carried from the window as though she'd been a dream after all.

CHAPTER 34

W ittendon woke, his head full of nightmares. Why couldn't he just dream of flying like Sarak always did? Yes, flying would be nice. Instead there was the thick wall of blackness, a hole like a tunnel leading to more blackness. It was always there in his dreams, but in Zinnegael's wood, it pressed on him. Somehow, he knew that outside of the blackness of his dreams there was light, but he couldn't see it or touch it. He only smothered in the dark.

He had spent two days sitting in Zinnegael's cellar while she attended to the forest fire and what she called "business." Now, Wittendon crawled out of the cottage, expecting to see a great change, but everything was as it had been before. Except, perhaps, that the tea had gotten cold. The white sentry cats sat regally cleaning their paws. The plate of pastries sat on the table next to the jar of cream. The trees swayed in the wind and when Wittendon sniffed he could smell the lavender and rosemary in the garden. But he could smell something else too. Slowly, he walked from the hut, through the forest, and into the bright afternoon. The woods across from him were gone—completely gone. In their place lay a flat, empty field, gray from ash and dust. In the distance, he could hear the hondsong howled in mourning.

"Cookies are not the only thing I offer," Zinnegael said, coming up beside him.

"What is it, exactly, that you offer?" Wittendon asked.

"A chance," she said simply. "A chance to change the world you know is wrong. Have you met the boy?" she asked after a pause.

"He will not speak to me."

"You stole his father."

Wittendon sighed. "I did what—"

"What you were commanded to do," she finished for him. "Now perhaps it is time to do what you know you should do."

Wittendon did not answer her. He did not even look at her. He began walking across the ashen field and did not look back. The slave Jager would be executed when the blades were completed. Wittendon did not know about finding magical spears, fighting his own father, or what to do with the powers of a Greylord. But he knew that Jager was an innocent man. He had always known it. It was a place Wittendon felt he could begin. A place of pitch black versus stark white. The Greysmith's child had lain helpless for most of the previous day while the cats rubbed a healing balm on his face and neck and drizzled warm tea into his mouth. When he had come to, Wittendon had seen him— really seen him—for the first time. At the mines he had watched the child only from a distance. Here he could see the deep blue eyes, solid as stone and clear as water. Here he could sense the boy's hostility. The child would not look at him. Hours they had sat together waiting for the smoke to clear, and hours had turned over in bone-cold silence.

Watching him, Wittendon began to see, not only what his race had taken from the boy, but that his race had grown accustomed to taking things, easily and without any thought to the consequences.

Wittendon walked through the ash and around the dogs' land. He wanted to run from the hondsong, but forced himself to listen—to hear the grief and loss in every word. When he was clear of the dead land, he shifted into his wolken form and sprinted. In less than three weeks,

Jager would be eating a last supper. It was time, at last, for Wittendon, eldest prince of the dictator Crespin, to act.

~

Fourteen Years Ago

LOERWOEI KNELT IN THE GARDEN, PRUNING BACK THE LIMBS THAT SHOT out into long stalks without forming a bud. They took energy, but would never flower. She related a little too much. Her gardener had been creating tonics and teas that had done much to keep the unseen wound from spreading, but Loerwoei knew she was still getting sicker; and a permanent solution had yet to be found.

One of so many permanent solutions yet to be found, she thought to herself. Loerwoei could not yet bestow the stone on Wittendon—he was still too young. And she could not keep it much longer in her care. Soon, the king would feel it and then he would know—each of the tiny lies she had piled onto one another—like crystals forming around an impurity in a jar of honey.

When her grandmother had given the stone to her all those years ago, it had been with a warning. "Hide it, child, until you know the one on whom it must be bestowed." That part had been easy. As soon as she'd looked into her first babe's delicate face she'd known that the gem must someday be his for he made her heart strum with even more energy than the stone had. But in hiding it, she'd already failed once—Crespin had felt it, found it, and taken it deep in his treasure cave. Through her unlucky accident in that cave, she had it again, but she knew she would not be able to hide it forever.

The shadow her gardener cast was long by the time she made her way to the rose bushes.

"I have missed you," Loerwoei said, touching the stone in her cloak.

"It is a feeling that will not soon leave you," the gardener said, kneeling beside the queen and shoving a hand into the loose dirt.

Loerwoei looked up. She had started to notice the way the cloak rounded on the gardener's belly when a strong breeze blew. "You are leaving," Loerwoei said.

"But not without saying good-bye," the gardener said. "Please remember that. When I am gone."

There was something in the final phrase. "Where is he?" Loerwoei asked.

"For now, his majesty sleeps soundly. I prepared a special tea for our lord." The gardener stood, dusting off her knees, the gentle round of her abdomen protruding slightly as she brushed her dress free of dirt.

"Take the stone with you."

"I cannot, my lady. It burns my hand with the hate I carry for your king. To hold it, for me, would be death."

When they looked at each other, they knew that, at this point, almost anything for her would be death. Loerwoei held out her hand, a small sachet of seeds in her palm. The gardener took it, pressing her own fingers against those of her queen.

Wittendon had come when he heard his mother weeping. Loerwoei had pulled him to her lap, the stone in her cloak humming with happiness when she did. It was then that the trumpets sounded and the Königsvaren spilled forth, one long unified howl before they stampeded into the night, hunting the renegade gardener. Loerwoei buried her face into the soft hair on her son's head.

"Wittendon," the queen said, as calmly as she could when the sobs pressed hard against her throat, screaming to break free. "Come with me to the hill above the Grey mines. I've a hope to add some moonflower to my tea tonight."

WITTENDON MADE IT TO THE WOODS OUTSIDE THE HEAD CITY WHEN darkness settled heavy across his shoulders. The moonflowers had begun to open and their musky breath hung in the air like an invitation. Wittendon followed an overgrown path thick with the seven-petaled flowers until he came to a clearing with the softest moss he had ever felt. There he wrapped his cloak around himself and fell—exhausted—

into sleep. Yet just as the blackness of his dreams began to enfold him, a bright streak sliced through, like lightning in a fog.

Wittendon jolted awake. The cave—he had seen it—the cave of his dreams. And just like in his dreams, his legs ached to take him there. Only this time the dream had ended and still his legs throbbed, pressing him to move.

In the dark, the clearing looked strangely familiar. He realized that it was perfectly still—no bugs buzzed, no bats screeched. From the corner of his mind he caught a piece of the dream that had rattled him awake, the bolt of an animal, black as death with slashes of sterling white across its coat. And then the dream began to form into memory. He had followed the animal with his brother when they were very young. Dusk had been descending. The animal had moved through the trees. Someone else had been there with them, tending them—the gardener who was Zinnegael's mother. But she had been a stone's throw away and distracted, busy gathering moonflowers for his mother's favorite tea. He and Kaxon had run after the animal. The gardener had followed them calling, but they had ignored her. They were Veranderen princes and she was a human servant. Before she caught up to them, they had found an overhang at the far end of the soundless meadow, and hidden there.

Wittendon stood now in the clearing, fully awake and rubbing his head. The foliage had grown and changed since his childhood, but looking around, he knew the hidden tunnel was to the northwest—a tunnel with something inside it that he could *not* remember. Whatever it was had frightened him like nothing had before or since. As the half-memory took hold, his body began to tremble and his stomach felt weak. Kaxon had stayed near the opening of the tunnel and cried. Kaxon, who had once snapped the bone of his forearm completely in half without shedding one tear, had bawled the entire time, his face buried up against a stone wall.

It was jarring, the recollections with the gaps in between. Wittendon could not help but feel that there was a reason he had wanted—needed—to forget this place. But now that he was here, he felt almost as urgently that he needed—wanted—to remember it. He walked to the edge of the clearing and, just as he'd known he would, he could hear the steady drum of water. In front of him was a large rock that he and Kaxon had climbed over. The sound of water grew louder, grinding against rock as Wittendon walked toward the noise.

And then, though it had been impossible to see from the clearing, he came upon the dark overhang of rock with vines that hung down, perfectly concealing the opening Wittendon knew was there. Water dripped from the overhang and Wittendon held his cloak over his head and stepped, as he had all those forgotten years ago, toward the blackness.

It seemed crazy to walk towards something that had scared him so much as a child. Yet the cavern pulled at him with answers to lost questions. Wittendon felt his way along the wall of the cave until he came to the opening of a narrow tunnel. It was smaller than he remembered it, tall enough for his kind, but just barely.

Wittendon stared into the dark tunnel. For several minutes all was blackness in the cave. But then, in the distance, he saw a stab of light no bigger than the head of a pin. His head flooded with stories his mother had told him—stories he hadn't thought of for many years—dashing legends of ancient human princes, cats cast out and hunted, shifter-pirates annihilated by the king. His mother had often told him of a stone. It was shiny as the sea and smooth as glass, a globe of a gem that would fit snugly in a grown man's hand. The story nagged at him as a tiny green light flickered in the dark belly of the tunnel.

His mother's gem. His father's treasure room. A secret tunnel. The pieces clicked together in his memory like the outside of a jigsaw puzzle—the border forming, the center still empty. Wittendon felt as though his legs were being pulled through the tunnel. It was the same feeling he'd felt as a child, but instead of magical excitement, he felt a sense of dread curl into his gut. He shook his head, trying to remember what he'd been doing before he came here, where he'd been going, why he'd changed course. But all he could feel were his legs moving forward, his eyes focused on the path in front of him.

Soon the walls narrowed and the ceiling became low while the sound of water increased to a great roar. The pinprick of light grew bigger. Oddly it was the light that stopped him. There was something about it—something *wrong*. He shook his head, forcing himself to step backward, one foot, then the other. As he pushed against his legs, his memory started to clear. He had been planning to free Jager, not hunt around in tunnels for things he could barely remember. Slowly, he walked backward, afraid to turn his face from the strange light ahead of him almost as much as he was afraid to go toward it. Instead of the light, he thought of the boy's bright blue eyes, staring at him stubbornly without speaking. Those eyes were clear in every way the glow in front of him wasn't. Wittendon pulled back from the aura, and escaped out into the night.

CHAPTER 35

C arina breathed into the darkness—slow thin breaths as though rationing the air that surrounded her in the musty dimness of the trunk. From the darkness of her tiny prison, she could hear the sounds of the wolf Wolrijk, stalking through her house, knocking over drawers, pawing through clothes.

Kicking the trunk into which he had thrown her, he spoke to himself, "This is not the one I want. Where is he?" She shuddered at the voice—gravelly, angry. "But if I take her, there is a chance that the boy will come."

Carina had known that the Night Hunter was evil. But now, listening to him speak to himself as though he was split in half, a fear of his derangement crept into her. The wolf would not have what he wanted. Even if she had to die to ensure that. Carefully with the fingernail of her thumb she scratched into the wood underneath her. Her nail cracked and the bed of her finger bled, but still she scratched. "I will not be found. Go to Humphrey."

When the wolf forced her from the trunk into which he'd pushed her, she pulled out a blanket, leaving it dangling. The trunk slammed shut on the quilt and she tried to scream, but his hand held her mouth. The paw was scarred and mauled as it ever had been, but when it held her lips, she felt almost as though a palm of flesh pressed into her face, not the foot of a beast. His scarred face loomed over her and he laughed. "You are much loved, my dear. That is good." Now even his voice sounded human, but perhaps it was just the madness creeping through her for in his hand he held a broken vial with a bitter liquid that seeped into her mouth. In moments she felt as though spiders were crawling across her skin and up the walls, as though a snake uncurled itself inside her belly and spoke to her, as though a thousand fingers covered her eyes and stabbed her neck. She thought she saw the stars fall from the sky until only a black abyss stared at her and then her mind failed and she thought no more.

~

PIETRE AWOKE WISHING TO SCREAM, BUT THE SOUND STUCK STRANGLED in his throat.

In the girl's hut, Pietre dreamed in ways he never had before. Every dream was bright, clear, and—strangest of all—perfectly remembered. He had dreamed Humphrey standing in a sea of ash, his father encased in a room of flame and Shining Grey, the terrifying wolf Wolrijk peeling the skin off his own skull and laughing.

When he told Zinnegael about his dreams, she looked at him with pity and said, "That is the way of these woods, my dear. Your dreams will be strange, and sometimes strangely accurate." She always talked to him like that—like she was three hundred years old when he guessed she was no more than two years his senior. Turning back to her stove, she had concluded, "You'll get used to it."

Pietre doubted it. It'd been over a week and he still felt the same shock from the dreams every night.

Zinnegael poured two mugs of warmed chocolate. Pietre went to get the plates down to set the table. He had tried to hate Zinnegael like he hated the prince, but it was impossible. The prince reminded him of the loss of his father, but the girl witch reminded him somehow of his father himself—the laughter and food, the security and protection of her small hut. Pietre did not know why she needed him, but he did know that he hadn't exactly been taken by force—collapsing into the path of the cats couldn't quite count, and afterwards they had done much to revive him. The witch girl herself had promised to try to retrieve his mother and keep her safe. Strangely, Pietre trusted her.

Last night Pietre had dreamed of his mother and it had been the worst of the visions yet. He woke insisting that Zinnegael send a cat after his mother immediately. He needed to see her, to feel her face. He needed to subdue the haunting that plagued his sleep.

WOLRIJK SAT IN THE OLDEST LIBRARY WITHOUT EVEN A CANDLE TO light it. The darkness reminded him of the cellar of his old hut—his only sanctuary—though it was now filled with the breathing of the unconscious woman. If there was one thing he'd learned from King Crespin it was that if you wanted to get under someone's skin, you did it through a loved one. Wolrijk now had bait and something to barter. He had watched the hut constantly for two days and when the boy had not returned, he'd sent a spy to patrol the woods outside the village. Wolrijk would wait. He was a patient wolf—the most patient in all the land. And while he waited, he had plenty to do.

After taking Pietre's mother, Wolrijk had returned to the castle and searched the room of the trainer Sarak. King Crespin claimed he wanted information on the female Sadora, but it was clear that Sarak was the sibling of most interest to the king. Ever since the king had found the witch's wood, he had watched the trainer hawkishly, followed his movements, censored his correspondence. In addition to being interested in the trainer, it was clear that the king was interested in Sarak's parents. What wasn't as clear was *why*, although when King Crespin started wondering about people's parents, it wasn't because he hoped to invite them over for brunch.

In Sarak's room, Wolrijk had found several books on combat and magic, a closet full of fine robes, and a carefully folded note from the trainer's old nanny—soft, yellowed paper, heavily creased from much reading. Most of the words were blathering sentiment and motherly instruction, but on the upper right corner of the paper was a wax stamp of Sarak's father's house. Wolrijk looked at it closely, tracing a gnarled nail along the lines left in the wax. Some were deep as though they had been made millennia ago; some were shallow, as though they had been scratched into the seal later. For several minutes Wolrijk sat tracing only the deepest lines of the seal. It was not a stamp Sarak would recognize. It was not a stamp most people living in the head city would recognize. But hiding in the deeply etched lines, it was a stamp Wolrijk recognized.

In the last two lines of the letter the old nanny had written, "Your parents were sealed many years ago at the Monastery Girrodan, in the lands above the northern sea. It is in this same monastery that they have been laid to rest."

The old wolf smiled and walked to a table, pushing open a guide to northern monasteries. It was full of elaborate pictures of the Girrodan cathedral and pages of family lines. The line of the trainer's mother was easy to find. The line of his father was not. Wolrijk pawed open an ancient book of Veranderen history and in it he found only a few short pages on Tomar's escape—a great leap from a window, a special agility and speed possessed by few others, the way his family had been hunted and questioned. Wolrijk knew plenty about all of that. And the pages seemed to contain little else. But Wolrijk was used to looking for things in unusual places.

Although most wolves were not known to be able to do much with magic, Wolrijk was an unusual wolf. Opening the history book once again, he bit the pad of his paw until a faint trickle of blood rose to the surface. Holding the bloody paw above the enormous book, he carefully turned the thin pages one by one until at the end of the sixth chapter, the bloodscript began to appear—shimmering at first until Wolrijk held his palm closer to the page so that the script formed into clear, red words—notes jotted in Crespin's young hand: *The search for Tomar has failed, ended at the River Rylen where traces of the metal Pallium have been found, and with it the answer to a great mystery. The metal Pallium can resist the Grey, temporarily absorbing its powers. The river has been searched—less than one gram of the Pallium collected. This has been taken into my possession to be reserved for future use.*

Wolrijk closed the book with some satisfaction and absently licked his wound. Wolrijk knew much about the River Rylen. After his brother's death Wolrijk had spent many years in a secluded hut at its edge. There he had learned of the metal Pallium and its power. He probably knew even more about it than Tomar had. Pallium had the power to contain, but it also had, when used in a certain way, the power to hold things together that weren't meant to be held together. That old River Rylen held other secrets too. It was an anomaly—flowing north not south, and emptying into the northern sea. Tomar, who had spent almost as much time at the river's edge as Wolrijk had, would have known this as well.

In the morning, Wolrijk would send a missive to the head monk of the Girrodan monastery. He expected the monk had records of the deceased—papers about Sarak's parents and, more importantly, the original stamp for the family seal.

Wolrijk re-folded Sarak's note along its well-worn creases. It smelled of love, of use, of history. In one gulp, the ugly wolf ate it— the paper scraping his throat, then sitting dry and empty in his stomach.

CHAPTER 36

Pietre had spent most of the last two days trying to find a suitable weapon. The cats had not yet brought his mother, or even any news about her. In fact the only thing the cats had brought were whispered rumors that his father was soon to be executed. Pietre's dreams would not let him believe it. Still, he wanted to be prepared to fight for his parents. Or—he thought, feeling a little sick—to avenge them.

Pietre had spent almost every minute since arriving in Zinnegael's wood taking missives to miners and artisans, gathering weapons and recruiting those skilled enough to craft more. They had accumulated tools and scrap metal, even bringing together things of the women folk —heavy pans, thin needles, kitchen knives sharp enough to make quick work of gristle and bone. It was not enough. It was never enough, but it was a start. A forge had been erected to sharpen swords, re-shape spearheads, and melt down metal to create crude blades and spikes.

Pietre had expected the search for his own weapon to be exciting, but the swords were too heavy, the spears too long, and the arrows wobbled at his inexperienced hand. The hunt for a weapon had made him feel more like a young, ignorant child than a hero on a mission. Even the lowly slingshot, a weapon he'd used since he was a small boy, seemed impractical. Slingshots were well and good for killing birds for supper or chasing away squirrels in the garden, but he had a hard time picturing himself running after wolves throwing stones that would bounce off their hides until, eventually, he ran out. The thought made him shudder.

Now the sun was poised to set and he stood watching it—still weaponless. It was odd to sit in the woods while the sun sank low—a fat, dark garnet against the plum-colored sky. It sent beams of color across the horizon to bounce off the clouds. Who knew sunset could be a beautiful thing? Until he'd come to this wood, Pietre had known sunset as nothing short of deadly. Even now, he was programmed to run. He could feel his mother's worry with each inch the sun sank. In one of his dreams, she had sat knitting until every last ray of sun had vanished, and then she had put her head on the table and cried. Yet she had seemed to know he was still alive.

In the last dream—the dream of his mother in the trunk—his mother had left a message for him. She wouldn't have done that if she'd thought he was gone. Of course, since that night, his mind had refused to dream her again. He had dreamt Humphrey, Markhi, his father, even the prince he hated. But his mother's place contained only darkness. Which was worse than all the nightmares in the world.

Pietre rubbed the stone in his pocket, worried. Most of the rough bits had now been rubbed off and the stone was becoming perfectly smooth. It was still mostly gray with hints of blue and green at various points throughout the shimmering, metallic lines that streaked across the stone. He took it out of his pocket to look at it. It was the shiniest object he'd ever possessed. His nervous fingers had helped with that too. Parts had been dull, nearly black when his father had first given it to him, but now every bit seemed to gleam in the sun.

The weight felt perfect in his hand, as though his father had fashioned it for him and not just found it in the mines. Pietre remembered how it felt to pound the wolf general in the head—solid and precise. He smiled and reached for his goatskin flask of water. The skin of the flask was stretched long from use and felt sturdy and leathery like the slingshot beside him.

Pietre paused. He drank the last drops of water and held the stone up to the mouthpiece of the flask. It fit inside. He dropped it down, then held the open end of the flask firmly closed in his hand and whipped the other end at a nearby branch. The heavy stone hit it squarely and the wood snapped in two. Secure it its goatskin wrapping, the stone didn't fly off like a normal rock in a sling would have. Instead, it stayed with Pietre. He could strike but keep his stone. Pietre tried it again on a mound of dirt, then an old beehive. He knocked off berries and flowers, then apples and nuts. The pit of a peach split open. Each time, the stone in the goatskin hit its mark with more deliberate weight and surety. He aimed at a rock and struck. The center crumbled and the rock fell open like a book.

"Well, well," a voice said, coming up behind him. Pietre was caught off guard and hurled the stone towards the voice. Zinnegael stepped aside, light as a cat, though it nearly struck her arm.

"I see you've found a weapon," she said

He used it to crack a large geode, the shimmering crystals crumbling out.

She clucked her tongue in approval. "Of course, you might now get thirsty," she said, noticing the flask. "But I suppose we can do something about that." She smiled. "May I ask exactly what you've got in there that can split rocks as though they were stale biscuits?"

He dumped out his stone and held it up for her to see. "Ah," she said. "Interesting choice. A gift from your father, is it not?"

"Yes," Pietre said, trying to remember when he'd told her that.

The sun had sunk low while a partial moon had begun to rise. The two luminaries hovered just above the horizon like cousins across the dinner table.

"May I hold it?" she asked.

The rock seemed to grow heavy in Pietre's hand and he hesitated. With effort he held it out to her, the stone shimmering white, which seemed odd to Pietre. He'd have expected it to catch more of the red glow from the setting sun.

She took a deep breath and slowly extended her hand. The index finger touched first and the blackness spread through her veins almost instantly, darkening her finger and blistering the tip white.

"You—" he said softly, drawing it back. "You cannot touch it."

"True," she said, nursing her hand and nodding as though a suspicion had been confirmed. "There are few who can."

CHAPTER 37

J ager finished the last blade. The late afternoon sun spilled through the window, combining with the red glow of the forge. Jager held up the scythe, letting it catch the bloody light. He might as well have fashioned a blade for his own execution. Now that his work was complete, the king would have no more use for him. Jager set the blade down and sank into a wooden chair, holding the long chain that shackled his ankle to the table.

When his supper came tonight, it would be his last. But waiting for the inevitable did not make him feel better. He stood up and dug through the box of tools for the Grey dagger he'd hidden there. He put it near his boots, then went back to the forge. It was still hot enough to hammer a small rod he'd made from the last bits of remaining metals in his smithy—his own scraps, as well as various other bits of metals left by other smiths—some of the shavings so small or unusual he wasn't even quite sure what metals he was combining. He'd even added the last bits of the old Grey that the former smith had used to paint the blades. From all that, he'd created a rod, which he now began to pound into a thin, pointed lock-pick that he hoped would spring his ankle free. It was a ritual he had performed every evening for the last week. Tonight he noticed that his thoughts drifted away from his tool,

228

away from an ever more unlikely escape and back to his wife and son. He found an unexpected sweetness in his thoughts—a different type of escape.

Just as the sun sank beneath the horizon, Jager heard the footsteps outside the door of the smithy. When the prince Wittendon entered, Jager was surprised. It had been a while since he had seen the king's eldest. Jager tucked the lock pick he'd just made into the blackened pocket of his apron. Wittendon handed him a basket—his last meal—a small quail and a bowl of sweet pudding.

Jager ate it slowly, turned away from the Verander, wishing to spend time now only with his thoughts. When they took him to the gallows, as they very soon would, he planned to make a break for it, although he knew he wouldn't get far. Still, he would die knowing he had tried to the end.

Jager finished and turned to face the prince, only to find that the Verander was holding the small dagger of Grey Jager had made for his escape attempt. Jager could not help but gasp.

"I found it by your boots," Wittendon said.

"My liege," Jager began.

"I assume it fell from the table," Wittendon added, pausing. "Odd utensil. Unusually shiny."

Jager was about to make excuses and then just laughed—he was going to be executed anyway. "These are unusual times."

"So I keep hearing," Wittendon replied. "Well then, let's get on with it. Relieve yourself and I'll take you to some special quarters tonight."

When Jager returned, Wittendon had put the dagger in the slot Jager had sewn in his boot. "Clever design," the prince said.

Jager put his hand deep into his apron pocket and gripped the key he'd made, slipping it in his sleeve before he began to put on his boots. The prince knew of his plan and there was nothing left now but a final desperate attempt. As Jager finished knotting the laces of his boots, he slipped the new key into the lock of the shackle and quietly turned it. He expected to hear nothing as he had heard every night for the last few days, but somehow the alloyed pick he'd created while lost in thoughts of his family made a tiny click and the lock snapped open.

Jager ran.

No guards waited outside. Jager guessed that since the prince had been sent, the guards had been dismissed. Jager only knew one route well enough to travel quickly at night, and his feet found the path to the mines. The road would be fairly empty—Veranderen and wolves had little reason to travel that way. Though he had no idea what to do when he reached the guard.

Jager darted from darkest point to darkest point and waited for the sounds of the prince to be at his back. He was halfway up the base of the hill before he heard the steady footfall of his captor. The prince moved evenly, briskly. Jager knew he could not out-pace him for long, but if he could get to the mines he could hide there. If only he knew how Pietre had done it. No Verander would have the strength to follow him into the mines. Of course, what he would do after that was a problem. There was no way out except for the entrance. He supposed he would be left to starve to death or that a band of well-paid humans would be sent in after him. But if he could get to the mines, then perhaps he could find another way out of them—a turn he had missed, a narrow place to squeeze through, a thin wall that could be pickaxed until it broke.

"Seriously?" Wittendon grumbled to himself as he heard the man pick up his pace, stumbling up the footpath. He hadn't anticipated an escape. He knew the wolves of the guard would surely kill the prisoner he intended to free if he didn't hurry.

He stayed in his flesh form, but it still took less than five minutes to catch up to the human. "Friend," he said at Jager's back.

Jager pulled the crude Grey dagger from his boot and stumbled back.

"Friend," Wittendon repeated. "Do you think I allowed you to keep that blade because I wanted a fight?"

Jager threw the dagger without a pause.

For the second time that week, a knife sank into Wittendon's upper chest.

Jager ran again, assuming the Verander wounded, but Wittendon threw the dagger back so that it landed with a thud in the dirt at Jager's feet. He slid to a stop, staring down at the knife.

"Friend," Wittendon said again, more firmly this time.

"Do not pursue my family," Jager pleaded. "And be quick with it." He bowed his head against the fatal blow he expected.

"That seems a little dramatic," Wittendon said, picking up the blade, wiping it on his cloak, and handing it to the man. "And what exactly does 'friend' translate to in the human dialect?"

Jager looked up, unsure of what to do or say. Gingerly he took the dagger Wittendon handed him. "Your chest?" he said.

"Yes, well, it still surprises me too," the prince remarked. "Now about these mines...I suppose you know them just as well as anyone."

"And better," Jager said slowly.

"Good. Because someday I might like a tour."

Jager just stared at him.

"But before the wolf guard hears us and betrays us both, I'll show you part of a system of tunnels I've just recently become acquainted with."

Jager looked at him suspiciously.

"You don't think that boy of yours flew here, did you?"

Jager gasped, but Wittendon ignored it, moving a stone in the hill-side a foot to the right and revealing an opening Jager never would have found.

"But Pietre—" Jager began.

"Did not use this tunnel," Wittendon finished. "That is correct. But you'll find there are many tunnels connected underneath this land."

The newly-freed captive started to step through the opening and stopped. Turning back to Wittendon, Jager held up his hand, palm forward. The prince looked at him for a moment, then slowly raised his own hand. Their palms met in the human way—flesh to flesh. "Thank you," Jager said, before turning into the opening of the tunnel.

Wittendon nodded. "A cat waits in the tunnel to escort you to your village. Don't be concerned if she talks like a poetry book."

"Poetry," Jager said, "would be the least of my concerns tonight."

WOLRIJK HAD BEEN WATCHING THE OLDEST PRINCE FOR A WHILE NOW. Everyone assumed that when you were in love you acted strangely. Wolrijk wouldn't know. What he did know—and what everyone else seemed to forget—was that there were other reasons to act strangely. Wolrijk followed prince and prisoner. One moment two dark silhouettes were on the side of the hill just south of the guard, and then in a blink the human was gone.

Wolrijk waited until Wittendon had slowly descended the hill, and then he followed the path the two had taken. It led in ragged switchbacks up the hill. Twice Wolrijk made his way up and down the path and twice he found nothing. Pausing at the bottom, he looked up once again. Carefully he gauged the distance, searching the outcroppings to his left and right. When he was nearly to the top of the switchbacks, he saw it—a large stone that could be pushed to the side, revealing a narrow crack. Pulling his ribs in tight, he squeezed through. A few steps further and the blackness was complete.

Slowly he made his way along the high, dank walls of the cavern, feeling for any dips or drops, pressing his body against the right side of the rock so as to be guided through the most perfect blackness he had ever known.

The caverns stretched on for miles, winding and forking. Wolrijk was careful to note each direction change, each unusual smell. But as the caves wound further in, his thoughts started to muddy. He walked more slowly, wondering whether or not he would be able to find his way out. At a certain point, the cavern narrowed. Wolrijk pulled his shoulders back, inching forward and panting until finally through a small hole far ahead, a tiny light blinked on. The light grew bigger as Wolrijk pushed through the last lengths of the tunnel into a cavern where the man holding the light turned. A human with an old wrinkled face—nearly as patchy and ugly as Wolrijk's own—leaped forward, making the sign of the seven—thumb and forefinger extended, hand upside down. The man ran at the wolf with a small blade. Yet, even at the peak of life, a man was no match for the Night Hunter. This one, old and cracked as dirt in the sun, had barely lifted his weapon an inch before the mighty wolf was at his neck.

The lantern fell with a crack and then the light went out, encasing the tunnel again in blackness.

BLACKNESS WAS WHAT THE CAT ELLZA HAD BEEN WAITING FOR. Quickly—before the wolf realized that the old man had not been alone —she ran. The supporting beam was at the south end. It was to be collapsed in case of emergency. The keeper, Winterby, dead. The malformed general in their halls. She barreled into the beam with all the speed and force she possessed.

WOLRIJK HAD BEEN SLOWLY MOVING FORWARD, FOLLOWING THE sounds of paws that obviously knew these caverns better than he did. All at once, the running stopped and there was a loud crack. He felt it first, then breathed it as the dust began to rise. He had been crawling low to the ground, feeling the dips and turns of the tunnel with his forepaws. Now he turned blindly and ran back the way he'd come. He was relieved at last to stumble over the old man's body, ready to squeeze his way into the narrow canal, but the rock above him trembled, crumbling down as stones rolled over the opening. Wolrijk turned and ran to the only other open hallway. Behind him, he could hear the walls as they collapsed, could feel the gritty dust settle beneath his feet and in his fur.

As he ran, the path seemed to go up until he reached a small crevice, barely more than a crack in the stone. No man would ever fit through. Wolrijk wasn't sure he would either, but with his paws stretched out, his shoulders and hips were narrower than a human's. Besides, there were no options left to him. Deftly, he squeezed through the tight space hoping it would open up, though as he crawled through, it only got tighter. The minutes crept like hours and his breath came in short, ragged wheezes. He had to keep his front paws out long and his shoulders squeezed in tight, pushing himself along with his hind legs. His heart hammered into his head and he thought he was going to be sick when, finally, in front of him, a small breeze touched his face. He sucked the clean air in and pushed forward until after several long minutes the tight burrow released him—scraped and panting—into the night. He stumbled out near the top of the hill; and found himself facing the Grey mine.

Being so close to the mine's opening weakened him further and for several minutes he sat, breathing heavily. When he had rested enough, he turned back to inspect the small fissure. It was not a point through which any man could crawl, but it was a place through which a young boy could wriggle. This was how the boy had gotten the stone.

Wolrijk smiled his ugliest smile. Wolrijk didn't like the idea of an arrogant child wandering around with a stone he'd stolen from the mines. Wolrijk had taken the mother. He could take the father as well. Two prizes. Soon enough the boy would find his way to the wolf.

CHAPTER 38

Wittendon stood before his father with the news. Wolrijk stood at the king's right—fresh scrapes along his belly and front quarters—while several of the members of the Königsvaren stood at attention near the back. "The Greysmith is escaped, my lord," Wittendon said.

The king stood quickly, fury spreading over his features.

His wolf guard took a step back, but Wittendon remained unmoving. "The shackle was open. The room empty."

Crespin banged his staff on the floor, sending streaks of black smoke across the tiles. "How? How was it broken?"

"Not broken, my lord. Open. Picked by a tool of his own creation."

Cursing, the king flung his robe back and turned. "Go for him," he said to the wolves. "Search the woods. And if you cannot find him there, go hunt his soon-to-be widow as a ransom."

"Shall I go," Wittendon asked bowing.

"Don't be stupid," the king snapped. "The Mal begins in six days. You've more important business than digging through leaves and human hovels."

"And General," the king said, turning to Wolrijk. "Perhaps the human has escaped execution for now, but in every record it will appear that he has not. I will not have gossip seeping through this kingdom that a middle-aged human can just waltz out of the king's domain. Is that clear?"

Wolrijk nodded.

"Then go," the king shouted to both general and guards.

The Königsvaren broke into a run, a trumpeter issuing a rally to the hunt. Other wolves joined them as they ran, whipping through the woods like winds of death, until they were a great mass of gray fur and yellow teeth, capable of covering acres of forest in minutes. Still they ran for hours, finding nothing.

Wolrijk ran ahead and was gone until deep in the night when he returned to the pack. "Brothers," he said, "the village will give you answers sooner than the owls and bats of this wood. Come."

HUMPHREY NOW KNEW MANY THINGS. HE HAD SEEN COUNTLESS creatures slip beneath the earth, had heard whispers of a rebel band called the Septugant. He knew one of the dog sentinels was dead while the other had barely survived the forest fire. The survivor could remember little—only that after the flames encased his brother, another creature, white as an angel, had reached out and dragged him by the hind leg to somewhere higher and cooler than the flames. The surviving dog had lain low on the ground, drifting in and out of consciousness, and when he had come to, the white creature—and every other living thing—was gone.

Since then a few other dogs had entered Zinnegael's woods, and among some of the dogs a subtle rallying had begun due to the fiery death of the head sentinel Silva. "For Silva," they whispered, touching necks—a pass code of sorts, an agreement to leave their packs and fight alongside a crew of humans, cats, and other creatures. Humphrey was surprised more dogs didn't join them. Since the fire, several water sources had become contaminated, food was scarce, and—oddly— pups had started to go missing. Humphrey had never heard of such a thing; dog pups were well watched, and not easily stolen. Some of the olders whispered the word 'pet,' a term Humphrey had only ever heard once when he'd seen a bright yellow bird in a dingy metal cage. Humphrey didn't like to think of it and closed his eyes to shut out the memory, listening to the free-singing birds of the wood.

Listen. That was mainly what Humphrey did. He had expected a *mission* to mean daring and adventure, but so far it had meant lots of sitting, a bit of hiding, and hours of lonely listening. He missed Markhi. He missed Alekas and her willow-soft coat. He missed Carina and the gentle way she had combed the rotherem through his fur. Rolling around in a bush of it could never compare. But more than anything, he missed Pietre. It had been several weeks since they had seen one another.

Humphrey lay down among the dead leaves and placed his head to the ground wishing to sleep.

The sound started as a gentle throb—something like the sound of a flowing creek. And then it increased into a rumble that was soon thunder in Humphrey's ear. Lifting his head, he watched as the wolves of the Königsvaren flowed through the forest. He did not expect to be seen, and was surprised when one struck him on the back. "Speak, loner," the wolf commanded in his harsh wolven voice. "Have you seen a human man come through these parts?"

Humphrey shook his head as though groggy from being awakened and the wolves pushed onward, the thunder of their feet fading, though it headed in a direction Humphrey knew all too well. Adventure. Of course it would come when he was about to take a nap. He stood slowly, stretched once. And then, on paws as big as Carina's dinner plates, he ran through the darkness.

PIETRE WOKE BEFORE THE CATS, JUST AS DAWN BEGAN TO BREAK THE blackness into gray. His shoulders were shaking, his body weak. He did not know how Zinnegael withstood the dreams of this place. He got up and dressed, ready for the day's instruction. Ever since he had arrived the animals had been training him. His legs were strong from jumping, his arms sore from climbing. His shoulder ached from practice with his new weapon. Zinnegael had sewn a special new goatskin for his stone—a long, skinny sack with a netted opening where the stone rested. This, she promised, would allow the stone to make physical contact with his enemies. "And you're going to want that," she'd said. Looking at her hand, wrapped in a tight bandage, Pietre hadn't argued.

As morning yawned into a pale purple sky, cats and dogs gathered on a field deep in the wood. Yesterday Pietre had run with the few rebel dogs who had joined Zinnegael's rebel band; today he was supposed to skulk with the cats. Savah disliked his word for it. "Stillness training," she called it. But whatever the name, it meant that he moved as quietly as a boy of thirteen possibly could. He had gotten good at it. He could now move with a gentle padding of foot, shift like a shadow, and breathe as a corpse. Or, as the wild little Emie pointed out, very nearly so.

"Impressive," Zinnegael said, putting out raspberry donuts and hibiscus tea for their morning meal. Her finger was still covered with ginger-scented gauze. "Who'd have thought a boy your age could move like a whisper in the leaves."

"You're one to talk," he said, grabbing a donut. "You wander around all day like you're eighty."

"Well, one day I will be. Why not practice now?" she said, lifting the teapot and wincing.

Pietre stopped chewing. "How is your hand?" he asked.

"Oh this?" she said. "Don't worry about it; in fact, I'm really quite pleased."

Pietre looked at Zinnegael like maybe the wound had gone to her brain, but she ignored him. "And how was your sleep?" she asked, pouring the tea.

"The usual," he replied. "Haunted."

She sat, but he remained standing. "You have not brought her," he said after several minutes. "You have not fulfilled your promise."

The witch pursed her lips and carefully unfolded a napkin.

"She is gone," he said, stating it like a fact instead of a question.

"Your mother has been more difficult to locate than anticipated, yes," Zinnegael said. "Your home is empty. And you were correct about the message—there is one scratched into the trunk—one about going to the dog Humphrey."

Pietre closed his eyes to see the same darkness that greeted him when he wished to dream his mother. "And my father?" he asked.

"I must tell you," she said, "and I am sorry, but according to all accounts of my spies, including that of the Veranderah Sadora, he was yesterday executed by the king." Zinnegael sighed. "The rebel captain sends her condolences—"

"I do not need her condolences," Pietre said. He walked to the east to watch the purple haze as it drifted up over the horizon. It could not be. He knew from his dream that his father had seen the hut—his mother's deserted room—the covers of the bed tucked in tight and flat. His father had wandered from room to room, leaving doors open, touching everything. And then his father had smelled something—waxy, familiar. In the dream, his father's skin had prickled and he had reached for something in his boot just as a figure came into view, backlit by a single candle in the tool room.

The growl of the unseen one had filled Pietre's head like a thousand screams and then the hut had been empty—each corner swept, each piece of furniture in perfect order, each door *closed*. Pietre had woken weeping. Perhaps Zinnegael was right. Maybe the dream was just a lost hope trying to make room in his mind. But he needed to know. "I have to go there," he said. "I have to go home."

She set down her mug, though Pietre could see that she was not surprised. "It is a dangerous road. I almost lost a cat several nights ago when they went in search of your mother. The village is heavily guarded and the humans are unnaturally on edge." Pietre always thought it strange the way she referred to humans as though she was not one of them. "Besides," she continued. "Your training has just begun. You are not yet ready to leave."

Pietre actually laughed. "Well, I wasn't quite ready to come either."

Zinnegael smiled and stirred her tea. "That, I suppose, is true."

Zinnegael looked at Pietre for a long minute. "Go then. Find your mother. I will try not to be too jealous if you do."

The 'if' hung in front of Pietre like a screen of smoke. Zinnegael seemed to realize this. "I did not mean 'if,'" the witch said. "One way or another, you will find her. She is part of you and can never be wholly lost."

That was even less comforting.

"Oh, and the cats did find something just before dawn when they went again to your hut, hoping for clues about your mother." Zinnegael pulled a short, shiny object from her apron. "Though I doubt it was your mother's." The sharp dagger in her hand glimmered.

Pietre took it and looked at it carefully. "Not my mother's," he said, running his finger carefully near its edge. "But this blade was fashioned by my father. He has been there."

The witch sighed.

"You doubt?" he asked.

She didn't answer. Instead she said, "Are fathers really so worth finding?"

Pietre was taken aback. He realized he had heard much of Zinnegael's mother, but nothing of her father. "Have you no wish to find yours?" he asked suddenly.

"Hard as I try," she said, "I have never quite been able to lose him."

Pietre started to speak, but she stopped him. "Perhaps your father was lovely. I just worry that you may be placing too much stock in the impossible."

"Really," he replied. "And this from the girl witch whose mutilated mother was saved by a band of extinct animals."

"Touché," she said, holding up her teacup in a mock salute. "And may your life and that of your parents be as unlikely as mine."

Pietre smiled and handed the blade back to her. "Keep this safe for me," he said. "Until I need it."

Zinnegael nodded. "Will you go after this Humphrey then?"

Pietre looked at her. For a long time he didn't speak. He'd done much for Zinnegael's cause—much in a very short amount of time. He'd brought a knowledge of mines and miners, craftsman and weaponry. He'd trained his body and his mind—grown strong. In the safety of Zinnegael's wood, he'd defied his king in dozens of ways, proving himself a rebel if ever there was one. And yet he was hidden and protected in Zinnegael's wood just as he'd once stayed hidden and protected in his mother's house—hidden and protected while others were not. You could call yourself a rebel all you wanted, but until the time came to step forward and you actually stepped forward, you were still just a boy in a hiding game. It didn't matter if you were hiding behind the laws you'd kept all your life, or your mother's skirts, or a box stacked high with sharp new weapons. Pietre looked at the witch and smiled. "When your mother leaves you a bloodied message on the inside of a trunk, it hardly seems right to ignore her."

CHAPTER 39

It was late in the morning when the wolves of the Königsvaren found the hut. The front door was broken and askew, the flowers dead. But each room was darkened, tidy, and perfectly empty. The wolves flowed through it like a flood—overturning beds, chairs, and the small table, pulling out drawers and clothes.

"Enough," Wolrijk barked. "They are not here. Let this town be devoured inch by inch until they are found."

The wolves streaked through the streets like locusts, consuming all in their paths. Livestock were torn apart, their hearts gobbled out. Flowers, herbs, and crops were crushed. The few drunks or sickly beggars who had not fled were kicked aside.

The white wolf Zinder came up from the rear of the pack, weaving through the throng of wolves until he ran shoulder to shoulder with Wolrijk. "Brother," he said. "Will you destroy these innocents when the guilty have obviously fled?"

"I am your general, not your brother," Wolrijk responded. "And someone must pay when the guilty are not here to do so themselves. Such is our law."

"Someone must pay when the guilty are *dead*—that is our law," Zinder growled.

"Someone will pay," Wolrijk repeated.

Their argument stopped at the main street of the village. A group of men had gathered at the head of the road. They were armed with crude weapons, farm tools, and stones.

"Look," Wolrijk said as sweetly as possible in Zinder's ear. "Volunteers."

~

SEVEN ELDERS STOOD IN FRONT. THE FIGHT WAS ALREADY LOST. EVEN if they could conquer the throng of wolves in front of them, they would be hanged for their murders—one man for every wolf fallen. And there were many many wolves.

The chief elder stepped forward. "Is there a problem, General?"

"You house a fugitive in your midst. Offer him up and all this is over."

"We harbor no one, good wolf. We welcome you to search our lands and houses, but beg you to do it without violence."

Wolrijk snarled. "You will beg for more than that if you do not produce the human Jager."

Another elder stepped forward. "He has not been seen in this sector for months. Your own leader prince made the arrest. Besides we received news that he had been executed."

Wolrijk swore to himself, realizing his mistake. "He has been *sentenced* to execution," the wolf explained. "And will be most shortly. Now bring him forth."

"He is not here," the chief elder said.

Wolrijk merely growled and stamped his foot. A group of wolves advanced.

Another elder spoke, desperate. "His wife has gone missing as well. Perhaps he came for her and fled."

"His wife is missing?" Zinder asked, interrupting.

"And the boy too," the elder said. "Though we suspect he may have remained in the woods too long one night."

Wolrijk stomped again to silence them, glaring at Zinder.

"The slave went missing two nights ago," Wolrijk said. "You will have to theorize about your delinquent womenfolk later."

"The human did not say when the wife went missing," Zinder said quietly to Wolrijk, trying to look him in the eye. "It could have been two nights ago as well."

Wolrijk looked away from him. "Search them," he shouted.

The wolves flew toward the band of men in a mass of hair and snarls. The men lifted their weapons as though stunned, unsure of how to protect themselves without killing a wolf.

The chief elder fell first, bringing his shovel down on the head of a wolf while two other wolves leapt at the elder's throat. Other men attacked, but as the battle progressed, the group of men thinned and weakened, pushed back toward the line of houses behind them.

Only two of the elders remained—the youngest with a sharp kitchen knife and an old elder as gray as dusk with a spade in one hand and a hammer in the other. "Please," the older man begged. "He is not here."

Wolrijk howled a halt. "Then offer one who is," he said to the old man.

Immediately the elder laid his spade at the general's feet. Wolrijk was surprised. He had expected the battle to resume quickly, had expected the humans to value their lives enough to fight to life's end as any of his kind would have.

"Weakling," Wolrijk said, disgusted. "I will also need one other man for every wolf fallen."

"Your math is amiss, good leader," Zinder broke in. "More of them have fallen than us. The debt is paid—our law satisfied."

"Our law," Wolrijk shouted, "is filled at my command. Now fall back."

Zinder paused a moment, then stepped back into the pack.

"A man for every wolf," Wolrijk repeated. "And then we will leave your houses and families alone."

For a moment the mass of sweaty, bloodied men froze. Then, quietly, one by one, they began to come forward laying their weapons at the general's feet.

The youngest elder stepped forward just as a voice spoke from the back of the pack of wolves. "No," the voice said.

Wolrijk whirled around, expecting to see the obnoxious peace-monger Zinder in the distance. Instead he saw an enormous animal moving forward with a boy on its back. "No," the boy called again, entering the rear ranks of the wolves. The boy swung an ugly brown goatskin sack over his head, then struck the first wolf in his path. The wolf fell, then another. Quickly the boy carved a path through the mass of confused animals, striking more quickly than they could rebound, as the large dog bit at their faces and necks.

"The law is met," the boy said, reaching Wolrijk and facing him. To his countrymen he shouted, "Resume your arms," though no one moved forward to do so.

Wolrijk growled and stepped toward the boy.

"He was my father," Pietre said. "I am here. The debt is paid." Pietre dismounted from Humphrey and stood to face Wolrijk, his sling at his side.

"So it appears you did not linger over long in the wood," Wolrijk said.

Pietre did not answer, but stared the wolf in the eyes.

Wolrijk bared his teeth. "Do you then know the whereabouts of your renegade father?"

Humphrey growled and Pietre put a soft hand to the dog's neck.

"No," he said pausing. "I do not."

"Pity," Wolrijk said, breathing heavily into the boy's face and then smiling. "If you wish to give yourself up in your father's stead you may place your weapon at my feet, and the rest of these"—he motioned with his head toward the humans—"can go."

"You wish my weapon," Pietre asked pointedly, "to be placed at your feet?" Pietre held the stone near Wolrijk's face.

The wolf hesitated for half a moment and again the boy met his eyes.

"Zinder," Wolrijk commanded, taking a step back. "Relieve this babe of his slingshot."

Zinder came forward from the pack. "At my feet, child," the white wolf commanded.

"As you wish," Pietre said, slamming the stone into Zinder's front paw. The second-in-command crumpled under its force, and the goatskin pulled the stone back into Pietre's hand.

Wolrijk breathed heavily, feeling weak. Zinder moaned.

"I am not entirely sure his weapon wishes to depart from him," Humphrey said, stepping aside so Pietre could move a pace closer to Wolrijk. "Your lieutenant has had some issues in retrieving it."

Wolrijk scanned the pack of wolves for the largest among them. "Gog," he barked and the black animal ran forward. "Take it from the boy."

Quickly, Gog leapt at Pietre, but just as quickly a hammer struck the wolf's skull with a loud crack and the animal fell to the earth, twitching for a moment until all movement stopped.

"No," the gray-haired elder said. "It begins to appear that there are others whose weapons do not wish to depart their hands."

Wolrijk took another step back and Zinder got unsteadily to his feet.

"The Mal begins in just a few days," Pietre said. "The king will be busy, his nerves short. You can notify the king that the prisoner Jager is reported *dead*"—Pietre's voice caught for a moment on the word before he continued—"and that the debt for the other wolves' lives has been paid." He looked over the bloodied street of his childhood. "As it has been many times over." Pietre swallowed, catching sight of the body of the chief elder.

Humphrey continued for him. "Or you can return and tell him you have failed to conquer even one young boy and that you will need more from his army to return and complete your task. Such news would please him I believe."

Wolrijk growled. Already some of the wolves at the back had fallen out of rank and run toward the woods.

Pietre began to swing his weapon in slow circles at his side. It whirred through the air, gaining momentum with each turn.

Wolrijk's face twitched. "We will be back," he snarled. "When I deem it appropriate to receive the full payment for the debt." He looked the boy in the eye and then walked carefully to the woods, the wolves following.

Zinder limped at the rear, pausing beside Gog's body, head bowed for a long moment before he turned to follow his pack.

THE REMAINING TWO ELDERS OF PIETRE'S VILLAGE SAT IN AN OLD INN while women cried in the other room preparing the bodies of the dead.

Pietre stood between the two elders, not wishing to sit.

"Your father—he has destroyed us," the younger elder began. "This animal," he said, gesturing to Humphrey.

"No," the oldest elder interjected before Pietre could speak. "He has only sped up the clock. This land would have destroyed us either way. It is time to decide if we will let it."

The younger man crossed his arms and did not reply.

"A rebel army gathers," Pietre said. "If you wish it, Elder, I will send an ambassador with instructions."

The old man held his head in his hands and sighed, looking to his younger council member for consent.

"As if there is any other option now," the younger said.

"Jager did not have many options either," the older said gently. "Would you rather he had meekly wandered to the gallows? Is that what you want for our race?"

For a moment the young man looked very tired. The two elders paused, staring at each other. Finally, the younger sighed and shook his head.

"Send him," the old man said. "Send the ambassador."

"The ambassador," Pietre said, mounting Humphrey and preparing to leave, "is a *she*. And she is a cat."

CHAPTER 40

The cave from the voiceless meadow had called Wittendon back.

Maybe it was because he could not face Sarak and with him another practice for the Motteral. Maybe it was an intense curiosity about his mother's stories and the cave's connection to them. Maybe it was that the freeing of Jager had ignited a bit of madness in him. He could still feel the human's palm against his own—the connection they had shared. It hadn't been an alliance between slave and master. It had been a gesture between friends.

But there was something more. The cave called him, like the darkness of his dreams, promising to reveal pieces of his past that had been clipped from his memory, promising to fill holes he'd felt ever since his mother's death. They were promises too tempting to ignore.

Wittendon stood at the entrance of the cave, looking into the darkness, waiting for the blinking of the tiny light. He reached into his cloak and felt the long sharp pick that he'd helped himself to at the smithy. It was the final tool Jager had made to break the lock. The pick had been dropped on the floor of the smithy when Jager fled and Wittendon had picked it up before following him. He'd meant to give it back to the Greysmith, but in the hurry of escape he'd forgotten. The metal—a strange alloy concocted from bits of stray metals—had been made into a long, needle-thin blade attached to a clumsy hump of metal at the end. It was nothing more than a crude, metallic ice pick, though perhaps crude wasn't really the right word. It was quickly made and the handle was rough and uneven, but the blade, seemingly delicate as a woman's arm, narrowed to a piercing tip that could not be bent or broken. It reminded Wittendon of his mother.

Wittendon lit the torch he had brought and stepped inside. Unlike the mouth of the cave, the inside was humid, stifling, and strangely ancient. The ceilings were low, the walls narrow. Above him, long, sharp rocks jutted down and he had to navigate his head through them like he was walking through a maze. The floor was hard rock at first, but it sloped down a steep incline and the further into the earth he went, the more slippery it became. He felt he was walking on a bed of slugs, though the color was unnatural, auroral. And yet, for all mystery of this place, the disorientation, he felt something familiar here. With each sludgy step, his foreboding grew.

The small light became more intense as he approached—like a single star on the darkest night. A tremor rumbled through the tunnel, almost imperceptibly moving the walls and floor. Wittendon shifted into his wolken form. He let out a low growl, which curled and echoed through the cavern. As the sound of his own voice came back to him, a memory of his childhood screams came too.

He and Kaxon had gone into the tunnel while the human gardener had stayed back, terrified and shouting—calling into the tunnel and pleading with them that they return to the meadow, insisting that if they didn't come back she would leave and go for help. Wittendon didn't think she would dare—the king would have had her impaled with hot iron for letting them go into a cave. And yet she had gone—run through the wood as Kaxon had cried in the mouth of the tunnel and Wittendon had howled in its bowels.

Wittendon shook off the memory and walked on, a hundred feet down. The slime beneath him grew more solid, crunching beneath his feet like pebbles, only different somehow—disturbing, nagging. Wittendon bent down to duck a large stalactite and there to the right, lay the skeleton of a Verander—long dead. The bones of a near-immortal. He took another step, heard the unholy crunch again, and then the memories washed over him like a tsunami. They were not pebbles; they were bones. Bones of his dead ancestors mixed with the rotten remains of others. He took a breath to steady himself—the acrid smell, the stifling heat of the tunnel—they were the result of all these bodies—hundreds of them—breaking down and returning to the dust. He stood within a giant compost box. Right on cue, he noticed the worms, creeping through the remains, climbing over the thick skin and fur of his feet. Expert with the dead or not, his stomach wrenched.

He remembered too much now, though it came to him in mis-formed chunks like a dream. The human gardener returning with someone—though it was not his father. And something at the end of the tunnel—something that was still alive, something that had killed those who were now the bones over which he trod. Wittendon remem-bered screaming and then—at once—he remembered raising his hands at the monsters, all the force of his young magic pouring from his fingers.

Wittendon stopped. Magic. At his hand. The memory was clear and, as he began again down the steep path, he felt as though a thick veil was lifting off a corner of his mind. He had come to this place with the cocky swagger of a young prince. He had left with his station and power diminished—a verlorn, soon-to-be-motherless misfit in his father's kingdom.

Abruptly, the tunnel ended. It opened into a great round room that Wittendon could not clearly see. He breathed heavier and felt cold. The light that had been in front of him went dark, as did the torch in his hand. Then there was nothing but blackness and a silence that fell just as thick.

Wittendon had seen nothing yet. He could still return to the surface, but to step forward, to step forward would mean death. He did not know why he would step forward, except that he had done just that all those years ago. He had stepped into this room, only to be saved by his mother whom the gardener had fetched. His mother would not come this time; she could never come to him again. Wittendon hesitated, and then stepped forward.

The lives within the cavern stirred, the air shifted. A pale green light seemed to ignite, a hazy, thin cloud at the edges of the room. The chamber was wide and open. Wittendon stood to his full height and grasped his sword. "Show yourself," he called. All around him the haze thickened and trembled as though it were laughing. Wittendon took another step forward. The walls were smooth, though barely visible. And the room, even in darkness was quite full of all the most precious things of his father, all the wealth of his race's history—books with pages of gold and platinum, iron breastplates with blood red gems at their centers. Now when his feet crunched over the earth, he knew that it was rubies, emeralds, and sapphires that shifted under his weight. And there, in a dim circle hung twelve thin spears—the blades of Crespin. Wittendon might have laughed at the discovery, except that around him the green mist began to glow. It gave him enough light to see clearly. The twelve spears were positioned in a protective circle around a display stand that stood empty. Four prongs of dark, unusual metal stood atop the stand, open like an empty claw. Wittendon closed his eyes and remembered what it had held all those years ago—a strange jewel—metallic, round, and shimmering.

When he opened his eyes he felt almost as though he heard a voice, a soft voice that could not have come from the glowing green mist that now threatened to blind him. "The human tool," the voice said in his head. The voice was familiar, an echo of her voice as he had heard it all those years ago. Only then his mother had been telling him to use another weapon—the jewel. He turned around to look for the voice, the voice he knew so well and the voice he feared to hear in this tunnel more than any other. But there was nothing behind him except darkness and nothing ahead of him but death.

The mist began to coalesce, taking the shape of three figures. At first they were faceless, although gradually eyes began to form within the mounds that became three heads. After the eyes came crooked, sharp noses, and long, wispy mouths. Three assassins—the greatest the king had ever fought. Mördare. The word came to Wittendon from a place as deep inside himself as this room seemed to be in the earth. The Mördare were the darkest myth of his race—the half-life killers that formed every young child's worst nightmares. Hundreds of years ago, they had come from across the seas with a pact to end the rule of King Crespin. They had been the greatest leaders of north, south, and east and had come to slay the one who had taken the earth for himself and would not share its power. Crespin had defeated them, as he had countless others. Yet these had gone down only after a great battle that had sapped much of the king's strength and aged him hundreds of years. Because of this, Crespin had cursed them, cursed them to remain imprisoned—forced to protect those very things they had wished to acquire.

The Mördare stood before Wittendon, donned in misty battle garb. Veranderen rulers. The assassin phantoms now spoke as one in a ghoulish voice. "You should not have come here, prince fool. We were not permitted to spare even one as great as your mother, and we shall not now spare one as quivering and weak as the king's first son."

Wittendon took his sword and held it high, but again the murmur in his head spoke to him of the tool and he felt the weight in his pocket as if Jager's pick were made of lead. As a child, Wittendon had fled to the corners to cry while she—his mother—had flown through the tunnel to save him. This time, Wittendon forced himself to gaze at his attackers.

"Well," one laughed, his voice high. "Perhaps he has become more his mother's child after all."

"No matter," said another. "Even she could not match us."

"Although," chattered the third, "she was the only one to leave these walls after we had struck. And more beautiful than any we had seen," he concluded, licking his misty lips.

Wittendon swung at them with his sword, the vapors of their bodies parting easily, their laughter bouncing off the smooth walls and echoing so that it seemed thousands of them were in the room.

He swung again and again; sweat matting the fur of his face. The ghouls cackled—rotted fangs hanging from their mouths, their own stink putrid and smothering. "The son of the king is a rare treat," the ugliest one said to the others. "Family members are such delightful pieces of revenge."

Gasping for breath Wittendon swung his sword above and beside them, trying to think.

One of the Mördare raised his own weapon—a heavy scythe, barbed at the tip and so golden it glowed. The ghoul swung, and struck. Wittendon felt a sharp pain and the air rushed from his lungs. The second of the Mördare hit him across the knees with a blackened club and Wittendon weakened and fell.

Think, he told himself, but the familiar voice came back into his mind. "Do not think," the voice of his mother said, sounding almost annoyed. "Obey."

Wittendon reached into his pocket and grasped the pick. It was so small, so thin, so light. He pulled it out. He remembered his mother as she had held the gemstone—swinging it at the head of the first Mördare just as he had stabbed at her heart. The phantom had staggered back and she had grabbed Wittendon and run back through the cave, taking Kaxon at the end, and then they had spilled out into the night.

Wittendon staggered to his feet and took a careful step forward.

"Obey," she whispered.

Wittendon nodded and looked into the empty eyes of the Mördare. "I am Wittendon," he said. "Son of Loerwoei, and the last known Greylord of this earth." He struck the middle phantom. It smiled for a moment about to laugh, then stumbled. Wittendon jabbed again, this time aiming at its throat. It withered into a gust of foul air. The others howled, rushing forward with their weapons, trying to defeat him before the pick could penetrate them as well. But Wittendon felt stronger at once. He took a step to the side, swung at the head of one, stabbing its eye, and then moved through the mist of its withering form so he could strike the other directly to the heart. They sank into a dim haze.

The mist whirled and writhed around his feet, hissing and murmuring. "It is clear that your desires have changed; you wish for more now than to please your father. Indeed your father would not be pleased, good princeling, but we thank you. You have freed us from our damnation and we return to you now that which was always your own."

The room went dark. Wittendon turned, hoping to see his mother standing behind him. Hoping to see that she had been returned to him after all these years, after dying from the invisible wound the Mördare had given her while she had scooped him into her arms. She was not there. Wittendon picked up his sword, his body growing hot with anger, with loss. And then, in his hand, he felt his sword grow hot too. He touched it with a finger and the dank air around it steamed. Returning it to its sheath, Wittendon retrieved the torch and focused his anger, his heat. Then, as he had seen Sarak do a thousand times with a simple act of magic, the flame leaped up from the cinders at its tip. "My magic," he whispered. "It is returned."

With the Mördare gone and his torch re-lit, Wittendon could look at the room at his leisure. There was wealth beyond any he had seen or imagined. There were the twelve thin blades of Crespin, shining as though new. There was the stand where as a child he had seen the gem, the four prongs now empty. He touched one of the prongs—a mysterious metal he didn't know, which cooled his finger instantly. "Thank you," he said, hoping she could hear. "When we fled all those years ago, I told you that the next time I would obey. In exchange you said you would not tell father. I'm glad you reminded me. I'm glad I could keep my promise." He took his hand off of the empty jewel stand. His mother must have run with the gem when they were leaving. Wittendon felt a strange satisfaction at that. Her heirloom had been returned to her after all.

SADORA SAT IN THE DANK LIBRARY, HER CANDLE BURNED TO A NUB. She didn't like to steal the documents that comprised her nation's geography and distant history, but there were many things she needed to know. The metal Pallium could do more than contain. It could absorb. It could neutralize. It could even repair or restore. The ancients had attempted to utilize it as a mineral in healing—using it to stave off bleeding or seal up breaks of skin and bone, though they had quickly abandoned the practice because in order to heal, the Pallium had to consume. Early patients would find themselves with a wound healed, but a portion of memory, magic, or strength missing. The exchange was simply too risky.

Only traces of the metal were left in the land and they could only be found in the River Rylen—a river that held, she was learning, many secrets. Secrets, she began to suspect, that were related to those she was sure the king's general was keeping. She had often wondered about Wolrijk and his excessive scarring. What could cause and seal wounds like that?

The wick of her candle flickered and she knew she would have to leave soon. Turning with an ancient scroll tucked into her cloak, the light quivered and she hit the corner of something, stumbling. It was an old picture that had been turned around and wedged behind an even older document, a parchment book with rules. Much of the glass in the frame was already broken, though several more shards cracked and clattered to the floor when she bumped it and again when she tried to right it. Carefully she held her candle in front of her so as not to step on any of the shards. The candle illuminated the faces in the portrait, twelve Veranderen seated in a circle. Sadora stopped. She had never seen an image of the Elders. No one had. As far as any knew, all depictions had been destroyed when Crespin came to power. The candlelight flickered across each face and then Sadora gasped. There, pictured at the center of the broken portrait, was a tiny replica of the thing she'd been searching for all her life. She opened the locket that hung at her heart, fingering the engraved coat of arms—the pieces of her life clicking together as the candle reached its end and went out.

CHAPTER 41

The Motteral Mal opened in flame.

The king stood atop a tower in the center of the amphitheater. He welcomed North, South, East, West. He wished the competitors luck and grace. He bowed to the ladies of each court. And then he lifted his arms above his head and the fire burst forth around him. He shot above it, suspended in the air. More flames poured from his mouth and fingers. His shaggy hair swirled around his face like a great meteor in the midst of the flame. He threw more light from his arms in streaks and swirls of color. And then from every edge of the arena, magical courtiers released an intense burst of firelights—azure, emerald, fuchsia. So many that the amphitheater warmed and the spectators gasped and clapped like children.

A small room sat at the top of the amphitheater with eight guards stationed at its door. Wittendon slipped into the royal box and took his seat. Sadora came and sat beside him. "Your father certainly understands a show," she said.

"Yes," Wittendon said, standing and stepping away from her. "Appearances are his specialty."

"Well," Sarak said, walking over from the corner near a window.

"It appears the son of the king has decided to show up after all. Do you know how many times you've stood me up for practice lately?"

"Yes," Wittendon said, "I do." The prince stood in flesh form, adorned in battle sashes of crimson and gold. His breastplate was a shimmering series of copper discs that moved with his body so well he could almost forget they were there. His legs were wound with sturdy yet thin fabrics that would help to protect the weak skin of his flesh form. His sword hung loosely at his side in a golden scabbard with the king's crest upon it.

"Well, at least you look the part," Sarak said snidely. "Like father, like son."

Wittendon gave him a hard look. "Enjoying these seats I've secured for you?" he finally asked.

"Delightful," Sarak said. "I'll remember them when your father hangs me after you get your hide kicked by some twelve-year-old Verander who actually attended his practices."

"Well," Sadora said sweetly. "I'm feeling a bit parched. I'm just going to step out for a minute and find some refreshment. Anyone else need anything?"

Trainer and pupil just stared at each other. Sadora left with a clink of jewels, a swish of gown, and a pointed look to her brother.

Below them dancers leaped toward the center of the field—the females lifted upon the backs of the males to form a shape like a moonflower.

"You are angry," Wittendon said when Sadora had left.

"I am worried," Sarak replied, looking out towards the edge of the area where the first round of competitors was preparing to be released to the field. "But it comes out feeling the same."

"I'm sorry," Wittendon said. "There were other matters—"

"I'm sure there were," Sarak said, glancing in the direction his sister had gone.

Wittendon wished he could tell Sarak the entire story. Instead he said, "I brought you a gift." From his pouch he pulled a short, sturdy knife that had come from Jager's smithy. There had been dozens retrieved by the Veranderen guard who had been sent to search the

257

smithy. This particular dagger was made of steel and the workmanship was unusually fine considering the short time Jager must have had to create it.

Sarak stared at it a little greedily, but did not reach out to accept it.

"You're an idiot if you don't take it," Wittendon said.

Sarak still didn't speak, but held out his hand to take it.

"There. Now you can cut your noose if I do badly today."

"Or tomorrow. Or the next day." Sarak turned the weapon over in his hand. "The tournament lasts almost a week; you've got plenty of chances to get me executed."

"All the more reason for you to be nice to me," Wittendon said.

Sarak looked up and lifted an eyebrow, then smiled, shaking his head. "I thought it was my job to crack the jokes around here."

"You missed your cue," Wittendon said, almost smiling.

"At least Kaxon will be out there to pick up your slack and make your crazy father happy."

Wittendon's smile vanished.

Sarak saw it and looked to the door. "He is a bit late, isn't he?"

Wittendon didn't answer at first. Six magicians lined the field. They broke maidens from cages then transformed them into birds, caught them, and caged them again. "It's a stressful time," Wittendon finally said.

"It's still weird for Kaxon," Sarak replied. "He's never late, especially for things like this."

"You mean the biggest event of his life?" Wittendon said. "No, he's not."

Sarak looked away. "So you've noticed he's been acting strange lately?"

Wittendon nodded.

"I haven't even seen him in the kitchen for weeks." Sarak said. "All his favorite wenches must be weeping." Sarak smiled, but Wittendon's expression didn't change.

The smile fell from Sarak's face and he sighed. "I'll be glad when the whole of this madness is over and our lives can return to normal."

Wittendon looked at his friend for several long moments. They had known each other since childhood. They had dug worms in the gardens, built shanties in the woods, camped, hunted. They had been the only boys without mothers in this long-lived race and, despite their differences, it had woven them together tighter than any mutual hobby or social class could have.

"Sarak," Wittendon began. "These are strange times. Promise me you'll take care of Kaxon if he ever needs it and I'm not here."

Sarak just stared, surprised at the earnestness. "Of course," he said. "I mean, what else would I do? But…lately, it's like, everything has been so different."

Wittendon pursed his lips. "I know." He was about to say more, but just then the king stepped onto the field with his staff aglow.

"Let the battles of this, the 12,000th year of the Motteral Mal, begin," Crespin roared. A bell tolled, two of the arena doors opened, and two warriors dressed much like Wittendon ran through the doors, straight at each other without hesitation or a nod to the crowd. A great cheer rose up. The century-awaited game had begun.

PIETRE RODE HUMPHREY LIKE A HORSE. HE WAS NEARLY THE SIZE OF one and with Pietre on his back, they could thunder from town to town at three times the speed Pietre could have moved on foot. Humphrey ran as though attached to wings while Pietre rang a large bell, and called men and dogs to arms. The Mal provided them with a window of time to openly gather troops to their cause. Still they had only a few more days before the summer solstice, before the Septugant would need to act. Pietre and Humphrey ran through the towns ringing and shouting out the names of those whom the Veranderen had destroyed or taken. They ran through the dogs' lands too, and though many dogs and even their young had gone missing recently, they always shouted the same name—the name that had come to represent all that was senseless and needless in King Crespin's kingdom.

"For the murdered sentinel Silva," they cried until their voices fell hoarse. "For Silva!"

∾

Wittendon stood in the darkness of his battle chamber, waiting to be released onto the field for the last match of the day. Sadora entered with perfect silence, but he sensed her presence as he always did. "How did you get in here?" he asked without turning.

"It wasn't through a tunnel in case you were wondering," Sadora said laughing. "You'd be surprised what a guard will let a pretty face do."

"No," he said. "I wouldn't. What do you wish?"

The room was pitch black, though his eyes had begun to adjust. He could see the golden bangles that lined her wrists and a slender rope of the same color that circled her waist.

"I've come to wish you luck," she said.

He stiffened.

"Though at this phase, you'll hardly need it."

Her fingers searched for his arm in the dark. She found his forearm first and slid her slender fingers down to his wrist and into his hand. His skin tingled at every point her fingers touched and he wanted to pull back.

"I am not a toy," he said angrily.

"I know," she said, pressing something thin and cold against his palm. "I am sorry—more sorry than you can know—that you were ever made to feel like one. We begin, all of us, to feel like figures on a chessboard. Wooden, immobile, positioned forward and back at another's will. This feeling of compulsion must never become a reality, especially at times of war." She took a breath. "Please," she said, pressing the object into his hand again.

After a pause he closed his fingers around it.

"Good luck, dear Wittendon," she said quickly, and left.

Wittendon felt the cool, thin metal warm in his hand. It was a delicate piece—like a fish's scale. Or—he fingered it again—a rose's petal. It was one of the pieces of the broken hilt. A reminder of his power before he had known what power he had. Carefully he held it against the hilt of his blade, concentrating. He felt it join with the metal and melt into the hilt, just where his hand always held it.

A bell tolled, the door rose, and blinding sunlight streamed in. He raced onto the field, pressing his hand to his hilt and thinking of his mother.

~

THE BELLS OF THE CITY RANG OUT, DROWNING OUT THE SOUNDS OF Pietre's tinny instrument, although he still rang it shouting names. Men gathered to the center of the town, armed as usual with blunt objects, sharp tools, and their wives' best knives. Pietre assembled the groups into rank according to age and size, and gave detailed directions to the rebel camp deep in the woods. His margin of opportunity was brief. As long as the cheers and screams of the Mal sounded in the distance there would be few wolves and no Veranderen to hinder them. But at dusk every town must fall silent, every family go about its business as though men and boys had not left en masse to join the Septugant.

Pietre was surprised at the ease with which human men were recruited. He was almost equally surprised at the scanty numbers of dogs. Their lands had been burned and branded, innocents killed, and lately many pups had gone missing—taken, the rumors went, and given as pets to royals who had come from other lands to view the Motteral. Even with such humiliation, for every fifty men who marched forth, only one or two dogs scrabbled from their packs, and even those seemed to leave their packs in shame.

Pietre knew Humphrey was upset about this. A council had been arranged with Markhi and the arch hounds of the other nine packs. They would meet in the morning, though the gathering did not seem to hold much promise of support. Land and life, it was clear, did not mean as much for the dogs as language and independence. For the dogs those two virtues wrapped around each other so tightly that Pietre started to see how they choked everything else out. Or, as Humphrey put it, "Those stubborn mutts are going to strangle themselves with their precious words."

The last bell of the evening shook with a crack that seemed to loosen Pietre's bones.

~

WITTENDON'S SWORD CLANGED AGAINST THAT OF HIS OPPONENT. THE tall, wide Verander was hairy and thick-skinned even in his flesh form and had already gained two points more than Wittendon. The first round allowed no magic and no shifting, just a sword and any strength or cunning you had to use it. Wittendon had expected to do well, but with every point lost he grew more nervous.

Wittendon's opponent snarled, his humanish teeth streaked with brown lines of decay, his skin pocked from battles and training. "You move like a willow in the wind," the Verander said to Wittendon. "And soon you will snap like one of its branches in a gale."

Wittendon pressed forward with all his weight, though he found his feet often sliding back through the dirt. Brown Tooth struck Wittendon's shin and he stumbled back even further, losing yet another point. The Verander hovered over him, banging his weapon like a hammer against Wittendon's head. The prince fell down, but managed to block the next blow from his position on the ground. He blocked like that again and then again. He remembered something his mother had said about willows—their wood was soft and often bent in the wind; they were much more likely to withstand a storm.

Steadily, Wittendon regained his footing. He blocked once more and then he struck and struck again. He stood against his opponent, not with weight this time, but with flexibility, cadence, and skill. His arms and shoulders moved together rhythmically, like the ticking of a clock. Brown Tooth took a step back, then another. The sound of their swords connecting drowned out the noise from the crowd. Wittendon could hear nothing now but his blade, could feel nothing now but its connection with that of his opponent. Soon his attack became more intense. He pierced the other Verander's side then stabbed his shoulder. Brown Tooth growled and held up his sword to block. With an enormous movement, Wittendon brought his own weapon down and as he did his opponent's blade snapped.

Brown Tooth fell backwards and when he did, Wittendon pressed his sword to his throat. "Did you say something about a branch?" Wittendon asked as the king came to the field and held Wittendon's arm up—victorious.

Wittendon sheathed the sword, willing the metal petal to disconnect from the hilt and fall into his hand. He held it tightly, feeling his mother and Sadora in its weightlessness. Without meaning to, he looked to the royal box and smiled.

CHAPTER 42

When Wittendon returned to his bed, tired and sore, Zinnegael sat perched on his bedpost like a long, skinny owl.

"Your magic," he said, taking off his armor. "You use it in the oddest ways."

"Such is my destiny. Well, that or to sell roadside souvenirs—the tea leaves were a little unclear there. But anyway, what's the point of being super human if you go about using it for all the usual things?" she asked.

"If you were anyone else perched in my room late at night, I'd assume you hadn't just come for tea, but knowing you—"

"Well, I certainly am never opposed to a good cup," she said. "But it's true—that is not my main reason for being here tonight."

Wittendon sat on the bed and she came and sat next to him. He wondered how it would have been if they had grown up together like Sarak and Sadora.

"Well?" Wittendon said, taking off his shoes.

"I just came to tell you that you need to win the Motteral Mal."

Wittendon laughed. "Because?" he asked. "Wait—let me guess.

You have a fondness for the game and would love to see your brother become the next Chancellor of the world?"

Zinnegael crossed her arms. "Because only by winning will you be able to empower the *Zonnesteen* in the correct place without being disturbed."

"The zonne-who?"

"Steen," she said. "*Zonnesteen*—stone of the sun. Stone of the *source*."

"Well," Wittendon said sarcastically. "Glad you cleared that up. And you need me to do this because?"

"Because how else will the appointed one be able to take it to the Sacred Tablet and change the course of our world forever?"

"So I'm going to empower a stone and then give it away?"

"Yes," she said.

"And whoever I give it to is going to take it to the tourist attraction at the top of the hill that lovers go to and kiss for luck?"

"Exactly. The Zonnesteen will be placed in that little dip at its left —the spot people spit in for victory."

"Of course." He banged his shoe on the floor. Caked on dirt came off in stinky clumps.

"And who, exactly, will be taking it?"

"A human."

"Which one?"

"The one who shows up to take it from you, of course."

"Naturally," Wittendon said, wrinkling his nose at the smell of his own feet. "Well, I'll do my best. You know you really have more in common with our father than you'd like to believe."

She made a sour face, but even in the squinchy lines of her eyes— especially the copper one—she didn't look entirely convinced that he was wrong.

"And how exactly will I empower this zonne-whatever?" Wittendon tossed his shoes.

"You going to clean that up?" she asked, nodding to the pile of dirt and grass clods.

He shook his head. He could be found out and tried as a traitor at any moment. Why waste precious time on sweeping? "The stone?" he reminded her.

"Yes. The stone of the source." She pushed the dirt to the corner of the room with her foot. "I'll show you where to empower it—it's a lot more secluded than the Tablet, but it gives a nice, clear view of the sun and moon, which you'll need. And then that night you'll know what to do. The ancient writings indicate that it should be instinctive, like having a baby."

"Wonderful," he said. "Because that's what I've always wanted to do." He looked out his window to the hills. "And why don't you empower it yourself? Why don't we sneak up there right now and get it over with?"

She sighed as though explaining something to a very dense child. "For starters," she said. "I haven't even got the stone—that's another order of business to be dealt with. And for middlers, it has to be done at the summer solstice—the night of the fullest moon on the shortest night just at the moment when moon and sun gaze upon each other across the horizon. It should be about the time you would be winning the Mal." She nodded as though to confirm this detail. "And for finishers, *I* can't do it."

"Why?" he asked. "You are the most powerful among us."

"Because," she responded, "I am not a werewolf."

He grimaced at the word, but she ignored it.

"Through this stone, you will take something from your own and give it to someone else. I cannot give something to another when it is not in my possession to give. You, werewolf prince, can give it."

"You ask me to take something from my own people?" He looked at her, all the sarcasm and joking gone.

"I ask you to alter the sun and moon that control this world," she said, meeting his gaze. "A change that would alter the balance of power among the races."

"You make it sound as though it will hurt my people."

"It will take another people up to the same standing."

"But only the same? Not greater?"

"That, brother, is a question I cannot fully answer. It will create a level field. What happens on the field after that is not for me to say."

"And why can't we create a level field in some other way? A new constitution perhaps, with another ruling council. It could even maybe have humans included as some of its members. Like the Septugant."

Zinnegael cocked the eyebrow above her green eye. "That is a lovely idea. I'll just go present it to King Crespin and the Veranderen right now."

Wittendon glared at her. "Look, I know it wouldn't be easy, but it does seem possible. Different races are already gathering to support the Septugant after all. I just don't understand why the entire world has to change."

Zinnegael sighed and sat on the bed beside him. "Crespin—for all his shortcomings—has done one thing for his people. There is no war. It has made his people forget what war can mean. It is not brief, brother. It is not a few days of battle and all is ended. It is months and years of fighting, bloodshed, strategy, advances, and retreats."

Wittendon tried to interrupt, but Zinnegael held up a hand. "It is more gruesome than you or any of your kind can imagine. I believe, and Sadora concurs, that changing the suns, and with them the current balance of power, would significantly reduce the death toll and eliminate conflict of any significant length."

Zinnegael pressed her dress down flat over her knees before continuing. "In addition," she said. "You must understand that under the red sun, with the power it and the ever-hanging moon grant to the Veranderen, no war of any length is likely to be successful. When one group is in possession of significantly more power, convincing them—as a body—to let that power and position go is difficult, almost impossible. The power is too alluring. Even if some are willing to contain and control their powers for the greater good, many will not."

"Which means?" Wittendon asked.

"Which means that after years of war, even in the event that we win and establish a new constitution, it will be shaky at best. The Veranderen are so powerful. They will want to return to that dominance."

"So changing the suns *will* reduce my people."

Again Zinnegael sighed. "To be truthful, no one is entirely sure what will happen at the sun change, but yes, we can assume that some of your powers will be *adjusted*."

Her words should have hit him like a fist, but Wittendon found that they didn't. Having spent much of his life without power, it was easier than he cared to admit to see things from the other side. Yet, having his power so newly restored, he was somewhat hesitant to lose it—a fact that also supported Zinnegael's argument. Of course, that didn't mean he was excited about her plan.

Wittendon looked at her and then flopped back on his bed. "I must think on it, sister."

"Then think. And watch. Both should do you good."

She left by vaulting over his bed and out the window using her staff.

He laid his head on his pillow. "Stone of the sun," he murmured, wondering why that should seem familiar. "Stone of the source." Suddenly he sat up, banging his head on the wooden headboard behind him. "The Sourcestone," he whispered.

CHAPTER 43

They met at dawn. Ten dogs walked from the cool shadows of the woods like dewy phantoms. They were all known for their intelligence, strength, and loyalty to the pack, though each had different gifts—one lean, long and intensely fast; one beautiful, her voice a song; one heavy and strong; one agile; one brilliant; one secretive; one ancient; one hunter; one planner; and Markhi, with his perfect sense of smell and almost infallible ability to track. Yet while their bodies, abilities, and voices were different, they shared one quality: none looked happy to be there. Markhi put on a good front, but his eyes were tired and his body seemed to sag.

Humphrey cleared his throat and Pietre began to speak. He had scribbled a few arguments to make the night before, but now that he stood before grumpy, snarling, sometimes bored dogs, the paper served only as something he could crinkle nervously between his fingers while he stammered through his thoughts about how the Septugant needed the dogs in order to succeed. Needed their strength and numbers, their speed and teeth, their noses and words and talents.

A laugh rang out from the circle of shaggy faces, gentle and singsong sweet. "But why, dear boy," the beautiful one seemed to hum.

"Why does this conflict need to exist at all?" At the music of her words, Pietre could not remember or at least not explain.

"Why?" Humphrey said, not nearly so enchanted. "Your land lies blistered. Your head sentinel dead. Food sources have become scarce—especially surrounding the burned firelands. Your kin begin to taste their hunger, a hunger that will only deepen as the dogs' ribs grow sharp against their skin. Not to mention the more shocking fact that the pups have begun to vanish—twenty-seven in just the last few days."

"'Tis true," grumbled the ancient one. "It happens every hundred years. No one quite knows why."

"But of course we know why," barked the battle planner. "They use them. They give them as gifts during the Motteral Mal."

"It's never actually been proven," the old one grumbled.

"Yet even if it was," the singsong voice replied. "And do not think me harsh—only realistic—it happens but once a century. As for the burning and the sentinel—the king will soon repay us in more land, and the good Silva, while valiant and strong, was but one."

"But one," sputtered the agile one who was also a female. "And our young gone too."

"Yet it is true," said the planner. "Assuming we *can* conquer a force so great that it has survived for thousands of years, what benefit would it bring us compared to the small losses we occasionally encounter?"

"And our voices," the fluted one said.

"Our stories," the elder continued.

"Our experience," the secret-keeper chimed in.

"Are but frivolity if we cannot fight when wrong is done to us," Markhi said suddenly. "It is true that at present our losses have not become catastrophic. But with Crespin as king, there is never a guarantee that this will continue. What if he did *not* wish to reimburse us our land? What would we do? What could we do? In this conflict there is a chance to unite with a cause greater than our whole."

"And yet still very nearly doomed to failure," the planner pointed out.

The dogs fell quickly into a rough babble of argument. Pietre sat dazed, but Humphrey stared at them hard and waited, then stamped his enormous front paw three times. It shook the ground and one by one the faces turned to glare at the stranger in their midst.

"You prattle on about pros and cons," he growled. "You worry for your young taken as pets, about food sources and security. You defend yourselves with words about your language as ancient as the sun. You are already as pets to the king—to be spoiled and pampered or beaten and abandoned at his whim. Your language, your history, your break from the wolves whom you claim to despise—what does it mean, what weight does it bear when you quiver at the command of a master while you let those weaker, and yet more loyal to you, falter and fall while you close your eyes, hum your tune and turn away? You sing your songs—songs of loyalty, bravery, and love. Yet, how many of you have been—or known those—housed or fed, bandaged or buried by the soft-fleshed humans, the humans who even now gather and rally for causes in your defense? The humans who, even in their own poverty, have begun sending parcels of food to the packs of dogs suffering as a result of their scorched lands. While the Veranderen, who have so much more, still do nothing to supply food to our hungry packs near the fire-land, do nothing to aid us at our time of need. Stay and keep your language and your history for all the good it will do you when others join together as friends and allies, making sacrifices of love that have the potential to bring about changes on your behalf, changes that will never happen if you just sing about them and walk away."

Humphrey stepped back, the circle of leaders silent and scowling.

"And you, human child, what do you think?" asked the strongest dog. "Is this conflict, your race, worth sticking our necks out for, worth sacrificing many of the things that are of most importance to us?"

It was not meant to be an insulting question, only an honest one.

Pietre pressed his lips together and stuffed his paper into his pocket. "The humans," he began, "are not always as honorable as the dogs. We are a race that sometimes abandons its own in a way the dogs never would, a race that is cowering in a way the dogs never are, a race that sometimes uses each other in a way the dogs never would." He looked down. "And yet we, more than any other races, have shown a willingness to join with others, stick our own necks out for others, and allow others into our midst, even when they have been cast out from their own. We are a race that harms, but also forgives; a race that understands that sometimes to gain something, something else must be sacrificed. We are far from perfect, good dogs, but part of our strength lies in understanding that."

The singing dog seemed to hum her disapproval, but several of the others were looking at Pietre, deep in thought.

Markhi raised his paw to signal a vote. Each dog cast his ballot and when all were tallied, Markhi sighed. "It is even," he said flatly, looking with sad eyes to Humphrey and Pietre.

"So?" Pietre asked.

"There is nothing we can do," Markhi concluded. "A majority must rule for the dogs as a group, to act."

Humphrey snorted and walked in disgust from the dogs. Pietre knew Humphrey had always wished to be a full-bred dog. Now Humphrey seemed proud that he was not, that he could not be bound by their laws, prejudices, and inactions.

"We will meet again in three days," Markhi told Pietre. "And discuss it further."

Pietre nodded respectfully to each dog, trying to make up for the hole of Humphrey's absence, and left.

THEY MET AT MIDDAY. WOLRIJK HANDED THE LETTER TO KING Crespin. It was written in a lavishly scripted hand—a hand that had clearly spent far too many years in a monastery with not enough to do. The prose was almost as flowering as the handwriting. The writer gave his greetings to the king, his compliments, his apologies for missing the great tournament on account of his oath-bound commitment to a life of silent meditation and humble service.

The king flipped through the pages impatiently, slowing occasionally to nod or scowl. At the back of the pile were two documents: one to seal Lila Friedenszdotter and a foreigner known as Mar together in life. And another to close them in death. Included with these documents was a flat, metallic seal. Crespin held it up to the light, rubbing his thumb over the intricate etching several times before dragging a sharp nail down its center, leaving a thin, jagged slash through the otherwise perfectly preserved disc.

"That will do, General," he said. "You may go."

THEY MET AT DUSK. WITTENDON STOOD BY THE DOOR OF THE CAVE and waited for Sadora's thin shadow to emerge from the bushes. He had secured a position in the Mal that would advance him to the second level, as had Kaxon. His father was pleased. Which no longer concerned Wittendon.

After the prisoner Jager had escaped, his father had burned the smith's clothes and tolled the execution bells. But that wasn't enough for the king. Several of the Königsvaren had been demoted to starve with the Blødguard while each and every human servant who had brought Jager food or been in the smithy to pump bellows or feed the fire had been ordered hanged. Hanged. Wittendon knew his father knew that those servants were not responsible for Jager's escape. But the king wanted his presence to be felt. He wanted to be absolutely sure that any rumors of the escape were silenced. For this over fifty innocent humans would die as soon as the Mal was over.

Wittendon had always known his father to be strict and immovable, but he had never considered him rash or purposefully cruel. Now Wittendon realized that his father could be both. Wittendon did not know the servants who would be hanged, but he had seen them bringing food to Jager, sometimes sharing a laugh when they thought no one was looking. He had seen several of them help the smith feed metal into the crucible above the fire and pump the bellows when it had been necessary—the sweat pouring off their gaunt faces, hissing as it hit the fire or the hot floor. And he had seen their faces as they had been walked through the courtyard, their hands tied in rope. They did not know why they were being led to the prisons adjacent to the gallows, only that they would not be able to tell their families where they had gone.

Wittendon sighed. His father was correct about him in one thing. Wittendon had the weakness called pity. And Wittendon was fairly certain that it would do him no good. Yet he couldn't help but step toward it instead of away. To show the blades to Sadora would be the last step, the final treason against his father, his race. It would begin the process to "level the field" as Zinnegael had put it. Level. That was how Wittendon had felt with Jager when he had freed him—not superior as he'd been taught to feel toward the humans, not inferior as his father and his kind had often made him feel. And yet to lead Sadora here—it could change everything—his people, his position, his beautiful city. Wittendon paced nervously in front of the cave. Being level with the human Jager had felt more right than anything he'd ever felt in his land. And yet the right thing, Wittendon realized, would come at a price.

Sadora arrived shortly and without a sound. "You have found them?" she asked, her voice so full of wonder and surprise that Wittendon wasn't sure if he should be gratified or insulted.

"Yes," he answered, holding up a branch that blocked the mouth of the tunnel so she could step through.

"And they lie here, unguarded," she asked.

"Guarded no longer," he replied, swatting at a bug and not bothering to elaborate.

"You are a mystery to me," she said at last.

Wittendon wasn't surprised. Lately he had become a mystery to himself.

Sadora stepped carefully through the low mouth of the cave and then walked ahead of Wittendon and his torch by several paces, unencumbered by memory or trauma. Wittendon followed slowly, surprised at the dread he still felt in the tunnel—not the deep foreboding of his prior fear, but a cautiousness that came from knowing what had lain ahead. The sludge turned to pebbled bits and suddenly Sadora let out a scream. She stood in front of the skeleton, felt the bleach white rock under her feet, the worms, the death. She turned, grabbing Wittendon by one arm as if to pull him away. "The myth," she hissed. "It is the Tunnel of the Mördare. It is death."

"No," he said. "Not anymore." He held her arms firmly in his hands so she would not run. He couldn't help but enjoy the way her soft humanish skin felt under his fingertips, especially in the near darkness. He stepped back to shake away the feeling and she stepped back, still trembling.

"How?" she asked in a whisper.

"Oddly enough—through a lot of brainless risk and a human-made pick," he responded.

Her forehead furrowed as though she was trying to remember something. Wittendon found himself fighting the urge to touch the line at the bridge of her nose. *She is not the same girl as you thought her to be*, he reminded himself, striding forward. "You may shift if you wish, though there is no need."

Behind him he felt her body ripple and grow, absorbing more of the light and air. He shifted too, not liking the feeling of being shorter and weaker than she. She walked forward and took his elbow. "Forgive me," she said, seeming embarrassed. "I feel as though the marrow in my bones has turned to cream and sugar."

"You are forgiven," he said, leading her through the tunnel and pausing at the point where it opened into the great room. There was no blackness, no haunted green haze, no misty voices shaking with scornful laughter. But there was a single low hum that Wittendon was sure had not been there before. It gave him pause.

Fortunately so.

The blade whizzed past him as his foot crossed the threshold.

CHAPTER 44

Sadora stepped aside with so much speed that it seemed the blade hadn't quite surprised her. Wittendon was surprised. When last he left this room everything was docile and lifeless. Now eleven of the long blades of Grey hovered in the air pointed at them.

With a quick movement of her hand and a muttered word, Sadora lit each torch in the great room, the one in Wittendon's hand blazing so high and thick he had to hold it away from his body to keep from being singed. In the brightened room, he noticed that the blades were not pointed at *them*; they were pointed at *her*.

Slowly she unsheathed a narrow sword. The long tips of Grey shook like angry snakes. Two flew at her. She struck one with the blade and knocked it into the other, but not before four others were released as though shot from giant, invisible bows.

Wittendon finally came to his senses. He drew his sword, grateful he had brought it. He cut each of the blades from their wooden shafts and they fell to the earth, but only for a moment. As seven more hurtled toward Sadora, the four on the ground reformed. Only one remained in place, and for some reason that made Wittendon more nervous.

"I need," Sadora said, panting and striking as though she were swatting at flies, "two minutes. Can you give me that?"

Wittendon nodded, swinging just as wildly with his sword. Eleven blades gathered together in a clump of deadly metal pointed at Sadora. Wittendon could hear them move before he saw them. Quickly, he jumped in front of Sadora. Each blade stabbed through his flesh with the usual sickening sucking noise. Wittendon still wasn't used to it.

Sadora gasped. If she had been the lady in waiting he had once thought her to be, she would have fainted. As it was she held her arms above her head and stood perfectly still.

Wittendon felt his skin close, forcing the blades out with a pop that might have been funny if Sarak's sister wasn't in mortal danger.

Again the long tips of Grey hovered, preparing their attack, but Sadora didn't move. She faced them with her arms held high, her face and neck exposed, her eyes closed. They buzzed and shot toward her but just as they did, she shouted out a word—ancient and beautiful, thick and terrible. The word sprang forth like a weapon. The blades halted, shuddered, and burst—shards of the Grey raining through the air like sharpened hail.

Wittendon held his hands over her head and pulled her face and body into his, surrounding her as much as possible with his limbs and head. Enough scratches from the shards could still destroy her.

"It is not over," she whispered into his chest. "The worst is not begun and I have nothing more with which to fight it."

Behind her on the wall hung the last remaining blade. It creaked from its position like an old man moving from his bed. Even as it rose to the air the shards at their feet began to reassemble. It would take longer this time, but in less than a quarter of an hour all the blades would face them again.

Sadora held her weapon by her side and began whispering incantations—some wild and quick, some slow and complex. None halted the blade of Grey now pointed at her heart. She swung at it and it moved away from her with such speed that Wittendon could barely see it move. She sweated and panted, chanting and stabbing until after several minutes her voice fell silent. The blades at their feet were rejoining to their wooden shafts.

"Move away," Sadora shouted to Wittendon as the eleven sprang again into the air and the twelfth dove straight at her heart. Impulsively, she closed her fingers around the locket just as the blade pierced her hand and bore into the metal of the pendant on the way to her heart. She stumbled back at the force of the blow, shrinking into her flesh form, and screaming at the pain in her hand. Then, at once the eleven spears fell to the ground and in another moment the one at her chest did too.

Wittendon ran to her expecting to catch her as she fell dying, but she stood—silent and stunned. Slowly, she took her hand from the locket, blood flowing from the gash at her palm's center. The locket at her chest was a mangled mass of metal, but the skin beneath it had not even a scratch.

Wittendon stepped back and she stared at it. With her free hand, she tore a sleeve from her cloak and wrapped it tightly around her hand.

Then she bent to the earth and picked up the fallen weapon. She knocked the end to the ground and the eleven remaining spears stood upright like slender soldiers at her command.

"You," she said to Wittendon without looking at him, "are a Greylord."

"Yes," he said. "And you?"

She turned to him, her skin glowing golden white like the inside of a flame. "I am the oldest born of the last surviving elder—your father's mortal enemy."

"Well that explains a few things—like why all the spears were enchanted to attack you."

With a swoop of her hand, she gathered the blades to her.

"But this part?" Wittendon said, gesturing to the now-obedient weapons.

"For this part," Sadora said. "I have only a guess." To herself she murmured, "Close to my heart indeed." She fingered the mangled locket.

Looking to Wittendon she said, "Growing up I had no idea who I was. When I was quite young and my nanny died, I was given three commissions: to always wear this locket, to remember my name, and to obey my brother as though he was the oldest. I didn't like the last nearly as much as the first, but I did my best to fulfill this dying instruction.

"And then ten months ago, I began to wonder if I was going mad. I always felt as though I was being followed, saw strange shadows cross my path, noticed cat-like statues where I was sure none had been. To appease the haunting of my mind I started to research the extinction of the cats, which led me to notice the seeming extinction of other lines within our own race. It was a bit shocking—the families of Veranderen who sometimes vanished without a trace."

Sadora pressed on her wounded hand. The blood had begun to soak through her wrapping. "I became involved with the Septugant rebellion; I met more cats than I ever could have imagined. And then very recently while researching metals, these blades, and several other things in the dingiest wing of your father's libraries, I found a portrait. The canvas was torn and dirty, the frame broken in half, but it was clearly the Circle of Elders and at its center stood a man who wore on his robes a clasp—I did not connect the fact that the metals were the same—but the clasp bore the exact same crest as the locket I've worn since my infancy."

She held her hand above her head and sat down, looking pale. "It could have been a fluke; this locket could have been a bauble purchased by my mother at some ancient shop in our land to the north. But the eyes of the man in that portrait—it was like looking into Sarak's face."

"Then this metal," Wittendon said, sitting beside her and reaching out to finger the locket at her neck, "is Pallium—the same that deflected the blade the first time. But—" Wittendon paused. "Tomar did not overcome the blade."

"No." she said softly. "He jumped from a window and fled. Your father called the blade back. But today Crespin was not here to do so.

The blade found its mark and bore with all its strength into that mark. But its strength was not sufficient. Pallium is a metal with the strange property that it can contain or deflect many other powers. I, with my accidental shield, overcame Crespin's blade of Grey. As such, it—and the eleven blades connected to it—are mine." The blade hummed again, but this time almost in pleasure.

"We should go," she said, standing.

When she did, the blood drained from her face and she quickly sat down again. "Of course the Grey is still the cursed Grey," she said, nursing her pierced hand.

"Let me look," Wittendon said gently.

"I'm not sure you should unwrap—" she began, but he was already removing the makeshift bandage. The wound still flowed in lines of red that showed no signs of clotting. He frowned, touching her palm. She winced, but let him. With the rag, he wiped the blood from her palm as best he could, holding the back of her hand gently.

"I'm sorry," he said. "I really thought there was no danger left in this room." He pressed his other hand against her palm, hoping he could exert enough pressure to slow the blood flow.

Her hand was hot, but the fingers were soft and smooth. He found he liked having them wrapped in his own large hand.

"It is not your fault," she said. "I knew what the blades could do, though I underestimated their strength—a mistake my father never would have made."

Wittendon pressed firmly against both sides of her hand. "I could carry you to Zinnegael. She will know how to mend it."

"Wait," Sadora said. "I think what you're doing is helping. The pressure seems to be slowing the blood. Just let's sit here for a few moments before we move again."

Maybe she was captain of a rebel force; maybe she'd tricked Wittendon into the tunnels the first time and then asked him to do a dangerous, nearly impossible task; maybe she was his father's sworn enemy. But he was in a dim room sitting close and holding the hand of a beautiful Veranderah he'd been interested in since he'd thought to have interest in such things. She'd asked him to wait. Wittendon wasn't an idiot. He held her; and waited.

Her smooth hair pressed into his chin and he could feel her breath against his chest. It *was* growing steadier and stronger. He uncapped one hand, venturing a peek at her wound, and stared. He'd expected to see the huge hole, torn flesh, congealing blood. Instead, the blood was gone and a thin sheet of skin had sealed over the wound.

"A little gruesome, is it," she asked, trying to get a peek.

He moved one hand off of hers and she gasped. Carefully he placed three fingers over the spot where the Grey had pierced her. The tips of his fingers shimmered as her skin thickened into a firm white scar.

"Stop," she said abruptly.

Wittendon pulled one hand away from hers, feeling embarrassed.

"I wish," she began, tracing the shimmering scar. "I wish to remember this day. Don't make the scar vanish completely."

Obediently, Wittendon took his other hand off hers. She held it up to the light of the torch and turned it right then left. "Who knew such things were possible?"

"Not me," Wittendon mumbled.

She smiled. "Wittendon, lord of the Grey," she said. "This is amazing." She looked into his face with the glee of a child and the wonder of a woman.

Wittendon could not help it. He leaned down and kissed her.

THE SPEARS FOLLOWED SADORA OUT OF THE TUNNEL, LIKE DUCKLINGS after their mother. Wittendon held her other hand—the one without the scar—and traced the fingers with his thumb.

They walked in silence until they had passed the bones and Wittendon finally said, "What was the word you uttered? The word that shattered the other blades?"

"My name," she said without explanation. "In the ancient language, the name I was told not to forget."

"Good thing you didn't," Wittendon said and paused. "It was well chosen—beautiful, dangerous, resolute."

"Yes," she said without embarrassment or pride, and then added abruptly. "Does it bother you? My destiny set on your father's destruction?"

"Well," he said slowly. "Every relationship has its bumps."

CHAPTER 45

Pietre stood near Humphrey, surveying the armies on a field below. Zinnegael said they marched in three days. She said it was imperative that the attack occur on the night when the moon filled into a great disc of summer light. The night that happened to be the last night of the Motteral Mal. Somehow, attacking an enormous force when they were strongest, gathered together, and armed to the teeth wasn't the most appealing battle strategy to Pietre.

Zinnegael came up beside him and looked over the men on the field. There were also several women and even a few older children practicing with sticks and swords. "A motley crew, aren't we?" she said like she was proud of that fact.

Humphrey laughed and trotted down to the field to help a young boy select a weapon. Pietre wanted to laugh too, but the sound just wouldn't come out. The closer they came to battle, the easier it was to see why the dogs were so cautious with their alliances. Pietre looked down at the weapons and troops. The fact that they were together was largely his doing. The men and women carried knives and pitchforks, spears re-fashioned, and old swords sharpened and cleaned. Yet to look at them Pietre knew that they might as well have been holding children's paper fans for all the good it would do them; and guilt swept through him. Had he gathered his people and lined them up like cows at the slaughter barn? Turning to Zinnegael he blurted, "Why the last night of the Mal?"

"Because," she said, "despite how things look on the outside, there is much hope. It lies, unfortunately, with two unlikely not-quite-allies and some very fortuitous timing."

"Great," Pietre mumbled.

"It will be," she said, winking. "Just watch."

The pitch black Ellza—her shoulder patched since collapsing the uppermost tunnel—came and stood beside her mistress. "Another group of fighters has arrived, my lady."

"Very good," Zinnegael said. "Sent by Sadora?"

"Yes."

"Well, then, I must go and greet them."

Zinnegael and Ellza left, and Pietre stood on the hill—happy to be alone for a moment in the silence. After a few minutes, however, Pietre started to feel as though someone stood behind him, watching, although he had heard no one approach. He turned, expecting to see one of the messenger cats and was surprised instead by Alekas's pretty cream-colored face.

"Good morrow, she-hound," Pietre said, bowing slightly. "Have you come to join us?"

"I am neither brave nor particularly cunning," she began. "And my greatest asset has always been one of kindness." She looked out over the field of sparring humans. "Which I am not sure is the best strength at times such as these. But I have news for Humphrey—ill-timed I'm afraid, but news that must be shared."

Pietre nodded to the place on the field where Humphrey stood, just as Savah came to join Pietre on the hill. Savah stared as the dog departed, purring in a way that hummed like gossip. "She does not plan to fight, does she?" the cat asked.

"No, actually. She does not. But why do you state it like that?"

"My boy," the cat laughed. "I suppose you are too young and too human to see it, but the she-dog is thick with child."

Pietre gaped at the field below, watching Humphrey jump away from a club leveled at him by the young boy practicing.

"Now come," the cat said. "My mistress awaits."

CHAPTER 46

Round two of the Motteral was grueling—some said the most grueling of all. It lacked the energy of the first round and the desperation of the last. It was fought in wolken form, but without weapon or magic. This round relied on speed, skill, and a bit of improvisation. It also relied on teeth—a lot of teeth.

It was teeth that were facing Wittendon right now. The canine teeth were bloodied and looked so barbed Wittendon wondered if the large Verander in front of him had actually sharpened them. His breath was bad too.

The Verander pulled his head back, rearing to strike like a snake. Wittendon let his body relax, counting slowly to himself. *One...two...* and then he jumped up, funneling all his energy into his legs. He pounded into his opponent, knocking the breath out so that he staggered back. But it was only for a moment. The Verander ran toward Wittendon, his head down like a hammer. Wittendon, still recovering from the last impact, took the hit in the forehead and moaned. His thoughts went foggy—drifting to a song his mother used to sing to him that seemed suddenly the perfect thing to be humming in the middle of a potentially life-threatening tournament. "When the sun sinks low, and the moon shines high," he murmured, standing unsteadily. It wasn't until he got to his feet and his head began to clear that he realized the other Verander should have been on his chest and bearing down on his neck. Looking around, still seeing stars at the corners of his eyes, Wittendon saw the Verander, lying unmoving on his side with a small pool of blood forming under his snout. The arbitrators at the side were counting, "Nine...ten." One raised his hand and the round was declared.

Wittendon went to the Verander and sang a few more lines. "When the night goes black and the stars retire. It's then you'll go to sleep." He doubted it would have been much appreciated if his opponent had been conscious, but maybe it would sweeten his dreams until the healers got him back on his feet.

Sadora waited for Wittendon at the side of the field. "Fortunately your head is harder than anyone anticipates," she said as they walked to the dinner cart.

Wittendon smiled, still a little fuzzy-headed, and followed her.

On their way to the dinner cart, they passed Kaxon. Wittendon gave him a thumbs up. Kaxon glanced at him and returned the gesture, though it was distracted; and his brother's smile—usually one that ate up half his face—looked more like a limp fish making a final squirm before its death. Wittendon wondered why. His brother had done just as well as he had, better even. At this point Kaxon had several more points, even though they'd won an equal number of rounds. Perhaps Kaxon was just not as far ahead as he had hoped or expected to be. Or maybe he dreaded facing Wittendon as much as Wittendon dreaded the thought of facing him.

SARAK STOOD IN THE PRACTICE ROOM ALONE. ALONE WAS SOMETHING he was getting used to, but that didn't make it any nicer. Wittendon and Sadora were now always together or entirely missing—which was pretty much the same thing. Sarak wondered where their hiding place was. He wondered it with a little resentment and then felt guilty about that. Hadn't he wanted them to be happy? Hadn't he felt terrible for

Wittendon when it seemed the whole thing might not work out? Sarak swung his sword, feeling it grow hot and cold with his shifting feelings. *Control it*, he thought to himself, *and your feelings will follow.* He swung the blade steadily, so hot it seemed to sizzle away the moisture that hung in the air. Silently, he moved through his evening practice, legs bent then straight, arms flowing from his body like water dragons through the sea. It felt good. It had always felt good. No wonder he'd become skilled enough to train a prince—he'd spent too much of his life alone to be anything else. The thought gave him some comfort. And Wittendon was doing well in the Mal. Surprisingly well.

Sarak spun through the room, always knowing where his feet would land, always anticipating the weight of his sword, the place it would strike if he had had an opponent to face. The sword, the magic, the control—like a dance, they soothed him, made him feel he had a place in this world, this world that otherwise would have rejected a nameless orphan. Sadora had her looks, her fashions, her laugh. He had a steady hand and a talent with magic that surprised even the king. Sarak had not really wanted to fight in the Mal. He had always known that as one without a confirmed parentage he would not be able to and so the desire had never taken him; he was one to flow with his lot in life instead of kicking against it. And yet an opportunity to prove himself at the Mal—to show himself as the powerful Verander he was, to be one with his people in a way that had, as an orphan, eluded him— he couldn't help but feel a pang for the chance. As it was he would have to shine through Wittendon. Something he didn't begrudge exactly, but found that he wasn't cherishing either.

Sarak tossed his sword to the side of the room where it landed perfectly in its spot on the weapons wall. He'd done it hundreds of times and it made him smile every time. Quietly he took a grandiose bow, only to be jolted upright by the sound of clapping.

"Most impressive," the king said as Sarak fell to one knee, bowing. "You fight like a king or one nearly destined to be so."

"Thank you, my lord," Sarak said, not daring to rise. Indeed, the king did not release him as he usually did with a wave of his hand.

"Your work with my son," the king continued. "It is admirable."

The king paced tight circles around the kneeling Sarak. "Although it remains to be seen in the coming round whether you've managed to coax any hint of magic out of his stubborn fingers."

Sarak tried to smile, but felt like his cheeks were wobbling. "Yes, my lord, it remains to be seen."

The king stopped in his pacing and looked down at Sarak. For one brief moment, Sarak thought the king would raise his flaming staff and crush him like an unwanted mouse in the pantry, but all at once the king relaxed, bidding Sarak rise, and clapped him on the back as if in congratulation. "Yes, child, you've done quite well. Let's hope it continues."

King Crespin smiled—his sharp wolven canines pressing down over his lower teeth—and left.

Sometimes, Sarak thought, it wasn't the worst thing to be an orphan. Wittendon had a father. And his father was terrifying.

CHAPTER 47

S he offered him quiche.

"The full moon," Pietre began, ignoring Zinnegael's tiny plates and mugs of tea. "Why is it necessary for our attack?"

She pushed a plate to him, along with a little tin fork and napkin. He pushed them away. "I am not the only one with these questions," he said. "The troops ache from days of practice and nights on hard ground. They begin to long for their wives' stew almost more than freedom itself."

"Such is the way with men," she said. "Now have some food and a cup of tea because my answer is neither short nor easy."

She took a bite herself, chewing slowly before she began. "This land was not always thus. In the time before our time, a small sun shone, blinding and white."

"Yes, I know," Pietre responded, ignoring his meal.

Zinnegael unfolded his napkin for him, then dropped three sugar cubes into his tea and gave it a stir. "Do you?" she asked. "In human lore, there is much talk of the hot, white sun, but little known of the moon that also shone. The moon hung off of its earth, which hung off of that sun—connected by its mass, its force. This moon reflected light only because of the grace and majesty of that powerful sun."

Pietre nodded.

"This ancient moon, though bright, could only be seen in the darkness of night and then only when the sun was in position to bestow her light to it."

"The moon was not always seen?" Pietre asked.

"Correct," Zinnegael said. "In fact, the moon was often *not* seen. When the worlds were changed and the Veranderen came to power, all of that changed. The humans became weakened by the dullness of the sun just as the Veranderen power steadied and grew constant like the moon."

Pietre picked at his breakfast.

"The stone must be placed at the summer solstice in the year of the Motteral Mal because it is only then that the powers of moon and sun balance equally in the sky. The moon at its fullest point, the day at its longest. The *Zonnesteen* can be empowered only as the sun is setting and the moon rising, both giving equal light to the earth. It is then, during this moment of symmetry, when a Greylord's power is greatest. After that, the stone can be placed in the Sacred Tablet by one of pure heart, thereby bestowing the worlds with power to change. Man will have the potential to rise in power becoming level with shifter—"

"Anybody home?" a voice broke in.

Zinnegael turned to see Wittendon's tall frame stooping through her door, followed by Sadora's willowy figure. Pietre scowled and turned away.

Zinnegael stopped in her story and shooed them out. "Be a couple of dears and wait outside in the kitchen. You'll find a tart just about ready to come out of the oven."

Zinnegael turned again to Pietre. "In the last changing of the suns," she said, "the werewolves held almost all the power. They held the stone, empowered the stone, placed the stone. Our current world reflects that imbalance. Now there is need for help from all the races. Now there is a chance for something better. The Veranderen and humans have always worked best and been strongest together, and with the other races, but only when unified by will. So it was with the Sourcestone at the very beginning before it was corrupted. So it can be with the Sourcestone again—empowered by one race and placed by another with the help of both dog and wolf. Such a change *could* create a world with more power and peace than we have ever known."

"*Could?*" Pietre asked, his face hard.

"Of course it would take a good deal of cooperation."

"Is cooperation just another word for the humans doing the bidding of the stronger races?"

"In this case," she replied. "I'd say the humans have a good deal more to gain than anyone else."

"Only because we are on the lowest rung of the ladder already."

"Indeed," she said. "But the truth still remains that others will step down somewhat while the humans step up."

"As they should," Pietre said a little harshly.

"Which doesn't change the fact that the Veranderen rebels have much to lose through this upheaval. As do the dogs. As do the cats and even the wolves. While the humans stand only to gain."

She paused, puttering with the quiche. "If only we could find the stone—"

Pietre stopped scowling and looked up sharply. There was something in her tone, something distinctly cat-like. When she met his gaze, he expected to see her with eyes like slits—slits that let in only the amount of light that was exactly necessary. But when he looked, the eyes were the same round discs of green and copper they always were.

"Tell me of the stone," Pietre said, feeling afraid to hear it.

Without blinking she replied, "It is a stone of perfect roundness. Dull when left to itself, it begins to glimmer and glisten only when handled—polishing to a shine that could rival even the glow of the fullest moon. Originally passed through those known to the werepeople as Greylords, it was lost soon after all known Greylords were thought to have been eliminated. Unlike the Grey, the Sourcestone does not discriminate. It will devour the hand of a human or melt the bones of a shifter. The only ones who can touch it are the Lords of the Grey and those humans with pure motive, kind heart, and deepest love."

Pietre stood. He was glad he hadn't eaten much quiche as now his stomach reeled. "No," he said. "It is the last gift from my father and you ask me to give it to you."

"Oh no," she replied. "I ask you to do something much harder. I ask you to give it to the one who took your father in the first place."

Pietre plunked back down into his chair as though he'd been punched.

Wittendon walked slowly into the room. "Your walls are thin, prophetess."

"Yes," she said. "I know."

Pietre held his weapon tight in his hand and pushed past Wittendon, toward the door, but before he could leave, Humphrey pounded through, nearly knocking him down and not even noticing. "You must grant her safe haven, my lady, you must."

Zinnegael stirred her tea, raising an eyebrow. "Who, good dog?" she said, though something in the lines of her forehead seemed to know the answer.

"She," he barked desperately. "She to whom I have been joined. I told no one," he said. "I considered it a matter between her and me alone. But now—" He stopped to take a breath. "Now she bears our young and she must"—he looked pointedly at Pietre and then at Zinnegael—"she must be granted safe haven."

Zinnegael continued to stir. Pietre watched her. When he had first met the witch, all he could see were her disconcerting, mismatched eyes. Now he barely noticed them and saw instead a face that was simply Zinnegael. As she sat stirring her tea, Pietre noticed that stirring was something she always did when strange or troubling news came to light. Stirring was something she did, Pietre realized, when she was nervous.

"Have you told her of the blood lines from which you descend?" Zinnegael asked.

Pietre thought it an odd question considering the fact that Humphrey hadn't even told Zinnegael.

The dog-wolf looked at her for one long minute. "Yes," he said. "But only just now."

"And how has she taken the news?"

Humphrey paused again, seeming to think about this for the first time. "With increased concern for the pups. And for me."

This seemed to worry Humphrey as he said it. But Zinnegael seemed pleased by the answer. "In that case, she is welcome here. None will or can harm her here. Not yet anyway."

PIETRE LET ALEKAS HAVE HIS BED THAT NIGHT. SHE DECLINED IT OVER and over until Pietre said he would be sleeping on the floor no matter what, so she could waste the soft mattress or not. He lay on the floor near the bed, staring at the stars through the thin ceiling, an opaque blanket of what seemed to be flower petals that served as Zinnegael's roof. He had known these constellations all his life. Would it hurt so much to know them a few years longer if he did not surrender the stone?

He fell asleep counting the stars and woke with a burning sensation in his hand. In his sleep he had grasped his weapon and begun to swing it. It soared in the air above his head, but with each whir of the sling, his hand hurt more. He stood quickly, trying to release it from his grip, only to find that he couldn't. It burned through his hand and up his arm. Soon the bedposts had burst into flame and the room was quickly consumed. Alekas fled, crying from pain of labor. The fire spread to the gardens around the hut. It ate its way through the trees, murdering his countrymen—their shouts rising up like curses to his ears. It tore through the land, finding his father and mother, leaving ashen silhouettes in their wake.

Humphrey jumped out at once, confronting the fire, looming above it, but even he was not strong enough. In moments Humphrey was gone, as was Alekas. Her tiny pups cried for her and then screamed as the flames engulfed their innocent, blind bodies. Still, Pietre could not release the stone. He looked down at himself and saw a man patched together like the general Wolrijk—with ugly scars that seemed to be all that held him in place.

Pietre woke sweating. His hands were hot and swollen even though the weapon lay far from him, glowing in its makeshift sheath.

THE NEXT MORNING PIETRE WENT TO WITTENDON AND DROPPED THE stone in his lap. It didn't burst into flame or melt the shifter's bones as Pietre had hoped it would. Wittendon looked up, about to speak, but the boy had turned away, walking toward the woods.

CHAPTER 48

W olrijk waited near the edge of the wood. Waiting was something he'd mastered long ago. He expected the king would one day be surprised at how well he had learned that forced patience. It had allowed him to trick the foolish Kaxon into opening a book he never should have seen and then to commission a blade Wolrijk hoped to make useful to himself. It had allowed him to see the Veranderen prince set the Greysmith free. It had given him time and the element of surprise in capturing the smith once he returned home.

The young boy, of course, was the reason the Night Hunter had captured both father and mother. Revenge was not something Wolrijk was willing to shortchange. But after being defeated twice by the boy's simple weapon, revenge had grown into something more. Wolrijk suspected that after he killed the boy, the stone would be surprisingly useful—perhaps even more than Kaxon's extra-long blade. And tomorrow—the final day of the Mal—Wolrijk needed strength. The wolf had followed the child's scent from the village to the verdant wood of the witch, and skirted now near the cliffs at its eastern edge. Wolrijk gritted his teeth. The boy had caused him no little grief, but now the child would be easy. For he often wandered.

Wolrijk walked to the herb he had discovered years ago. It was a humble little plant that could mask a wolf's scent perfectly. Now it gave Wolrijk an advantage in this rebel-filled corner of the land. None had detected him and he was sure the boy wouldn't either. Wolrijk rolled once more in the herb before finding cover in the bushes to wait. Late in the afternoon Wolrijk saw the boy walking alone.

Pietre passed Wolrijk's hiding point and stopped to sniff at the air as though a familiar scent had caught him. He turned, looked around, then stooped down to examine the broad-leafed herb that grew near the edge of a steep, rocky drop above the River Rylen. The boy moved the leaves to the side, noticing that the rotherem had been crushed, and looked up in alarm.

The wolf leapt from the shadows, his energy and teeth directed at the sling at the child's side. "Empty," the wolf hissed, circling Pietre. "Where is it hiding, man-pup?"

"I lost it," Pietre said.

"Filthy liar," Wolrijk growled; yet he could not feel the power of the deadly metal anywhere near the child. "No matter," Wolrijk said. "That will make my original goal that much easier." He sprang at Pietre, expecting an instant victory, but the boy leaped to the side more quickly than Wolrijk had thought possible for a human boy.

"You stand, unarmed, before a cliff," the Night Hunter said as he ran at Pietre again.

Pietre stepped backward, picking up several rocks, which he threw at the enormous wolf. The animal shook them off. "Do you expect to wound me with a handful of stones—I who was torn apart from top to bottom long before your time?"

Pietre picked up another handful and threw them. "Wouldn't be the first time a pebble disabled you."

The wolf growled, wishing to tear him to pieces instead of simply pushing him over a cliff, but he could hear footsteps in the distance and was not inclined to get caught alone by a pack of dogs or even a band of rebel humans. He ran a third time at the boy, plowing into him. Pietre held to the wolf's ears. Wolrijk bit at his face, tearing the lobe of Pietre's ear before pushing him backwards and over the precipice.

~

PIETRE SCREAMED, TUMBLING DOWN THE STEEP FACE OF ROCK. HE grabbed at stones and twigs, tasted the dirt and minerals of the dust rising all around him, saw the colors of the earth for the millions of variations they were instead of the simple reds, browns, and greens he usually noticed. Below him he heard a sound like the whizz of an arrow. Seconds later his hand caught on the hilt of a dagger whose tip was embedded miraculously into the side of the cliff. Pietre clung to it, his body cut and bleeding.

He wondered how long it, or he, could hold. He wasn't strong enough to pull himself up and, even if he had been, the rocks above him were too loose for foot or hand holds. His fingers ached and the muscles in his hand and forearm began to tremble. Beneath him he could hear the waters of the river hitting the rocky cliffside—like the beating of ancient funeral drums.

His bicep and shoulder burned and he could feel his grip loosen. For the first time, he was glad he had given the stone to the prince. He was glad his parents were already gone and would not grieve him. He was glad Humphrey had Alekas and a soon-to-be brood of pups.

Pietre closed his eyes as his trembling fingers slipped when suddenly his wrist and shoulder seared in pain. Pietre hung in the air, held in place by the large prince in wolken form. The prince stood, balanced like a mountain goat, on an impossibly small outcropping of rock.

"My arm..." Pietre moaned.

In another minute, Pietre's body hit the ground above the precipice and he groaned. His arm felt like it hung from the wrong place, his wrist throbbed, and his ear bled. Wittendon climbed the cliff with impossible lightness.

He took the boy by the arm and held Pietre's body firmly while, with a sudden movement he jerked and re-placed the boy's shoulder. Pietre howled at the pain, then sat on the ground, wanting to throw up.

"Here," Wittendon said, tossing the blade beside him and wrapping bandages around a few of Pietre's cuts. "Zinnegael can suture your ear. It's not as bad as it looks."

"Suture?" Pietre asked.

"Put a few stitches in."

"With a needle?"

"Unless you'd rather she used a sword."

Pietre would rather she used some painless type of magic, but he didn't say so in front of the prince.

"Where did you find this dagger?" Wittendon asked, wiping his hands on a clean rag he'd taken from his cloak.

"I didn't," Pietre said. "It hung from the mountainside and I grabbed it."

"You're delirious."

"I am not. It—" Pietre stopped, trying to remember. "It was just there."

Wittendon sat beside him and picked it up, weighting it as though it was familiar. "This?" he asked. "This dagger was hanging from the mountainside?"

"Yes," Pietre said, finally sitting up to look. In a moment he had grabbed it from the prince. "But how?"

"You know it then?"

"It was my father's—found in my home, left at Zinnegael's hut. So how…"

The question hung, just as the blade had—stuck.

"Come," Wittendon said.

They walked together back to the camp near Zinnegael's hut. Pietre polished the dagger with his dirty shirt, and looked carefully for the very first time to the prince's face. The Verander had not shifted back to his flesh form; his face was covered in light gray hair and two fangs rested against his lower teeth. But Pietre noticed that his eyes never really shifted—always a bright steel color—sharp and careful, cool and steady, surprisingly kind.

"Thank you," Pietre said.

Wittendon shrugged. "I'm pretty good with the injured. And the dead. Good thing you didn't *fall* into that category." Wittendon sniggered.

Pietre's mouth crinkled up. "That is possibly the worst pun I have ever heard."

"All in a day's work for a traitor to the king."

"Sounds like a long day," Pietre said, and then after a pause he asked. "How did you know I was there?"

"Young boys are not the only creatures who like to wander into the woods without telling anyone. And I have very good ears."

"What did you hear?"

"I heard a scuffle and a voice I have always disliked."

"Mine?" Pietre asked.

"Of course not," the prince replied.

AT A NARROW POINT OF THE RIVER, THE WHITE WOLF ZINDER SWAM across, then followed a jagged, well-concealed deer path up the side of the cliff.

He rested at the top by the broad-leafed plant before taking a leisurely roll in the rotherem's oily leaves.

He could also hear extremely well. He could throw decently too. Years ago his father had taught him to hold an object in his mouth and toss with the strength of his neck. And years ago, his mother had shown him that even the mighty Grey could not harm him if he first took a sip of the sandy waters of that old river. As for taking things that weren't his—that he had learned after his parents had disappeared. He did it best of all.

He hadn't taken anything for many years, but he'd been gripped by the desire to see the surviving sentinel and when he'd crept into the camp, the blade had been left on a table by a pot of tea. The other wolves would call it madness, but Zinder had felt as though the God of the Sun called to him through that blade, and he'd taken it. Of course, maybe it hadn't been a god at all. Maybe it was simply that he'd known Wolrijk was lurking around these woods as well. Maybe it was not destiny, but a desire calling to him—an increasing urge to undo the things he'd begun to suspect Wolrijk planned to do.

~

THAT EVENING AFTER SUPPER, SADORA MET THE TROOPS WITH PIETRE by her side. Zinnegael was right. Pietre was starting to like her. She had a mind that could organize things—even masses of grumpy, hungry humans—into orderly, competent, intimidating groups that became easily loyal to her.

Tonight as she assembled the troops, twelve spears stood behind her. They stood, Pietre noticed, on their own and seemed to follow Sadora with the same devotion as everyone else.

Quickly, she separated the groups into eleven equal sections, appointing a leader to each. The men she chose as captains were surprisingly different—several were so old Pietre wasn't sure they'd even make it to the gates. The oldest remaining elder from Pietre's village was among them. Some were short, others balding and thin. Only one looked the part of a burly warrior with arms thick as tree branches. But this one had a twitchy eye and stuttered so badly that Pietre wondered how Sadora had ever learned his name.

Sadora stood at the top of a small scaffold and with one gesture raised the spears aloft. "As many of you know, one of our tunnels has been compromised, the noble keeper Winterby dead. Because of this, we have deemed it unsafe to move any of our troops through this or any other passages into the head city. There is but one ancient mine entrance to the hill now—a tunnel so narrow that only the most agile could fit." She looked for a moment to a group of cats lying on the lawn. "I trust that it will come to good use."

Ellza seemed to nod without moving her head or blinking her eyes.

"However," Sadora continued. "The rest of us will have to enter the city in a more usual way. The head city has exactly twelve entrances—remnants from a time when twelve elders ruled this land. The entrances are guarded by twelve Veranderen. On the appointed day and at my signal, each captain will remove the guard from his post with one of

301

these blades." With a gentle crook of her finger she sent eleven blades through the air like arrows to each captain. Pietre was surprised the old ones didn't keel over from heart afflictions, and it did seem that the stuttering one trembled a bit.

"Do not kill the guards if you can help it," Sadora said. "If the cause of the Septugant is to succeed in the long run, we must learn to offer kindness and compassion in return for the cruelty that has often been shown to you."

A few of the men grumbled at that part as Sadora continued, "After the guards have been removed, the gates will open and the troops pour through. We will converge at this area." She pointed to a magical diagram in the air. "Understood?"

The crowds below her roared until she banged her own spear on the scaffolding for silence.

"Sleep men, for tomorrow we march."

CHAPTER 49

Pietre woke as the night tiptoed into morning. Today was the final day of the Motteral Mal. By the time the sun set that evening, they would have converged on the Hill of Motteral, hoping to place a stone and change the world. He and Humphrey would be leading the troops up the hill. If Wittendon could just win, it would be easy, well easier. But Zinnegael was bustling about with teacups and leaves—and when she looked down into the pattern the leaves had formed in her cup, she sighed.

Pietre pursed his lips.

"Bad news?" he asked.

"Depends on your definition," she said. "Just be prepared for a lot of things."

"Could you maybe be a little more specific?"

"Well," she said, looking into her tea, "there are madmen. Oh, yes, definitely that. There will be a veritable deluge of crazy werewolves wandering around."

"Great," Pietre muttered.

"And traitors, of course. You don't need prophetic tea for that— you can always expect them."

"Okay," Pietre said, feeling like he really wanted to go back to bed.

"Oh, and Pietre," she concluded. "Just be sure to get the stone from Wittendon."

"Why?"

"So you can place it, of course."

"Why would I place it?" Pietre asked. "What about Wittendon?"

"Wittendon is to empower it. A human must place it."

"Wittendon will be stronger and faster and better positioned for placing it."

"If Wittendon places it, then nothing will change." Zinnegael paused. "Well, perhaps Wittendon himself would change, but not for the better. A werewolf must empower it and a human must place it. You must learn to work together."

"We are working together," Pietre said. "We'll be on the hill, protecting his back."

"He will not need you to protect his back," Zinnegael said. "He will need you to place the stone. And though he may not seem to appreciate it at the time, he will eventually. You watch."

Pietre opened his mouth, then shut it, then opened it again and said, "Isn't there a prophecy or something? My mother said in the old stories there was a great one needed."

"Yes, dear," Zinnegael said. "That's you."

Pietre actually laughed. "That's not me."

"You'll have to do," she replied, pulling several rolls from the oven.

"But not just anyone can fulfill a prophecy."

"Why on earth not?"

Pietre shook his head. "Because that's not the way they work. I mean why have a prophecy if anybody can just walk up and fulfill it?"

"I did not say anyone could," Zinnegael corrected.

"Yes, you did."

"I said anyone who would could."

"Stop rhyming," Pietre said, his voice rising.

Quietly, Zinnegael looked him in the eyes. "Prophecies are often there not to tell us what will happen, but to tell us what can happen—to show us our potential, what could be if we work hard enough. Not to mention the fact that a prophecy isn't usually fulfilled by one person. It takes a village to be the chosen one, that's what I always say."

"That makes no sense," Pietre said.

"Well, fortunately for me, I did not say it made sense, only that it was true," Zinnegael replied. "A prophecy is naught but some beads of words strung together—preferably in rhyming couplets. Its fulfillment, if fulfillment is to be, is a lot of work by a lot of people willing to see it through to the end. Even if the end is bitter. Or, one could hope, bittersweet."

"There is no great one," Pietre said, putting the idea together as though tasting a new food and not really liking it.

"Oh, there are plenty of great ones," Zinnegael said. "The trick is finding one willing to do the job." With that Zinnegael hurried him out of the door of her hut, tucking a crescent roll into his jacket pocket as though he was going on a day hike, not marching to his potential death.

CHAPTER 50

Kaxon waited at the base of the hill, as the dawn spread its purple fingers across the sky. His palms were sweating and he gripped his scythe harder than necessary. He didn't get it. Even at age eighteen, his life hadn't exactly been pristine. He'd learned to sneak out of his bedroom at age ten, pulled pranks, told lies, passed most of his school exams with a little "help," and of course there were his productive hours in the kitchen with the wenches. But the long-tipped Grey scythe was different—a step up from his usual crimes. It bothered him that this was the first thing in his life that he was perfectly sure both his mother and his father would disapprove of. His father would consider it weak, dishonorable. His mother might have thought so too, but more than that, he imagined that she would worry for the damage such a blade could do. Not that damage was what Kaxon intended to do—not *that* much anyway. He just needed an edge, something to pierce a little deeper and disable his opponents a little quicker.

What he couldn't quite excuse was that he planned to blame Wittendon if he got caught. Wittendon who clapped him on the back every time they passed, Wittendon who would have happily skipped out on the Mal and let Kaxon have it all to himself if the rules had allowed a royal son to bow out.

A bugle sounded and the final ten contestants walked out onto the field for Round Three. Each was adorned in golden mail, the fur of their heads tipped in burgundy paint. Around their necks hung capes of various colors, representing the house and lineage into which they were born. Kaxon and Wittendon both wore shades of red with amber and yellow pictures embossed with magical thread that shifted into different battle scenes as the capes blew in the wind.

A second bugle sounded and a group of ten female Veranderen strode onto the field to remove the capes and grant a kiss. Sadora stood behind Wittendon and whispered something in his ear as her lips brushed his cheek. Kaxon had chosen a curvy brunette who wore too much perfume and couldn't stop giggling at the crowd.

He gripped his scythe tighter.

At last the third bugle sounded. The Veranderen were blindfolded and led to different starting positions at the base of the hill. When all three bugles sounded together, the blindfolds would come off and the hunt would begin.

WITTENDON WAS LED TO A THICKET OF WOODS. THE BLINDFOLD ONLY heightened his other senses. He could hear the crowds at the base of the hill—their voices and cheers pulsing with the fervor of a deadly stampede. He could smell the musty layers of leaf under his feet, a patch of closed moonflower behind him, the lichen on the trees. He could feel the swaying of branches near his face and the shade they provided. He was grateful for that. Several of his opponents, he suspected, were at positions more vulnerable than his—near rocky cliffs, by deafening rivers, in the center of fields baking with morning sunlight.

At once the screams from the crowd hushed and Wittendon's body tingled. For several seconds even the wind seemed to stop and then three lonely notes poured over the hillside.

"Luck," the guide whispered, whisking the cloth from Wittendon's eyes, and running.

Wittendon opened his eyes, expecting—he wasn't sure what—but something terrifying. Instead, he stood on a shady hill—so quiet, so beautiful, so still. For the briefest moment Wittendon wished to forget the Mal, forget his errand with the stone. He wanted only to sit down on a soft blanket with a warm lunch. He realized in another minute that that was the very danger of his position and that it could be just as deadly as the rockiest cliff. Even so he did not immediately move. He needed to hear, needed to feel.

All at once he felt too much. The ground in front of him seized. One of the trees near him lifted its roots and pounced. At least that's how it looked. Wittendon dove to the left so that the thick trunk would not crush him, but as his paw-like hands hit the earth, the ground mounded up around his legs, so heavy and thick he stumbled. More earth rose around him burying all but his face in a shell of mud that hardened instantly. A vine from the fallen tree wrapped around Wittendon's neck and a tall Verander walked from behind where the tree had stood. "It was easy to see that the rumors of the verlorn prince were true," he said. "Still, I did not expect it to be quite so easy. I can only assume you made it this far because of your father's position." The easterner named Koll raised his hand about to send a flare for one of the overseers of the game, but with an intense bite, Wittendon snapped through the vine that surrounded his throat and—summoning all his feelings of courage and strength—he jerked out his arms and legs, cracking the thick casing of earth like a clay toy.

Wittendon thought of his mother, of Sadora, of Sarak—of all that was solid in his life. He thought of the boy Pietre with his steady blue eyes. Wittendon held out his palm to calm the earth in front of him, and then, raising his arms overhead, he used his magic to lift the enormous, fallen tree trunk and throw it at his opponent.

"You should not always believe the rumors you hear."

Koll jumped from the tree though it caught his back paw and Wittendon heard a small crack.

Below them, Wittendon could hear a collective gasp, whispers, and the word 'magic' as it pulsed through the crowd rising into a cheer. So the secret was out. It felt good.

The Verander Koll steadied himself on his good leg, then jerked his scythe from his scabbard and dove toward Wittendon.

Their blades met in a crack as loud as the crashing of the tree and for several minutes they maneuvered through the shady woods, neither able to gain an advantage. Their fight was so well-matched that Wittendon began to feel it was almost meditative—peaceful in its steadiness—just like the wood. The wood. Wittendon focused his energy on it, the calm seductive nature. He thought of walks with Sadora, picnics with his mother, lying on the softest moss for rest in the shade of a giant oak. Rest. He thought intensely of rest, and he gripped his blade. In one quick movement he nicked Koll on the cheek, sending all of his thoughts of peace, fullness, and sleep to the weapon's tip. The Verander staggered back, then fell, curled into a soft slumber, a tiny drop of blood hanging on his cheek like a good-night kiss.

Wittendon touched the wound with his finger so that it would not continue to bleed and whispered, "You deserved worse." Then from his palm, he shot a white flare into the sky. An overseer would come quickly with a group of healers to carry Koll like a baby down the hill. Embarrassing, yes, but in the history of round three defeats, definitely not the worst way to go.

In the distance, Wittendon saw another flare go up—this one in red to indicate a significant injury. No, not the worst way to go at all.

Wittendon walked to the edge of the wood, feeling strong. For a minute, Wittendon thought about how easy it would be to just compete at the Motteral Mal, make his father proud, become a leader of his land, and then grow old and fat. But that minute passed and Wittendon looked up the mountain, to the small overhang where the stone would need to be empowered—the place Zinnegael had called *Steenmacht*. Another flare went up. Three Veranderen down, six to go. Wittendon sheathed his blade and broke into a run.

THE STUTTERING MAN WALKED UP TO THE GATE, HIS HEAD HUNG LOW, A bucket of fish in his left hand, his fishing spear in his right. Masses of humans milled around the gates, awaiting entry. By mid-morning all of the Veranderen and wolves had gotten through and now the humans lingered, papers in hand, hoping for their chance to catch a glimpse of the famed tournament. The stutterer—called Damiott by the old maid-servant who had found him abandoned as a child in the woods—was glad for the crowds. They shielded his own scruffy band from suspicion. Still, he was puzzled at the idea of his own kind eager to watch the match of the Veranderen.

A woman next to him practically giggled in excitement though Damiott considered her well past giggling age. "Can you believe it," she said. "Once every hundred years. I think we're going to get in."

Damiott nodded.

"You know they say the youngest son of the king is breathtakingly handsome," she babbled on. "In flesh form of course. One look," she murmured, "just one. And tales for generations." She sighed in delight.

Damiott looked north for the captain's signal and fidgeted with his bucket.

"Come now," the woman said, moving closer. "Tell me it's not just the most exciting thing of our lifetimes."

Damiott desperately wanted to say, "It's *not* the most exciting thing of our lifetimes," but all that came out was, "N-n-n-Nt. I. I." And then he stopped.

She wandered off muttering, "Of course I'd wind up talking to the village idiot."

Damiott the idiot, he heard chanted in his head, just like it had sounded all those years of his childhood when he had worked cleaning washrooms in the king's court. He breathed deeply to calm himself and a small tremble shook the ground beneath them—a tremor you would notice only if you were waiting for one. Damiott had been waiting for one all his life. He stepped forward to the guard, set his bucket down, held his papers out and then—more calmly than he'd ever spoken a word in his life, he took his "fishing spear" and stabbed the guard under his arm. The Verander crumbled, unconscious. Lifting his bucket, Damiott walked serenely through the gate—a steady line of humans, Veranderen peasants, and a dog or two following him, as though they were all at the head city for a once in a lifetime event. As indeed they were.

~

KAXON STEPPED OVER THE VERANDER'S BODY. HE HADN'T EVEN unsheathed his weapon on this one. All he'd needed to do was create a simple illusion—two actually. The Verander had jumped over the part he'd considered water, onto the part he'd considered earth; and into the sinking pit.

One leg was broken and he'd howled like a child, though he must have been a couple hundred years old. Kaxon had to resist the urge to throw the dirt back in and cover him up so he didn't have to listen to it. He had passed only one other Verander who had cried—and that one had had his limb blown off by an explosion his opponent had hidden in the ground. Kaxon wasn't looking forward to meeting the foe who liked to detonate his opponents. Perhaps Wittendon would be a gentleman and do that one in for him. Of course, even if he did, there was still the largest, most experienced finalist to defeat—the one who had been a finalist in the last three Mals, the one who had sent his opponent down the hill on a stretcher, unconscious and dripping blood from a broad gash across his chest.

All at once the vegetation in front of him burst into flame. Kaxon was angry he hadn't heard the Verander approach and wondered at once if it was the explosion guy—he seemed to like heat. Other trees were catching now and soon Kaxon was surrounded by a ring of flame that got smaller and smaller as it moved in on him, like a wall in the scary stories his nanny used to tell. Sweat began to mat Kaxon's fur and the only colors he could see were the black of the smoke and the red of the flames. Poison of unnatural types was not allowed during the Mal. Smoke, however—totally legal.

Kaxon hit the ground, lying as low as possible with his sash pressed hard against his nose and mouth. The ground just under him felt oddly cool compared to the hot air everywhere else. Kaxon focused on the cool, pulled as much of it into him as possible. The more he did, the deeper he felt the earth and the cooler it became. Mentally, he burrowed beneath layer after layer of soil, searching for the cool wet areas and then—bingo—he found an underground river. It was just below him—probably part of the Grey mine. He focused on the water with every bit of brain and magic he could muster and pulled it up, gathering with it any moisture he could find in the layers of dirt. Just as the wall of fire nicked his paw, the water burst out—shooting him up into the air so that he stood atop a great geyser. He smiled, enjoying the cool, wet water at his feet, and the look of shock on his opponent's face. Kaxon recognized the Verander Peigh. Short and lean, he was the smallest of the finalists, and close to Kaxon in age.

Kaxon let the water collapse. It doused the remaining flames with plenty left over to throw his opponent to the ground. With any luck, Peigh would get knocked into a tree trunk and lose consciousness. But luck wasn't what the Mal was about. Peigh got to his feet and raised his blade to the sky. Kaxon could tell that he was feeling for any electric current in the air, which he would then send through the water to Kaxon's feet. It would have been a nice move.

Kaxon drew his own blade and banged it against his opponent's. Both of them felt a bit of the shock that had gathered and took a step back. The short one actually laughed like they were brothers playing too rough behind their nanny's back. Kaxon liked that. Maybe they could be seated together at the celebratory ball after this was over, but only if Kaxon could defeat him without sending him to the infirmary for several weeks. He re-sheathed his blade and gathered the water that was trying to seep back into the earth, forming it into a ball in front of him. He threw it at Peigh. With an easy movement Peigh caught it and threw it back.

"I was hoping you would stab it," Kaxon said.

"So I would be drenched from head to foot?" Peigh responded.

"It would hardly destroy you, but it would have given me a good laugh," Kaxon said, gathering the ball of water again, this time with more concentration. He hated to do it, but he had just seen a flare go up behind Peigh's back. Whoever had won the match was not far off and would find them soon enough. Kaxon needed to make this quick. Into the ball, Kaxon gathered twigs and rocks, leaves, and an unlucky lizard —these would be a distraction. At the center of the water ball, he gathered something else—something he hoped he could find enough traces of in this water from the Grey mine.

Peigh watched the ball carefully, his hand on his blade.

Kaxon suspected he was heating it. Heat was too easy in the Mal, which made it a bit of a weakness. You felt angry or scared or pressured and you went for heat. Heat was making Peigh sweat; heat was predictable and, even though it was a risk, Kaxon was counting on that. He flung the enormous ball of water at Peigh and just as Kaxon had hoped, Peigh stabbed it with a super-heated blade so that it evaporated on contact. Down rained the dirt, leaves, and sticks. The lizard hit the ground and scampered away. A deluge of pebbles battered Peigh's head and shoulders and then, just as it seemed it was done, a small ball of compact mineral with traces of the Grey fell from the cloud. The clump was not as heavy as several of the others, but it was more potent. The stone hit Peigh with a solid plunk and the Verander collapsed.

Kaxon waited for several moments to be sure he was really down and then sent up his flare. He walked over to Peigh and kicked the small mineral stone away, examining the bump on Peigh's skull. It wouldn't be pretty, but nothing that would keep them from sharing a goose leg at the final ceremony. Peigh's blade lay near his body and Kaxon picked it up.

For a minute he considered abandoning his scythe and taking Peigh's normal one. But then he thought of the stump of exploded wolken leg. He thought of the largest Verander and the way his blade gleamed—polished and sharp against the sun. He thought of the crowds below. And he thought of his father—watching from his box, waiting for a win. *Two to go*, Kaxon thought, *and then I can bury this cursed weapon and forget it ever was.*

CHAPTER 51

S adora walked through the midday crowds in a blood red dress that matched Wittendon's ceremonial cape. Around her neck she wore the necklace of dull metallic petals, though the broken locket hung underneath her dress, as close to her heart as ever.

Everywhere she went people smiled and murmured. Several curtsied and then teetered with gossip as she passed. People seemed to think that when you were pretty you couldn't hear a thing. Most of the *doting* ladies of the court hated her sincerely. It was this—this tendency of the high-birthed ladies to smile and gush, then mutter to another about your ignoble birthright or coy plottings for the prince— that had driven Sadora first to the lonely dark libraries, and later to the ancient, ugly tunnels. In the end it was those seemingly abandoned tunnels that had cured her of her exclusion. She had friends in the Septugant, friends of all sorts and races. She could feel them watching her now as they milled through the crowds, slowly and steadily changing their positions, making their way, step by shuffled step, to a deep nook on the eastern slope.

She hoped they would make it before the injured gate-keepers were discovered. With each lieutenant she'd sent a rebel Verander to hide the unconscious gatekeepers, tend the bleeding with a special powder she had made, and stand in for them until it was time.

From a distance Sadora caught a glance of the general Wolrijk. He turned to her for a brief moment and she looked into his eyes—scarred, darkened, odd, like peering into the eye sockets of a mask. Quickly the general dipped his head in a respectful bow as a flare shot up. It was Kaxon's by the look of it, curly, showy sparks floating to the earth. Wittendon's flare was much more direct, a straight line to the sky. She hadn't seen it for the better part of an hour. She fingered her necklace and chewed her lip. Without Wittendon they would fail. The Septugant would be dispersed, forced to wait and then regroup in another hundred years. She looked constantly to the healers, who collected the downed Veranderen. If Wittendon was injured, it would be partly her fault—largely her fault. Not only would they fail, but the only other Verander as dear to her as Sarak would be harmed because of a plot she had helped form.

For a minute, her perfect posture sagged.

Then the stutterer Damiott caught her eye and risked a wink. He would have been struck with a club if a Verander or guard had noticed the gesture to a lady of the court. None did. She nodded to the man, a touch of smile on her face. The ladies of the court would not have lent her as much as a hair pin, but these humans and dogs and rebel Veranderen would offer their lives, and gladly.

Her only wish—the wish she hoped would not turn to regret—was that Sarak would forgive her when all was done, for he had been her best and only friend for so many years.

She knew he waited impatiently for her in the box, dreading each minute he had to sit alone with the solemn king and stoic guards. "I'm sorry, brother. Your wait will run long today."

HE WAS THE ONE WITH THE SWORD, NOT THE EXPLOSIVES. AND HE HAD drawn his pretty blade almost immediately—obviously preferring weaponry to magic. Not the best choice considering Kaxon's unseen advantage in the weapon's department.

Again and again Kaxon struck the sharp-fanged Verander called Quidin. Each nick from the Grey refused to seal and the Verander seemed to ooze with blood. Even the crowd below had noticed—they had begun stamping and calling with an ardor that turned Kaxon's stomach. Blood was unusual among their thick-skinned, quick-healing race. Blood was part of the novelty and thrill of the Mal. Yet, with each nick of his blade Kaxon felt the simplicity of his life fade.

"Will you not quit when it is clear that my skill exceeds your own," Kaxon asked.

"Nothing is clear until all is complete," Quidin responded, getting a good jab in below Kaxon's armpit. The sting angered Kaxon and he pulled back, just as Wittendon could be seen jogging up the hill. Apparently, he had beaten the Verander with the explosives. Kaxon knew he was out of time. He swung his scythe in a tight quarter circle, plunging it into Quidin's shoulder—at least two inches deep—deeper than he had really intended to go. The Verander gasped in pain too intense to scream. "Your blade," he choked.

Wittendon turned suddenly, seeming to hear what Quidin had said.

"Smarts," Kaxon said, finishing Quidin's sentence and hoping that Wittendon would wait at a distance.

"No," the Verander Quidin said.

Wittendon ran to them with a speed only a body as long and lean as his could.

Quidin had begun to tremble, the blood pouring out of his shoulder.

"I'm sorry," Kaxon said, looking at his opponent in a way that was truly fearful and full of regret, "but I have come too far." Again he brought his scythe back and swung, aiming at his opponent's chest as though to drag the curved Grey through his ribs. But just as the weapon was about to hit, Wittendon ran in front of the Verander—like a frightened and stupid rabbit—taking the weight of the blade along his side in a jagged line that extended from shoulder to waist.

"No," Kaxon screamed, dropping his scythe.

"No," Quidin whispered, fainting finally from lost blood.

"No," Wittendon said firmly. He stood in front of his brother and shook his fur as though he had just swum through a creek—droplets of water and blood showering Kaxon.

"Forgive me, brother," Kaxon begged. "You were not my target."

IN THE DISTANCE, KING CRESPIN STOOD AND STEPPED OUT OF HIS BOX. What was Kaxon doing, pleading like a lover, weaponless and exposed? The king sprinted to his sons just as Wittendon sent up a red flare.

Wolrijk followed close to the king. The two of them stopped at a distance—the afternoon sun at their backs—and watched.

Wittendon picked up Kaxon's blade and tossed it back to him with a roar that shook the branches above them.

"My liege," Wolrijk said, gesturing with his head to Kaxon's blade. The king saw it suddenly—the blade Kaxon held—the way the metal tip was just brighter than it should have been. It was a tell-tale sign of paint enchanted to cover extra inches of the Grey. The king saw something else too, something Wolrijk hadn't yet noticed—he saw the way Kaxon stood, shaking and confused at the line on Wittendon's side that shimmered gray, instead of red.

"By the elders," the king whispered, connecting each secret his sons had so carefully concealed from him. "Move," the king said firmly to Wolrijk, not wanting him to see.

"But my lord," Wolrijk began.

"Back," the king commanded.

Wolrijk obeyed, moving back several lengths and waiting for his next order. Even the king remained at a distance, watching carefully.

Kaxon held his blade tightly, though it still hung at his side. Wittendon held his scythe in front of his face in challenge, waiting.

"Who are you?" Kaxon asked, staring at the gash now fully sealed.

"Someone who is just figuring myself out." Wittendon nodded at

Kaxon's blade. "As are you. Come now, our father waits, anxious to declare a winner."

Kaxon frowned, then growled, lifting his blade in front of his face. Each brother paused for a long moment. Then, like two lightning bolts touching the earth, the scythes of the brothers met—the clang of the metal carrying to the crowd below. The throng gasped and cheered at the noise from the two figures so far up the hill they could barely be seen.

Sarak, on the other hand, had a fabulous view. He sat in the king's box, relieved Crespin was finally gone, but confused by what he saw. Kaxon's hesitation had been just as baffling as his ferocity now was. Wittendon and Kaxon fought like demons—screeching, scratching, and flying at each other. The movements of their blades might as well have been the movements of their hands—as innate and powerful as natural-born parts. And yet, they fought like brothers too, each anticipating the others' movements in the same way Sarak knew how Sadora would move in dance.

It was beautiful and terrible all at once. Sarak watched Kaxon slash at his brother with the force he would have used to kill a poisonous snake. It seemed like the world had turned upside down.

Silently the king was considering a plan for himself and his kingdom. He could simply allow Wittendon to defeat Kaxon. With his obvious advantage, it would be inevitable. Kaxon would not enjoy this, but he would be spared the shame of a disqualification. But if Wittendon won this way, the king would lose a chance he wasn't sure he could afford to lose. If Kaxon was disqualified; if Wittendon was forced to fight another instead, Crespin might be able to eliminate an enemy he had lately wondered how to dispose of gracefully.

With a mighty clap of his hands and a golden spark from his staff, the king strode forward. The battle between the brothers halted, as did any sound or movement from the crowd below.

"My son," Crespin said, looking to Kaxon and summoning the long-bladed scythe with a slight gesture of his hand. Carefully, the king ran his finger up the shaft, stopping at the point where the metals joined. The king sighed, as though disappointed. "My son," he repeated.

Kaxon looked at his father. "Call the match. They do not know," Kaxon said, gesturing to the crowd. "Please Father, call the match. Give the position of Chancellor to Wittendon, but spare me."

"I am sorry, my son, but I cannot."

Kaxon seemed to crumple. Wittendon wished he could hand him a toy like he had when they were young, and make it better between them. "Call the match, father," Wittendon said.

"That's right," Kaxon said, straightening a bit. "Wittendon wants you to call it too." He stared daggers at his brother. "The blade you hold—it is not mine."

"What?" Wittendon asked.

"They were switched in the battle. Look," Kaxon said, pointing to a small flower engraved on its handle. "A moonflower. His lady's favorite."

Wittendon said nothing, only stared.

"Hold it, brother. See how well it fits your hand."

The king examined the engraving on its handle, slowly and thoughtfully, then held the blade out to Wittendon. "Hold it," he said. "Warm it."

Wittendon did not move.

"Perhaps," the king said, "the two of you have forgotten who still rules this kingdom. Hold it." He threw the blade with force toward Wittendon's body. Instinctively, Wittendon caught it. He held it for several moments, looking from his brother to his father then back to his brother again.

"Now give it back to me," Crespin said. Wittendon did. The king held the warm hilt, turning it several times. He then held it up to the afternoon sun so that it caught the light.

"Too clever for his own good," Crespin muttered, turning the hilt away from the sun. "I am sorry, Kaxon, it is clearly yours. The Grey-smith made sure of that."

Kaxon looked to his father who held out the scythe. Between each petal of the moonflower was a carefully etched letter of Kaxon's name —an etching made of old, unstable Grey that darkened when the blade was warmed by another.

Without a word or an apology, Kaxon walked from the field.

"Kaxon," Wittendon called, but his brother ignored him. "Kaxon. There is still opportunity in these times to create honor for yourself." Wittendon took a step forward. "Kaxon," he shouted, but his brother did not look back.

The king looked to his oldest son, whispering so no one else could hear, "You, lord of the Grey, have a great advantage. However it is one of natural gifting and as such you may—by the terms of this game— continue. Nevertheless, and especially under these circumstances, I cannot in good conscience declare you conqueror on a disqualification."

Wittendon raised an eyebrow and waited.

"I have recently received information clarifying Sarak's parental line. He is of high lineage. Though not traditional, it is permissible in such unusual circumstances as this to allow one of equal blood to step in and fight in the place of another."

"Fight Sarak?" Wittendon asked.

"Yes," the king replied, turning his back to his son. Crespin walked the distance back to Wolrijk and held out Kaxon's long-tipped scythe. "Return it to my box," the king commanded. The scarred wolf took it in his mouth, careful to avoid the Grey tip, and obeyed.

Standing on the side of the hill, the king raised his staff and called, his voice amplifying across the kingdom, "The warrior Kaxon is no longer qualified for this competition. In his place will stand one dark and bold with magic and strength to rival kings past. Come forth, Sarak —son of the ancients—child of Tomar."

Below the audience seemed to have been struck perfectly dumb. And then, beginning with a few voices and rising to a wave of sound so great it shook the rocks and beams in the mines below the hill, the crowd broke out into a mighty noise. "Hail, Sarak, son of Tomar. Hail, Wittendon, the once-verlorn prince." The names rocked back and forth in the crowd, combining eventually into a hysterical scream.

The king had to admit he was pleased. A lost lord. An underdog prince. A way to destroy the child of Tomar and with him the witch's prophecy about Crespin's own destruction. It couldn't have turned out more nicely if he'd been plotting it for years. Regally, he strode from the field.

~

FROM HIS SPOT IN THE BOX, SARAK LOOKED AROUND. ONE OF THE black wolf guards came to his side to escort him to the hill. "Is it I?" Sarak asked, and the wolf looked at him as though he was half-brained or half-bred or both.

"There is no other," the animal responded, pointing with his nose to a scythe near the corner he had brought for Sarak to use.

Sarak sat there for a moment, picturing Kaxon as he had raised his blade—willing to chop it through his brother's neck if the chance arose. Now Kaxon was gone and he, Sarak, an orphaned nobody was to enter the Mal. *Son of Tomar*. The words made him almost dizzy. He would fight his best friend whom he had trained. Not only that, but the king seemed perfectly thrilled about it. Try as he might, Sarak couldn't quite put it all together. Wolrijk came into the box and dropped the Grey-long blade in the corner. Sarak looked at it.

"The world has gone insane," Sarak muttered.

"No my lord," a voice behind him said quietly. Zinder stepped up beside Sarak. "The world has always been thus. You have only just now had cause to notice." And with that, the white wolf turned and grabbed the extra-long blade with his mouth. He ran, heading for the hills as though on some desperate errand.

Sarak had never heard a wolf gasp, but Wolrijk clearly gasped. The general turned to look for the king who was still at a distance on the hill. Then, cursing, Wolrijk followed after the white wolf at a ferocious speed.

"Insane," Sarak repeated to himself. The black guard stared after the other wolves for only a second before regaining his composure.

"Come," he said, leading Sarak out onto the field and into the fevered cheers of the crowd below.

CHAPTER 52

The dogs walked steadily in the direction of the Motteral Mal. If all had gone as planned, Humphrey, Pietre, and the rest of the Septugant had gone through the gates hours ago and were now waiting at the base of the eastern slope. If all had not gone as planned and Wittendon was defeated, the rebels would soon disperse and return to their homes. That would be the easiest thing. There would be no choice for the dogs to make and all would go back to what it had been.

Markhi knew that most of the dogs were hoping for this outcome. In the unlikely event that Wittendon did succeed long enough to empower the stone, the dogs were faced with a decision—a decision they had been arguing about for days. None of them wanted to fight, but the packs near the burned wood grew hungrier. Even worse, no less than two hundred pups had gone missing this week—more than were recorded for any other year of the Motteral Mal. A terrible hondsong had arisen in their camps, mothers and fathers weeping and singing for their lost babes. And yet, to fight did not mean to win and to win did not mean any guarantee of freedom for the dogs. Their race was strong without language, but it was not nearly as strong and every single one of them knew it.

In the long green meadows outside the capital, the outline of the Hill of Motteral rose up in front of them and their walk slowed.

~

ZINDER DROPPED THE WEAPON AS WOLRIJK CAUGHT UP TO HIM, grabbing at his hind legs with his teeth and toppling the large white wolf to the ground.

"You've gone mad," Wolrijk growled, kicking the other wolf and snarling.

"No more than anyone else," Zinder said, getting to his feet.

"Give me the blade. I need to return it to the king."

"Oh, yes, you'll *return* it, I'm sure. The king's welfare is certainly your central concern."

"As though it is yours."

"Mine has become clouded in the last several weeks, it is true, but your purpose—your mission as general—I do not think it has ever been cloudy or compromised. I think you have always known what you wanted and what you were going to do. And I don't much think it involved the king."

Wolrijk growled. "It has always *involved* the king. Just not quite in the expected ways."

With a harsh laugh, Zinder kicked the blade to Wolrijk. The general stopped it with his front paw.

"Go on," Zinder said. "Pick it up. Use it. I'm sure you'll find that terribly easy to do when fighting with it in your *mouth*."

For a long moment, Wolrijk looked at the white wolf.

"You know you're not the only misfit in this world, don't you?" Zinder asked, stepping closer to Wolrijk.

"I know there are no others like me on this earth," Wolrijk responded.

"Perhaps," Zinder said. "But there are others with eyes that watch and ears that hear. I've noticed you know much about magic and history—" Zinder paused. "For a wolf."

Wolrijk struck him without hesitation—sharp yellow claws across his eyes and one ear. But Zinder did not even take a step backwards.

"I am a strange creature pieced together as well," Zinder said. "Only my stitching is on the inside."

"Well, soon you will need some on the outside also," Wolrijk said, striking again and clipping off Zinder's other ear while taking a step closer, his teeth bared.

Zinder stepped toward him as well so that very little space was left between their faces. "You convinced me to swear allegiance to the king. I watched him go on witch hunts where he cared not how many wolves fell. I tended their torn flesh and carried them home. I felt Gog sweating in the asylum where he might have been healed except that he was pulled out to be used again. I suffocated as the land of the dogs burned leaf by leaf. I pulled the only surviving sentinel from the ashes, and I felt my feet drag under the dogs' songs of mourning."

As he said it, the great body of dogs crested the hill. Hearing the last part of the argument, they stopped, staring at the two powerful wolves alone on the foothill in front of them. Wolrijk bit at Zinder's muzzle, dots of blood pricking up along Zinder's white face.

Zinder did not seem to notice the dogs or any pain. "I heard decrees as they came forth from the king—food withheld from the miners, tightened security to the human villages, the Greysmith to be hanged. Even before then I have smelled blood when humans screamed in darkened forests, caught whispers of rhymed prophecy with misty endings, and sensed uprisings at every corner of the land."

Slowly the dogs formed a wide circle around the two wolves. Wolrijk growled, but did not move.

"Ever since I was a pup," Zinder said, his face so close to Wolrijk's that he could feel his breath as though it was his own, "I have heard each and every edict to kill the half-breeds created in this land. You have only encouraged them. Yes, I have watched you, my friend, watched you better than any others have thought to do."

At Markhi's command the dogs stepped two paces forward, the circle tightening.

"I have seen," Zinder continued, "how you took out the prior general, Grender, by poisoning the minds of those ignorant, jealous wolves. And I heard you tell the king about the innocent pups of the she-hound Hannah."

The dogs stood shoulder to shoulder now, not even leaving enough air for a breeze to blow through the wall of muscle and fur. Markhi growled with a deep, steady hum.

Zinder continued, "I have watched you abandon your own, attack all others, and plot against the king you formed a band to protect. I know the hut in which you keep the human boy's parents drugged and barely alive. I know you were hoping he would come for them, so you could trap him, too." The blood-soaked white wolf laughed in Wolrijk's face. "And most importantly, I know why there is so little of the powerful Pallium remaining in the River Rylen and I know what you have used that metal for." Wolrijk jumped forward, landing on the wolf's chest, pinning him to the earth.

Zinder gasped and then laughed again. "It is difficult, General Wolrijk, to wear a skin that is not your own." Wolrijk growled so low the ground beneath them trembled and then he struck into Zinder's belly with his paws. "You may remove my skin if you wish," Zinder said. "I have no desire to see, hear, or smell more than I already have in this world. But others do desire it. They will want their families back, their lands renewed. I daresay the boy Pietre longs for his mother's embrace, as do the pups you have taken. I often longed for my own mother. But she was one-eighth dog and went missing one day when I was quite young. Strange how that happens in this land of the great red sun."

Wolrijk stabbed Zinder's neck with three nails of his forepaw and Zinder's head fell back. The dogs let out a war cry—shrill and united and terrifying.

Zinder turned to them, his head in a pool of blood on the ground. "You will find the boy's parents in a shack on the south-western edge of the River Rylen. There you'll find answers to many riddles. As for your own young—you'll find many of them in a room adjacent to the north ballroom, though if you don't join in the battle that is sure to come, you can count on never finding them at all."

Wolrijk struck Zinder one final time in the jugular, and the blood burst forth as quickly as the dogs lurched forward—a mass of teeth, hair, and revenge. The general barreled through the dogs, tossing them aside like dolls. Others moved in and Wolrijk stood on his hind legs— his front paws daggered, his eyes wild. He slashed and hit and crushed them. Kicking three dogs to the side and grabbing the scythe in his mouth, he jumped over the last line of dogs and ran back to the head city, faster than any creature the dogs had ever seen.

Markhi ran to the nearly dead wolf and stood at his side. Pointing to a band of heavy-set dogs he said, "Go to the place by the river; find the boy's parents. And you," he said to one of the sweetest singers. "Try to find the room that contains our young; send word as soon as you do." He turned from them back to the crowd. "Leaders of the packs, come. We cast now our final vote. Do we stand by and watch? Or do we run forth to avenge?"

CHAPTER 53

The sun widened as it began its descent. The moon was just now peeking up over the bottom of the horizon.

Wittendon didn't wait for Sarak to shake off his shock. He ran for the spot that jutted out of the mountain like a tiny nose on a too wide face. Hawks had roosted there and Wittendon suspected many couples had made their way over the rocks to sit on the overhang and watch the sun set and the moon rise. Here it felt like you were dangling off the edge of the earth, the valley darkening, soon to be quilted in stars.

The sun dipped lower and the moon rose—two fraternal twins about to switch places. Wittendon put his hand in his pouch and touched the stone. A warm pulse beat through him, like a small electrical current charging his muscles and blood.

It was his mother's gem. He had known it as soon as the boy had dropped it in his lap. How it had gotten from her to him was luck or destiny or some weird combination of the two. Wittendon's only guess was that the queen had found some unlikely place to hide it. Or rather, some ridiculously logical place—like a mine filled with solidified trickles of the metal the stone had once created.

Wittendon walked to the place of empowerment—the *Steenmacht*.

It looked like nothing more than a small cairn at the end of a rocky goat path, a small cairn with its top stone missing. Here the light of the sun and moon would meet. Here the stone would be given power so that a human could place it in the Sacred Tablet in order to change the suns. The Sacred Tablet was a national monument. But this spot was nothing. The tiny cairn sat on the left side of the overhang, looking like you could kick it over if you were in the mood. Yet it was this little tower of stone, this place where lizards had slept, where birds had pooped. It was this place that would start to change the world.

Wittendon pulled the stone from the pouch, its smooth surface fire to his blood. The evening sun touched the back of his neck, level almost with his chest. He turned to check the position of the moon and there, standing less than twelve inches from him, stood Sarak.

"So your dad's a loon," Sarak said, kicking off a boot and dropping a rock out before putting it back on.

"You know you could have won just now," Wittendon said. "I had no idea you were there."

"Which is why I was the trainer, and you the student. But you're right," Sarak said. "The son of Tomar would have straight up stabbed the son of Crespin in the back. Which just goes to show what I've been thinking."

"Which is?" Wittendon asked, watching the moon as it rose, and trying to sound casual.

"That your old man has lost it. I'm not the son of Tomar anymore than you're the son of the winter fairy."

"My father isn't crazy," Wittendon said abruptly. "He's dangerous."

"Which can be the same thing."

"Which are much too much the same thing," Wittendon concluded. "Sarak, you should go."

Sarak gave him a funny look. "I thought we were supposed to battle. I didn't realize this was a brunch I hadn't dressed for."

"It's not a brunch," Wittendon said looking away, but not quite in time. The bottom of the sun had reached the point on the horizon where the top of the moon touched. Wittendon felt it even before he saw it—the light that burst through him.

Sarak took a step back and stared. "No," he finally said, looking at Wittendon's eyes—eyes that had begun, just barely, to glow. "No."

"Yes," Wittendon said. "It is my duty and destiny."

"No," Sarak said. "They were just stories, bedtime tales, crony talk." He reached down and touched the hilt of his blade—and Wittendon could see that he was clicking together memories like pieces of a puzzle that suddenly made sense. The way the weapons room had buzzed with Wittendon in it, the hilt broken to petals, the day on the hill when every lightning bolt that had weakened Sarak seemed to ignite Wittendon.

"My old nanny," Sarak said stammering. "She knew all the old songs, told tale after tale. The human slaves used to laugh at her and say she was crazy." Sarak stopped and looked at Wittendon. The sun and moon hung almost equal on the horizon, the light from both moving toward Wittendon. "But she wasn't," Sarak concluded. "I *am* the son of Tomar. My father gave her to me to fill me with our history and our secrets without arousing any suspicion. And so I would know who I was when the right time came." Sarak paused. "Which I guess is now."

"You should go," Wittendon repeated. His power began to surge into the stone.

"You will destroy our kind," Sarak said. "That is what is written and sung of the lords of the Grey."

"I will only grant strength to other kinds."

"Who will crush us."

Wittendon held the stone over the *Steenmacht*.

"Stop!" Sarak said in a voice Wittendon had never heard him use before. "The stone will grant power that will go too far—tip the balance of the world in the favor of men."

"It will only bring them to equal ground."

"Equal ground is a myth. Soon enough they will rise up in power. They can create and command tools. Friend, they can subdue and use the Grey. Please listen—the balance will tip in the favor of men."

"Well, perhaps they will do more with it than we have. Perhaps they will not hunt innocents in the night. Or pit brother against brother. Or send friends to destroy each other."

Sarak laughed. "Perhaps you have lived too long in a palace. Do you know what the humans are capable of? Some abandon their weak or malformed purposefully in the woods to be consumed. Others drink liquids that alter their minds to the point of confusion or sickness. They turn beggars away, leave widows to work and sweat out their days, mock and jeer at those they perceive as weaker than themselves."

"Only because we have pushed them to it—given them lands devoid of growth, torn families apart without warning, forced them to pay for these robes and blades while they sit in piles of mud and feces until their skin rots off." Wittendon paused looking at his friend. "I am sorry, Sarak, but I trust men more than wolves."

"Supposing they *are* as good as you imagine—what if in the course of centuries, men turn to beasts and hunt our kind?"

"If that should happen then all is lost."

"No," Sarak said. "If that should happen, then *we* are lost. Only us, Wittendon. Control the magic, my prince. Protect us."

"I cannot control it," Wittendon said. "It takes from me what it wishes to have. That is the fate of the Greylord. That is why I am here."

"No, you cannot control it because you have not the desire."

Wittendon turned back to the stone, his eyes glowing brighter. "Go," he said.

"No," Sarak whispered. "I am Sarak, son of the surviving elder Tomar, and I will not let you bind us captive to another race." Sarak lifted his blade, holding the top of the shaft and bringing down the blunt end of the hilt on Wittendon's head.

Normally such a hit would have brought Wittendon to the ground. Now with the power of the stone, it was like a raindrop on his scalp—Wittendon barely bothered to shake it off.

The sun and moon sat almost level now. Sarak couldn't use the Grey blade—it would only make Wittendon stronger. He sheathed his scythe and pulled out the small knife Wittendon had given him as a gift and said, "It is good to know you have finally found your magic."

Wittendon looked at him, his body shimmering.

"It is unfortunate you haven't had the last twenty years to play with it." Sarak took the dagger, muttered an incantation, and stabbed the short, strong blade into the mountain. "Tricky stuff, magic."

From above rocks began to crumble, falling on Wittendon's body and all around him.

Wittendon turned to his friend and said, "Sarak, please just go." But Sarak was concentrating and heating the rocks. Quickly, they began to steam, ignite, and melt.

Wittendon cradled the stone. He had to keep it intact; it could not melt. He held his body stiff, yet calm. He gave the stone every thought of every winter day he could remember. To Sarak he sent other feelings of cold—each memory of his father's rejection, the feeling in his stomach the day his mother fell ill, the cool of her skin the day she died. There were plenty of icy, sad days in between. He used each and every one against his friend. Then he raised his hand to the mountain and froze it. Sarak pushed back with the heat of the anger he had felt at never knowing his parents, at hearing his nanny mocked by the nobles and townspeople, at losing his aunt after his nanny died. Sarak melted through Wittendon's icy barrier until each Verander was pushing with a wall of energy—one hot, one cold—against the other.

Sarak's skill was greater. He stepped forward slowly, inch by inch, moving the heat closer to Wittendon and the stone. He was close enough to feel the warmth in Wittendon's veins and lungs—warmth Wittendon had to maintain to survive. Sarak smiled. With his brain and body he pushed into that heat and Wittendon looked at him, panicked.

Wittendon felt his body burn—his own fingers softening the metal of the gem in his hand. Quickly, before it could melt, he placed the stone on the *Steenmacht*. As he did, the centers of the sun and moon fell into perfect alignment. Light streaked over Wittendon's face and then—at once—he exploded.

Sarak was thrown back against the side of the mountain—his shoulder crushed, the side of his face and arm torn open and bruised.

When Sarak staggered to his feet, Wittendon stood unharmed in front of him—light pouring from his eyes, his skin, his mouth. "You cannot stop me now," Wittendon said calmly.

Sarak stood for a moment, shivering from the pain in his side. "You're right," he said. "I am lord of nothing, much less the Grey." He stepped beside Wittendon, blinded from the light. "I am not as powerful as you, but I, too, can give this stone a touch of my essence, my desires. You would make this change permanent. I can take that permanence from you, from this stone. If and when our kind cower in fear, this stone will have the power to return the red sun and, with it, the strength of our race." Sarak took a deep breath and reached toward the stone.

At once, Wittendon felt a different sort of power—a small surge. His friend had placed a finger upon the stone.

"No," screamed Wittendon, pushing at Sarak. "It is too much; it will kill you."

"But it will not kill us all. If the time should come that man becomes beast, we are not lost; the power of the suns can again be reversed." Sarak's finger grew white.

The sun sank down a breath as the moon rose. Sarak trembled and collapsed. The light pulled back into Wittendon, leaving just a glimmer in his eyes. "Sarak," he whispered, bending down. "Sarak," he repeated, shaking him. The body of his friend—the one who had taught him to catch a frog, trained him in his first use of a sword, walked with him to his mother's grave, the man he had planned to ask for Sadora's hand—lay cold and still.

Wittendon knelt on the cliff as the first star broke open the fading sky. The Septugant waited for him, the stone hummed, his father expected him. But Wittendon, lord of the Grey and now Chancellor to the king—bent forward, held Sarak's dead fingers, and cried.

CHAPTER 54

Wittendon slowly carried Sarak down the hill. Below him, he could hear the murmur of the crowd as it rose up to meet him. He had not sent up a flare, nor did he intend to until what he planned to do was done. Laying Sarak on the ground beside a thick, red-barked tree, Wittendon stood still, pulling into himself all of the ice he had thrown at Sarak in their last battle and recalling all the fire Sarak had thrown at him. These elements he let swirl and collide inside of him. Then, holding both arms out over the ground, he raised up four walls of earth surrounding his friend and quickly shot out the heat, followed by a burst of cold. He did this several times in a row until the ground around his friend had melted and hardened, melted and hardened into walls stronger than any metal or rock their land had known. With one final burst of energy he sealed the top of the tomb and, pushing with all his magic, he forced the sanctuary beneath the dirt. Wittendon sat on the ground panting. After a few more moments, he raised his right arm and sent a simple black plume into the air. The crowd gasped. It had been many centuries since they had seen the flare signaling that a competitor had died.

THE KING STOOD IN HIS BOX AND THE THREE BUGLES CALLED OUT A mournful wail followed by the howls of wolves and Veranderen. Wittendon turned his back on his father's box and began to walk to the eastern slope. As Crespin watched his son he caught a glimpse of an animal that looked like a cat slipping over the hill in the distance. The cat was deeply black, though its coat shimmered purple when the rays of the sinking sun hit it and the cat's eyes flashed as blue as the skies in Crespin's dreams. Crespin shook off a shudder as Wolrijk slipped quietly into the king's box, released the other guards, and stood patiently at the door.

"He has conquered," Crespin whispered. "My destiny is secure." Raising his staff to declare Wittendon the winner, the king opened his mouth, but Wolrijk stopped him.

"No, my lord," the wolf said quietly. "It is not."

Crespin turned to look at his general. Wolrijk's fur was bloodied, his face torn. "What happened to you?" the king asked.

Wolrijk stood in front of the king, looking him directly in the eyes and holding the stare for several long seconds. "Do you not know me?" he asked. "I who played for years at your side. I who fashioned the staff you now hold. I who marked you for a great leader yet to come— a leader who would not compromise. I was right. When you destroyed the elders, you spared none—not even my brother. And when you took him, you murdered me too. In my grief, I fled to the hills by the gorge, discovered a place to hide. I ate fish, stole eggs, and foraged for berries. You rose to power. You defeated any who crossed you, made treaties, found love. I panned for gold in the lonely stream, hoping to sell it and hide myself in a distant land. But I found something better— traces of the same metal Tomar had studied all his life. An ore strong enough to defy an unconquerable king. I found that it could not only repel the Grey, but bind flesh and vein together. I found that it could transform a lonely crazed creature. I killed a wolf, and remade myself." Wolrijk laughed and, holding Kaxon's scythe with his paw in a way that seemed unnatural for a wolf, he stepped closer to the king. "All these months, when you looked into my eyes, I thought you would know me. It brings me some satisfaction that you could not see past the scars." With a deft turn, Wolrijk struck the king in the shoulder with the three-inch blade.

The king crumpled to the ground. "Draden?" the king said. "Can it be?"

Wolrijk laughed and kicked him in the jaw.

"Draden," the king repeated, blood pouring from his shoulder and trickling from his chin.

Wolrijk stood on his hind legs, murmuring words of an ancient tongue. The fur broke along his back, like seams of a child's doll bursting apart. His front paws turned to hands with daggered nails, his legs lengthened, his body grew tall. The wolfish face broke and contorted—half man, half animal—bleeding and splitting in the places where the scars had run along it. And though his body was distorted and malformed, it was clear who he was.

"I am Draden, Nadenszbror. You and then your sons will die at my hand and I will claim this kingdom." He shoved the wounded king against the throne. It cracked under the weight of its leader, gem and cement crumbling beneath the king. With his good arm, Crespin groped for his staff.

Wolrijk stood to his full height and laughed. "You cannot use that weapon against me."

Crespin stood. With his good arm raised he spat out a spell, sending a burst of energy into Wolrijk, pushing him back. The king grabbed Wolrijk's neck and lifted him into the air, but only for a moment before Wolrijk kicked Crespin in the gut, knocking him to the floor.

Wolrijk held the Grey blade to the king's neck. "I must thank you," Wolrijk said, "for the idea of the extra-long blade. You were right all those years ago—it's the perfect thing for killing the unkillable."

Crespin rolled free just as Wolrijk stabbed at his neck. The king kicked Wolrijk's legs so that the shifter stumbled. Without pause the king grabbed at the scythe, but couldn't reach it with his good arm.

Regaining his footing, Wolrijk laughed. He kicked the blade aside, then lifted the wounded king up as if he were a mouse and tossed him against the northern wall of the royal box. The northern wall collapsed, burying the king and leaving nothing but his hand visible, his staff on the floor several inches from it. Deliberately, Wolrijk lifted the scythe as though to drive it through the king's hand, but instead he brought it down on the top of the king's staff—the bauble cracking and dimming until nothing remained but the smoking, blackened glass.

Wolrijk walked to the hill and stood at its center. To the crowd below, he shook the scythe and shouted, "I am Draden, Nadenszbror, known to this kingdom as the General Wolrijk, Night Hunter. With the king's most noble *consent*, I claim my royal right as brother to the elder Naden and will participate in the Motteral Mal in this the year 12,000."

The crowd seemed to break—a wave of noise and confusion, alarmed and overjoyed. At the sidelines, ladies clucked to each other about the excitement of Crespin's cloying tournament—each new development more exciting than the last, while the king's guard exchanged shocked glances, looking at the distant figure of their trans-formed general and then to the southern wall of the king's box.

Wolrijk could see Wittendon's thin frame near the east side of the hill. Stretching in a way the wolf-turned-shifter had ached to for years, Wolrijk ran towards the prince—salivating for the hunt.

CHAPTER 55

Sadora had seen the black flare, had watched Wittendon walk across the hill. In a gush her world had emptied out into nothing. All these months she had moved quickly, steadily. But now, slowly, she walked to the king's box. Near a creek, she picked three dark purple calla lilies and laced them through her hair. She had felt it the moment Sarak died—a crushing burst in her own lungs. He had not been struck; she was sure of that. It was as though he had been consumed. She, it was true, had been consumed long ago, but she had never expected to take her brother with her.

When she got to the king's box, the northern wall was destroyed while the others that faced the crowd remained intact, concealing what Wolrijk had done. The general, she well knew, was a traitor and a madman, but not an idiot. With her foot, she tapped the king's staff, pushing it to the side and letting it roll to the edge of one of the unbroken walls. Beneath the rock, she heard the king groan. Gently she raised one hand and the rocks began to move, slowly at first and then more quickly, creating a whirlwind of stone above the king's weakened body. Moving her weight, the rocks, metal, and gems of the desecrated throne and walls lifted; she shook them to the floor in a gentle heap of rubble and dust.

"My lady," the king said, groaning and reaching blindly for his staff. "Your power is great. I confess I did not expect it. Thank you."

"Do not thank me," she said.

The king did not respond, but looked for the first time very carefully at this woman whom he had considered to be nothing more than a beautiful implant to his land. "No," he whispered. "It cannot be." His shoulder where Wolrijk had pierced him bled continuously and several of his bones were broken, but he did not make a move to stop the flow of blood. As well as he could, he stood on the leg that was still sound. He held out his hands and, looking past Sadora, he said, "To me."

His ruined staff shivered and rose to one hand, but still the king waited, his other arm trembling and outstretched.

"Perhaps," she said, calmly, "you are looking for this." She held both arms above her head, her hair and eyes reflecting the setting sun. The long-tipped spear, the one that had followed her out of the cave, flew into her hands. She lowered the weapon, and pointed it at the king.

He gripped his own staff, his arms cut and bleeding. "Why then," he asked, "have you saved me from another who had equal, perhaps greater, claim to my life?"

"Because," she said, not appearing to relish her task, "he cannot destroy you in the way I can."

Without pause, Crespin sent a blinding light toward her chest. She did not move to protect herself, but the light broke before reaching her as though shattered. She stepped toward him.

"My life has not all been balls and fashions, laughter and frills. It has also been time spent searching for a family line that didn't seem to exist, for a place in the world that I hoped could fill the empty parts of who I was."

Crespin ignored her and struck again, his spell shattering. The force of his own magic pushed too much weight onto his broken leg and caused him to stumble. He knelt there on one leg before her, his eyes flashing, his shoulders firm and proud. "I will not beg for mercy, if that is what you expect."

"I do not expect it. And you will not receive it."

339

Crespin pushed up with his good leg, barreling into Sadora's small frame. She pushed his body back with the strong wooden handle of the spear, though she did not pierce him with its tip. The king stumbled again, his bleeding shoulder splattering on the hem of her gown. Again he rose. "You will not kill me without first feeling the strength that has kept me in power for nearly a millennium," he said.

"I have no intention of killing you," she said. "It is my destiny to *destroy* you." She paused to look at the king. "You have been deceived by your first in command and duped by a giggling socialite of your court. Your youngest son has fled in disgrace. Your world, as we speak, is being transformed by those of lowly hands. It is a transformation made possible by the wife whom you unwittingly slew, the half-breed daughter left from another union, and your eldest son. This kingdom will crumble, the laws of nature shift. There is, my king, precious little left to you worthy of destruction. But I will do my best."

He struck her again, this time using his staff as a blunt weapon and this time hitting his mark—a line of blood and a rush of bruising sprouted on her cheek as she moved aside to avoid the full force of his blow.

"This blade," she said carefully, holding the spear. "It was formed to do more than just murder. It was formed to rob families of their magic, their position in this society, their dignity and power. How many?" she asked, dodging another hit. "How many grandchildren and great-grandchildren from those last elders roam in our midst? How many of them use magic for good or ill in this world? The bloodlines of those elders have been ruined or made verlorn, their progeny left to rot in graves or slums. All the weakness of humans with none of the craft. It was this I first noticed before I knew who I was or who I would become."

"The families of the elders would have been too intense of a threat. The kingdom was fragile," Crespin said.

"The slaughter of the elders was tragic," Sadora said. "But the deterioration of their family lines—of the innocents of their blood—was more than that; it was under-handed; it was weak."

As she spoke, light from the setting sun formed a fiery halo behind her. "Even Wolrijk survived only because he discovered a metal more powerful than the Grey. The same metal that saved my father, the same metal that granted this spear to my control."

Sadora held the spear in front of her chest like a talisman. "This blade could kill you," she said. "But there are things that can do worse." She moved the spear to her side and Crespin noticed the mangled locket around her neck.

"The necklace," he said, springing upon her, knocking her to the ground. He grabbed the locket with his good arm and tore it from her throat, standing before her and holding it triumphantly above his head. Quickly, he held it to the still-bleeding wound in his shoulder. Instantly the wound sealed itself and the king laughed, though in another moment he put his free hand to his shoulder and fell to his knees.

Sadora stood up. Her back and chest hurt, her cheek throbbed.

"You will not have it back," he said stubbornly, clutching the locket, pushing it against his broken bones.

"No," she said. "I will not." She sat on a large piece of rubble and sighed. "All my time was not spent at royal galas. I spent a good deal of it hiding musty, stolen scrolls and trying to figure everything out."

The king hissed a curse at her. He stood on legs with bones that had healed, yet he trembled and the hand that held the metal locket hung limp at his side as though it was too heavy to lift.

"Did you think," Sadora asked, "that Wolrijk was scarred beyond your recognition because this metal had powerful restorative properties?"

The king did not answer. He concentrated only on his breathing, drawing it in in slow, wheezy pulls that seemed to take all his energy.

"The metal Pallium is unusual—a metal of containment, useful, but not entirely predictable. Many metals conduct energy. This one traps it. My father used it to temporarily contain the power of the Grey and thus resist it. That is why it did not sap his strength. Or mine. Wolrijk's use of it, like Wolrijk's use of so many things, was somewhat perverse. Many naturalists believe certain metals to have energy. Pallium is no exception. It has energy so potent that it can be used to heal. The problem is that even as it heals it continues to contain. Wolrijk could

JEAN KNIGHT PACE & JACOB KENNEDY

use it to heal, or rather to hold together, only because he allowed it to contain or absorb a great many other energies—his sanity, his humanity, his senses of reason and love, his potential, his sweetest memories of his own dear brother. He maintained his magic, he multiplied his power only because he allowed this metal to take a part of him and absorb from him all his goodness. It was a dangerous trade."

At last the king collapsed, gasping for breath. "What have you done?"

"I?" she replied. "I have done nothing. You have done it all—or nearly all—for me. And to my credit, King Crespin, I did just sit here and try to explain it to you. The metal has restored parts of your physical body, but only by absorbing other energies from you—your wishes to ruin me, your strength, your magic. Those feelings you have carelessly poured into the Pallium as we've been sitting here and the metal has contained them; it has contained *you*." Sadora stood. "And I must congratulate you, dear king, for you must have some goodness left in you, which you have kept to yourself. Otherwise I expect the metal would have consumed you entirely."

At last the king let the mangled locket fall from his hand. It rolled slowly to her feet. She stepped away, careful not to touch it now, and held the long-tipped spear in her hand.

"The Grey could not destroy the Pallium when one was made to deflect while the other was created to destroy. But now both have been filled with destruction and, as so many things of that nature, they will eagerly take care of each other." With a movement more powerful than any would have expected from the satin-gowned lady of the court, Sadora stabbed the tip of the Grey into the mutilated Pallium. The Pallium twisted around the blade of the spear, both metals hissing at each other like warring reptiles until in a burst of white and gold, they were gone.

Crespin looked down to see himself transformed into his flesh form. He was small and balding, his lips a thin line of feeble pink, his skin nearly hairless, except for a few patchy, black tufts along his chest.

Conqueror conquered now descends.
To meet his own most bitter end.

Sadora picked up the wooden shaft that remained now that the Grey spearhead was gone. She turned from the king. "You are free to go, Verander Crespin. As free as the descendants of those you destroyed." Sadora walked from the crumbled room to the battlefield where her people and friends waited just over the hill

The king tried to follow her, but was too weak. He sat for a few moments in his trembling flesh form. And then staggered away toward the wood.

CHAPTER 56

Alekas looked at the hill, the sun sinking steadily behind it. They had at most an hour before it set completely. Sadora had left, giving instruction to the rebels to find their positions without her. Pietre stood at the front of the troops, if such a ragtag group could be called that, but Humphrey hung back with Alekas, laying his muzzle on her head at the spot just between her ears. Constantly it felt as though her belly squirmed. It would not be long now before her first litter of pups was born—quarter breed pups, doomed to death unless this crazy plot worked. After a minute Humphrey moved his head off of Alekas and followed her gaze to the top of the hill.

"Though I fully intend to see you again," he said. "It is possible that we may never be able to speak."

"Though not with words, we will always speak," she said. "Do what you have to do to protect the innocents."

"I will," he said, touching her nose with his. Then, letting his muzzle rest for one long moment on the soft fur of her neck, he closed his eyes and took a deep breath before he ran through the ranks to meet Pietre at the front.

～

On Humphrey's back, Pietre led the force of humans and rebels over the first foothill. This part was easy. None were yet aware of their presence, much less who they were or what they were doing. But before the rebellion could succeed, they had to find Wittendon and get the stone. And now they were not the only ones looking.

Pietre could see the Tablet at the top of the hill where the stone had to be placed. And he could see the sun, touching the horizon.

The old stories said that the prophecy called for one of pure heart. And Zinnegael had told him that the circumstances called for him. He wondered which was right. If either was. Pietre knew that he did not have a pure heart, and he knew that the circumstances could be altered. It was in his power to ask another to place the stone, or to abandon their designs completely.

Pietre climbed off of Humphrey's back, watching the hills in front of them and waiting. Silently, he bent to pick up several round stones for his sling.

"Don't be afraid," Humphrey said, sensing his sadness and nudging a smooth, round stone toward him.

"I'm not afraid," Pietre said, picking up the stone and placing it in the pouch by his sling. "At least I'm not afraid of them." He gestured out to the hills in front of them.

"Then what are you afraid of?" Humphrey kicked another rock— this one sharp and large.

"Me," Pietre said miserably, picking up the stone, weighting in in his hand and then tossing it away in favor of a denser, smaller stone. "I'm just a child."

"Undoubtedly," Humphrey answered. "So what's the problem?"

Pietre picked up three more rocks, dusting them off, checking their edges and choosing one with several small, jagged ridges. "Children don't do great things. At least, not me."

Humphrey cocked his head to the side. "You saved me. I was just a tiny, helpless thing. Now look." He held up a huge paw. "With luck, the small things you do will grow into big ones." Humphrey looked

345

ahead and Pietre knew he was thinking of his unborn pups. Humphrey continued, "Many desire to do good, but to desire and do are separate virtues. You used both when you saved me."

"I ignored both when I didn't save my parents."

Humphrey moved his body in a way that looked a lot like a shrug. "You could not have saved your parents."

"See," Pietre said. "Then how can I save anyone else?" He tossed down one of the stones he'd just chosen.

Humphrey used his foot to push it back towards Pietre. "You are thinking of the end, which seems impossible, and the beginning, which seems faltering. You are forgetting about the middle—the most important part, the part where you change."

Humphrey nudged Pietre's pocket where he used to hold the stone. "Much like a plain, rough rock that can be transformed into a beautiful, powerful gem. The gem was always there, but it had to be smoothed, then recognized, then used."

Pietre held his pouch, now heavy with several strong stones. "I'm not very fast," he said at last.

"That's okay," Humphrey said. "I will be your speed."

Pietre looked into the wide brown eyes of his friend—he who had so much to lose if they didn't succeed. Pietre climbed onto Humphrey's back and together they thundered forward, running along the thin string of hope that had bound them together since the beginning.

WOLRIJK RAN AT WITTENDON'S BACK. THE PRINCE WAS HUNCHED over, looking towards the top of the hill as though he thought he was the only creature there. Wolrijk raised his blade, about to swing it across the back of the prince's neck, when Wittendon swatted a hand as though hitting a fly. A thick vine flew down and smacked Wolrijk across the face.

The Verander let out a roar and Wittendon turned to face him.

"I bet you think that was cute," the wolf-man hissed.

"What was cute was the fact that you thought I wouldn't hear you pummeling toward me, like a child playing at war."

"You call me a child?" Wolrijk asked, laughing. "I who have been of this kingdom since before its conception."

"Whatever I choose to call you, I don't have time for your stupid game," Wittendon said. "Here, take my crown—it's yours." Wittendon tore off his crimson sash and tossed it at Wolrijk's feet.

Wolrijk stepped on it, grinding the fine fabric into the sandy stones beneath him. "I'd rather play my game *now*. And you won't give me the crown because I'm going to take it."

In the distance a trumpet blasted and a wolf captain shouted, "The king's box; it is destroyed." This cry was repeated among the ranks, trickling to the crowd below.

Wittendon looked to Wolrijk.

"He was my first order of business."

"*You*," Wittendon said clearly, "cannot kill my father."

Wolrijk swung the blade so swiftly back and forth at Wittendon's stomach that the metal looked like scissors opening and shutting.

In the distance, they heard the howling that shook the air. "The king is gone," the captain bellowed.

Wolrijk's blade stopped. "Gone?" he whispered.

"As I told you," Wittendon said.

"Without aid, he will die soon enough from the wound I inflicted. As will you."

"I will do no such thing," Wittendon said, stopping the blade at once with his own weapon and pushing Wolrijk back.

The wolf-turned-Verander may have been a crazed lunatic bent on usurping the kingdom, but Wittendon was broken-hearted and furious with everyone he'd ever cared about. That was its own kind of lunacy. Wittendon sheathed his blade and pointed all ten fingers in front of him like they were tiny harpoons. Behind Wolrijk trees began to fall. They hit the ground in rhythm, like a line of dominos getting nearer. Wittendon smiled. Two trees fell on either side of Wolrijk. Abruptly, Wittendon clenched his fingers into tight fists. Instantly the trees burst into flame.

347

"All the better to cremate your body," the wolf growled, but as he conjured a tornado of stone to dump on the flames, it was clear that both shifters would need more than a quick blade or a burst of magic to conquer the other.

~

Now that Pietre was standing staring down the sun, it didn't feel as terrifying as he'd expected. Until the drums began. From across the hill at the king's box, he could hear the Veranderen guard calling, "She has come—leaving a purple lily of mourning—to avenge her brother's death."

"Find the lady of the lily," a whispered shout rose into the air like an army of ghosts. "She who has robbed us of the life of our king."

"Sadora," Pietre murmured. The drums grew louder—a chilling sound in the land of the red sun—the march of Veranderen hunting one of their own, armed with weapons tipped in the Shining Grey. The chants of the guard and the crowd arched over the hill like a song of banshees—Veranderen wailing the coming death of their traitorous comrade.

Sadora wasn't one to do things by mistake. Pietre guessed she'd left the flower for a reason. And he had a guilty feeling that it involved leading the king's guard away from the Sacred Tablet, away from himself, and down the hill.

"The king's blood splattered like water," the head wailer sang, inciting the troops. "His body lost from those who mourn."

The king's full guard—both wolf and Veranderen—gathered at the opposite slope of the hill and then, at the blood-curdling signal of the head captain, they stormed forward over the grass like a pestilence of crickets darkening the hillside. Pietre could hear their feet as they tore up and across the great hill. Even worse, he could feel them, thousands of tiny earthquakes barreling toward his captain.

"Madmen," he whispered. "Check and double-check."

~

SADORA STOOD AT THE CENTER OF THE HILL, LESS THAN A MILE AWAY from Wolrijk and Wittendon and a bit further from the boy. Dropping a flower in the king's box hadn't been her best plan ever, but she'd had to do something. She had heard the guard coming up the hill to check the box. When they found it destroyed, she knew that they would have combed the hill one way or another. As it was, they were now looking for her, not a prince they didn't yet know was a traitor, or a small boy who needed a shiny stone. Just her. And presumably when they found her, they would stop looking for anything else. She sighed. Fulfilling your destiny sounded grand, but now that it was done and the king destroyed, it would have been nice to enjoy the years ahead.

She walked to the freshly disturbed dirt that she knew marked Sarak's grave. It would be a logical place for them to find her and she wanted to be as near to her brother as possible. Sarak had always made difficult things better. She took one of the two remaining flowers from her hair and rested it on the dirt.

The thundering of the guard shook the ground beneath her and she took a deep breath, ready to be driven through with the first tooth or Grey-tipped scythe that came at her. The line of muscular wolves and Veranderen crested on the darkening horizon, and stopped. "My lady," said the one in the forefront—the wolf known as Rorof. "You must now come with us."

"Must I?" she asked, holding the shaft of the blade of Crespin.

Rorof gave the broken weapon an odd look and said, "My lady; it is clear that your grief over your brother maddens you. Now come. Even the asylums of our land are better than a lonely hill."

"An asylum," she asked, feigning surprise. "The king who has reigned for 900 years is gone, and you speak to me of asylum. It is difficult to believe."

Behind the wolf Rorof, another growled low. His voice was joined by others, though soon silenced by Rorof. "You will have the best our land can offer you."

"Which is, as I understand it, a noose after a decent meal."

"On some occasions, yes, it well may be."

She raised the shaft of the spear above her head and moving it in circles brought a heavy, dark cloud above the wolves. Rorof lowered his body and the guard behind him did the same, bracing for attack.

From the cloud, Sadora pulled a jolt of energy, which she held at the shaft's tip. Rorof looked to it, calculating.

Sadora took a deep breath. She would never be able to take them all with one puny lightning streak, but it would take out a few and frighten many more.

She tightened her grip on the shaft with the bolt and Rorof pawed the earth. Both paused, letting the adrenaline build and bracing for its release when a voice spoke from behind Sadora.

"And what if she didn't do it?" Kaxon asked, stepping in front of Sadora. "She is not the only one who has cause for madness on this day. Nor is she the only one that would do evil to our king."

"Kaxon," Sadora said, too shocked to notice the reaction of the guard.

"You may come with us as well, my disgruntled prince," Rorof said, though without the civility he'd expressed to Sadora. "No noose awaits you or asylum either, although with the disgrace you will surely suffer throughout your life, you may wish it had been thus."

"Ah," Kaxon said. "I see you understand my predicament then. That is very much what I was thinking when I came to my father and —" Kaxon gestured to the point on the hill where his father had been.

"There we found a flower just as this one," Rorof replied, nodding to the flower that lay on Sarak's grave.

"There's a whole creek bed of them right near the royal box."

"Kaxon," Sadora said.

"Do not try to protect me just because I am kin to your love," Kaxon replied.

"I will take you both," Rorof replied, looking from one to the other, confused.

"You will not," Kaxon replied. "You will take only me. The blade that spilled my father's blood—it wasn't hers. Which is fairly obvious. Did you not notice that she's fighting with a *stick*. The blade belonged to me." He laughed, a sad, sick sound that rose from his throat like choking. "You know, that extra-long blade, three-inches of Grey—it even had my name on it. Can you believe it?"

Rorof just stared at him.

"I couldn't quite believe it either, but it's true. A little gift from a too-smart Greysmith." Kaxon staggered around, like a human drunkard.

"Kaxon," Sadora said for the third time, raising her voice. And with that, Kaxon swung around and smacked her on the mouth. "Enough," he shouted. "Now go."

The flesh of her lip split open, and she held her hand to it in shock more than pain. "I will not leave my brother's grave. You go."

"Fine," he said. "Consider it the last favor I do for my brother." And with that he ran straight into the outstretched weapons of the Veranderen, collapsing as his chest and neck hit the blades.

Sadora stepped back and gasped. "Kaxon," she whispered one final time.

"My lady," the wolf Rorof said, turning to her. "Tell me truly: did you kill the king?"

"No," she said clearly. "I did not."

He bowed briefly and said, "Then pay your respects to your brother if you must, but be careful on this hill. It has brought more death today than it has in all the years since its first."

After they left, Sadora sat down for the first time that day. She wanted to cry. They would see more death before it was through— death of the good as well as bad. She had known this at the start— known what war and revolution entailed. But watching Kaxon fall for her sake, she felt it deeply for the very first time.

IN THE DISTANCE, WITTENDON HEARD A CRASH. THE GUARD, IT seemed, was dealing with something else on the hill. The sun sat low and fat. Wolrijk had conjured a group of snakes that hissed and writhed at Wittendon's feet. Using his scythe to vault over them, Wittendon jumped and ran toward the sounds of voices. Wolrijk followed. For somebody who was 1,000 years old and had spent the last several centuries cramped into the incorrect body, Wolrijk was fast. Wittendon had to stop just before he reached the noise in order to face Wolrijk again, but he'd made it several lengths up the hill. In the fading light he could see the Tablet—a simple round stone, pocked and ancient. It looked nothing out of the ordinary, but at its left was a small indentation—an indentation you would assume had been formed from millennia of rain pooling there. That was where the stone needed to go. Placed by the hand of a human. If a human managed to show up.

Wolrijk tore a handful of hair from his neck and held it in front of him. Quickly each hair grew into thin golden daggers that reminded Wittendon of the ice pick that had killed the Mördare. That couldn't be good. Wolrijk tossed one at Wittendon. It was impossibly fast. It struck his tricep and hurt, but no more than a needle would have. Wittendon pulled it out.

Wolrijk smiled then spat on the others. They sizzled at their tips and Wittendon moved back a step. Four dozen needle-like daggers, now poisoned at their tips with the wolf-man's saliva. In the distance, Wittendon heard Sadora shout something that sounded like his brother's name. At that moment, Wolrijk smiled again and pulled his arm back, releasing the daggers. Wittendon couldn't think what to do—he stepped back once again, tripped over a rock and fell. It wasn't his most graceful escape. But it worked. Only two daggers hit their mark—one at his side and the other on his forearm.

Both had barely hit him, but stung like death. Wittendon moaned and stood up. "I don't have time," he said, but could say no more. As soon as he was on his feet, he wanted to sit back down again. His head felt like a sandbag and his vision was almost entirely marred so that he could see only out of the corners of his eyes. Turning, he saw Wolrijk grab another wad of hair. Taking the Grey blade of the scythe, Wittendon quickly scooped out the needle at his side, and immediately started to feel better. Trying to hold the small end of the scythe without cutting his finger off, he jabbed at the other needle in his forearm. When it was released, his head cleared, though by the time he had his vision back, Wolrijk was ready to spit again.

Wittendon's own mouth felt like he'd swallowed a layer of the chalky river sediment. He paused at the thought and then pointed to the ground, pulling a chunk of it up. Whitish-gray soil lurched into the air, and Wittendon threw it towards Wolrijk's mouth just as he opened it. The wolf-man coughed and Wittendon swiped the hair blades with his scythe, cutting them in half.

Cursing, Wolrijk lunged at him with his own scythe—chopping and swinging with a force he hadn't before. Wittendon stepped back once, then twice. They were nearer to Sarak's grave now and Wittendon focused on his friend. In his mind he could see Sarak swinging the scythe with a level of skill he was sure Wolrijk didn't possess. He pictured Sarak's movements and mimicked them—faster and faster. Just as he had in the first round, Wittendon felt the outside sounds melt away and heard only the clang and click of their swords. He had forgotten the sun, the stone, the tournament. He threw Wolrijk to the ground and the wolf-man's head hit a large stone, his eyes rolling back. To Wittendon's left a voice murmured,

Bravo, my princeling,
but you waste precious time
dancing and mincling.

"That's not even a word," Wittendon said. "And would you care to step in?"

Wolrijk had begun to moan and would soon be getting up.

The cat just purred.

"I'll get the stone to the top of the mountain; I'm on my way," Wittendon said, turning to run.

"But you see," the feline said. "That would do no good. This feat must be accomplished by the pure one."

Wittendon just looked at her. It was the calico Savah and she sat there in the midst of an empty battlefield cleaning her paw.

"Pardon, my liege," she said at last glancing at him. "But you are not he. The stone must be given to the one who is."

"I don't suppose," Wittendon said, watching Wolrijk through the corner of his eye, "that you would like to tell me who this man is?"

"He who is himself called stone, formed by two of steady heart—solid as the earth itself and streaked as such, but not with gold." She turned, apparently considering the question answered, and pranced away with her tail in the air.

"Feline demons," Wittendon muttered.

Wolrijk got up, holding his hand to his head and growling—a deep menacing sound that made Wittendon's innards vibrate. Wittendon looked to the top of the hill. Wolrijk's gaze followed and then, slowly, he began to laugh.

Rhythmically, Wolrijk hit the bottom of his scythe on the ground—two taps, followed by seven quick ones, then two more very slow, then one loud boom.

"You're such a sweet little hero," Wolrijk said, still laughing. "The sash you threw at me, the mysterious errand. Do you think I haven't been around long enough to have heard the prophecies? Though it would have been easier if your father hadn't destroyed so many of the ancient books. Even great minds cannot remember all the pieces. As it is, I'm just starting to put them together."

Wittendon could hear the marching. It began at the bottom of the hill and moved quickly toward them.

"I am still general of the king's guard," Wolrijk said.

Wittendon leveled his scythe at Wolrijk and ran recklessly toward him. Wolrijk stopped the blade with a quick movement and pushed him aside, casting a spell that made Wittendon's tongue feel like it had twisted into knots. The king's troops came into view—both the strongest wolves and most powerful Veranderen of the land.

They halted when they saw their mute prince and the newly transformed general. "Do you see that noble altar atop this mountain? That which is found in our histories and mythologies, that which has been here ever and always since the beginning of our time?" Wolrijk asked.

The head captain nodded.

"Destroy it," Wolrijk commanded, "and quickly."

~

THE KING'S GUARD WAS NOT TRAINED TO QUESTION. THEY MOVED LIKE a wave toward the stone. Yet, as the troops closed in on the Tablet, a tiny animal moved into view in front of the army. At the sight of the creature the entire group halted. The animal swished its tail twice and mewed. The wolves of the group took a step back, some touching their foreheads to the earth in a prayer their race used to ward off evil. The cat stretched her front legs as though preparing for a nap and then, in an impossibly quick movement, she sprang at the head captain's face, clawing him with all four paws.

"Now," the little cat Emie hissed. From the bushes and trees shot dozens of cats, some small, some huge—claws extended, teeth exposed. They ran at the guard as graceful and swift as fish, though strong and thick-skinned as elephants. They tore at the flesh of their enemies, breaking the necks of some who crumpled in helpless heaps. As the cats fought, a group of humans and green-cloaked Veranderen with ornate 7's embroidered across their chests formed a wide circle around the top portion of the hill.

Eleven spears gleamed in the near-darkness—their tips shimmering like the moon. The cats scampered back to the ranks of the Septugant and for one long minute nothing happened.

"The blades of Crespin," the wolf Rorof whispered.

"Crespin's blades no longer," a voice replied from the crowd. "Good Rorof, it pains me that you did not join our force," Sadora said, coming forward. "And though it brings me no pleasure to fight one such as you, we cannot let you destroy the Tablet." She paused, smiling weakly. "I have not yet even kissed it for love."

"You gave me your word," Rorof said.

"And my word was good," she replied. "I did not kill the king. I did not so much as spill a drop of his blood. But I do lead this rebel band. Return and you shall have mercy at our hands. Continue, and these blades—the very blades the king used to secure his reign, will spill the blood of our good people. Please," she said, sincerely. "They are blades intended to kill an unkillable race. Return."

"You know that is not a thing the Königsvaren can do," Rorof said. Lowering his head, he released his troops. They tore through the most vulnerable humans with ease as Rorof barreled toward Sadora. She lowered her shaft. Rorof's face was white, his fur a light, shiny gray. Sadora was determined not to kill him. When he leapt at her, she ducked, her body almost flat against the earth. As his body sailed over her, she drove the spearless shaft into the air above her, hoping her estimation was right. It struck Rorof's hind leg, shattering the bone. The wolf landed in a heap a pace away from her. Running to him, she raised her shaft again, bringing the bottom end down with all her force onto the center of his forehead. "There," she whispered, as he slumped to the earth. "I might be a fool, but I've tried to return the good turn you did to me. You should be passed over as quite dead."

Behind her, she could hear the cries of the humans in her army falling and giving way, but she could also hear the swishing of weapons—human-made weapons stronger than any the king's guard had known. Several of the miners carried hammers and picks, which landed with loud cracks on the heads of the wolves, although they couldn't harm the Veranderen force. To her left, she could see the stutterer Damiott swinging and jabbing with his Grey spear. A group of four Veranderen had surrounded him—which was four more than she feared any human could handle. He moved back and forth, jabbing and turning with the spear. Just before she reached him, the last Verander fell, not quite dead perhaps, but maimed beyond recovery. Sadora willed herself not to look at the fallen of her own kind and stared instead into Damiott's triumphant face.

"I see you have this area covered," she said. Then she turned and ran into the fray to help the others.

※

WOLRIJK PRESSED AGAINST WITTENDON WITH THE CONFIDENCE OF A conqueror. Wittendon let him. Above them on the hill, the humans fell like gnats before his race. There was no *pure one* in sight. And Wolrijk would not rest until Wittendon's blood flowed in a stream down this hill.

Near the periphery of the battle just above them, Wittendon saw Pietre standing to the side, looking for someone. *The boy*, Wittendon thought.

Wolrijk noticed Wittendon staring at the child, held his weapon steady and grinned. "The child," he called up the hill to the wolves. "Kill him."

"Have you gone mad?" Wittendon asked, but it could barely be heard over the howls of the wolves. Wittendon saw that Humphrey stood beside Pietre, but even with the enormous dog, the two figures on the hill looked impossibly small.

The Veranderen remained to fight the Septugant while the wolves ran at the boy. The wolves seemed glad to do it. They knew the child—the village orphan who had pushed his way through gates and guards, who had struck and weakened wolves with his sling. And Wolrijk was not the only wolf who enjoyed revenge.

STEADILY, PIETRE BEGAN TO SWING HIS SLING—THOUGH IT WAS JUST A normal sling with a normal stone. In his other hand, he held the dagger his father had made. It was more weaponry than he had ever held, but looking to the mass of predators that ran for him, he knew he was a blade of grass on a field about to be plowed.

The wolves howled with the same blood call Pietre had heard every night of his childhood when the Blødguard had run through the woods in eager pursuit.

Pietre released his stone. It sailed away from his sling and landed with a quiet plunk on the forehead of one of the wolves. The animal stumbled and fell, but all the others—hundreds of them—still ran at Pietre. Humphrey leaned back on his hind legs, ready to jump and tear into the sea of wolves, ready to fight until he himself was shredded to a skeleton. Pietre loaded another stone, swung, and released. Again, it struck with a small plunk, but this time the noise seemed to echo over the hill—sounding as though hundreds of new footsteps had begun to pound the earth behind them.

"Can there be more wolves that come now from behind?" Pietre whispered to Humphrey, sad as he looked to the empty Tablet. Humphrey turned to face their new foe, about to attack when a line of dogs rounded the hill and barreled past him toward the stream of wolves that was about to overtake Pietre. The wolves did not slow, nor did the dogs and when they met, it was with a deafening crack of bones and teeth—dozens of animals driven to the earth almost before Pietre had time to blink.

The dogs fought first in silence, fully focused on the enemy in front of them. They jumped and bit, dodged and ran. Some fell, but most pressed into the force of wolves that stood against them. As they did, their voices rose up—in snatches of song at first—a shrill note, a mournful howl; then broke into lines and verses as haunting and steady as death. The melodies swayed above the wolves in triumphant tones while the harmonies dipped into the worst dreams the wolves had known. Perhaps the dogs would not speak or sing again when this night was through, but today they sang into the bones and blood of their enemies. Some wolves fled to the woods without a scratch, others whimpered at the feet of the dogs who tossed them aside where they lay shaking. Those who stayed to fight moved left when they had meant to go right, jumped when they had wished to duck, finding their attacks distracted and misplaced.

Pietre stared entranced, his sling slack at his side. The dark form of Ellza appeared at his side. "My child," she said. "Your time has come. You must let the dogs now do the work always intended for them to do."

Humphrey faced the cat.

"You," she said. "Go with the boy and never let it be said that half-breeds have no place in this land."

Humphrey did not need to be asked twice.

∾

358

WITTENDON SAW PIETRE DISAPPEAR FROM THE MASS OF WOLF AND dog, and turned. When he did, the hook of Wolrijk's scythe caught him in the neck. It missed his carotid by a breath, but it brought Wittendon down and when he fell, Wolrijk pounced, landing on his stomach, prepared to rip at his chest with razored teeth.

Wittendon gasped for breath, trying to push the wolf-man off of him. For the first time since the clamor had begun around him, Wittendon noticed the screams of the crowd below. They had no idea what was going on, what had happened to their king, or who it was that fought the king's guard. They did not care. They screamed now for blood, for battle, for a taste of things they did not understand because most of them had been shielded from death their whole lives. They screamed for Wolrijk to kill and as soon as Wittendon freed himself from Wolrijk's teeth and stood up, they screamed for him to fight back. It was a sound Wittendon wished he could ignore, though now that the terrible noise had caught his attention, it was difficult to let go.

Wittendon's chest bled into his torn clothes and his flesh felt like it had gotten caught in the cook's meat grinder. Not all of the bites were intensely deep, but Wittendon could see bits of his skin hanging from Wolrijk's teeth, which made him almost as dizzy as if he'd lost pounds of blood.

"It is finished," Wolrijk growled, circling him. "Your rebellion falters, the wolves fight with vengeance at my command and it seems that I might even get my revenge on that precious little man child. Your father and friend are dead. Your lady will soon be too. Your brother is gone. Soon, I will win my rightful rule of this land and at my hand, your father will look like the Flower Prince and all but those most faithful to me will ache for what will then seem the gentleness of his reign."

Wittendon put his hand into his pouch. The stone was still there, but what good could it do? What Wolrijk said was true. Wittendon's body quivered; the rebels fell fast at the hand of the trained Veranderen soldiers; and the boy would be attacked or stampeded before Wittendon had the strength or opportunity to get to him. Still, he had no desire for Wolrijk to know of his mother's stone, much less own it.

With a quick movement of his hand, as though wiping sweat from his face, Wittendon dropped the gem into his mouth, intending to swallow it and thus carry it with him to his grave. But as soon as the stone hit his tongue, his body felt like it had erupted with lightning. Light shone from his nails and the ends of each hair shot up from his skin, tipped with white. He took a deep breath and as he did, the skin across his chest stretched and healed. He ran his hands over his face and arms and legs, sealing every nick and cut.

Wolrijk stepped back a pace and below them people screamed and howled and cheered at the burst of unexpected light.

Bending over, Wittendon picked his scythe up from the ground and as soon as he touched it, Grey ran up and down along the hilt until the entire weapon was shimmering and hardened with the metal. Quietly, he held it in front of his face in challenge. "Do you, Wolrijk, know now who I am?" The stone moved in Wittendon's mouth like part of his tongue—each word a shot of light from his mouth.

Wolrijk tried to grimace, but as he returned the challenge with his own blade, his hand trembled.

"I am Wittendon, son of Loerwoei, and Lord of the Grey."

Wolrijk licked his dry lips.

"You are not the only one with secrets. You will not rule this land, nor will my father if he lives," Wittendon said. He lowered his blade and plunged toward Wolrijk. Wolrijk struck with his own blade several times, staggering back as Wittendon cut his shoulder, side, and arm. Each wound bled continuously.

Wolrijk panted, then threw his scythe to the side and held only his claws in front of him. "And I am Draden. But perhaps you are right to call me Wolrijk, youngling, for that is who I have become. A creature stitched of the Pallium—its grains embedded in the creases of my nails and seams of my flesh." Quickly, he slashed Wittendon across the face. Wittendon touched it and, though the blood slowed, it did not heal entirely.

Wolrijk advanced, aiming his sharp claws at any exposed part of the prince. Wittendon, likewise, stabbed at each piece of Wolrijk's skin that he could reach until both of their bodies gaped with hundreds of small wounds that would not seal. Wittendon held the gem tightly in his mouth—the last piece of his mother he possessed.

Strangely, at this moment, he thought of her beauty, not her power —of her graceful step, her long hair, her delicate fingers. At once, Wittendon stopped, offering a tiny murmur of thanks. Again Wolrijk swiped with his daggered nails and at once Wittendon returned the blow—not to the skin of the wolf-man as he had been doing, but across the tops of his fingers. He was careful not to hit the Pallium-seamed nails, which he thought might deflect the force of the Grey. Instead, he aimed just below, lopping off each finger at its center—left then right. The deformed creature howled in a way that seemed to pull the earth into itself.

He ran at Wittendon, teeth bared. Wittendon held his blade in front of his body—ready to pierce his crazed opponent, but just before the tip of Wittendon's blade swung into Wolrijk's bloodied flesh, Wolrijk leapt over scythe and prince and ran through an empty field toward a pine wood at the northern foot of the hill.

Pressing down on the stone in his mouth one last time, Wittendon could feel the pull of the Grey beneath him in the mines. Above him, several of the Veranderen—both of the guard and the rebellion—staggered and fell. The wolves slowed in their attacks, breathing heavier and running more clumsily.

In a moment the boy Pietre appeared in front of Wittendon, carried on the back of the dog.

Slowly, Wittendon spit the stone into his hand and below him the crowds erupted into screams and cheers. With one voice they began to chant, "Hail Wittendon, Lord of the World." Wittendon gripped the stone, feeling the jolt of power flood his veins, and paused. The hill, the head city, this continent, their world. His. All he had to do was raise his arm and release the golden flare. The sun was almost gone. No human would make it to the peak anyway. With one hand Wittendon held the stone; his other palm he opened toward the sky about to release the winner's flare. Pietre stared at him long and hard as the roar of the crowd grew louder.

Quietly, the boy whispered, "My prince, I need the stone."

361

Wittendon looked down at him. Oddly, he had forgotten he was there. "I can take it," Wittendon said. "In just a moment. My speed is needed anyway."

Pietre shook his head, barely daring to move. "No," he said. "I need it."

"You defy me?" Wittendon asked. "I said I could take it."

At Pietre's side hung his sling—one lonely, plain rock from a lonely, plain stream the only weight at its bottom. It was a grain of dust against the gleaming prince with his white tipped fur and glowing face. With one quick circle, Pietre pulled his arm back and launched the rock at Wittendon. The stone landed soundly on Wittendon's forehead. Pietre expected it to bounce off like a pebble hurled at a stone-wall, but the prince-king staggered back, grabbing his face, though he did not fall. With a growling scream, Wittendon sprang at the boy, his blade aimed at Pietre's neck. Humphrey moved faster than Pietre—shoving the boy aside so that Wittendon's blade missed his neck and instead sliced up the side of Pietre's face—a burst of blood where his ear had been.

Wittendon raised the blade again, then paused. The boy's injury was familiar—blood flowing from the child's ear just as it had after he'd been attacked by the wolf Wolrijk. Only worse. Wittendon gripped his blade, trying to think why exactly he was holding it up against a child.

In his pause, the boy reached to the earth to grab another stone. "The rock," Wittendon whispered, dropping his blade. "Solid as the earth itself."

Pietre placed the stone into his sling, but did not yet release it. Beneath them the crowd screamed like waters breaking a dam. "Kill the human rebel, oh king. Kill him." Wittendon shook his head and stepped back. Pietre looked at his prince—his king—with a determined defiance, a desperate fear, and a blink of something smaller, but brighter than everything else. "Please, Wittendon," Pietre asked, the glimmer of hope leaking into his voice.

Wittendon looked at the steely blue eyes of the boy for one long breath. "Catch," Wittendon said, throwing the empowered gem to

Pietre. The boy jumped onto the dog who ran swift and straight—a sound pouring from the animal's lips—not a howl like the wolves, nor quite a song like the dogs, but a single piercing note—clean and straight as a streak of light.

The Veranderen guard had broken through the Septugant defense at the top of the hill and now aimed their great force at the Tablet. Wittendon ran through the angry ranks to face them, his eyes glowing. Pointing his fingers to the hill, the prince-king pulled the Grey from its depths. The ground rippled and rose—a jagged ridge of rocky Grey between the guard and the mountaintop. "Stop," Wittendon bellowed. "I am Wittendon, Crespinszon, Lord of the Grey, and—for about four more minutes—Chancellor and Ruler of this, the known world."

In confusion the armies stopped, weakened by the jagged Grey ridge that had risen in front of them. Then one shouted, "You are no more than a traitor to the king."

"And perhaps his murderer as well," another chimed in.

They staggered forward against the Grey ridge, just as the boy and dog crested it, headed like lightning for the Tablet. The sun hung a sliver above the horizon, pausing in good-bye. The dog threw the boy toward the Sacred Tablet and in the next instant blackness soaked the earth—heavy and complete. The stars sank into the darkness and the moon quivered and faded.

Wittendon could see nothing. He knew Veranderen and wolves stood only feet away, but he could not see them and any noise that came to his ears sounded muffled, as though he had been sealed in a jar. Everyone else must have felt it too because no one moved against him. No one moved at all. In fact, in the next few minutes a haze came into Wittendon's head that felt strangely like sleep. His body sagged and grew tired, while odd images leapt up into his sub-conscious like dreams—shifting and rocking in his mind: the boy fallen to the side of the Tablet, his body knocked over like a butterfly in a tornado, the half-breed licking the child's chin, then sinking down into sleep, the stone glowing and growing until it burst from its perch into the sky, hanging in front of the old moon and pushing it away.

Pretty dreams, Wittendon thought hazily to himself, then mumbling he hummed a few bars of the lullaby his mother used to sing him,

When the sun sinks low and the moon shines high.
When the light falls down out of purple sky.
When the night goes black and the stars retire,
It's then you'll go to sleep.

"Prophecy," Wittendon murmured as he drifted further into sleep. "From my cradle she has sung it."

CHAPTER 57

P ietre woke to darkness like none he had ever experienced. The blood where his ear had been was crusted into a scaly lump and his body hurt. He reached out blindly until his hand felt the soft fur he knew to be Humphrey. Finding the rise and fall of Humphrey's breath, Pietre scooted over, ready to lay his head on the animal's side when, to the east, a splinter of light broke the intense blackness. It stared at him above the horizon like a lustrous eye just opening. Beside him, Humphrey moaned in his sleep. The new sun rose quickly, pushing back the night over the eastern base of the hill and working its way up. As it moved, the people stirred. When the light hit the surviving Veranderen, they sank into their flesh forms, some still sleeping, some jolted awake.

"Humphrey," Pietre said, shaking his friend. "Humphrey, it comes."

The animal rolled over, lifted his head, then sank down again. Pietre pushed on him again. He wanted to talk to him one last time before the light hit; he wanted to hear his voice. "Humphrey," he said. "We did it; we won. You are free."

Humphrey lifted his head again, his eyes glazed. He looked at the boy as though he still couldn't see him. "Humphrey," Pietre said again.

"Thank you. You threw me to the Tablet. You did it just in time." Pietre paused. "And Humphrey, Humphrey you sang—the most beautiful note I have ever heard."

Slowly, Humphrey smiled, then opened his mouth to reply, but just as he tried to speak, the sun crept over the mountain and touched the animal. A sound came from his lips that surprised them both—not language, not hondsong, but a crude sort of bark. Humphrey said nothing more, but placed his head in Pietre's lap. Pietre stroked the dog-wolf's neck for several minutes, letting the tears run down his cheeks and drop onto the half-breed's fur.

Above them a small bright sun found its way over the hill and into a crisp blue sky. Beneath them, the hillside staggered to life. From the base of the hill, three sharp bugles sang out and just below them, Pietre could hear Sadora's voice. "Prepare your weapons and wait for my signal."

Pietre waited too. He expected to feel the trembling earth as he had yesterday. Instead, after more minutes than he had expected, he was greeted with a shrill whistle followed by the steady barking of the dogs. It was good enough. The rebel troops streamed down the hill.

The Veranderen forces, now all in human form, stood and re-grouped, but most were completely unarmed in robes that hung loosely from their smaller human frames.

The Septugant ran into the weakened pack of Veranderen and wolves, plunging human-made spears and swords into thin human flesh while the wolves howled to one another, speechless and confused. Quickly those who survived were forced down the hill. When nearly to the bottom, their Veranderen captain turned to the others and called, "Stand down." His haphazard troops fell back, waiting several paces down from their leader. He walked forward—stout, pale, and unarmed. Normally the wolves of the Königsvaren would handle these negotiations, but normally the wolf-guard was not a howling, wordless, messy mass of noise.

Sadora went forward to meet the Veranderen captain, the bladeless shaft in her hand, two of her men at her side. Pietre watched from behind.

"My lady, I do not know how it has come to pass, but you have won. More than won," the captain said. "Will you now slaughter my—our—kind as you tear through a city filled with thousands of them? I beg you," he continued, "three hours to gather our people and flee the city."

"You may have until dusk," she replied. "Those who wish to stay and live in equality and peace may hang a piece of green fabric above their doors. Those houses, we will pass over; the rest will be taken, emptied, and re-filled with the families of this rebellion. Is that understood?"

"Yes, my lady," he replied. Beside him stood a wolf—silent and sulking—his foot set in a hurried splint.

Sadora paused. "I am glad to see, good Rorof, that you are recovering from yesterday's blow."

From deep in his belly, Rorof growled, each tooth visible to the new leader of the head city.

Sadora closed her eyes sadly. "Our troops will supervise the evacuation. You will find camps on the north and west sides of the city, though I hope that many choose to stay and live in peace with the other races since one way or another, this will become their new way of life."

The captain replied merely by bowing. Then he turned down the hill to give orders to the defeated forces.

Pietre watched as Sadora stood on the hill for several minutes listening to the bugles wailing and the messengers shouting as they ran past houses. Then she struck the spear shaft to the earth, whistling shrilly, and the rebel troops streamed through the crowds at the base of the hill to supervise the evacuation. "Fight only if necessary. Spare as many as possible," she called. Under her breath, Pietre heard her mutter, "There will be enough unrest and violence as it is; we've no need to aggravate it."

Pietre walked slowly toward the city below. In his pocket he could feel something heavy. He hadn't yet dared to reach in and touch it, but as the long form of Wittendon came into view he felt its weight more keenly.

～

SADORA STOOD AT THE NORTHWESTERN GATE AND WAITED FOR HE WHO was no longer a prince or a king. Inside the palace walls she could hear her troops streaming through the castle—hunting down nobles who tried to hide or resist. Humans were cheering and marching and joining her troops, some of the Veranderen were fighting or running or screaming like children in tantrums. The wolves and the dogs were uncomfortably silent. To the north, a steady stream of Veranderen and wolves had begun leaving the city—heavy bags tied to their backs, children at their sides crying and asking questions. *It's hard to feel like the good ones*, Sadora thought, trying to remind herself how much worse it could have been, trying to remind herself she had given them a choice.

Wittendon met her at the gates without looking her in the eyes. Together they walked into his mother's garden. Much of it had been trampled. Sadora saw Wittendon's hair—now tipped in white—rise up in anger. He raised his hand to pull the earth up and create a gate around the garden, but nothing happened. Again Wittendon raised his arm, this time murmuring an incantation as well. Still not so much as a cloud of dust stirred from the earth.

"Oh dear," Zinnegael said, coming up behind them. "This will never do. Especially not when this garden was formed by a human and shifter working side by side." Quietly she stood beside them, focused and careful. Slowly the vines from the morning glory began to wind around the thorny branches of rose bushes. Both plants climbed steadily to the height of a man, forming a fence. In front of this sprang a dozen or more Dewberry bushes—their thorns nearly as sharp as the humans' swords.

When she was done, she stepped forward toward a branch of the sterling rose and plucked two blooms.

"How is it possible," Wittendon asked, "when magic has escaped the rest of us?"

"It has not *escaped* you," she said, handing him a flower. "Though I suspect that you will now feel the strength of your magic change with the moon; and nearly non-existent in the sun. You will find many things now driven by the course and strength of the moon and sun." She handed the other flower to Sadora. "But I am not a shifter—my insides are wound in unusual lines that allow unusual things. Why do you think your father wished the half-breeds extinct?"

The sun hung high in the sky—bright as a coin. They walked through an open courtyard, where several of the troops, done with the supervision of their quarters had come to receive further orders. Sadora sent several after food and then she, Wittendon, and Zinnegael stood alone and silent.

"Well then," Zinnegael said after several quiet minutes. "I need to see what mischief the cats have found. They haven't been alone in a city for centuries—the local fish market will never be the same."

When she was gone, Wittendon turned to Sadora, casting the flower Zinnegael had given him to the ground. "Did you kill my father?" Wittendon asked abruptly, still without looking at her.

"No," she replied. "Though he no longer has power and has fled to the woods as he caused many to do before him."

"But he lives?"

"Yes," she said, "*he* lives." Sadora paused, taking a deep breath, "But Wittendon..." She stepped nearer to the once king.

Wittendon stepped away. "I'm sorry," he said, "Sarak is gone."

"I know," Sadora replied. "I felt it the moment it happened. You did what you had to do. As did he. We all did."

They paused again before Sadora continued, "And Kaxon," she said slowly, "Kaxon did more than he had to do."

"Kaxon?" he said, looking to her at last.

"Yes," she said, handing Wittendon her rose. "He came back, but now he is gone as well."

"You know this?" Wittendon asked.

"Yes," she replied. "He gave himself up to save me."

Wittendon stood without speaking for so many minutes that Sadora turned to leave him with his grief.

"I didn't feel it, in case you were wondering," Wittendon said abruptly. "We weren't *one*. Hardly wound together as twins."

Sadora wanted to look down, but forced herself to gaze into his face.

"But I wondered if he would come back," he said. "Leaving didn't seem like something he would do."

At the center of the head city a plume of dark smoke rose up. Sadora knew the purpose of the great fire. Bodies could not be left to rot in the streets. "Come," she said. "Let us go inside while others handle this business."

"No," he said, looking to the hill. A muscular human carried a shifter still in wolken form. All those who had died in that form remained so. "No," Wittendon whispered, running toward the body.

"Give him to me," he said to the human.

The man turned to Wittendon, but did not immediately obey. Damiott came down the hill and gestured to the peasant. "G-go on," he said.

Turning back to Wittendon, the man held out the body like it was a rag. "My lord," the human said, his voice turning down on the word 'lord' like a frown.

Wittendon carried his brother's body to the garden. "Where is the witch?" he said, the pitch of his voice rising. "Where is the bedeviled sorceress when I need her?" He placed the body among his mother's favorite flowers and walked to the edge of the garden like he expected Zinnegael to appear there, then kicked his foot into one of the old rose bushes, blood beading on his humanish skin like dew.

"Where is she," Wittendon shouted at Sadora. "I cannot now do this without her."

Sadora looked at him, slow tears running down her cheeks. "Yes," Sadora said, finding an old shovel in the corner of the gardens. "Yes, you can."

For a minute Wittendon just held the shovel, tears streaming down his chin and onto his clothes. Then with one powerful movement, he stuck the shovel into the ground and began to move the dirt. Sadora went through the garden gathering sweet herbs, which she laid upon the body. The sun sat high and Wittendon dripped with sweat. After several hours, the two of them lifted Kaxon into the earth and then both of them—Wittendon with the shovel and Sadora with her hands—covered Kaxon's body with dirt. Sadora reached into her hair, pulling the last dark lily from it. Gently she placed it on the mound of dirt. "Come," she said.

Wittendon fingered the soft petals of the lily. "He always did like you," Wittendon said.

"He did not do it for me," she replied. "He did it for you." Sadora handed him the sterling rose he had dropped earlier.

Wittendon looked into Sadora's coppery eyes, then reached out and placed the pale rose behind her ear, letting his fingers trail down the side of her cheek.

Pietre burst through the gate, startling them. "Have you done it?" he asked, breathless.

Sadora looked to him in surprise. "Done what, brave child?"

"Have you brought them? Come and see." The boy ran through the halls of the palace into the street to the side. "Look," he shouted. "They come." Jumping on Humphrey's back, the two of them raced to the thin figures coming across the square accompanied like royalty by a band of stout, short hounds.

Pietre sprang from Humphrey and ran to them. His father caught him in his arms as though he was a small child. His mother touched his hair, his eyes, his cheeks. She moved her hand to the bloodied spot where no ear was and for one long minute she closed her eyes. Humphrey waited to the side, respectful, until Carina broke free from her family and knelt beside him, stroking his muzzle as though it was silk. "It seems, good creature, that you have carried on the work of your mother after all." With a twinkle in her eye, she removed her hand and said, "And I hear you carry on her blood line as well."

Humphrey pressed his body against Carina, touching her hands with his cool nose as though in thanks. At once the group was caught up by part of the crowd and carried to the great hall. The new sun hung low and into the room ran humans, dogs, green-robed shifters, and a few shy wolves. Several men at the end of the procession carried a fat pig, roasted with tubers and greens that lay in heaps on the platter around it. "It is finished, my lady," one of the captains said.

"There is much work still to be done, but I think it can wait until morning."

Throughout the city and the great hall, torches were lit. One of the Septugant began to play a long metal flute and before long dancing began.

Sadora wanted to enjoy the music, the dancing, the food, but it reminded her only of Sarak, of graves, of loss. Before long, Wittendon came to her and took her hand. The two of them exited the hall, wandering along the empty corridors of the palace. Shortly, they heard footsteps behind them. Wittendon turned with his blade outstretched, but in front of him stood only the boy with the silent dog.

Humphrey walked in front of them as if to lead the way. Pietre stepped in behind him. Wittendon looked away from the scab at the side of the child's head and sheathed his weapon. The four walked quietly for a very long time, feeling far away from the feast that carried into the streets—songs filling the air, stomping, laughing.

"Zinnegael has suggested a contract," Sadora said at length. "To protect the dogs."

"What of the cats?" Pietre asked.

"The cats she is less concerned for. The large cats will always be free and powerful. The small ones feisty, crafty, and fast. No, she worries for the dogs."

Humphrey let out an indignant sniff. Pietre stuck his hands deep into his pockets, then stopped. "The stone," Pietre said. "I have it— your stone."

Sadora stopped to look at him. "You placed it and then you took it again?"

"No," Pietre said. "I placed it and then when I awoke, it was with me again. Here," he said, holding it out to Wittendon.

"It is not mine," Wittendon said, "and never was. I think you are meant to keep it; and to keep it safe. At any rate I think it best kept out of my hands." Wittendon looked at the stump where the child's ear had been. "I am very sorry," he said. "Have they not found the ear? Zinnegael could heal it in a breath."

"No, my lord," Pietre said.

"Do not call me that," Wittendon responded.

Pietre ignored him and continued, "Zinnegael sent the cats to look for it, but they found nothing. She thought it odd. She said usually the cats can find a needle in a haystack."

"Well," Wittendon said. "Ears are different than needles. Maybe one of the felines ate it."

"Hardly," a voice from the shadows said.

All four stopped. From the darkness stepped Ellza and her sister Savah.

"You speak," Wittendon gasped.

"But of course," Ellza responded. "We are not of the four races. We are not bound by the laws of the stone."

"Or any except our own," Savah added.

Humphrey growled.

"However," Ellza continued. "We have lived too long in the shadows to easily jump into the sun and we prefer it thus. We will remain silent; we find much wisdom in this. Together the two chanted,

> *Others do not appreciate*
> *that which they do not understand.*
> *We will sit in quiet*
> *keeping the riddles of this land.*

Pietre mumbled, "And we're back to rhyme." Wittendon and Humphrey both smiled and when Pietre looked up, the cats were gone.

Outside, the sun sank beneath the horizon, stars twinkled, and a small, bright moon glowed. They watched through a tall arching window.

"Thank goodness it is not blackness," Wittendon said and each of them laughed nervously. Far in the distance they could hear the wails and mourning songs of the evacuated Veranderen as the noise carried through the night air. Sadora chewed her lip and Wittendon put a gentle hand at the small of her back.

At once, a ruckus rose up from the already rowdy celebration—whoops and barks and cheers rang out. Quick short steps ran toward the group. Wittendon again unsheathed his sword, but it was only Carina who burst into the hallway, followed by Markhi and Borl. "She has birthed," Carina called to them, bending down to hug Humphrey. "Seven strong pups!"

Pietre looked to Humphrey whose face glowed as bright as the waning moon. "Freeborn," Pietre said. "Quarter-breed pups and allowed to roam as they were meant to do." Markhi bowed in respect and Sadora kissed Humphrey's head as Wittendon sheathed his sword and smiled. Outside, a group of dogs raised their speechless voices to the moon and howled their congratulations—not hondsong, but beautiful still.

PRONUNCIATION GUIDE

Character Names (in order of appearance):

Zinnegael (Zin-ə-gayl. The 'ae' form a long 'A' sound as it male)
    Savah (Sah-vah)
    Pietre (Pee-ay-tray)
    Crespin (Kres-pin)
    Grender (Gren-dər)
    Wittendon (Wit-tən-don)
    Kaxon (Kax-on)
    Wolrijk (Wohl-rike. The ij form a long 'I' sound as in kite)
    Hannah (Ha-nah)
    Carina (Car-ee-nah)
    Jager (Jay-gher)
    Humphrey (Hum-free)
    Sarak (Sa-rək)
    Sadora (Sah-doh-rah)
    Koll (Kohl)
    Tomar (Toh-mar)
    Naden (Nay-dən)
    Loerwoei (Loor-way or Loor-ə-way)

Draden (Dray-dən)

Markhi (Mark-hi. Long 'I' sound as in kite)

Winterby (Win-tər-bee)

Zinder (Zin-dər)

Rorof (Rohr-off)

Dorak (Dohr-ack)

Gog (Gahg)

Silva (Sil-vah)

Ellza (El-zah)

Borl (Borl)

Emie (Ee-mee)

Damiott (Day-mee-ot. The 'O' is short as in shot)

Peigh (Pay)

Quidin (Qui-din. Both 'I's are short as in bib)

Terms:

Veranderen (Vər-an-dər-ən): Wolf-shifters. This word refers to them as a people and as the plural. Generally, they are able to shift at will and have strong magical abilities. They comprise the ruling class. Verander—Singular. Veranderah—Feminine (singular)

Blødguard (Blewd-gard): The lowest class of wolves, starved so they will hunt humans after dark.

Königsvaren (Kəh-nigs-vah-rən): The wolf class that forms the king's guard.

Motteral (Mah-tər-ahl): The hill on which the Sourcestone was once placed and the highest point in the land.

Motteral Mal (Mah-tər-al Mahl): The tournament held among the Veranderen every hundred years at the summer solstice.

Shining Grey (shi-ning gray): The metal that can weaken or harm Veranderen.

Verlorn (vər-lorn): Term used for a Verander without magic.

Wolken (wohl-kən): The wolvish form of the Veranderen.

Septugant (sep-tu-gahnt): Those who wish to rebel against the king and usher in a Seventh Era.

Mördare (mərh-dah-ray): The half-life assassins the king uses to protect his treasure.

Rotherem (roth-ər-əm): An herb that can mask a wolf's scent.

Pallium (pal-ee-um): A metal that can contain or deflect energy.

River Rylen (Ri-lən): Main river.

Zonnesteen (zohn-ə-stayn): The stone of the sun.

Steenmacht (stayn-mahkt): The place where that stone can be empowered.

ACKNOWLEDGMENTS

Writing a good book takes a lot of collaboration. We'd like to take a few minutes to thank those who helped this little project along its way. First, a thank you to Ink Smith Publishing, which originally took this book on and published it.

Secondly, we'd be horrible people if we didn't give a huge shout out to our beta readers: Becca, Emilee, Catherine, Vanessa, Anna-Lisa, and Rebecca. They gave valuable input and support to the book. In addition to these ladies, we've had tons of support from friends far and wide, new and old. It's been touching to see the love and enthusiasm exhibited by people we haven't seen face-to-face for years. We have truly amazing friends.

And, finally, the largest thank you to our families. Some of our siblings have promoted the book like marketing monsters and have given much needed tech and social media support. Our older children have cheered us on, read different versions of the book, and told us that it definitely deserves to become a bestseller (they may be a wee bit biased, but it's still nice to hear). Equally amazing (and blindly biased) are our spouses. Thank you, Kip and Cara, for making life better.

ABOUT THE AUTHORS

Jean Knight Pace is the co-author of *Grey Lore* as well as the author of *Hugging Death: Essays on Motherhood and Saying Goodbye*. She has had essays and short stories published in *Puerto del Sol*, *The Lakeview Review*, and other literary magazines. She lives in Indiana with her husband, four children, six ducks, and a cat. You can find more about her at jeanknightpace.com.

Jacob Kennedy is an ER doctor who dreams werewolves and tournaments in his free time. He is also the co-author of *Grey Lore*. Find him on Facebook @jacobkennedybooks.